From the Bri
Isaac Asimov Comes a Galaxy of Breathtaking Wonders

A starship captain's astonishing discovery changes the present, the future . . . and the past in Robert Silverberg's:
THEY HIDE, WE SEEK

A diplomat's bizarre journey with a cunning alien philosopher becomes a lesson in life—and living—in David Brin's:
THE DIPLOMACY GUILD

When the world's ruling family entrusts a rebellious young man with a delicate quest, death awaits among the stars in Poul Anderson's:
THE BURNING SKY

Ancient alien ruins reveal awesome, hidden secrets in Robert Sheckley's:
MYRYX

The sole survivor of an abandoned enemy ship ensnares a crew of explorers in the deadly mysteries of a lost civilization in Harry Turtledove's:
ISLAND OF THE GODS

Worlds of Science Fiction from Avon Books

ANOTHER ROUND AT THE SPACEPORT BAR
edited by George Scithers & Darrell Schweitzer

100 GREAT SCIENCE FICTION SHORT SHORT STORIES
edited by Isaac Asimov, Martin H. Greenberg, & Joseph D. Olander

TALES FROM THE SPACEPORT BAR
edited by George Scithers & Darrell Schweitzer

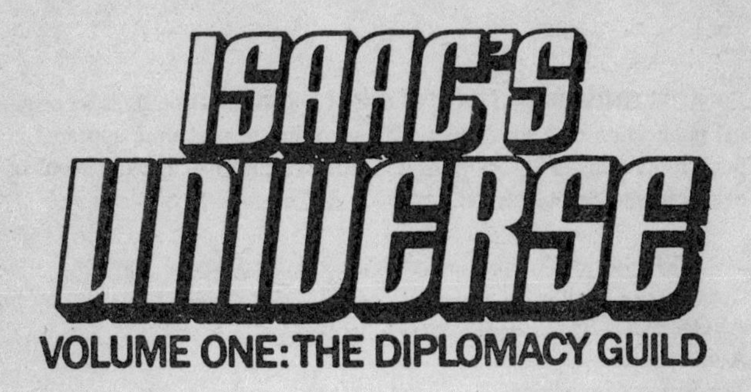

VOLUME ONE: THE DIPLOMACY GUILD

EDITED BY
MARTIN H. GREENBERG

WITH AN INTRODUCTION BY ISAAC ASIMOV

AVON BOOKS  NEW YORK

To Madeline Claire, with love

ISAAC'S UNIVERSE: THE DIPLOMACY GUILD (Vol. 1) is an original publication of Avon Books. This work has never before appeared in book form. This is a work of fiction. Any similarity to actual persons or events is purely coincidental.

AVON BOOKS
A division of
The Hearst Corporation
105 Madison Avenue
New York, New York 10016

Cover illustration by Martin Andrews
Published by arrangement with the editor
Library of Congress Catalog Card Number: 89-92473
ISBN: 0-380-75751-6

First Avon Books Printing: April 1990

Printed in the U.S.A.

RA 10 9 8 7 6 5 4 3 2 1

Contents

Introduction

INVENTING A UNIVERSE

ISAAC ASIMOV

WHY HAVE I GONE TO THE TROUBLE OF INVENTING A universe for other writers to exploit?

No, it isn't the money or the fame. Most of the royalties and all of the fame will go, as they should, to the authors who actually write the stories in this book and (it is to be hoped) in later companion pieces. My own return is, as it should be, miniscule.

But there are other reasons and I would like to explain them at some length, for among other things, they involve my feelings of guilt. Now guilt (for those of you who have never experienced the emotion) is a dreadful annoyance, souring one's life and making one unable to enjoy properly any renown or riches that come one's way. One is bowed down by its weight and is rendered fearful of the (usually imaginary) accusing eye of public disapproval.

In my case, it came about this way. I hadn't been writing for more than ten or fifteen years when I began to have the uneasy suspicion that I was becoming rather well known as a science fiction writer. In fact, I was even getting mentioned as one of the "Big Three," the other two being Robert A. Heinlein and Arthur C. Clarke.

It only got worse as the decades continued to fly by. We were not only cursed with prolificity, but with longevity, so that the same old Big Three remained Big for nearly half a century. Heinlein died in 1988 at the age of 80, but Clarke is still going strong as I write this and, obviously, so am I.

The result is that, at present, when there are a great many writers attempting to scale the mountainside of science fiction, it must be rather annoying for them to see the peak occupied by elderly has-beens who cling to it with their arthritic paws and simply won't get off. Even death, it seems, won't stop us, since Heinlein has already published a posthumous book and the reissue of his old novels is in the works.

Thanks to the limited space on the shelves of bookstores (themselves of sharply limited number), large numbers of new books of science fiction and fantasy are placed on them for only brief intervals before being swept off by new arrivals. Few books seem to manage to exist in public view for longer than a month before being replaced. Always excepting (as some writers add, with a faint snarl) the "megastars."

"So what," I can hear you say in your warm and loving way. "So you're a megastar and your books are perennial sellers and the economic futures of yourself and your eventual survivors are set. Is that bad?"

No, it isn't bad, exactly, but that's where the guilt comes in. I worry about crowding out newcomers with my old perennials, about smothering them with the weight of my name.

I've tried to justify the situation to myself. (Anything to make it possible for me to walk about science fiction conventions without having to skulk and hide in doorways when other writers pass.)

In the first place, we started in the early days of science fiction—not only the Big Three, but others of importance such as Lester del Rey, Poul Anderson, Fred Pohl, Clifford Simak, Ray Bradbury, and even some who died young: Stanley Weinbaum, Henry Kuttner, and Cyril Kornbluth, for instance. In those early days, the magazines paid only one cent a word or less, and there were *only* magazines. There were no hardcover science fiction publishers, no paperbacks, no Hollywood to speak of.

For years and decades we stuck it out under starvation conditions, and it was our efforts that slowly increased the popularity of science fiction to the point where today's beginners can get more for one novel than any of us got in ten years of endless plugging. So, if some of us are doing unusually well now, it is possible to argue that we earned it.

Secondly, from the more personal standpoint, back in 1958 I decided I had done enough science fiction. I had been successful in writing nonfiction of various types and it seemed to me I could make a living if I concentrated on nonfiction (and, to tell you the truth, I *preferred* nonfiction). In that way I could leave science fiction to the talented new writers who were making their way into the field.

So from 1958 to 1981, a period of nearly a quarter of a century, I wrote virtually no science fiction. There was one novel and a handful of short stories, but that's all. And meanwhile, along came the "New Wave." Writing styles changed drastically, and I felt increasingly that I was a back-number and *should* remain out of science fiction.

The trouble was that all this didn't help. The science fiction books that I published in the 1950s refused to go out of print and continued to sell steadily through the 1960s and 1970s. And because I wrote a series of nonfiction essays for *Fantasy and Science Fiction*, I remained in the consciousness of the science fiction public. I was therefore *still* one of the Big Three.

Then, in 1981, my publisher insisted (with a big INSIST) that I write another novel and I did and, to my horror, it hit the bestseller lists and I've had to write a new novel every year since then, in consequence.

That would have made me feel guiltier than ever, but I've done various things to pull the fangs of that guilt. For instance, I have, quite deliberately, decided that since my name has developed a kind of weight and significance, I would use it, as much as possible, for the benefit of the field rather than of myself.

With my dear and able friends, Martin Harry Greenberg and Charles Waugh (and occasionally others), I have helped edit many anthologies. More than a hundred of these have now been published with my name often in the title. What these serve to do is to rescue from the shadows numbers of stories that are well worth exposing to new generations of science fiction readers. Quite apart from the fact that the readers enjoy it, it means a little money to some veteran authors, as well as a shot in the arm to encourage continued production. The thought that the presence of my name might make such anthologies do better and be more efficacious in this respect than otherwise makes me feel fine.

Then, too, a number of novels by young authors have been published under the "Isaac Asimov Presents" label. In this way, the young authors get perhaps a somewhat better sale than they might otherwise have, and even (perhaps) a better break at the bookshelves.

I have even granted the right to make use of some of the themes that I have developed in my own books. There is a series of a dozen books, for instance, that have the generic title "Isaac Asimov's Robot City." They are written by young writers who have my express permission to use my Three Laws of Robotics, and for each one I write an introduction on one phase or another of robotics. The books are doing well, actually, and it is clear that the presence of my name doesn't hurt.

Then another way of using my name usefully came up. Marty Greenberg suggested that, rather than have writers use a "universe" I had already invented and made my own, I invent a brand-new one I had never used and donate it to some publishing house that would be willing to have writers produce stories built about the concepts of the "universe"—and, of course, that we find the writers who would want to try their hand at it.

I agreed enthusiastically. After all, I had just devised a new background for my 1989 novel, *Nemesis,* one which had not been used in any piece of fiction I had written before, so I did not foresee any great difficulty in inventing an "Isaac's Universe" for other writers to use. (The use of the word "Isaac" in the title was Marty's idea but I snatched at it eagerly. There are well over sixty books that I have written—by no means all anthologies—with either "Asimov" or "Isaac Asimov" in the title, but none with "Isaac" alone, until this one.)

In making up a new "Universe" there were some things I couldn't abandon, of course. We would be working within our own Galaxy in which I postulated the existence of 25,000,000 star systems containing a habitable world, the whole being linked together by devices that made it possible to travel and communicate at faster-than-light speeds. The short-hand for this is "hyperspatial travel and communication."

I have this in my "Foundation" universe, and the other novels I have been connecting to the Foundation, but from here on my Universes part company.

In my Foundation series and the novels related thereto, the Galaxy contains only one intelligent species—our own. All the habitable worlds have been colonized by human beings so that we, in effect, have an all-human Galaxy. I may have been the first to write important novels based on such a theme, and the reason I did it was to pare away the complexities that would arise from a multiplicity of intelligences. I wanted to be able to deal with humanity and its problems in a detailed all-human manner, making them even clearer by showing them through a Galaxy-wide magnifying glass. This I have ended up doing—albeit imperfectly, of course, since I am no Shakespeare or Tolstoy.

However, I was well aware that there was the alternative multiple-intelligence Universe. We see that now constantly on such television shows as *Star Trek* and in many of the older "space opera" stories. There we always have the risk of a failure of imagination that leads to the portrayal of other intelligences as differing from ourselves superficially by the possession of green faces, or antennae, or corrugated foreheads, but allowing these changes to leave them, clearly, primates. You can't really blame *Star Trek* for this, since they have to have human beings playing the roles of other intelligences, but in science fiction stories in print, having all intelligences primate (or, if villainous, reptilian) seems insufficient.

E. E. Smith's *Galactic Patrol* and its sequels had a multi-intelligence Universe that had its intelligences encased in radically different physiologies and this I found satisfying when I read the stories as a young man. I was particularly pleased with the feeling Smith labored to give of a communal *mental* feeling among individuals who had nothing *physically* in common.

It was something like this, then, that I wanted for my Universe, but I wanted to make my Universe more specific in its description of the different species and more concerned with the various political, economic, and social problems of the Galaxy. It was to be less space-operaish and more quasi-historical, a melding to some extent of "Galactic Patrol" and "Foundation."

I wanted a Universe with millions of planets bearing life, with the indigenous life on every planet unique to itself and with differences limited only by the imagination of the writer. However, there are only six *intelligent* species—widely different in nature:

1. Earthmen.

2. An aquatic race, vaguely analogous to Earthly porpoises.

3. A fragile, skeletal insectlike species adapted to a low oxygen atmosphere plus neon rather than nitrogen.

4. A sinuous, limbless species, possessing fringed flippers, however, that are snakish in a way.

5. A small, winged species adapted to a thick atmosphere.

6. A strong, slow-moving, blocklike species with no appendages, and adapted to a gravity higher than Earth's.

The intelligences each control more than their native planets. They can be pictured as going through the Galaxy, colonizing and settling planets suitable to themselves. In general, a world suitable for one is not particularly desirable for any of the others, and with plenty of each variety, there is no push for going to the enormous expense of modifying a planet to suit one's own kind. The intelligences can therefore live together in the Galaxy without treading on each other's toes. There is nothing to fight over unless there is an inability to overcome the unreasoning dislike of one species for another because, of course, each appears incredibly ugly to all the others, and each may have social customs and ways of thought that are distasteful to the others.

Yet the various intelligences need to be in contact, since trade among them is useful for all, and since advances in technology by one species may be useful to others as well (and each intelligence has its own specialties in technology, some of which are unpalatable to the others for one reason or another), and since disputes may arise occasionally and there must be some form of political/social machinery to settle them. There are even occasional dangers that might require Galactic cooperation. What's more, each intelligence may be split up into several mutually hostile subcultures.

So, you see, the Universe I invented (and which I described in considerable detail to the publishers and to the writers who were willing to chance working within it) supplies plenty of problems, some of which would certainly be beyond my imagination to handle well, and has broad enough limits to allow the writer a great deal of personal room for his own visions.

You can see how it works out in the sampling of stories in this volume, which (we very much hope) will be but the first of a series. Good reading—and if you like it, write and say so. It will lower my level of guilt, and I can always use that.

THEY HIDE, WE SEEK

ROBERT SILVERBERG

NOBODY HAD ANY GREAT INTEREST IN ALTERING THE long-established galactic balance of power, least of all Captain Hayn Wing-Marra of the *Achilles*. But one thing does lead to another, and immense consequences have a way sometimes of hinging on very small pivots. In this case, the pivot was nothing more than the fact that Captain Wing-Marra, who was eleven cycles old, had spent one lifetime as an organic chemist and another as an archaeologist before he had gone to space.

It was the passion for organic chemistry, still alive in him after all those years, that had brought his Erthuma-registry starship and its crew of nine, seven Erthumoi and two Naxians, to the vicinity of the gaseous nebula W49. What they had set out to do was to explore a large molecular cloud, a spacegoing soup of complex hydrocarbons, which was certainly of scientific interest and probably had some economic value as well.

What they found nearby, hidden on the far side of the cloud, was a main-sequence star, which had four or five planets, most of which had moons. That was unexpected but not particularly surprising. The galaxy is full of stars, hundreds of millions of them, and nearly all of them have planets.

At first glance neither the star nor its planets nor any of the moons seemed particularly out of the ordinary, either, though one of the planets was close enough to Earth-type to be of potential use to Erthumoi. There are, however, plenty of worlds like that.

But a second glance revealed that a Locrian ship was already present in the unknown star system. It was parked in orbit around the second planet, and Locrian scouting parties were apparently at work both on the planet and its moon. That didn't make a great deal of sense, because the second planet was the Earth-type one, with a dense oxygen-nitrogen atmosphere very low in neon and other noble gases. Locrians are not at all comfortable in places like that. Nor would the airless moon be any more inviting to them.

So it seemed appropriate for Captain Wing-Marra to take a third and rather less casual glance. Which he did; and after that nothing would ever be quite the same for any of the six races of the galaxy that were capable of interstellar travel.

Until the discovery that a Locrian exploration force was working the same territory he was, the molecular cloud—nearly thirty light-years across and laden with marvels—had seemed quite interesting enough for Captain Wing-Marra.

"Do you see?" he said to Jorin Murry-Balff, who was his Communications. "Not just piddling little hydroxyls and ammonias. That's cyano-octa-tetrayne there— HB_9N. Eleven-atom chains, Murry-Balff! And there! That's methanol, by all the stars! CH_3OH!" Wing-Marra reached toward the spectrometer's dazzling screen, shining with swirls of amber and topaz and carnelian and amethyst, and tapped this brilliant swirl and that one. "And this—and this—"

Murry-Balff didn't seem impressed. "Doesn't every molecular cloud have stuff like that in it?"

"Not this intricate, most of them. Those are very big molecules out there. Formaldehyde—H_2CO. Vinyl cyanide—H_2CCHCN."

"Formaldehyde? Cyanide? Sounds pretty deadly to me."

"Don't be an idiot. Those are the chemicals of life, man!" Wing-Marra leaned close, staring into the screen. Information moved in dizzying whorls before him. The spectrometer, whipping its scan-beam tirelessly across the vastness of the molecular cloud, provided color-analog displays of each organic compound it detected, reports on mass configuration, a three-dimensional distribution arc, and an assortment of other quantifiable factors. "Look, there's formic acid. And five or six amino acids, or I miss my guess. You and I and the snakes downstairs and everything else that breathes and metabolizes are built out of that stuff. And for all we know, we're alive at this moment only because wandering clouds like this seeded the newborn planets they encountered with just this sort of organic material."

Murry-Balff shrugged. "I'll take your word for it, Captain. Chemistry was never my field. Cosmology neither." A red glow blossomed on his wristband. "If you'll excuse me, sir—there's data coming in now from our planetary probes—"

"Dismissed," Wing-Marra murmured.

It was embarrassing for him to see the speed with which Murry-Balff, who ordinarily was in no rush, left the observation deck. Perhaps I was too ebullient for him just now, Wing-Marra thought. Or too intemperate. Certainly I was running off at the mouth a little about those molecules.

He wondered whether an apology was in order. They were old friends, after all. Murry-Balff and Wing-Marra were natives of the same Erthuma world, Hesperia in the St. Dominic's Star system. The other five Erthumoi on board came from five different worlds, none within a hundred light-years of any other; that fact alone gave the two Hesperians a certain sense of fellowship that went beyond the pseudomilitary shipboard formalities. On the other hand, Wing-Marra thought, it's Murry-Balff's problem, not mine, if the contents of that molecular cloud don't interest him. The cloud is what we came here to investigate. Before we're through with it he'll have had to learn the formulas for a hundred different hydrocarbons, like it or not.

Wing-Marra peered at the spectrometer screen once again, and within moments he was lost in wonder.

His capacity for wonder—exultant, transcendent intellectual excitement—was one of the many contradictions out of which he was constructed. Wing-Marra was quiet and self-contained, a tall, pale, ascetic-looking man who believed in setting limits and abiding by them. To some that seemed odd and even quaint, considering that he had spent the last three cycles of his long life roaming the virtually limitless reaches of the galaxy. Wing-Marra himself saw no inconsistency in that. The way to cope with the crushing weight of infinity, he thought, was to behave as though one were capable of setting boundaries to it.

And though he seemed in many ways a passionless man, his fascination with the intricacy of the organic molecules was intense to the point of obsessiveness.

Six cycles back—his life now had encompassed eleven all told, a span of nearly a thousand Erthuma years—he had been struck suddenly by a waking vision, a startling hallucinatory display. He was living then on the sultry world called Atatakai, where the air seemed as thick as fur. Suddenly in the red evening sky he saw inexplicable pulsing points of light, which cavorted and leaped about in a wild whirling dance.

As he watched, astounded, he saw two of the shimmering light sources come together to form a pair, and then a third and larger one seize them both, and then even more complicated unions take form. And all the while the giddy dance went on. The whirling lights were strung like serpents across the sky. He had never seen anything so awesome. The patterns of their sinuous movements were elegant, compelling, sublimely beautiful. It was a revelation. It seemed to him that he was looking right into the heart of the universe, into the deepest secrets of creation.

Then, to his even greater amazement, one serpent seized its own tail in its mouth, and, ringlike now, began a fierce gyration so imperious that he fell to his knees before it, stunned and shaken. There was a powerful truth in that furiously whirling serpentine form—the truth of what, he had not the vaguest idea—and under the impact of that vision of the innerness of all things he trembled like a leaf in a storm. After a time he could no longer bear to watch. He closed his eyes; and when he opened them again he beheld only the cloud-choked crimson sky of Atatakai.

But the memory of the bewildering, overwhelming vision would not leave Wing-Marra's mind; and in the end he had had to seek help in regaining his mental balance. A zigzag trail through a variety of therapists and therapies brought him at last to a flat-faced dome of silvery metal that listened to him for a time and said finally in a brusque impersonal voice, "Your hallucination is not original. You are not the first to experience it."

Wing-Marra felt as though the autoshrink had spat in his eye.

"Not—original? What the hell do you mean?"

"Another has had this vision before you, in early times, in the very distant past. It is the dream of Kekule. This is true. I have consulted the archives."

"Kekule?"

"You are a chemist. This is true."

"Why—no," said Wing-Marra, puzzled. "Not true. Not at all."

"Then you have studied chemistry," said the machine, sounding a little irritated. "This is true."

Wing-Marra thought. "I suppose so, yes. Long ago. In my first cycle, when I was at the university. But—"

"A datum buried since your student days has surfaced in you. You have recapitulated the dream of Kekule," the machine told him again. "Such things happen. It is not a sign of serious mental disturbance. This is true."

"Kekule," Wing-Marra said wonderingly. "Who's that?"

There was the momentary hum of data-search. "Friedrich August Kekule. Erthuma of the Earthborn. Professor of chemistry at Ghent and later at Bonn."

"Where?"

"Ancient Earth places. Do not pursue irrelevances. Kekule, pondering questions of molecular structure, saw atoms dancing before his eyes, forming a chain. Later he dreamed again and perceived the pattern of the benzene ring. This is true. The episode is well-known."

"To chemists, maybe," said Wing-Marra. "I'm not a chemist." He felt disgruntled and obscurely let down at having paid good money to discover that the vision that had so irradiated his consciousness was a second-hand one. On the other hand, he told himself, probably it was better to hear that a phantom memory had come floating up out of some lecture of his student days than to be informed that he was going out of his mind. Still, he was in a sour mood as he left the autoshrink's cubicle.

His annoyance passed, though, and his fascination with the images that had so spontaneously leaped from the recesses of his brain remained and even deepened. He looked up Kekule and his work. Nineteenth century—my God, practically prehistoric! The dawn of science! A forgotten man, but for one great accomplishment, the theory of organic molecular structure. Kekule had demonstrated the tendency of carbon atoms to link together and to snare other atoms in their quadrivalent embrace.

And so that vision, second-hand or not, led Wing-Marra from one thing to another and another, forging ever deeper throughout all the years that remained to him in that lifetime into the study of organic chemistry. It was his hope to recapture some of the splendor and wonder of those dancing lights in the sky. It was his hope to know again that sense of being in contact with inarguable truth. His head was aswim with isomers and polymers, with alkanes and olefins, with aromatics and heterocyclics and aliphatics, with esters, ethers, aldehydes, ketones. The crisp symmetries of their bonding patterns offered him ineffable joy and held him in an ineluctable grip. And here he was, five lifetimes later, still pursuing the mysteries of the carbon compounds out here in this remote arm of the galaxy, forty thousand light-years from the home world of all Erthumoi and even farther from the planet of his own birth.

Now, throat dry, eyes wide and scarcely flickering, Wing-Marra gripped the handles of the spectrometer screen and guided its scanner this way and that across the face of the great molecular cloud. Radiant bands of colored light leaped out at him from the smoky vastness. He was staring into the miraculous core of creation.

Stars were being born in that dense black pit. Future worlds were coalescing. The unimaginable life-forms of a billion years hence would be assembled from those rich whorls of molecular soup.

Wing-Marra felt his spirit soaring, felt his soul expanding, going forth into the cloud, walking among the drifting wonders. It was an almost godlike sensation.

"Sir?"

Murry-Balff. The intrusion was maddening, painful.

Scowling, Wing-Marra made an impatient gesture without turning away from the screen. Whatever Murry-Balff wanted, it could wait.

"Sir, this is important."

"So is this. I'm scanning the cloud."

"And we've been scanning this nearby solar system, sir. The planetary probes have pulled in something very strange. Seems that we have company."

Wing-Marra spun around swiftly.

"Company?"

"Let me show you," Murry-Balff said. He touched his wrist-plate to a wall terminal. Instantly a data screen came to life across the room. It showed a green planetary ball. Another, somewhat smaller ball, bleak and lifeless looking, orbited it at an inclination of about sixty degrees.

"This is the second planet of the system," said Murry-Balff. "And its moon. I call your attention to the right side of the screen, near the planetary equator."

Wing-Marra thought he could see a dark speck.

Murry-Balff fingered his wrist-plate. The screen zoomed into enlargement mode. Now the green world filled nearly all of the picture. Something like a black spider hung beside it. Murry-Balff made another tuning adjustment, and the spider occupied the center of the screen.

It wasn't a spider. It looked more like some narrow-waisted wasp now: three dark, gleaming elongated cylinders, linked by narrow communication tubes. Six fragile leglike appendages trailed from the hindmost cylinder. At the other end were two faceted domes, rising like huge insect eyes from the front. Spiral rows of hexagonal ports wound across each cylinder's sides.

The thing was a starship. And not of Erthuma design.

"Locrians," Murry-Balff said quietly.

"So I see." Wing-Marra pressed his fists together until his knuckles cracked, and swore. Murry-Balff brought the magnification up to the next level. It was pretty grainy, but at this level Wing-Marra thought he could actually make out the insectlike figures of the aliens moving about behind the ports. He shook his head. "What in God's name would Locrians be doing *here?*"

The crew assembled fast, all but the Naxians, who needed more time. Snakes *always* needed more time, no matter what. Wing-Marra didn't feel like waiting for them. He kept the data screen lit and ordered Murry-Balff to maintain real-time tracking surveillance of the Locrian ship.

"We're under no obligation to withdraw," Wing-Marra said. "This is unclaimed territory and remains that way until they've established valid possession. Simply being the first to get here doesn't constitute valid possession."

"They aren't under any obligation to withdraw either," Linga Hyath, his Cosmography, pointed out.

"Understood."

"They might not agree that they don't have valid possession," said his Diplomacy, Ayana Sanoclaro.

Hyath and Sanoclaro looked at each other and exchanged quick, smug nods of satisfaction. Wing-Marra could usually count on them to think the same way and to express essentially the same ideas at approximately the same time. They were both wiry, long-limbed women with the gaunt, attenuated look that natives of low-gravity worlds generally have, and they appeared to be not merely sisters but twins: the same pale blue eyes, the same immense cascades of golden hair, the same thin, pinched features. The odd thing was that they were not at all related, but came, in fact, from worlds a thousand light-years apart. Some genotypes are strikingly persistent.

Wing-Marra said, "Are you suggesting that they might make trouble for us?"

"They might have serious objections to our hanging around here," Sanoclaro said.

"If they think there's something really worthwhile here,

they might defend their claim in a way we wouldn't like,'' said Hyath.

Mikoil Karpov, the Biochemistry, said, ''You imply that they'd take hostile action?''

''They might,'' said Sanoclaro.

Karpov blinked. He was a squat, broad-shouldered man, heavy jowled, densely bearded, from the chilly world of Zima, and his Erthumat was thickened by strong Russkiye inflections. ''You are talking about acts of war? And you are actually serious? The idea's absurd. Nobody makes war.''

''Erthumoi used to, not all that long ago.''

Karpov gestured emphatically. ''It was plenty long ago. Nobody fires on peaceful ships.''

''Especially across species lines,'' said the Navigation, a dark, soft, tiny, deceptively feminine-looking woman named Eslane Ree, who came from Doppler IV. ''The Locrians can see that this is an Erthuma ship. Maybe the Crotonites still like to squabble among themselves, or, from what I hear from our two, the Naxians. But those are Locrians over there. They don't even have a history of intraspecies warfare—why would they take a shot at us? I'm with Karpov here. We're spinning horrors out of nothing at all.''

''Maybe so. But what are Locrians doing here, though?'' Linga Hyath asked. ''Locrians don't ordinarily go sniffing around high-oxygen worlds. And from the looks of it, this one is particularly badly suited for them. Six gulps of that atmosphere and they'd be drunk for a month. They must have seen something out of the usual here that got their attention in a big way.''

''Who says?'' Eslane Ree demanded. ''Have we?''

Hyath shrugged. ''We've only just arrived.''

''Perhaps so have they.''

''But they'd have taken one look and moved on, since this world is plainly useless to them,'' said Ayana Sanoclaro. ''Unless they've spotted something. And if they have, my guess is that they'll go to great lengths, maybe to surprisingly great lengths, to keep us away from it.''

Eslane Ree gave the elongated blond woman a sour glare. "Paranoia! Hyperdefensiveness!"

"Foresight," Sanoclaro retorted. "Prudence."

"What are you advocating?" asked the Maintenance, Septen Bolangyr, who came from a high-ultraviolet world in the Nestor Cluster and whose skin, artificially hyped with melanin, was a lustrous purple green. "Should I activate the defensive screens, sir? Do you want me to get the cannons ready? If we are to go on a war footing, Captain, then tell me so right now. But I want the order in writing, and I want it with a date and a seal."

"Stay easy," Wing-Marra said. "We're a long way from fighting any space battles. What I'm going to do is contact these Locrians and find out whether we have a problem with them. But I hope you'll go along with my feeling that we ought to take a firm position about staying here, regardless of what they say."

"Even if they threaten us?" Hyath asked.

"They won't," said Karpov. Eslane Ree nodded in vigorous agreement.

"If they do?" Wing-Marra asked.

Eslane Ree said, "It would depend on the nature of the threat. We'd be foolish to stay here if they're willing to blow us out of he sky."

"*Locrians?*" Karpov said incredulously.

"Sufficient greed can turn any species warlike," Ayana Sanoclaro said, looking to her friend Hyath for support. "Even Locrians. The fact that the Six Races have avoided serious conflict with each other up till now is irrelevant. The evolutionary imperatives that have carried all six species this far have plenty of aggression buried in them, and the right motivation surely can bring that aggression to life. Locrians or no, if what they've found here is so valuable that—"

"We don't know that they've found anything, and—"

"How can we assume—"

"The unmotivated adolescent belligerence of these arguments is utterly—"

"The naïveté of—"

"More than fifteen hundred years of peaceful space

exploration behind us and we still regard ourselves as capable of reverting to the level of—"

"Not us, *them!*"

"Us too! Who began this whole—"

"Enough!" Wing-Marra said sharply. "Sanoclaro, tell those two snakes of ours—excuse me, those two Naxians—to get themselves on deck without any further delay. Brief them on what's going on. Murry-Balff, I want to be talking to those Locrians in five minutes or less. Bolangyr, work up an inventory of our battle stores, just for the hell of it, but don't activate anything, you hear, not a thing. The rest of you stand by and hold your peace, will you?" He glowered at the spectrometer screen, where clumps of gorgeous amide radicals and polyhydric alcohols were circling in a stately sarabande of astonishing colors. Whatever the Locrians were doing here, he thought, it ought to be possible to work out some kind of territorial agreement with them in half an hour or so, and then he would be able to get down to his real work. We are all rational beings. Reason will prevail. We of the Six Races have all managed to coexist in interstellar space for a very long time without any serious conflicts of interest. Why start now?

Why, indeed?

The Locrian gave its name as Speaker-to-Erthumoi. Murry-Balff had asked to talk to Ship-Commander, but Speaker-to-Erthumoi was the best he was able to get. Of course, they might be the same person, Wing-Marra knew. Locrians change their names as often as they change functions. Perhaps it was not even legitimate to regard Locrian "names" as names.

He put the transmission into image-stasis, freezing the communication channel. The Locrian would simply have to sit there on hold until the Erthuma captain had a clearer idea of the situation. Turning to one of his Naxians, Wing-Marra said, "Is this meant as an insult, Blue Sphere? Should I insist on speaking to Ship-Commander?"

The Naxian studied the motionless image of the Locrian that glittered from the frozen screen for a long while, assessing the information visible to it-her on the insectoid creature's seemingly impassive face. It is the extraordinary gift of Naxians to be able to read the emotional output—not the minds, only the emotions—of any life-form, no matter how alien to it. Greed, anger, lust, shame, compassion, whatever: All creatures are open books to Naxians. Even when all they have to work with is a static image on a screen. How they did it, no Erthuma knew. The various stargoing species of the galaxy had many sorts of intuitive powers that were difficult for Erthumoi to comprehend.

The Naxian seemed to be working hard, though. Meditative ripples and quivers ran the length of its-her pink, narrow snakelike body. So intense was Blue Sphere's concentration that it-she went into flipper mode for a few moments, extruding stubby fringed grasping organs from its-her otherwise limbless form, then absorbing them again.

"You may proceed, Captain," Blue Sphere announced after a time. "The Locrians intend no insult. Mere efficiency of communication is the most likely purpose. I suspect Ship-Commander is less fluent in Erthumat than this one. At any rate the Locrian's emotional aura is benign."

"But apprehensive," offered the other Naxian, Rosy Tetrahedron. "Definite anxiety is evident. The Locrian feels strong uncertainty as to Erthuma motivations or intentions in this sector of space."

"Fine," Wing-Marra said. "If they're as nervous about us as we are about them, there's hope for working something out. Reciprocity is the mother of security, eh, Sanoclaro? Eh? Old diplomatic proverb."

Sanoclaro didn't smile. But he hadn't really expected her to.

He killed the image-stasis and the screen came to life again. The Locrian could have walked away from the transmitter while Wing-Marra's colloquy with the Naxians was going on, but it was still there. At least Wing-Marra assumed that it was the same one. He stared at it. What he saw was a fleshless angular head much longer than it was wide, a lipless V-shaped beak of a mouth, a single giant glaring eye shielded by a clear bubblelike plate hinged at each side, a thin tubular neck sprouting out of a flimsy, skeletal six-limbed trunk.

The Locrian looked for all the world like a giant insect, a dry parched chitinous thing that would probably crunch if you hit it with the edge of your hand. Very likely they had evolved from some kind of low-phylum insectlike arthropods on their dry, chilly home world, which belonged to an orange K5 sun in the Cygnus arm of the galaxy. But there was nothing low-phylum about them now. They were chordate vertebrates with tough siliceous spinal columns to support their scaly gray green exoskeletons. And they had tough, shrewd brains in their narrow, elongated skulls.

The moment the stasis broke the Locrian said, "We request clarification, Erthuma representative. Do we speak with Diplomacy or Administration?"

"Administration. I am Hayn Wing-Marra, captain, Erthuma of Hesperia in St. Dominic's Star system."

The Locrian made a crackling sound that seemed like displeasure. "We request Diplomacy. It is a point of protocol. Transspecies discussions are protocol matters."

Wing-Marra felt like screaming. The last thing he wanted was to have to conduct this discussion by way of Ayana Sanoclaro, considering the wild suspicions she had just been voicing. But the Locrian was right: Contact across species lines in open space had to follow protocol. Reluctantly Wing-Marra beckoned to Sanoclaro, who gave him a little smirk of triumph and stepped into the pale yellow glow of the communications field.

"What we want to know, Speaker-to-Erthumoi," she said without preamble, "is whether you're staking a claim to the solar system that lies adjacent to our present position."

"Negative," said the Locrian immediately. Though the two ships were eighty-eight million kilometers apart at that moment, the communications field—a modulated-neutrino carrier wave operating through hyperspace—permitted instantaneous communication between them. For that matter, it would have permitted communication at essentially the same response time even if the ships had been at opposite ends of the galaxy. "No claim to this system has been recorded."

Wing-Marra held up both his hands. Making two circles out of his thumbs and forefingers, he moved them in an elaborate pantomime that he hoped would suggest the orbital relationship of the second planet and its huge moon. But Sanoclaro, without even looking at him, had already begun to ask the obvious next question.

"Are you claiming just the second planet, then? Or its moon?"

"Is there Erthuma interest in the second planet?" the Locrian countered.

The Naxian who called it-herself Blue Sphere moved outside the field's scanner range and signaled to Wing-Marra that it was picking up increased ambiguities and uncertainties. Wing-Marra, peering at the screen, sought to detect some change in the Locrian's expression, but Speaker-to-Erthumoi's rigid features showed not a flicker of movement. An integument that chitinous wasn't capable of much movement, or perhaps of any at all. Whatever clues the Naxians used in doing their little trick, facial expressions didn't seem to play an important role.

Sanoclaro looked to Wing-Marra for a cue. He indicated the spectrometer screen, ablaze with drifting hydrocarbon masses.

"We are purely a scientific mission," Sanoclaro told the Locrian. "We're here to study the molecular cloud. We have no territorial intentions whatsoever."

"Nor do we," said Speaker-to-Erthumoi. "We require only unhindered completion of our research."

Wing-Marra frowned. He was beginning to wonder if any of this was any business of his at all. If the only thing the Locrians wanted was to be left alone to snoop around the second world, and all that he wanted was to be left alone to study the molecular cloud—

No. The directives were very clear. When an Erthuma ship encountered a ship belonging to any of the other five races in open space, the Erthuma vessel, regardless of its own purpose, was required to file a report on the activities of the other spacecraft. Even though no one saw any serious risk of anything so farfetched and implausible as interstellar warfare breaking out, it behooved the Erthumoi—as the youngest and least experienced of the six starfaring peoples—to keep close watch on everything that their rivals might be up to. Assuming that their activities would never be anything but benign, regardless of the generally peaceful relationships that had prevailed among the Six Races since the first Erthuma entry into interstellar space, was folly.

He needed more information.

Making the planet-and-moon gesture again, Wing-Marra tried to depict the orbiting Locrian ship by moving his nose in a circle around the equator of the finger and thumb that represented the planet. Sanoclaro shot him a mystified look. Abandoning the pantomime, Wing-Marra whispered angrily, "Try to find out what the hell they're doing here, will you?"

Sanoclaro said, "May we inquire into the nature of your mission?"

Blue Sphere, still out of scanner range, signaled that increased agitation was coming from the Locrian. Or so Wing-Marra thought the Naxian was trying to tell him.

It was maddening for the captain to have to deal through this many intermediaries. Every ship carried a Diplomacy as a matter of course, but Wing-Marra hadn't expected to need to make use of Sanoclaro's services in this remote region. And the Naxians, though they were valuable interpreters of nonverbal messages in tricky situations like this one, weren't always easy for non-Naxians to understand.

Speaker-to-Erthumoi said after a long pause, "Our mission is exploratory also."

Wing-Marra pantomimed drunkenness.

Sanoclaro looked puzzled again. Then, smiling to show that she understood, she said, "But surely a high-oxygen world such as the one nearby can be of little practical use to Locrians."

Speaker-to-Erthumoi was silent.

"May we inquire whether the nature of your exploration is exploratory?" Sanoclaro said. "Or is there perhaps some other purpose?"

"Other," said the Locrian.

"Other than scientific?"

"Other, yes."

"Is its nature such that our presence here will disrupt your work?"

"Not necessarily."

"Then it is proper to conclude that the representative of the Galactic Sphere of Locria has no objection to our continuing to remain in this region?"

Another long silence.

"No objection," Speaker-to-Erthumoi replied finally.

Both Naxians now signaled that they were picking up *distress, resentment, suspicion, general contradiction of spoken statement.*

Wing-Marra fumed. He hoped Sanoclaro didn't think that having obtained the Locrians' permission for them to stay here was any sort of wonderful achievement. This was, after all, open territory.

He said under his breath, "I need to know what they're up to!"

Sanoclaro said, "Our captain instructs me to obtain data from you concerning the nature of your mission."

"I will reply shortly," said Speaker-to-Erthumoi. There was yet another lengthy pause. Then the image froze. This time it was the Locrians who had imposed the stasis, no doubt so Speaker-to-Erthumoi could engage in a quick off-screen strategy session with Ship-Commander.

Wing-Marra said to Sanoclaro, "If it's just a routine mapping mission, they shouldn't be as edgy as the Naxians say they are. When they come back on, see if you can pin them down about their reasons for landing scouts on that planet and its moon."

"What do you think I'm trying to do?"

"What I think," said Linga Hyath, "is that they probably were just on a routine mapping mission, but they found something on the second world or its moon that was way out of the ordinary, and so they're sticking around to take a close look at it, and they wish we'd get the hell out of here before we find it too."

"Thank you," Wing-Marra told the Cosmography. "Your grasp of the obvious is extraordinarily profound."

Hyath glared and began to reply.

"Save it," said Wing-Marra. The screen was alive again.

Speaker-to-Erthumoi—if that indeed was who was on the screen now—looked astonishingly transformed, as though it had been wearing a mask before and now had removed it. The hard, sharp-angled gray chitin of its all but featureless face had been opened back like the two doors of a cabinet, and what was visible now was the bare surface of its great staring glassy inner eye, the immensely penetrating organ that Locrians revealed only when they needed to see with particular clarity. Facing that eye was like facing fifty Naxians at once. It seemed to be seeing right into him. Wing-Marra felt stripped bare, down to bone and tendon. He had never seen a Locrian in full percept mode before, and he didn't like it.

To hell with it, he thought. I don't have anything to hide.

He met the glare of that terrible eye without flinching.

The Locrian said, "Ship-Commander requests face-to-face contact with Erthuma-captain in order to continue the discussion in a more fruitful way. He proposes stochastic choice to determine which ship is to be the site of the meeting."

Sanoclaro looked inquiringly toward Wing-Marra, who nodded at once.

"Agreed," the Diplomacy told the alien. "Shall we flip a coin?"

"That method is acceptable."

"Do you want us to flip one?"

"We prefer to do that," said the Locrian.

Again Wing-Marra nodded. His irritation was mounting rapidly. Let them use a coin with two heads, for all he cared. What did it matter whether the meeting took place on his ship or theirs? He just wanted to get on with his work.

"Select your choice," said Speaker-to-Erthumoi. It held up its claw, revealing a shining six-edged coin of some bright coppery metal grasped between two of its numerous many-jointed fingers. One face of the coin showed some Locrian's beaky big-eyed head, and when the alien turned it over Wing-Marra saw jagged abstract patterns on the reverse.

"I'll take tails," Wing-Marra said.

"Tails?"

"The side that doesn't have the head."

"Ah."

Something happened off screen. Speaker-to-Erthumoi said, after a moment, "We have tossed the coin. Your selection proved to be correct. We will send a boarding party. How soon can you receive us?"

There was more grumbling, of course. Hyath and Sanoclaro, the suspicious ones, were convinced that the whole coin-tossing gambit had been nothing but a ploy to insinuate a Locrian force aboard the ship, perhaps so that they could seize it. Eslane Ree thought that was crazy, and said so. Mikoil Karpov, too, wanted to know why the two women were taking such an alarmist position. Even Murry-Balff, who usually went along with anything Wing-Marra said, thought it would have been a better idea to have sent the Diplomacy over to the alien vessel to conduct the conference. "If they're up to anything funny, better that they do it over there," Murry-Balff said. "And to her, not us."

Annoyed as he was by the paranoia of Sanoclaro and Hyath, Wing-Marra found nothing to amuse him in his old friend's frivolity. He was a cautious man but he saw no reason for fear. The risk was all on the Locrians' side. They were the ones who would be boarding a strange ship, after all. He couldn't bring himself to believe that they had anything so wild as an armed takeover in mind. No, the coin toss had probably been honest, and the Locrians could probably be trusted. Or else they were working up something so devious that no sane person could be expected to be on guard against it.

Within the hour a beetlelike hypershuttle brought a four-Locrian delegation across the gulf between the two ships.

It popped back into normal space astonishingly close to the *Achilles* and coasted in for a docking.

Four Locrians came scrambling through the access lock. They were taller than the tallest of Erthumoi, but so light and frail were their bodies—six pipelike limbs and hardly any thorax—that they seemed little more than walking skeletons.

By way of protection against the intoxicating richness of the Erthuma ship's atmosphere, they were wearing translucent spacesuits that hung about them in loose, awkward folds, like old baggy skin. Anything beyond a 10 percent oxygen concentration was dizzying to them, and furthermore they preferred to breathe air that was thinned by a substantial neon component, which the *Achilles* was unable to supply.

The first thing the Locrians saw was the spherical golden grille and trembling corkscrew antennae of the simultrans machine that Murry-Balff had set up in the center of the meeting room. They obviously didn't like it.

"There is no real need to employ this device," said one of the Locrians coolly, giving the translating gadget a fiercely contemptuous stiff-necked glare. "Your language holds no mysteries for us."

Wing-Marra had expected that. The other races were *always* scornful of Erthuma artificial-intelligence gadgets, because in one way or another they were able to manage most things without such mechanical assistance. The simultrans was capable of rendering real-time translations of anything said in any of the six galactic languages into any or all of the other five. Erthumoi, notorious for their general incapacity to master the ancient and intricate languages of most alien species, found the machine extremely useful. The others didn't.

But Wing-Marra suspected there was more to the Locrian objections to the simultrans than simple racial prejudice. With the simultrans offering instantaneous translation of anything said, no members of either species would be able to speak to each other in surreptitious asides unintelligible to the other party. Wing-Marra saw that as a distinct advantage for him, since some or all of the Locrians appeared to be fluent in Erthumat, but no one aboard the *Achilles* understood more than a smattering of Locrian. Evidently the Locrians saw things the same way.

Smiling grandly, he said, "Ah, but we feel it is only courteous to offer you this small assistance. You are already under the stress of having come aboard a strange ship, and you are compelled to conduct this meeting clad in spacesuits that doubtless must cause you some discomfort. We would not burden you with the obligation to converse in an alien tongue as well."

"But it is not necessary that we—"

"Permit me to insist. I am overwhelmed by your unselfishness but I could not bear the shame of having inconvenienced you so deeply."

There was a frosty silence. The Locrian looked—so far as Wing-Marra was capable of telling—extremely annoyed.

But after a moment the Locrian said, "Very well. Let us use the translator. You know me as Speaker-to-Erthumoi. I am accompanied by Ship-Commander and Recorder."

Three names, four Locrians, no indication of what was what or which was whom. Wing-Marra didn't even try to get an explanation.

"I am Captain Wing-Marra," he said. "This is my Diplomacy, Ayana Sanoclaro. These Naxians travel with us and will observe. They call themselves Blue Sphere and Rosy Tetrahedron. Jorin Murry-Balff, my Communications, will record our conversation. With your permission, of course."

"Granted," said Speaker-to-Erthumoi.

Within the helmet of its suit its head split open, revealing the great luminous beacon of its inner eye.

Wing-Marra shivered.

One of the other Locrians opened its eye also. Wing-Marra could not decide whether that one was Recorder or Ship-Commander. Did it matter? Perhaps they were *all* Recorder. Or all four were Ship-Commander.

Aliens, he thought. Go and figure.

The other two remained sealed. A safety measure, Wing-Marra suspected. Locrians were terribly vulnerable when their inner eye was exposed. The slightest pressure against it—the touch of a hand—could blind or even kill. Therefore they opened their facial hinges only when they deemed it absolutely necessary to do so.

Even in normal visual mode, Wing-Marra had heard, Locrians saw three-dimensionally, penetrating into the interiors of things. With the inner eye unveiled, he imagined that they could see right into his soul.

The two unveiled ones were watching him from opposite sides, as though trying to read all aspects of him. It was like being in the crossfire of two brilliant lasers. Wing-Marra understood now why they had asked for this face-to-face meeting. They wanted a chance to evaluate the nature of the Erthuma they were dealing with in a way that long distance conversation via neutrino wave could not provide.

Well, let them look, Wing-Marra thought. Let them look as long and as hard and as deep as they like.

The silent surveillance went on and on and on.

After a time he stopped finding it merely disagreeable and began to find it worrisome. He glanced toward the Naxians for an opinion. But they were calm. They lay motionless, placidly coiled side by side in a corner of the room, watching with unblinking eyes. They were in their limbless relaxation state. Evidently they saw no cause for alarm in this peculiar wordless interrogation.

At length one of the unveiled Locrians—not the one who had identified itself as Speaker-to-Erthumoi—said, "We believe that you are trustworthy."

"I am deeply grateful for that," Wing-Marra said, trying hard not to sound sarcastic.

"These are delicate matters in which we find ourselves enmeshed," another of the Locrians intoned. "We must operate from a position of absolute assurance that you will not abuse our confidence."

"Of course," Wing-Marra said.

"Let us come to the point, Captain Wing-Marra," said the fourth alien. "What we would prefer is that you leave this region at once, making no further investigation."

Ayana Sanoclaro uttered a muffled, undiplomatic grunt of surprise and anger. Wing-Marra's own reaction was closer to amusement. Was that why they had given him this elaborate scrutiny? That seemed a preposterous buildup for such a straightforward, almost simpleminded demand. Did they think he was a child?

But he restrained himself.

Carefully he said, "We have come a great distance, and we have significant research goals that we wish to carry out. Leaving here now is out of the question for us."

"Understood. You will not leave and we do not expect you to. As we have said, the problem we face here is delicate, and we would prefer to handle it without the complications that the intrusion of another galactic species can bring. But we state only a preference."

Wing-Marra nodded. He had forgotten how literal minded Locrians could be.

"Aside from our going away from here right away, then, what is it you really want from us?" he asked.

The two Locrians who had not opened their inner eyes now drew back the hinges of their faces. Wing-Marra found himself confronting four great blazing orbs. Within the translucent helmets, four sharp-edged alien beaks were slowly opening and closing—a sign, he supposed, of intense concentration. But he suspected also that it might connote Locrian tension, disquietude, malaise. Something about their stance suggested that: They held themselves even more stiffly than usual, practically motionless, limbs rigid.

The Naxians too now seemed distressed, probably from having picked up jittery auras from the Locrians. They had uncoiled and lay stretched taut, side by side, their eyes gleaming and bulging, their little transient flipper-limbs shooting in and out of their sides.

"It may be the case," said one of the Locrians finally, just as the silence had begun to seem interminable, "that we are not able to deal with the problem that we see here unaided. Indeed, we are quite certain of this. What we propose, therefore, is an alliance."

"What?"

"We will recapitulate. There is a problem in this solar system that causes us much concern. We would rather conceal it from you than share it with you; but because we have come to feel that we are incapable of solving the problem without assistance, specifically without Erthuma assistance, we are willing to regard the arrival of Erthumoi at just this moment as providential. And invite you to work with us toward a solution."

Wing-Marra felt a faintly sickening sensation, as though he were teetering on the rim of an infinitely deep mine shaft. What, he wondered, was he getting into here?

He looked from one Locrian to the next, four fleshless, forbidding insectoid heads whose alien eyes blazed like frightful torches.

"All right," he said. "Tell me something about this problem of yours."

"Let us show you," said the Locrian who was Speaker-to-Erthumoi.

The alien gestured to another of the Locrians—perhaps it was Recorder—who drew from the folds of its spacesuit a small brassy-looking metallic object that Wing-Marra recognized as an Locrian image-projecting device. The Locrian set it on the floor in front of itself.

"We came here," said Speaker-to-Erthumoi, "much as you did, simply to explore. We had no military or economic purpose in mind. As you already recognize, the planets of this solar system would be of little value to us. But in the course of our reconnaissance, we came upon something in the vicinity of the second world that aroused our curiosity. We investigated more closely, and this is what we observed."

Speaker-to-Erthumoi nodded. Recorder—if that was who it was—stared at the image projector until a warm golden glow, like that of a little sun, began to come from it. The device, Wing-Marra knew, was tuned to the Locrian's brain waves.

Suddenly the room blossomed into vivid color. A three-dimensional scene, so immediate in its presence that it seemed almost as though the wall of the *Achilles* had opened to reveal another world just outside, took form before Wing-Marra's eyes.

It *was* another world. Heavy-bellied orange clouds hung

low in a deep turquoise sky. The vantage point at which Wing-Marra found himself was just below the clouds, perhaps a kilometer above the surface. He saw dense blue-green forests below, broad rivers, a chain of huge shimmering lakes.

Far off on the horizon a smallish G-type sun was setting, streaking the air with brilliant bands of violet and gold. On the opposite side of the sky a moon had already begun rising, huge and oppressively close, perhaps no more than one hundred thousand kilometers away. Its bare, smooth, gleaming face was marked with the dark, rugged lines of what must surely be immense mountain ranges ringing shining ovals that might have been the beds of long-dry seas.

"What you see is the second world of the nearby system on a summer evening," Speaker-to-Erthumoi announced. "It is not an agreeable place. The mean temperature at the altitude of observation is approximately 315 K. It is slightly cooler at ground level, but still unpleasantly warm, at least by our standards. The atmosphere is composed almost entirely of nitrogen and oxygen, with substantial water vapor and minor components of argon and carbon dioxide. The atmospheric pressure is equally displeasing, approximately seven times as great, at surface level, as on Locrian-norm worlds. There are strong tidal effects, caused by the proximity of a satellite unusually large in relation to its primary, and a vortex of relatively cool air descending permanently from the poles creates constant strong cyclonic winds. Ordinarily we would not have continued our observations of such a planet beyond this point. However—"

The other Locrian made a barely perceptible movement. The focal intensity of the image changed, and Wing-Marra abruptly found himself looking at the second world from a point not far above the tangled canopy of a tropical jungle.

Winged creatures were moving slowly through the air.

"Native life?" Wing-Marra asked.

"No. Look again."

He narrowed his eyes against the brightness of the sky, doubly lit by the spectacular sunset and the cold white glory of the gigantic shining moon. What had seemed to him at first quick glance to be huge birds now appeared something quite other: humanoid figures with small stubby legs and two slender arms held close against their chests. From bulging humps below their shoulders rose two powerful limblike projections heavily banded with muscle and anchored by jutting keels on their chests; and out of those came the giant fleshy wings, far larger in area than the creatures themselves, whose steady stately flapping motions held them aloft.

Then one of the flying creatures turned so that its narrow, tapering head was clearly outlined against the sky, and Wing-Marra could plainly see the great curving bony crest rising from its forehead and the equally astonishing jut of its elongated chin. He had no further doubt. Another of the galactic races had preceded both Locrians and Erthumoi to this place.

"Crotonites?" he said, with a little involuntary shudder.

"Indeed. See, now, their base." Focus shifted once again, and Wing-Marra beheld the elaborate webwork weave of a Crotonite nest, spreading through the treetops to cover perhaps a hectare. The winged aliens, equipped with breathing masks to help them deal with an atmosphere whose chemistry was not much to their liking, moved busily back and forth, swooping down to land, disappearing within the strands of the delicate structure, emerging again and rising skyward with strong, unhurried strokes of their great wings.

"If there are Crotonites here," Wing-Marra said, "why haven't we detected any signs of a Crotonite starship in the vicinity?"

"No doubt it has been here and gone," said the Locrian. "So far as we can determine, the Crotonite base here has been established for quite some time. We regard it a semipermanent outpost."

Wing-Marra looked toward Sanoclaro. The Diplomacy's expression was solemn.

She said, "It might just be a world they could use, I suppose. Thick atmosphere, warm climate. Though the atmosphere doesn't seem poisonous enough to make them really happy, but they could work out some kind of adaptation to help them cope with all that oxygen. They seem to be doing all right with those breathing masks. Well, if they've filed a claim, we'll have to apply to them for permission if we want to make a landing and set up a base. But not if we're only going to make a ship survey of the molecular cloud. This solar system lies completely outside the cloud. Their claim wouldn't give them any rights to adjacent space."

"They have filed no claim," Speaker-to-Erthumoi said.

Wing-Marra frowned. "No?"

"Nothing. Nor have they made any response to our presence here. They seem to be making an elaborate point of ignoring us. It is as though they have not noticed us. Or you, we presume, since you evidently have not heard from them. They simply go about their business, setting out every day from that base and exploring the planet in an ever widening circle."

"Then I fail to see the difficulty," the Erthuma captain said. "If they don't care that others are here, why should you care so much that they are? This whole solar system's a free zone for everybody. And in any case there doesn't seem to be much here of any importance."

"You have not heard the entire story yet," said Speaker-to-Erthumoi. "They also have a base on the moon."

Another tiny movement by the Locrian operating the projector, and the lush tropical scene vanished in an instant. Its place was taken by something far more harsh: the barren, airless landscape of the second planet's moon. Now Wing-Marra found himself at the edge of what must have been an ancient sea. A shallow, barren basin of some white limy rock stretched to the horizon. Colossal mountains, their lofty summits unexpectedly eroded and rounded as they might have been on a world that had an atmosphere, rose to one side. The dazzling green bulk of the second world hung close overhead, filling the sky, terrifyingly near, seemingly about to plunge down upon him.

The Crotonites had woven a seven-sided Crotonite dwelling that sprawled over the brightly lit plain just at the edge of the mountains' shadow. And Crotonites, swaddled in individual pressure-bubbles that covered them, wings and all, from crested heads to stubby legs, were driving about in land-crawlers.

But their movements were incomprehensible. They seemed to be circling a big empty area a dozen or so kilometers from their base. From time to time one of the crawlers would abruptly disappear, as though it had been devoured by some unseen lurking monster; or one would wink suddenly into existence in the middle of the plain, as if popping out of nowhere.

"I don't understand," Wing-Marra said. "Where are they going? Where are they coming from?"

"We ask ourselves the same thing," said Speaker-to-Erthumoi. "Our answer is that the Crotonites believe they must go to great pains to conceal whatever they are doing on that lunar plain. And so they have generated a zone of invisibility around it."

"Can they do such a thing?" Wing-Marra asked, surprised.

"It would appear that they can. We see nothing; and yet we feel the presence of living beings in that empty zone."

Murry-Balff said, "What do your instrument readings show? If there are Crotonites moving around out there, you'd be getting infrared output. And if they've set up some kind of invisibility gadget, there might be some measurable light-wave distortion around its edges. Or various other forms of data corruption."

"We do not have instruments capable of measuring what cannot be seen," replied the Locrian, and there was a distinctly icy edge to its flat, unemotional voice. "What we detect is the emanations of intelligent beings, radiating in the Crotonite mind-spectrum, coming from a place that seems to be uninhabited and uninhabitable."

Wing-Marra said, "What do you think they're trying to hide? A weapons factory? A center for espionage activities? A laboratory for secret scientific research?"

"We have considered all those possibilities. They have varing orders of probability. But what we think is most probable of all is that they have discovered something of great value on that moon, and do not want any other galactic race to know what they have."

"That might explain why they haven't filed a claim to this system," Sanoclaro said. "Even though their occupation of the planet and the moon would ordinarily validate any claim. Maybe they didn't want to call this place to anybody's attention even to the extent of claiming it. They gambled instead that nobody else would find it."

"This is our belief also," said the Locrian.

Sanoclaro shook her head. "Bad luck for them that not one but *two* different galactic races stumbled on it right after them, against all odds. But sometimes it does happen that the needle in the haystack gets found."

Speaker-to-Erthumoi said, "What it is the Crotonites have discovered here, we have no idea, any more than we know how they are able to conceal it. But Crotonites would not remain in so hostile an environment without strong motivation. We wish to know what that motivation is: that is, what it is that they are concealing."

Wing-Marra laughed. "We thought *you* were the ones who had found something valuable here."

"What we found was Crotonites working here secretly in a zone of mystery. We wish to know what that zone of mystery contains. And so we invite you to enter into partnership with us."

"So you've already told us. But just what kind of partnership do you mean?"

"We have one asset to offer: the discovery that the Crotonites are hiding something. But we are unable to proceed beyond that. You Erthumoi can provide, perhaps, the asset we lack: the technology by which the Crotonites' shield of concealment can be penetrated. Let us work together to expose and exploit their secret. And we will share, half and half, in such profits as come from the venture."

"Half and half?" Wing-Marra said. "If there's something valuable on that moon, don't you think the Crotonites are entitled to a share, too? Or are you planning to cut them out of it altogether?"

"To be sure," said Speaker-to-Erthumoi. "We may have to divide the profits in thirds."

* * *

The discussion aboard the *Achilles* that followed the departure of the Locrian boarding party was very possibly the loudest and most vociferous that Wing-Marra had ever known in all the eleven cycles of his life.

Sanoclaro, of course, was horrified at the notion of entering into any kind of deal with Locrians, and urged Wing-Marra to head for the nearest Erthuma world at once and turn the affair over to the authorities there. But her friend Linga Hyath, to everyone's amazement, disagreed completely with her: She was all for finding out without any delay what it was that the Crotonites were hiding on the second planet's moon. If the cool and unemotional Locrians were so churned up over it, she said, then it was important to know what they had. Mikoil Karpov took the same position, and so did Murry-Balff, who was already bubbling with notions of how to break through the Crotonite data screen.

Eslane Ree, though, was on Sanoclaro's side. "This is simply none of our business," the Navigation said quietly, and when Hyath and Murry-Balff took issue with her, she said it again less quietly, and then very loudly indeed. For a small woman she was capable of astonishing ferocity when she thought the occasion warranted it, and apparently she thought this one did. "We're here to do scientific research. Not to strike bargains with aliens."

"You look on aliens as enemies?" Karpov asked.

"I don't look on them as friends," Eslane Ree shot back. "They tolerate us in the galaxy because they have no choice. We came muscling into a system that they had carved up into five nice slices while we were still using stone axes, and demanded our piece of it. Well, because interstellar war is currently obsolete, and the galaxy is so big that even the Five Races hadn't had time to explore it all, they graciously allowed us to become the Sixth Race. But they don't trust us and they don't like us, and they all think they're a whole lot wiser than we are, and maybe they are. We haven't been out in the galaxy long enough to know."

"We have achieved so much in such a very short time," said Karpov ponderously. "Is that not—"

Eslane Ree glared at him.

"In a short time, yes, we've figured out black holes and pulsars and hyperdrives and neutrino-wave communication, and maybe all that makes us think we're pretty hot stuff. But when it comes to galactic politics we're still strictly novices. If the Locrians want to do something dirty to the Crotonites, let them. Why should we risk getting drawn in? Because the Locrians tell us they'll cut us in on the profits? *What* profits? When have the bugs ever gone out of their way to cut us in on anything? How do we know what they're really up to? What they want to do is use us. And when they're through using us, they might very well get rid of us, if it turns out what we've stumbled across is something that's inconvenient for us to know."

"Madness," Karpov muttered.

"I don't think you have any right—"

"Please," said Septen Bolangyr. "It is my turn to speak."

Bolangyr, who usually was indifferent to discussions of policy, also argued in favor of keeping out of potential trouble. "We don't understand much about Locrian psychology and we don't even begin to understand the Crotonites," he argued. "All we know, really, is that both of them are older and probably shrewder races than ours, and that, as Eslane Ree says, neither of them have much respect or liking for us. Eslane Ree is correct. We're likely to find ourselves way over our heads if we get mixed up in some squabble between them."

"Wrong!" Karpov cried. "Such a great opportunity to learn! We must not turn our backs! Not only the mystery of this moon, but the mystery of Locrians, the mystery of Crotonites! Go among them, is what we must do! Engage them! Entangle ourselves! How else can we learn? How can we simply turn our backs at such a time?"

"Easily," said Eslane Ree. "We're scientists, not spies."

"And to involve ourselves in any such irregular trans-species dealings is completely unwise," said Ayana Sanoclaro.

"And for all we know the bugs are the bad guys and the bats are the good guys," said Septen Bolangyr. "We'll be putting our noses into something we don't remotely understand. That doesn't feel very healthy to me."

"But can't you see—"

"Won't you realize—"

"If you'd only stop to consider—"

And so on until Wing-Marra, running out of patience at last, cut through the uproar to say, "I make it three in favor, three against. All right. I cast the tie-breaking vote. We go in with the Locrians."

"No!" The word came from Eslane Ree and Ayana Sanoclaro in the same instant. "Impossible! Unthinkable!"

"And very stupid," said Bolangyr.

"Those who don't like it," Wing-Marra replied, "can place formal objections on file. We will take official notice and proceed as planned." To Eslane Ree he said, "This is a scientific mission, yes. But it's also an Erthuma spaceship, and all Erthuma ships have the responsibility of protecting Erthuma interests in space, which sometimes involves monitoring the activities of the other five stargoing species. That's what we're supposed to do, and that's what we're going to do. Clear? Good. Murry-Balff, I want to talk to you about what instruments we're going to use to scan the Crotonite lunar base. Sanoclaro, put together a Crotonite master psychological profile for me. I need to know what makes those bats tick. You have twenty minutes. Eslane Ree, park us around that second planet's moon and compute a landing orbit that'll put our groundship down somewhere in the neighborhood of the Crotonite base. Bolangyr, run the usual maintenance checks on all extravehicular-activity equipment. I think that's all for now." He paused a moment. "No. There's one thing more. Hyath, go down below and tell the snakes—excuse me, the Naxians—what we've just decided. Ask one of them to volunteer for the landing party."

"And me?" Mikoil Karpov asked.

Wing-Marra realized that he had provided an assignment for everyone except Biochemistry. But he couldn't see any immediate role for Karpov in any of this.

Then, with a pang, the captain remembered that they had all come to this obscure corner of the galaxy for a reason that had nothing to do with Locrians or Crotonites or galactic power politics. For a long sad moment he stared at the glowing screen of the spectrometer. Neglected though it was, it was still flashing bright-hued reports from the nearby molecular cloud. Through Wing-Marra's mind went roiling visions of esoteric hydrocarbons, life-giving amino acids, complex polyvalents of a thousand kinds, stirring about tantalizingly in that mysterious ocean of intricate gases that lay just beyond his reach.

He sighed.

"You keep an eye on the spectrometer screen," he told Karpov. "There's no telling what sort of significant stuff is going to turn up inside that cloud. And we aren't going to stop the whole mission dead in its tracks while we deal with this distraction. Not if I can help it. Okay? Okay. Adjourned."

They set up their camp in the long shadow of the great mountains, fifty kilometers from the Crotonite moon base: close enough so that the curvature of the lunar surface would not interfere with Murry-Balff's instruments, but not so close that the Crotonites would come running right over to put up a fuss.

The first thing Wing-Marra did was to send out an all-frequencies neutrino-wave announcement telling the entire galaxy that a joint Erthuma-Naxian-Locrian expedition had landed to investigate certain "anomalies" on a moon of the second planet of an unclaimed main-sequence star in the W49 nebula, where a Crotonite exploration team appeared to be already at work.

Murry-Balff said quizzically, "Sir, is that such a good idea? The Crotonites can't fail to pick that message up. Should we really be letting them know we're here?"

"They already know we're here," Wing-Marra said, amused. "Do you think we can put a groundship down right in their backyard without their noticing? What the message does is tell everyone *else* that we're here. In case the Crotonites have any idea of defending their turf against intruders. If we were to attempt a secret landing, they might feel it was safe to respond with an immediate lethal attack."

"Against a transspecies ship? But that would be an act of war!" Murry-Balff exclaimed.

"Yes, it would. That's why I want to make it difficult for them to proceed with it. Most of us operate under the sane and reasonable assumption that one species will never attack another, but I suspect the Crotonites may operate under the assumption that they shouldn't attack another species unless they think they can get away with it. If everybody for fifty thousand light-years around knows we've landed here, the Crotonites are less likely to undertake military action against us. Or so I hope."

In fact he had no real idea how the Crotonites were likely to react to anything, but he was prepared for the worst. The psychological profile of them that Ayana Sanoclaro had drawn up for him was profoundly disturbing in that regard.

Of the five senior races of the galaxy, the Crotonites were the least predictable and, potentially at least, the most dangerous. Only their preference for worlds with thick atmospheres heavily laced with ammonia and hydrogen cyanide, evidently, is what had kept them out of serious conflict with the other races. The worlds they inhabited were unendurable to the other species; the worlds they coveted were worlds that none of the others would want.

What set them apart from the other intelligent species of the galaxy, possibly even more than their metabolic differences, was the fact that they were the only one that had wings. Locrians and Erthumoi walked upright; Naxians were wrigglers; Cephallonians, aquatic; the ponderous Samians, when they deigned to move at all, rolled. But Crotonites were fliers.

On their home worlds they lived primarily airborne lives, moving slowly but with a strange grace through the heavy atmosphere, swooping and rising, rising and swooping. Lesser winged creatures were their food, caught always while in flight. They had no cities, only small transient settlements fashioned of twisted fiber, which they abandoned after only short periods of occupation. How they had ever attained the technological capacity to achieve interstellar travel was hard for Erthumoi to understand; but, then, it was hard for Erthumoi to see how any of the Five Races, except perhaps the Locrians, had managed to cross that difficult-to-attain threshold. Yet they all had, where thousands of other intelligent species had not. Some force had driven them, often against all biological and mechanical probability, to reach outward not only to their neighboring worlds but to the stars themselves.

Could it be, Wing-Marra wondered, that the force that had impelled the Crotonites outward was hate?

Certainly they manifested plenty of that in their dealings with the other races. They scarcely troubled to conceal their contempt for beings who had no wings. "Groundcrawlers," they called them or "mud-lickers" or "landslugs." So great was their disdain for all things wingless that they could not bear even to eat the meat of the unwinged, predatory carnivores though they were: It was shameful, they explained, to incorporate the flesh of landslugs into their own high-soaring bodies.

Once they had learned that various sorts of wingless mud-lickers had found a way of traveling between the stars, therefore, the Crotonites must have felt that they too would have to go forth into that vast darkness. And they had not rested until they also had solved the mysteries of hyperspace travel.

Once they did enter the community of starfaring races, they accepted the presence of those who already roamed the galaxy, because they had no choice about it. There was no way for them to maintain absolute isolation from the rest. Interstellar commerce requires a certain amount of contact with alien creatures, and it is economically suicidal to let racial prejudices get in the way of that. But they made it plain that they did no more than tolerate any of the others, and that in fact what they felt for them was loathing and enmity.

They did not, of course, carry those feelings to the extent of actual warfare. If there ever had been any such thing as interstellar warfare, it had gone out of fashion long before the first Erthuma starfarers had come upon the scene. One reason for that was the logistical difficulty of waging war on a galactic scale, even with hyperdrive-equipped vessels. Another was that in a galaxy of effectively infinite size there was very little motive for serious territorial disputes among six intelligent life-forms whose environmental requirements were all mutually incompatible. But the main reason, probably, why the Crotonites never acted upon their hostility toward the wingless was that they knew the wingless would not permit war to break out. Nothing was apt to draw the separate races together more swiftly than any sort of conflict that might lead to war. War was an expensive nuisance; war was a messy disruption; war simply could not be allowed. The Crotonites probably knew that they would be annihilated at once by a united all-species force if they ever gave vent to their deepest emotions, and that helped to keep the galactic peace.

Instead they cheated wherever they could, they swindled, they behaved toward the wingless in all ways as though matters of morality were unimportant. The wingless in turn bore little love for them. Erthumoi, who had their own not very complimentary nicknames for each of the other galactic races, called the Crotonites "bats," or sometimes even "devils."

And now Wing-Marra found himself camped fifty kilometers from a nest of them.

"This moon can't have been airless very long," Linga Hyath was saying. "Probably it was just as habitable as its primary world, once upon a time."

"You think so?" Wing-Marra said.

They stood, spacesuit-clad, arrayed in a semicircle around Murry-Balff as he bent over the bank of instruments that he had set up on the bed of the dry sea. There were eight in the group: Wing-Marra, Hyath, Sanoclaro, Murry-Balff, Eslane Ree, the Naxian Blue Sphere, and two of the Locrians. Septen Bolangyr, Mikoil Karpov, and Rosy Tetrahedron had remained behind on the *Achilles*.

Hyath indicated the towering mountain range that loomed behind them. "Those are very big mountains," she said. "The sort you'd expect to find on a moon like this. But look at the way they've been worn down. For most of their existence they've been subjected to wind and rain and the other geological forces of a living world. But of course an atmosphere will wander off into space if a world's not big enough to hold it by gravitational force and if it's warm enough so that the atmospheric molecules can move faster than the local escape velocity. There was a time when this place must have had an atmosphere pretty much like its primary's, I'd guess—these two are really a double-planet system, most likely with similar outgassing history—but the moon, large though it is, was too small, and too warm, to keep its air. Little by little the entire atmosphere was able to break free of the gravitational field here and escape. And eventually there was none left at all."

"How long ago did that happen, would you say?" Eslane Ree asked.

"Oh, quite recently, quite recently indeed," said Hyath. "Within the last two or three hundred million years, is my top-of-the-head answer."

Eslane Ree chuckled. "Oh. Only two or three hundred million years ago! That's your idea of quite recently?"

"Surely you understand that on the geological time scale that's only—"

"Hold it," Wing-Marra said. "I think Murry-Balff's got something."

The Communications had been leaning forward over his control panel, muttering to himself, shaking his head, tapping in data setups, wiping them out, tapping new ones in. Suddenly the board was alive with flashing lights.

"Okay," Murry-Balff said. "I think we have data capture."

Wing-Marra peered close. The readout was analog, but he could make nothing of the patterns he saw.

"What I've done," said Murry-Balff, "has been to plot light-wave deviation first. That's this information here. Assuming there's a zone of significant surface mass in that supposedly empty zone, it ought to have at least some relativistic effects on photons traveling through its vicinity, regardless of the visual data corruption that the Crotonites are managing to throw up around it. Okay. There it is." He pointed to a pattern in green and red at the side of his panel. It meant nothing at all to Wing-Marra. Murry-Balff said, "It's next to imperceptible, but that's what you'd expect of any sort of mass smaller than a continent, anyway. But the fact is that it *isn't* imperceptible. What I'm picking up is the bending I expected, right here—and *here*—that's an inferred computation of the required size of whatever's causing the perturbation. Those are the boundaries of the concealed object, see?"

"Show me that again," Wing-Marra said.

Murry-Balff made a quick gesture with his light pen.

"But that's enormous!" said Wing-Marra. "It's the size of a small city!"

"That's right. Not such a small one, either. The area is—umm—sixty-four square kilometers, plus or minus four. Now, we get the sonar in there and we try to see whether it'll penetrate the Crotonite data shield; and we discover that we can, more or less, although the perimeter data is likewise corrupt and has to be factored for a standard distortion deviation, which the little brain here in this box has been kind enough to work out for me. We bounce the sound waves through the invisibility shield, and luckily for us, the shield doesn't screen them out once we're inside and so far as I can tell does not corrupt our data, but returns us a clean readout. Which gives us the horizon profile of the concealed object."

"Where?"

"Here. You see? These ups, these downs. The skyline, so to speak, of the hidden city. And the mean elevation is—well, rooftop level, I make out to be eleven and one half meters, with a deviation of—umm—the tallest building is, let's say, twenty-one and one half meters, but there aren't many of those, and most of the others are, well, single-story structures—"

"Structures?" Ayana Sanoclaro said. "You've got actual buildings showing on that screen?"

The two Locrians were murmuring now in their own

harsh, clicking language. The Naxian, agitated, was rapidly thrusting its little flipper-limbs forth and retracting them.

"Didn't you hear me?" Murry-Balff said. "There's a city under the Crotonite screen. Now that I'm past their corruption line, I'll have the whole thing mapped out for you in less than fifteen minutes."

"A city?" Sanoclaro said in wonder. "The Crotonites have built a *city* on this airless moon? Under some sort of dome, do you mean?"

Murry-Balff looked up at her. "Did I say it was a Crotonite city? Do the Crotonites even build cities? There's no dome that I can see, at least not an actual physical one, though of course all I'm getting is shadow images, and it's possible that a dome viewed edge-on might somehow not show up on my screen. I can check that out from another angle. But you can see the building profiles, can't you?" He waved his hands grandly over the panel, which was still entirely incomprehensible to Wing-Marra. "There's nothing Crotonite-looking here. Look, these are streets and avenues. Crotonites don't ordinarily have streets and avenues, do they? And those are solid, rounded structures with vaulted roofs. I don't have the foggiest idea what they are, but Crotonite they aren't."

"But who—?" Sanoclaro demanded, gesturing bewilderedly. "It isn't one of ours, or we'd have had records of a landing here. It can't be Locrian. The Cephallonians would hardly build a settlement on a world that doesn't have a drop of water. The Samians—the Naxians—"

"Why does it have to be a city belonging to any of the Six Races?" Wing-Marra asked suddenly.

Everyone stared at him.

"What are you saying?" asked Eslane Ree. "That there's a seventh interstellar race somewhere that nobody knows about yet?"

"I don't know," Wing-Marra told her. "Right now all I can do is ask questions, not answer them." To Hyath he said, "You believe that this place once was as habitable as its companion planet, but that it's been airless like this for—how long? Three hundred million years?"

"Plus or minus a hundred million," said Hyath.

"Same difference." He closed his eyes a moment. Then, turning to the Locrians, he said, "You people were the first of the Six Races to achieve star travel, right? How long ago was that?"

"It was in the Eighteenth Era," one of the Locrians began.

"Translate that into Galactic Standard Years. Please."

After a moment the Locrian said, "You would think of it as approximately three hundred fifteen thousand years before the present time."

Wing-Marra nodded. By Linga Hyath's geological way of reckoning things, that was only a heartbeat ago.

He said, "And when you first got out into interstellar space, did you encounter any other starfaring races then, older races that are extinct now?"

"No," said the Locrian. "We did, of course, come upon the ruins of ancient civilizations which perhaps had been galactic in nature, though we do not believe that they were. But of living galactic races—no, no, we were the first of our epoch. And perhaps the first in the history of this galaxy."

"I'm not so sure of that," said Wing-Marra, half to himself.

His mind was racing. Knowledge he had not called upon in hundreds of years came bubbling now out of its deep hiding place.

In the second cycle of his life, flushed with the new youth of his first rejuvenation, he had turned his attention toward the remote past with much the same intensity as he had much later taken up organic chemistry. Archaeology then had been the center of his energies, and for decades he had pored backward into the yesterdays of his species, digging into the few hundred years of history that his native world of Hesperia could provide, then onward, deeper, to Earth, the mother world of all Erthumoi, where antiquity was measured in hundreds of centuries: Chichén Itzá, Pompeii, Babylon, Troy, Luxor, Lascaux. But even that had not satisfied his hunger for antiquity, for Earth was a young world as galactic worlds went, and the Erthumoi a very young race: The mother planet offered no more than thirty thousand or forty thousand years of past that had the richness and complexity he sought, and beyond that lay nothing but stray scraps of bone, scatterings of stone tools, the charred ashes of ancient hearths.

So he had gone out into the galaxy again, digging on worlds beyond the Erthuma sphere. At least ten thousand of the worlds of the galaxy had evolved intelligent life-forms. Only a relative handful of those had gone on to develop technological civilizations, and some of those were extinct: dead by their own hands, so it would appear. Of the survivors, only five, before the Erthumoi, had reached the level of interstellar travel. It was not generally thought that any of the extinct races had succeeded in traveling beyond their own solar systems. A widely held theory argued that there was a critical technological threshold that every race had to pass; the ability to achieve self-destruction invariably came sooner than the ability to attain interstellar flight, and only those races able to master their own self-destructive impulses would last long enough to master the mysteries of hyperspace travel. Many had not.

Wing-Marra had probed the ruins of dead alien civilizations in a dozen different star systems. But they too were disappointing to someone seeking vivid and immediate insight into the look and texture of the distant past. Even in the best preserved of them, not much had withstood the inroads of time: a faint line of stone foundations here, an empty burial vault there, some shattered walls, a battered fragment or two of strange jewelry, perhaps a bit of some unfamiliar and unrecognizable fossil, and not much more. That was all that remained. The youngest of those lost civilizations was one hundred thousand Galactic Standard Years old, according to his dating instruments; the oldest was five times as ancient as that. Mere traces, outlines in the sand.

But now—on a world where no one could have lived for hundreds of millions of years—

A city? A complete city, with a discernible street plan and buildings still so intact, after whole geological eras, that roofs still remained and the number of stories could be counted? No, that was archaeological nonsense, Wing-Marra thought. Whatever lay out there on that dead plain, it could not possibly be a settlement that went back to a time when this world still had air and water and vegetation.

But what, then? Perhaps, in the stillness and void of this lifeless moon, the familiar forces of erosion would not operate as they did elsewhere, and whatever was built here would remain through all the ages, undecayed. Why would anyone bother, though, to build a fair-sized city on so absolutely inhospitable a place as this world had become once its atmosphere had fled? And who would have done it? None of the Five Races, that seemed certain. And surely not Erthumoi.

A seventh galactic race, unknown to all the others?

It had to be.

It could not be.

This makes no sense, Wing-Marra thought. None whatsoever.

"What are you thinking?" Sanoclaro asked.

"A lot of things," said Wing-Marra. "But I don't have enough information. Do you know what we need to do now? We need to get into our buggies and ride over across there to take a close look at whatever it is that the Crotonites don't want us to see."

It was, of course, an outrageous thing to be doing. The ground vehicles were equipped with weaponry, and both Wing-Marra and Murry-Balff were carrying hand-model blasters, which were not uncommon items of male ornamental dress on their home world. The Locrians, too, were armed. But in all the cycles of his life Wing-Marra had never once had occasion to use his blaster against another living creature, and he doubted that Murry-Balff had either. As for using it against a member of one of the other galactic races—no, no, it was unthinkable for a member of one race to injure a member of another.

He was counting on the fact that the Crotonites were likely to feel the same way.

Besides, this solar system was unclaimed. If the Crotonites

had taken the trouble to claim it, they could have closed both the second planet and its moon to all other races, and backed that up, if necessary, by force. But they had filed no claim. Whether they had chosen that course for some unfathomable sneaky Crotonite reason or simply because they had been too confident that no other race would find this place was something Wing-Marra did not know. Either way, as things stood, they had no legal right to bar anyone else from landing here.

They could, naturally, keep trespassers from entering any base they had established themselves. But Wing-Marra had no intention of going anywhere near the Crotonite base. All he wanted to inspect was that big empty place out on the bed of the vanished lunar sea. That was no Crotonite base, was it? That was simply an empty place. How could they stop him from driving right up to it? From peering in? From entering it, if he could?

They would have to admit that there was something there, after all, before they could keep him from trying to look at it.

At first, it seemed as though the Locrians would not buy any of his reasoning and were going to refuse to accompany him into the plain. They were afraid of some violation of Crotonite territorial rights that would lead to big political trouble. The Naxian, too, was uneasy about going along. Naxians, because of their keen intuitive sense of what might be going on in any organism's mind, were usually confident of their ability to handle themselves in all sorts of bothersome situations. But Blue Sphere, like the Locrians, indicated that it-she would just as soon stay away from the Crotonite outpost.

Wing-Marra was unhappy about that. He wanted the Locrians and the Naxian along for a show of solidarity—the Crotonites were less likely to commit some hostile act if they saw that they'd be stirring up trouble with three of the Six Races at once—and also he valued Naxian intuition and Locrian cold-blooded intellectuality. But they would not give in.

"Very well," Wing-Marra said finally. "We'll just have to go without you, I guess."

Which broke the impasse, for the Locrians did not trust their Erthuma partners sufficiently to want them to get first look at the enigma on the plain without them, and Blue Sphere, although it-she plainly suspected that Wing-Marra was bluffing, apparently did not want to take the risk that he was crazy enough to mean what he said. So in the end they all went: a tri-species expedition, setting out in two ground vehicles across the hard flat limestone floor of the ancient dry sea.

They were still twenty kilometers or so from the zone of mystery when Eslane Ree pointed out a Crotonite land-crawler coming up on their left.

"Everyone into defensive mode," Wing-Marra ordered. "All weaponry armed and ready, but don't get overanxious. Let's just see what they do."

What the Crotonites did was to swing into a path parallel to theirs at a distance of perhaps half a kilometer, and ride alongside them. A little while later, a second Crotonite vehicle took up the same escort position on the right. Then a third appeared, hanging back to the rear. All three maintained constant distances from the Erthuma vehicles as they traveled over the plain.

"The bats watch us, and we watch the bats," Wing-Marra said. "And neither side makes the first move. All right. We wait and see, and so do they. How far are we from the edge of the zone, Murry-Blaff?"

"Seven hundred meters."

"Well, we'll have some answers pretty soon."

"Here," Murry-Balff said. "This is it."

Wing-Marra signaled and the caravan came to a halt. They seemed to be in the middle of nowhere. Behind them, far behind, lay the mountains and their camp, and some distance off to the south the Crotonite camp. Ahead of them, stretching out almost endlessly, was the bright, chalky, almost featureless plain that once had been the floor of a prehistoric ocean. The green second world, hanging overhead, seemed closer than ever, a massive, looming weight; and its brilliant light cast an eerie, chilling glow.

Right in front of us, Wing-Marra thought, is a city that may be half a billion years old. And we can't see a damned thing.

"Here come the Crotonites," Eslane Ree said.

"Yes. I'm aware of them. Let's get out and sniff around a little."

He was the first out of the vehicle. After a moment, one of the Locrians jumped out also, and then the other. Sanoclaro and Eslane Ree followed. Murry-Balff remained with his instruments. Blue Sphere, looking fidgety and troubled, stayed in the vehicle also. Wing-Marra beckoned to it-her to get out. Murry-Balff could do his work from the vehicle, if he wanted to, but Wing-Marra needed the Naxian by his side.

He took a few steps forward, wondering if he would feel resistance. But there was nothing. Nothing at all.

"Am I near it?" he asked.

"Another ten meters," Murry-Balff replied. "But the Crotonites—"

"Yes. I know."

From the right, the left, the rear, the three Crotonite land-crawlers came zeroing in, and pulled up in an open arc around the two Erthuma vehicles. Wing-Marra, though he knew the gesture was preposterous, let his hand rest lightly on the blaster strapped to the side of his spacesuit. God help us all, he told himself, if it comes down to stuff like that. But he felt he had at least to make the gesture.

The Crotonites were out of their land-crawlers, now, six of them, approaching him in the peculiarly dismaying waddling shuffle that they employed when they were forced to walk on the surface of a world. Seen close up, they were less frightful looking than when flying like devils through the air, because their huge wings were furled and swaddled within their pressure suits. That way, they appeared as short, plump, almost comical little beings, standing no more than waist high to an Erthuma. But they were, Wing-Marra thought, pretty evil looking all the same. The great ungainly bulk of the folded wings behind them provided an ominous reminder of their true forms, and their long sharp-featured heads, crested and bony chinned, had a harsh, repellent, monstrous look.

"Turn on the simultrans," Wing-Marra said to Murry-Balff.

The Crotonites, he knew, would never deign to speak Erthumat. And he knew only seven words in Crotoni, four of them obscene and the others profane.

"Who is the leader here?" asked the shortest and fiercest-looking of the Crotonites, one with diabolical yellow eyes streaked with bands of red.

Wing-Marra raised his hand. "I am. Captain Hayn Wing-Marra of the Erthuma research vessel *Achilles*."

"I am Hiuptis," said the Crotonite. "What are you doing here, Captain Wing-Marra?"

"Why, we've been out for a drive. And now we're taking a little walk."

"I mean what are you doing in this solar system."

"Carrying out chemical research. We're studying the molecular cloud nearby."

"And does the molecular cloud extend to the surface of this moon?"

"Not at all. But while we were in orbit up there we ran into some old friends from Locria, who suggested that we all come down here for a little rest and relaxation."

"Indeed," said the Crotonite coldly. "This moon is an extremely relaxing place. But I suggest that you enjoy yourselves elsewhere. If you continue in the direction you are traveling, you will very shortly be trespassing on a research center established by and operated for the exclusive use of the Galactic Sphere of Crotonis."

"Will we?" Wing-Marra said. "A research center, you say? Where? I don't see anything here at all." He took a deep breath and began to move forward, indicating with a small movement of his hand that the others should come with him. "It's absolutely empty out here, so far as I can tell."

Murry-Balff said softly, "You're within two meters of the shield perimeter now, sir."

"Yes. I know."

Wing-Marra took another step.

The Crotonites began to look extremely agitated. Their bright, beady eyes gleamed and flickered, and they shifted their weight awkwardly from one to the other of their short, birdlike legs. Wing-Marra imagined that they would be flapping their wings, too, if their wings were not pinioned within their pressure suits. As he walked forward, the Crotonites hopped along beside him, keeping pace.

"One meter, sir," Murry-Balff said.

Wing-Marra nodded and stepped across the invisible line.

It was like walking through a wall. Inside, everything was different. He was standing in a kind of antechamber, an open space that curved off to either side at a wide angle. Behind him was the barren plain, still visible, and straight ahead of him, perhaps fifty meters ahead, lay a zone of absolute blackness, so dense and dark that it could well have been the outer boundary of the universe. The space between the invisible wall to his rear and the blackness ahead formed the antechamber, which was brightly lit by drifting clusters of glowfloats and cluttered everywhere with alien-looking instruments. It was full of Crotonites, too, who were staring at him with a look on their demonic bony faces that was surely the Crotonite equivalent of the most extreme astonishment.

Murry-Balff, still monitoring everything from the vehicle, said, "There's a second shielded zone within the first one, sir."

"I'm looking right at it. It's black as the pit."

"It's totally light absorbent. But the sonar goes through. The city starts just on the other side."

The Crotonite who called itself Hiuptis tapped Wing-Marra urgently on his thigh. "Now do you see, Captain? Plainly this is a research zone, and delicate observations are in progress."

"Fascinating," said Wing-Marra. "I never would have believed it."

"You concede that we are carrying on research here?"

"Yes. Yes, of course you are. That's plain to see."

"Then I call upon you to cease this trespass at once!"

"Ah, but we're not trespassing, are we?" Wing-Marra

said lightly. "We're only visiting. It's a purely social thing. This is such a forlorn dead place, this moon. It's good to have the company of one's fellow creatures for a little while in a place like this. And as long as we're here, you really don't mind if we look around a bit, do you? What sort of research did you say you were doing, by the way? I don't seem to recall."

Hiuptis turned to the Locrians. "Ship-Commander!" the Crotonite cried sharply. "Will you be a party to this detestable intrusion also? I warn you that you will thereby involve the Galactic Sphere of Locria in the culpability, and our inevitable demand for reparations will extend to your sphere as well as that of Erthuma. You have been warned."

"We take note of the warning," said one of the Locrians solemnly. "To which we reply that we are here only because we wish to pay our respects to the representatives of the Galactic Sphere of Crotonis, now that we have become aware that you too are present in this unknown and unclaimed solar system where both we and the Erthumoi have separately been carrying out research programs of our own."

The Locrian's emphasis on *unclaimed* was subtle but unmistakable. Hiuptis made a sputtering sound. It was shifting from foot to foot again, so quickly that it seemed almost to be hopping.

Wing-Marra glanced around. The Crotonites within the research station were unarmed, but the six who had come out to intercept the Erthuma vehicles carried blasters. He wondered what the chance was that they would use them if he continued to press forward. Certainly Hiuptis seemed furious, but so far the only threat it had made was that there would be a demand for reparations. Did that mean the Crotonites were ruling out any kind of attempt to end the intrusion by force? Or was Hiuptis merely trying to lull him with some slippery Crotonite sleight of tongue?

He looked toward Blue Sphere. The Naxian seemed to be aware of what Wing-Marra needed to know. It-she signaled relative calm: The Crotonites were angry, were, in fact, fuming mad, but there seemed to be no immediate danger of actual violence.

Of course, even Naxians weren't infallible. But Wing-Marra decided to risk it.

He began to move forward again, toward the strange zone of blackness that lay before him.

Hiuptis and the other five blaster-equipped Crotonites hopped frantically along at his side. "Captain Wing-Marra! Captain Wing-Marra! Captain Wing-Marra!" Hiuptis cried, again and again, in increasingly excited tones.

The other Crotonites, those who had been operating the myriad scanning devices that were aimed toward the wall of darkness, were staring at him, frozen with astonishment.

"Do you mean to go in *there?*" Hiuptis asked. "Surely not! Surely not, Captain Wing-Marra!"

Wing-Marra turned toward his Naxian again. Blue Sphere looked troubled now.

They are afraid, it-she told Wing-Marra with a silent gesture. They are angry that you are in here where they do not want you to go, but they are afraid, also, of what may happen if you go in there. It is for your sake that they are afraid.

"Murry-Balff?" Wing-Marra said. "Do you have any reading on what's going on on the other side of the inner screen? Do you pick up the presence of any Crotonites over there?"

"I don't, sir, no. But that doesn't mean there aren't any, only that the sonar doesn't—"

"Right," Wing-Marra said. He looked toward the Locrians. "What about you? Can you try to see through that darkness and tell me what's behind there?"

The Locrians, after a moment's hesitation, unveiled their inner eyes, and turned their piercing three-dimensional vision toward the black void ahead.

"Buildings," reported one of the Locrians, its voice sounding oddly strangled.

"Buildings, yes," said the other. "Streets. A whole city is there."

"No Crotonites?"

"No living thing at all," the first Locrian said. "It is very quiet in there. It is extremely still."

"Fine," Wing-Marra said. "I'll take a look."

"Captain!" Eslane Ree cried, in horror. "No!"

"Captain Wing-Marra!" said Hiuptis, practically squawking with rage and frustration. "I forbid—I utterly forbid—"

"Excuse me," Wing-Marra said. "I'll be right back, I promise you."

Quickly, before he could change his mind, he stepped into the zone of darkness.

The first thing he noticed on the far side was that he was still alive. He had been prepared to die—eleven cycles might well be quite enough, he had often thought—but that had not happened.

The second bit of information that came to him was the amber glow on the arm-monitor of his suit that told him he was now in the presence of an atmosphere. An oxygen-based atmosphere, at that. He could probably take his spacesuit off altogether in here, though he did not intend to. This place was like a world unto itself, sealed off within the screens that shielded it. Perhaps the atmosphere in here was the one the city had had when this moon was still alive.

Then, as his vision adapted to the low light level within the inner shield, he saw the city.

It was stunning beyond his comprehension. Low buildings, yes—Murry-Balff's readouts had been right about that. In a perfect state of preservation, absolutely new looking, and so totally strange in their architecture that he felt as though he had wandered into a land of dreams. Everything seemed to melt and flow: domes became parapets, walls became balconies, windows turned to arches. All was fluid, and yet everything was fixed, solid, eternal.

Unfamiliar colors teased his eyes. He could almost have believed that he was seeing in some far corner of the spectrum, that these were the hues beyond violet, or perhaps the ones below red.

Wonderstruck, he moved forward, down a narrow street that seemed to widen invitingly as he entered it.

The movement, he realized, was an illusion. Nothing moved here. All was in stasis: timeless, silent, free from any sort of decay. There was no dust. There were no cracks in the walls. This was a city outside time, shielded against all harm. No tectonic movement within the depths of this moon had left its mark on these flawless structures. No meteors had come plunging through the airless sky to crash through these roofs. No spider had spun here. Moth and rust were strangers here. An eternity and a half might have passed since the builders of this place had taken their leave of it, but nothing about it had changed.

How was that possible? What spell of enchantment kept this place invulnerable against the tooth of time?

He went close, peering through windows that seemed opaque and translucent at the same time. There were objects in the buildings: artifacts, mechanisms. He saw things on shelves that baffled and awed and astounded him. Wing-Marra began to tremble. Should he go in? No, he thought. Not now. Not yet. He might be pushing his luck too far. Who knew what traps awaited him in there, to guard those ancient treasures against intruders? And yet, to think that all the wonders of an unknown technology were just on the far side of those shimmering walls—

He was choking with amazement. There was no place to compare with this in all the galaxy.

He touched a wall. It seemed to give slightly against the pressure of his fingertips. And then suddenly the sky above him was ablaze with the whirling snakes of the Kekule ring. The fiery vision of a gigantic organic molecule danced before him. It was none that he had ever seen or even imagined before; immense, bewilderingly intricate, joined in a thousand thousand places, holding forth the possibility of infinite complexity. He stared into it and it was like staring into a new universe. After a time he let go of the wall and took a few tottering steps backward.

The vision faded at once and was gone.

But the impact, lingering, was overwhelming. Wing-Marra's mind throbbed. He had to get away. He needed to come to terms with what he had seen. He could not bear to remain in this place any longer.

He swung about and ran through the silent streets toward the blackness, and burst through it, and stumbled out into the antechamber. The bright lights dazzled him painfully and he shrank away from them, covering his face for a moment, closing his eyes. When he felt able to open them again, he saw them all staring at him in wonder, Crotonites, Locrians, his own people, all of them appalled, all of them aghast.

"You are alive?" Hiuptis whispered.

"Alive, yes. How long was I in there?"

Eslane Ree said, "A minute or so. No more."

"It seemed like years."

"What was in there?" Ayana Sanoclaro asked.

Wing-Marra gestured. "Go in and see for yourself."

"Are you serious?"

"Go in!" he cried. "All of you! You've never imagined anything like that! I wasn't hurt—why should you be?" He looked down at the Crotonite commander. "You mean to say that you never went in there, not once, not any of you?"

"No," Hiuptis murmured. "Never. We thought it was too dangerous. We only scanned it from outside, and nothing more. The shields—we were not sure if they were lethal. Finally we risked a penetration of the outer one. But the other—the other—"

"So you didn't put the shields up yourselves?"

The Crotonite made a gesture of negation.

"No," Wing-Marra said. "Naturally you didn't. Neither the invisibility shield nor the decay-proof shield inside it. We couldn't figure out how you had done it, and of course you hadn't done it. You don't have the technology for that. Nobody in the galaxy does. You just stumbled on the whole thing, and you've been dancing around the edges of it. Well, go on in now! All of you! Go and see! My God, there are miracles in there! And who can even guess how old it all is? Fifty million years? A billion? It can sit like that forever . . . right to the end of time."

"Captain—" It was Linga Hyath. "Captain, you're getting too excited."

"Damned right I am!" Wing-Marra cried. "Go in there and see! Go in, will you? See for yourselves!"

Afterward, when everyone had come stumbling out, hushed and dazed and dumbfounded, a strained silence fell. The vastness of the wonders that they had seen seemed to have overcome them all.

Only the Locrians appeared able to come to terms immediately with that grand and staggering experience. To Wing-Marra's amazement they joined hands and pranced about in a weird, jubilant dance, rubbing their antennae together as they cavorted. No doubt they were already counting the profits that could be mined from the hoard of treasure beyond the shield.

It was then that Hiuptis came to Wing-Marra and said, in a dark, cold tone the Erthuma had not heard from it before, "You wingless ones will leave our research center now, and you will not return. You will obey without further discussion."

There was insistence in Hiuptis's crackling voice and menace and something else; the implication, perhaps, that everyone there needed a time to retreat and digest the meaning of the discovery. But mainly there was menace and insistence. Wing-Marra suspected that there might be real violence, despite all taboos, if they tried to remain any longer; and Blue Sphere backed up his suspicions with the blunt warning that the Crotonites were reaching a point of exasperation that might prove explosive.

"Don't worry," Wing-Marra told Hiuptis. "We're going to go. You can have the place to yourselves again."

The Locrians halted their strange dance instantly. One of them turned to Wing-Marra in amazement, its great eye gleaming, and said, "But our agreement—!"

Wing-Marra met its glare with one of his own. "We can discuss that later. I'm calling for a withdrawal. I'm not ready to take any further steps here. You can do as you please."

"Leaving this find to them?" the Locrian said, astounded. "Incredible! You actually mean to withdraw and let them have— "

"For the time being," said Wing-Marra. "Only for the time being."

The Locrian rose to its full height and waved its forelimbs furiously in protest. But Wing-Marra, turning quickly away, began to walk toward the perimeter of the outer screen, toward the ground vehicles waiting just outside it.

Sanoclaro came up beside him. "Are you serious? You're really just going to pull out now?"

He whirled to face her. "What do you think I'm going to do? Start a war with Crotonis over it? These Crotonites are half crazy with confusion and rage and greed and outraged pride and God knows what other emotions, all of them dangerous. They're right at the point where they'll kill to get us out of here, now. Do you want to see if they will?"

"But to allow them sole possession of such a find—"

"For the moment," said Wing-Marra. "Only for the moment. They're in possession, but they don't have ownership. Nobody does. They discovered it, sure. But they didn't claim it, which they probably thought was very clever. Then the Locrians found out about it and got us involved. I went in on my own hook, which the Crotonites hadn't dared to do, and discovered that it's accessible and full of incredible things. You understand this sort of stuff: You can see how muddled the claim is by this time. Let higher authorities figure it out now. The only thing that's certain is that nothing's ever going to be the same again in this galaxy."

"But what do you think the city is?" Sanoclaro asked.

"Something left behind by a race greater than any of the Six," said Wing-Marra quietly. "That's all I know. I couldn't begin to guess who they were. Or are."

"*Are?* But you said the site might be a billion years old!"

"It might, yes. Or a million. And its builders might have become extinct before there was vertebrate life on

Earth. Or they might still be out there somewhere, hidden away in some unexplored arm of the galaxy, or in some other galaxy entirely. Maybe we'll stumble upon them. Or maybe they'll come back from wherever they are and pay *us* a visit. Or maybe they'll never be heard from again. In any case, the damage is done."

"The damage?"

"There's a city full of a superior alien technology sitting here. Now that we know what to look for, we may find that there are fifty more invisible cities just like it stashed around the galaxy too, or five hundred, full of the most astounding gadgets anyone has ever dreamed of. You can bet that all that technology, if anybody can figure out what to use it for, is going to destablize the equilibrium among the Six Races that keeps this galaxy peaceful. Or worse: Suppose the builders themselves ever come back and decide to play with us—choosing sides among the Six Races, picking allies, making enemies, maybe looking for vassals—can you imagine what that will do?"

"Yes," said Sanoclaro quietly. "I can."

They reached the ground vehicle. Wing-Marra turned for one last look at the place where the city lay hidden.

He saw nothing. Nothing at all, only the bare bright expanse of the flat stark plain, and a few Crotonite groundcrawlers. He shook his head.

Everything will be different from now on, he thought. Nothing will ever be the same again.

"Let's get back to the ship," he said wearily. All his people stood waiting by the vehicles, each one of them seemingly lost in astonished recollection of the vision they had seen. "I need to put together some sort of a report," he said. "The whole Erthuma sphere will know about this place by tomorrow. The whole damned galaxy, I suppose."

"And then?" Eslane Ree asked. "What will we do after that?"

"Who knows? That's not my concern right now. I've had enough excitement. I've got other work to do, you know. I still want to see what sort of hydrocarbons are floating around in that molecular cloud." He allowed his eyes to close, and the alien city sprang to life behind his lids, strange dreamlike buildings stretching on and on to the horizon, and every one of them laden with implements and devices of unknown and perhaps unknowable use. He saw the vision again, bearing promise of chemistries beyond any chemistry he had ever known. His whole being throbbed with the recollection of what he had seen and felt behind that wall of darkness. A magical place, he thought. A place of wonders. And, maybe, of terrors. Time would tell.

Yes, he thought, everything is going to be different now, all throughout the galaxy. And, he suspected, he, too, would never be quite the same again. After such a vision, how could he be?

He smiled. Eleven cycles old, and he could still feel a little shiver of wonder now and then. That wasn't so bad. Of course, it took something pretty spectacular to get that kind of response out of him: a cloud thirty light-years wide loaded with complex organic molecules, say, or an alien city a billion years old. But he had lived eleven lifetimes, after all. After eleven cycles he couldn't be expected to react in a big way to anything ordinary. He had seen all the ordinary things before, too many times.

He shrugged. It would be interesting to stick around for another cycle or two, and see what was going to happen next.

"Okay," he said, beckoning them all to get back into the ground vehicles. "I think we're finished here for the time being. Let's go."

THE DIPLOMACY GUILD

DAVID BRIN

"ONE OR TWO PHILOSOPHERS HAVE SUGGESTED THAT you Erthumoi have taken on this queer obsession of yours because you live so hot and fast. You sense the chill currents of time upon your backs, and so feel a need to *copy* yourselves, in order to be two places at once."

Phss'aah's words flowed so smoothly from the translator grille that it was easy to lose track of the Cephallonian philosopher's train of thought. Anyway, I had been distracted for a moment by the whining of the miserable Crotonite, huddled in the corner. It was a pathetic figure, whimpering and mumbling to itself, flexing the broken remnants that had once been powerful wings.

One more burdensome responsibility. I had been cursing both fate and my boss's bureaucratic meddling for saddling me with the creature, cruelly scorned by its own kind . . . and yet an ambassador plenipotentiary from that powerful interstellar race.

The words of Phss'aah shook me from gloomy perusal of my newest guest. Remembering courtesy, I turned back to the huge tank taking up half the volume of my ship's visitor suite. The vaguely porpoiselike form within flailed water into a froth of bubbles, but the Cephallonian's visage remained calm and restrained.

"I'm sorry . . ." and I made the wet sound approximating Phss'aah's name as near as a descendant of Earth humans could form it. "I didn't quite catch that last remark."

Bubbles rose from the cetacoid's twin exhalation slots, and now I read what might be mild exasperation in the flex of his long snout. Instead of repeating himself, Phss'aah waved a stubby, four-fingered flipper-arm toward the aquabot that shared his tank. The bulbous machine had already planted a sucker on the glassy wall and spoke in its master's stead.

"I believe Master Phss'aah is proposing a hypothesis as to why humans—you Erthumoi—were the only one of the six starfaring races to invent robots. The notion is that it is because you have such short natural life spans. Being ambitious, your race sought ways to extend themselves artificially. In order to be many places at once, they put some of themselves into their machines."

I shook my head. "But our lives aren't any shorter than Locrians' or Naxians'—"

"Correction," the robot interrupted. "You are counting up an individual's *total* span of years, including each of his or her *consecutive* natural lifetimes. I believe you have had four renewals for a total of three hundred and four standard Earth years, Ambassador Dorning. But my master apparently believes your Erthuma worldview is still colored by the way existence was for you during the ages leading up to high civilization. In any event, you invented artificially intelligent constructs such as me well before learning how to Renew."

The machine—and Phss'aah—did have a point. Not for the first time I tried to imagine what it must have been like for my ancestors, facing certain death after only a single span of less than ninety standards. Why, at my first Renewal I was still barely formed . . . an infant! I'd only completed one profession by then.

How strange that most human beings, back in olden times, became parents as early as thirty years of age. In most modern commonwealths and nations of the modern galactic Erthumoi, you weren't even supposed to *think* about breeding until the middle of your second life, when you were mature enough to contemplate the responsibilities of reproduction.

All this time Phss'aah was watching me through the

glass with one eye, milky blue and inscrutable. I almost regretted that human-invented technology now enabled the Caphallonian to use his artificial mouthpiece as yet another veil to shelter behind. Though, of course, getting Phss'aah to rely upon this fancy assistant drone was actually quite a coup for me. The idea was to sell large numbers of such machines to the water race and then to each of the other Big Five, so that they would get used to what they now called the "bizarre Erthuma notion" of artificially intelligent, semiautonomous devices . . . robots. As the newest starfaring race, we newcomer Erthumoi could do with a chance to become indispensable.

"Hmm," I answered cautiously. "But the Crotonites"—I nodded in the general direction of my unwanted guest in the corner—"have even shorter life spans than natural, old-style humans, and they don't even Renew. Why then, didn't *they* invent robots? It's not for lack of skill with machines. They're quicker and more nimble than anybody, with unsurpassed craftsmanship. Lord knows they have easily as much or more *ambition* than anybody else."

The Cephallonian rose to breathe, then returned trailing bubbles. When he spoke, the wall unit conveyed an Erthuma translation, this time bypassing the robot.

"You reply logically and well for one of your kind. I do not know the answer to that. Certainly you and the Crotonites share the quick metabolisms characteristic of breathers of supercharged atmospheres. They, however, are oviparous fliers. You, on the contrary, descend from arboreal mammals. Mammals are gregarious—"

"*Some* mammals."

"Indeed." And some of Phss'aah's irritation briefly showed. Cephallonians do not like being interrupted while they are pontificating an elegant new theory. That was exactly why I did it. Diplomacy is such a delicate business.

"Perhaps another reason you invented intelligent machines was because—"

This time the interruption was not my fault. The door behind me opened with a soft hiss, and my own secretary-bot hovered into the guest suite, floating on magnetic waves induced in the walls and deck.

"Yes, Betty, what is it?" I asked.

"Messages received," she said tersely. "High priority, from Erthuma Diplomatic Guild, Long-Last Station."

Oblong, suspended in a cradle of invisible force, the machine looked nothing like her namesake, my most recent demi-wife on Long-Last. But, as it was imprinted with her voice and twenty of her personality engrams, this was a device one had to think of as possessing gender, and even a minimal right to courtesy. "Thank you," I told the auto-sec. "I'll be right up to take them."

Assuming dismissal, Betty turned and departed. From the corner of the suite, the Crotonite lifted his head and watched the machine briefly. Something in those catlike eyes seemed to track it as a hunter might follow prey. But this Crotonite wasn't going to be chasing flitting airborne victims above the forests of any thick-aired world ever again. Where once he had carried great, tentlike wings, powerfully muscled and heavier than his torso, now the short, slender, deep-chested being wore mere nubs—scarred from recent amputation.

The Crotonite noticed my look, and snarled fiercely through its breathing mask. "Plant-eating grub! Turn away your half-blind squinty vision-orbs. You have no status entitling you to cast them on my shame!"

That was in Crotonoi, of course. Few Erthumoi would have been able to understand so rapid and slurred an alien diatribe. But my talents and training had won me this post.

Cursed talents. Double cursed training!

By my own species's standards of politeness I should have accepted the rebuke and turned away, respecting his privacy. Instead, I snapped right back at him in my own language.

"*You?* You dare throw insults at me? You who are broken and wingless and shall never again fly? *You* who shame your race by neglecting the purpose for which you were cast down? Here, try doing this!"

I flexed my strong legs and bounded high in the half gravity of the guest suite. The cripple, of course, could not manage anywhere near that height with his puny legs. I landed facing him. "You are a diplomat, Jirata. You won your fallen state by being *better* than your peers, one of the first so chosen for a bold new experiment. Your job is now to try something new to your folk . . . to *empathize* with ground-walking life-forms like me, and even swimming forms like Phss'aah. To make that effort, you were assigned to me, a burden I did not ask for, nor welcome. Nor do I predict success.

"Still, you can *try*. It is the purpose of your existence. The reason your people did not leave you at the base of some tree to starve, but instead continue speaking your name to the winds, as if you still lived.

"*Try*, Jirata. Just try, and the very least you will win is that I personally will stop being cruel to you."

The Crotonite looked away, but I could tell he was struggling with a deep perplexity. "Why should you want to stop being cruel?" he asked. "You have every advantage."

I sighed. This was going to take a long time. "Because I'd rather like you than hate you, Jirata. And if you don't understand that, consider this. Your job is to investigate a new mode of diplomacy for your people. Empathy is the core of what you must discover in order to succeed. So while I'm away, why don't you try conversing with Phss'aah. I'm sure *he'll* be patient with you. He doesn't know how to be anything else."

That was untrue of course. Phss'aah gave me a look of exasperation at this unwelcome assignment. For his part, Jirata looked at the Cephallonian, floating in all that water, and let out a keening of sheer disgust.

I left the room.

"Actually, there are two messages of red priority," Captain Smeet told me. She handed over a pair of decoded flimsies. I thanked her, went over to the privacy corner of the ship's bridge, and laid the first of the shimmering, gauzy message films over my head. Immediately, the gossamer fabric wrapped over my face, covering eyes and ears and leaving only my nostrils free. At once it began vibrating, and after a momentary blurriness, sight and sound enveloped me.

My boss looked across his desk at me . . . the slave

driver whose faith in my abilities was anything but reassuring. He seemed to feel there was no end to the number of tasks I could take on at the same time.

"Patty," he said. "Sorry about dumping the Crotonite envoy on you. As I told you earlier, he's part of a new experimental program being initiated by the Seven Sovereigns' League. You'll recall that particular Crotonite confederacy suffered rather badly because they so magnificently bungled the negotiations at Maioplar fifty years ago. In desperation they're trying something radical, to completely revise their way of dealing with other races. I guess they're trying it out on us Erthumoi first because we're the weakest of the Six, and if it flops, our opinion doesn't matter much anyway.

"In answer to your last message—I *still* have no idea if the Seven Sovereigns' League has cleared this experiment with other Crotonite nation-states or if they're doing it completely on their own. Crotonite intrarace politics is such a tangle, who can tell? That's why the Erthuma Diplomacy Guild decided to farm out Jirata, and the two others we've received, to roving emissaries like you—so you can try to figure out what's going on away from the spotlight of . . . well, media and the like. I'm sure you understand."

"Riiight, Maxwell." I gave a very unladylike snort. Back on Long-Last, Betty used to chastise me for that. But I never heard any of our husbands complain.

"That's my Patty," he went on, as if he was sure my reaction would be complete enthusiasm. "For starters, you can fly the contents of the other message past this broken bat of a Crotonite . . . and your guest Cephallonian as well. It seems one of our survey vessels, the *Achilles,* has stumbled onto something hot. I mean *really* hot, involving Crotonites, Locrians, and snakes. Who knows, maybe the league's idea of using crippled bats as envoys may make just that bit of difference, so let's put this on high priority, okay?"

"As high as preventing a breakage of the Essential Protocols?" I muttered subvocally. But I knew the answer to that.

"Of course, nothing is to stand in the way of getting King Zardee to toe the line on replicants. If he gives you any trouble about that, you just tell that freon-blooded son of a b—"

I'd heard enough. "Good-bye, Maxwell," I said, and ripped the flimsy off. It instantly began dissolving into inert gas.

"Orders, madam?" Always the professional, Captain Smeet looked at me coolly, expectantly.

"Proceed to planet nine of this system, and please beam to King Zardee I'll wait no longer for him to *prepare* for my arrival. If he plans to shoot us out of the sky, let him do so and live with the consequences."

Smeet only nodded and turned to tell her bridge crew what to do. I could have asked her to take me wet-diving in the nearby sun of the Prongee system, and she'd have found a way to do it, keeping her opinion of crazy diplomats to herself. That was more than *I* sometimes was able to do, after listening to Maxwell for a while.

Why it was that success followed that awful old man around so, I could never understand. I talked it over with the other emissaries under his command and all were equally mystified. Once, in a rage, I asked him. His answer? "Delegate authority," he had replied smoothly. "Then ride their asses."

"Schmuck," I commented as the last of the flimsy evaporated. It would be a little while yet before I was needed back here on the Bridge, for the confrontation with Zardee. I had better take the opportunity to go tell Jirata and Phss'aah this amazing news Maxwell was so breathless about.

Naturally, the Cephallonian took it philosophically.

I was still blinking in shock at the sights and sounds broadcast by the *Achilles*'s crew, evidence for a powerful starfaring civilization preceding even the Locrians. But Phss'aah, reliable Phss'aah, had already found a way to weave it into the convoluted web of his own argument.

"Consider the action of the *Achilles*'s captain," he said through the glass-wall translator. "He might be said to have been reckless, risking his life so, plunging through the final barrier into that strange alien city."

"Crazed slug behavior," contributed Jirata in a grating growl. For my part, I was so startled and pleased by even this insulting effort at conversation that I beamed at him. Naturally, he snarled and tried to take shelter under a wing that was no longer there.

"Yes, perhaps it was illogical," Phss'aah conceded. "Particularly since one might have sent through surrogates first. Locrians, for instance, would have taken a few days to hatch one or more immature males, intelligent enough to be sent through and report back, but essentially worthless and expendable. Naxians, in turn, would have sent one of their many animal helper species, if available, some of which are brighter than any young Locrian male! The same applies to Samians, and their magneto-surrogates.

"But it was *Crotonites* who discovered this place. Irascible, contemptuous, companionless Crotonites. They have only themselves, and have often expressed a wish they were alone in the universe. No doubt as the Erthumoi and Locrians arrived, the Crotonites were in the process of selecting a 'volunteer' to press on through the second barrier, just as Jirata here 'volunteered' to be a new-style diplomat for his people and his league."

"Whatever the Crotonites' plans," I commented, "the *Achilles*'s captain made all such preparations moot by simply striding ahead."

The Cephallonian whistled a sigh of perplexity. "The problem with my theory is this: The captain had his *own* surrogates to use—robots! Why did he not use some? Why do you humans create such marvelous, intricate entities, then fail to use them when they are most needed?"

Phss'aah illustrated the usefulness of robots by stretching under the massaging fingertips of the water-model I had given him. Contented bubbles rose from his sighing blow-slits.

I shrugged. At the back of my mind I was feeling the clock wind down toward my encounter with a wily, dangerous monarch. "Sometimes we use them too much, and then they can be more dangerous than anything."

Phss'aah binked. He regarded me closely. "Well, that may be. Perhaps that may very well be."

An angry visage greeted me on my return to the bridge, glaring out of the communications tank. I had been sent on this mission because, among all the different styles of government used by various Erthuma nation-worlds, kingdoms were among the quirkiest, and I had the most experience in our sector dealing with the arrogant creatures known as kings.

No doubt that was why I had been saddled with Jirata, as well.

Some kings were smooth. But this one actually reminded me of Jirata as he growled at me.

"We are not accustomed to being made to wait," he said as I stepped into the communications lounge. Ignoring the remark, I curtsied in the manner customary for the women of this commonwealth.

"Your Majesty would not have liked to see me dressed as I was when you called. It took a few moments to make myself presentable to Your Majesty."

Zardee grunted. I felt his eyes survey me like a piece of real estate, and recognized covetousness in them. Amazing, how many Erthuma societies left their males with these unaltered ancient, visually stimulated lust patterns! And Zardee was nearly eight hundred Standard Years old!

Never mind. I would use whatever chinks in his armor I could find.

"I accept your apology," he said in a softer tone. "And I must apologize in return for keeping such a comely and accomplished lady waiting out at the boundary as I have. I now invite you to join me on my yacht for some refreshment and entertainment I'm sure you'll find unique and distracting."

"You are most gracious, Your Majesty. However first I must complete my task here and inspect your mining establishment on the ninth planet of this system."

His visage transformed once more to anger, and again I felt astonishment that the people of this system put up with a monarch such as this. The attractions of kingships are well documented, but sentimentality can become a disease if it isn't looked to.

"There is nothing on my mining world of interest to the Diplomacy Guild!" he snapped. "And I remind you that you have no authority to force yourself upon me!"

This from a fellow so atavistic, I had no doubt he would chain me to a bed in his seraglio were it in his power. I kept my amusement to myself.

"I am sure, Your Majesty, that you would not want it to get out among your Erthuma and Naxian neighbors that you have something to hide—"

"*All* kingdoms and sovereign worlds have secrets, foolish woman. I have a right to keep secrets from the prying eyes of outsiders."

I nodded. "But not when those secrets violate the Essential Protocols of the Erthumoi. Or is it your intention to join the Outlaw Worlds, and forego the services of my guild?"

For a moment it looked as if he was about to declare his intention to do just that. But he stopped. No doubt he realized that step might push his people just too far. The commercial repercussions alone would be catastrophic.

"The Essential Protocols don't cover very much," he said, slowly. "My subjects have access to Erthuma ombudsmen. I vet my treaties past guild lawyers, and my ship captains report to the guild on activities observed among the other five races. That is all that's required of me."

"You are forgetting to mention article six of the protocols," I said.

Blinking several times, Zardee then spoke slowly. "Exactly what is it you are accusing me of, ambassador?"

I shrugged. "Such a strong word . . . I am certainly not *accusing* you of anything. But there are rumors, Your Majesty. Rumors that someone under your authority is violating the portion of the pact forbidding the creation of fully autonomous replicants."

His face reddened three shades. I did not need a Naxian to tell me that I had struck home. At the same time, this was not *guilt* that I read in the monarch's eyes, but rather something akin to *shame*. I found his reaction most interesting.

"I shall rendezvous with your ship above the ninth planet," he said tersely, and cut the channel. No doubt Captain Smeet and the king's captain were already exchanging coordinates by the time I departed the comm lounge and headed back to the guest suite to see how things were progressing there.

I shouldn't have expected miracles from Phss'aah. After all, the Crotonite was my responsibility, not his. But I might have hoped at least for tact from a Cephallonian diplomat. Instead, I returned to find Phss'aah carrying on a long monologue directed at the cripple Jirata, who huddled in his corner glaring back at the creature in the tank. And if looks could maim there wouldn't have been much of anything there but bloody water.

". . . so unlike the other elder races, we Cephallonians find this Erthuma innovation of articulate, intelligent machines useful and fascinating, even if it is also puzzling and bizarre. Take your own case, Jirata. Would not a loyal mechanical surrogate be of use to one such as you, especially in your present condition? Helping you fend for—"

Phss'aah noticed my return and interrupted his monologue. "Ah, Patty. You have returned. I was just explaining to our comrade here how useful it is to have machines able to anticipate your requirements and capable of repairing and maintaining themselves. Even the Crotonites' marvelous, intricate devices, handmade and unique, lack that capability."

"We do not need it!" Jirata spat. "A machine should be elegant, light, compact, efficient. It should be a thing of beauty and crafsmanship! Pah! What pride can a human have in such a monster as a robot? Why, I hear they allow the things to design and build still *more* robots, which build still others! What can come about when an engineer leaves his creations to pass beyond his personal control?"

I felt an eerie chill. Glad as I was that Jirata seemed, in his own style, to be emerging from his funk, I did not like the direction this conversation was headed.

"What about that, Patty?" Phss'aah asked, turning to face me. "I have consulted much Erthuma literature having to do with man-created machine intelligence, and there runs through much of it a thread of *warning*. Philosophers speak of the very fear Jirata expressed, calling it the Frankenstein Syndrome. I do not know the origins of that term, but it has an apt sound for dread of destruction at the hands of one's own creations."

I nodded. "Fortunately, we Erthumoi have a tradition of liking to frighten ourselves with scary stories, then finding ways to avoid the very scenario described. It's called Warning Fiction, and historians now credit that art form especially with our species' survival . . . with the fact that we made it across the bomb-to-starship crisis time."

"Most interesting. So tell me, please, how did you come to decide on a way to keep control over your creations? The Locrians certainly have enough trouble, whenever a clutch of male eggs is neglectfully laid outside the careful management of professional brooders, and the Samians have their own problems. How do you manage your robots then?"

How indeed? I wondered at the way this discussion had, apparently naturally, just happened upon a topic so deadly and so coincidentally apropos to my other concerns.

"Well, one approach is to have the machines programmed with deeply coded fundamental operational rules or laws which they cannot disobey at cost of paralysis. This method serves well as a first line of defense. Unfortunately, it proved tragically inadequate several times. The machines' increasing intelligence enabled them to interpret those laws in new and innovative and rather distressing ways. Lawyer programs can be terribly tricky, we discovered. Today, unleashing a new one without proper checks is punishable by death."

"I understand. We Cephallonians reserve that punishment for the lawyers themselves. But I will remember to advise my council about this if we decide to purchase more of your high-end robots. Do continue."

"Well, one experimental approach, with the very brightest machines, has been to actually raise them as if they were Erthuma children. In one of our confederations there are several thousand robots which have been granted provisional status as junior citizens—"

"Obscenity!" Jirata interrupted with a shout.

I merely shrugged. "It is only an experiment. The idea is that we will have little to fear from supersmart robots if they think of themselves as fellow Erthumoi who just happen to be built differently. Thus the hope is that they will be as loyal to us as our grandchildren, and like our grandchildren, pose no threat even if they grow smarter than us."

"Fascinating!" the Cephallonian cried. "But then, what happens when . . ."

Point after point, he spun out the logical chain. I was drawn into Phss'aah's intellectual enthusiasm. This was one of the reasons I entered the Diplomacy Guild, after all—in order to see old things in an entirely new light, through alien eyes, as if for the first time.

In his corner, I sensed even Jirata paying attention, almost in spite of himself. I had never before seen a Crotonite willing to sit and listen for so long. Perhaps this cruel and desperate experiment of theirs might actually turn out useful?

Then Jirata exploded with another set of disdainful curses, deriding one of Phss'aah's extrapolations. And I knew that, even if the experiment worked, it was going to be a long struggle.

Meanwhile, I felt the tension of my upcoming encounter with Zardee.

Even with hyperdrive it is next to impossible to run anything like an "empire," in the ancient sense of the word. Not across starlanes as vast as the galaxy. Left to their own devices, the scattered colony worlds—daughters of faraway Earth—would probably have all gone their own ways long ago . . . each choosing its own path, conservative or bizarre, into a destiny all its own. Without oppositon, we tend to fraction our loyalties.

But there *was* opposition of sorts, when we emerged into space. The other Five Races were already there. Strange, barely knowable creatures with technologies at first quite a bit ahead of ours. In playing a furious game of catch-up, the Erthuma worlds nearly all agreed to a pact: to form a loose confederation bound together by a civil service. Foremost of these is the Diplomacy Guild.

And foremost among the rules agreed to by all signatories to the Essential Protocol is this: *not to undertake any unilateral actions which might unite other starfaring cultures against the Erthumoi*. In my lifetime, four crises have loomed which caused strife over this provision, in which some community of Earth descent was found to be engaged in dangerous or inciting activities. Once, a small trade alliance of Erthuma worlds almost provoked a Locrian queendom to the point of violence. Each time, the episode was soothed over by the guild, but on two of those occasions it took severe threats—arraying all the offending community's Erthuma neighbors in a united show of intimidation—before the reckless ones backed down.

Now I feared this was about to happen again. And this time, the conditions for a quick and simple solution were not encouraging.

Zardee's system lay nearby a cluster of stars very rich in material resources, heavy elements given off by a spate of supernovae a million or so years ago. Asteroids abundant in every desirable mineral were plentiful there.

Now normally, this wouldn't matter much. The galaxy is not resource poor. We are not living in Earth's desperate twenty-first century, after all.

But what if one of the Six Races embarked on a population binge? Still fresh among us Erthumoi is memory of such a calamity. Earth's frail ecosystem is still recovering from the stress laid upon it before we grew up and moved out.

Of course, the galaxy is vast beyond all planetary measure. Still, it does not take much computer time to extrapolate what could happen if any of the six starfarers decided to have fun making babies fast. Take our own species as an example. At human breeding rates typical of prespacefaring Earth, and given the efficiency of hyperdrive to speed colonization, we would fill every Earthlike world in the galaxy within less than a million years. Only one of the catastrophic consequences of this uncontrolled expansion would be the effect on the various life-forms already in existence on those worlds.

And then, of course, our descendants would run out of Earthlike planets. What then? Might they not chafe at the limitations on terraforming—the agreement among the Six only to convert dead worlds, never worlds already bearing life?

Consider the fundamental reason why there has never been a major war among the Six. It is their *incompatibility,* the fact that each others' worlds are unpleasant or deadly to the other five that maintains the peace. But what if overpopulation started us imagining we could get away with turning a high CO_2 world into an oxy-rich planet. How would the Locrians react to that?

The same logic applies to the other Five, each capable of its own population burst. Only their irascible temperaments and short life spans keep the Crotonites from overbreeding, for instance. And the Locrians, the first of the Six upon the spacelanes, admitted to one Naxian in rare candor that the urge to spew forth myriad eggs is still powerful within them, constrained only by powerful social and religious pressures.

The problem is this: What seems at first to be a stable situation is anything but stable. If the Locrians seem ancient from the Erthuma perspective, by the clock of the *stars* they are nearly as recent as we. Three hundred thousand years is a mere eye blink. The coincidence of all Six appearing virtually at the same time is one that has Erthuma and Cephallonian and Naxian scholars completely puzzled.

Yes, we are all at peace now. But computer simulations show utter calamity if any race looks about to take off on a population binge. And despite the Erthumoi monopoly on *self-aware* machines, all of the Six do have computers.

As my ship docked with the resplendent yacht of the King of Prongee, I looked off in the direction of the Gorch Cluster, with its rainbow of bright, metal-rich stars and its promise of riches beyond what anyone alive might need.

But not beyond what any one man might *want*.

Captain Smeet signaled the locks would be open in a few minutes. I took advantage of the interval to use a viewer and check in on my guests.

Within his tank, Phss'aah was getting another rubdown from his personal robot. Meanwhile, the Cephallonian continued an apparent monologue.

". . . that some mystics of several races explained the sudden and simultaneous appearance of starfarers in the galaxy. After all, is it not puzzling that creatures such as we water dwellers, or the Samians, took to the stars, when so many skilled, mechanically-minded races, such as the Lenglils and Forttts, never even thought of it, and rejected spaceflight when it was offered them?"

From his corner of the room, Jirata flapped his wing nubs as if dismissing an unpleasant thought. "It is obscene that any but those who fly should have achieved the heights. This news just received—that there may have been forerunners of great power—perhaps it means you Cephallonians and the others were created as *jokes,* left behind to plague we true fliers when we achieved our rightful place . . ."

I felt pleased. By Crotonite standards, Jirata was being positively outgoing and friendly. Like a good Cephallonian diplomat, Phss'aah seemed not to notice the insults and chose to answer the portions that seemed relevant to the thread of logic.

"Indeed, it is possible that the sudden appearance of the Six, all at roughly the same time, means that we all—or most of us—received some boost from this forerunner race. Consider this possibility then: that the forerunners dispersed upon the starlanes an *outwardness gene,* without which all planet-bound races would be doomed to an inward mentality. Of course this gene would only take effect here and there. In the case of my own race, it took hold against all odds, in a species which by all rights should never have even considered flight, let alone metal technology . . ."

Jirata let out a bark of agreement. I sensed a signal from Captain Smeet and shut off the viewer reluctantly. There were times when, irritating as he was, Phss'aah was utterly fascinating to listen to. Now, though, I had business to discuss, and no lesser matter than the survival of the Erthumoi.

* * *

"My industrial robots are mining devices, pure and simple. They pose no threat to anyone. Not anyone!"

I watched the activity on the surface of the ninth planet. Although it was an airless body, crater strewn and wracked by ancient lava seams, it seemed at first that I was looking down on the veldt of some prairie world, covered from horizon to horizon with roaming herds of ungulates.

These ruminants were not living creatures, though they moved as if they were. I even saw "mothers," who paused in their grazing to "nurse" their "offspring."

Of course what they were grazing upon was the dusty, metal-rich surface soil of the planet. Across their broad backs, solar collectors powered the conversion of those raw materials into refined parts. Within each of these browsing "cows" there grew a tiny duplicate of itself, which the artificial beasts then gave birth to, and which they then fed still more refined materials straight through to adulthood.

There was nothing particularly unusual about this scene. Back before we Erthumoi achieved starflight it was machines such as these which changed our destiny, from paupers on a half-ruined world, short of resources, to beings wealthy enough to demand a place among the Six.

An ancient mathematician named John Von Neumann had predicted the eventuality of robots able to make copies of themselves. When such creatures were let loose on the Earth's moon, within a few years they had multiplied into the millions. Then, half of them had been reprogrammed to make consumer goods instead—and suddenly our wealth was to what it had been, as twentieth century man's had been to the Neanderthal's. There was no comparison.

But in every new thing there are always dangers. We found this out when some of the machines *refused* their new programming and even began evading the harvesters.

"I see no hound machines," I told King Zardee. "You have no mutant-detecting dog-bots patrolling the herds, searching for mutants?"

He shrugged. "A useless, needless expense. We are in a part of the galaxy low in cosmic rays. Our design is well shielded. I have shown you the statistics. Our new replicants demonstrate a breakthrough in both efficiency and stability."

I shook my head, unimpressed. Figures were one thing. Galactic survival was another matter entirely.

"Please show me how the mechanisms are fitted with their enabling and remote shutdown keys, Your Majesty. I don't see any robo-cowboys at work. How and when are the calves converted into adults? Are they called in to a central point?"

"It happens right out on the range," Zardee said proudly. "I see no reason to force every calf to go to a factory in order to get its keys. We have programed each cow to manufacture its calf's keys on the spot."

Madness! I balled my hands into fists in order to keep my diplomat's reserve. *The idiot!*

With deliberate calmness I faced him. "Your Majesty, that makes the keys completely meaningless. Their entire purpose is to make sure that no Von Neumann replicant device ever reaches maturity without coming to an Erthuma-run facility for inspection. It is our ultimate guarantee that the machines remain under our control and that their numbers do not explode."

Zardee laughed. "I've heard it before, this fear of fairy tales. My dear beautiful young woman, surely you don't take seriously those Frankenstein stories in the pulp flimsies about replicants running away and devouring planets? Entire solar systems?" He guffawed.

I shrugged. "It does not matter how likely or unlikely such scenarios are. What matters is how the prospect *appears* to the other Five. For twelve centuries we have downplayed this potential outcome of artificial intelligence and automation for the simple reason that our best alienists believe the others will find the possibility appalling. It is the reason replicant restrictions are written into the protocols, Your Majesty."

I gestured down below at the massed herds. "What you have done here is utterly irresponsible . . ."

I stopped, because Zardee was smiling.

"You fear a chimera, dear diplomat. For I have already proven to my satisfaction that you have nothing to worry about in regards alien opinion."

"What do you mean?"

"I mean that I have already shown these devices to representatives of many Locrian, Samian, and Naxian communities, several of whom have already taken delivery of breeding stock."

My mouth opened and closed. "But . . . but what if they equipped the machines with space-transport ability? You . . ."

Zardee blinked. "What are you talking about? Of *course* the models I provided are space adapted. Their purpose is to be asteroid mining devices, after all. It's a wonderful breakthrough! Not only can they reproduce rapidly and efficiently, but they can transport themselves wherever the customer sets up his beacon . . ."

I did not stay to listen to the rest. Filled with anger and despair, I turned away and left him to stammer into silence behind me. I had calls to make, without any delay.

Maxwell took the news well, all considered.

"I have already traced three of the contracts," he told me by hyperwave. "We've managed to get the Naxians to agree to a delay, long enough for us to lean on Zardee and alter the replicants' key system. The Naxians did not understand why we were so concerned, though they could tell we were worried. Clearly they haven't thought out the implications yet, and we're naturally reluctant to clue them in.

"The other contracts are going to be much harder. Two went to small Locrian queendoms. One to a Samian solidity, and one to a Cephallonian superpod. I'm putting prime operatives onto each, but I'm afraid it's likely the replicants will go through at least five generations before we accomplish anything. By then it will probably be too late."

"You mean by then they will have mutated and some will have escaped customer control?" I asked.

"No, according to Zardee's data, it should take longer than that. But by then I'm afraid our projections show each of the customers will be getting a handsome profit from his investment. Soon the replicants will become essential to them and impossible for us to regain control over."

"So what do you want me to do?"

Maxwell sighed. "You stay by Zardee. I'll have a signed alliance of all his Erthuma neighbors for you by tomorrow to get him deposed if he doesn't cooperate. The problem is, the cat's already out of the bag."

I, too, had studied ancient Earth expressions during one of my lives. "Well, I shall close the barn door, anyway."

Maxwell did not bother with a salutation. He signed off more weary looking than I had ever seen him. And our labors were only just beginning.

The Cephallonian and the Crotonite weren't exactly making love when I returned to the guest suite. (What an image!) Still, they had not murdered each other either.

Jirata had become animated enough to attend to the internal-environments controller in his corner of the chamber. He had dismantled the wall panel and was experimenting—creating a partition, then a bed pallet, then an excretarium. Immersed in mechanical arts, his batlike face almost took on a look of serenity as he customized the machinery, converting the insensitively mass-produced into something individualized, with character and uniqueness.

It was a rare epiphany, watching him so, and coming in an instant to realize that even so venal and disgusting a race as his could cause me to wonder at the purity of their ideals.

Oh, no doubt I was oversimplifying. Perhaps it was the replicant crisis that had me primed to feel this way. Ironically, though they were the premier mechanics among the Six, the Crotonites' technical and scientific level was not particularly high. And they would be among the *last* ever to understand what a Von Neumann machine was about. From their point of view, autonomy and self-replication were for Crotonites, and in anyone else or anything else they were obscenities.

I wondered if this experiment, which had caused a noble and high-caste creature of his community to be cast down so, in a desperate attempt to learn new ways, would ever meet any degree of success. What would be the analogy for a person like me—to be surgically grafted crude gills instead of lungs and dwell forever underwater, less mobile than a Cephallonian? Would I, *could* I ever volunteer for so drastic an exile, even if my home world depended on it?

Yes, I conceded, watching Jirata work. There was nobility here, of a sort. And at least the Crotonites had not unleashed upon the galaxy a thing that could threaten all Six spacefarers . . . and the million other intelligent life-forms without ships.

Phss'aah awakened from a snooze at the pool's surface and descended to face me. But it was his robot that spoke.

"Patty, my master hopes your business in this system has been successfully concluded."

"Alas, no," I replied. "Crises develop lives of their own. Soon, however, I expect to get permission to confide this matter to him. When that happens, I hope to benefit from his deep thought and insight."

Phss'aah acknowledged the compliment with a bare nod. Then he spoke for himself.

"You must not despair, my young Erthuma colleague. Look, after all, to your *other* accomplishments. I have decided, for instance, to go ahead and purchase a sample order of three thousand of these delightful machines for my own community. And if they work out there, perhaps others in the Cephallonian supreme pod will buy. Is this not a coup to make you happy?"

For a moment I could not answer. What could I say to Phss'aah? That soon robots such as these might be so cheap that they could be had for a song? That soon a flood of wealth would sweep the galaxy, so great that no creature of any starfaring race would ever again want for material goods?

Or should I tell him that the seeds contained in these cornucopia were doomed to mutate, to change, to seek a path of their own . . . a path down which no foreseeing could follow?

"That's nice," I finally said. "I'm glad you like our machines.

"You can have as many as you need. As many as you want."

MYRYX

ROBERT SHECKLEY

AARON WAS IN ONE OF THE MOBILE FIELD STATIONS on Sestes, trying to defeat a quick-mutating fungus that had sprung up overnight and wiped out nearly ten thousand acres of mixed crops. After several hours of computerized search and simulated experiment, he came up with a self-destructing virus that stopped the fungus without any other side effects, or none he could detect in the short term.

When he got back to his headquarters, he found a message, automatically logged. It was from a Samian ship, requesting orbital data preparatory to landing.

It was the first time a Samian had asked permission to land on this Erthuma planet of Sestes. Aaron wished this historic occasion had come at a time when he was less rushed. Harvesting had just begun in the temperate regions of his farm. It was mostly automated, but still, especially with Lawrence gone, there was plenty to do. But it would never do to refuse landing permission. It was important to keep on good terms with the Samians, who occupied two planets in the system. The other two were occupied by Erthumoi like Aaron, and the fifth planet, Myryx, was unpopulated.

Aaron radioed the Samian permission to land. Soon a view of the alien ship sprang up on the screen, a reconstruction rather than a straight visual. Moments later Aaron's ground telemetry picked up the ship's identification signal. It was a Council ship.

That was unexpected. The Council, which coordinated the affairs of the five planets of the Minieri system, rarely sent out its ships on official business. It was more efficient to work with the modulated-neutrino carrier waves that linked the six civilized races of the galaxy. But sometimes face-to-face discussion was needed for crucial or sensitive issues.

The ship landed within the hour. Samian atmospheric requirements were rather different from those of Erthumoi. But Samians were a durable race, well able to tolerate for a while conditions that would kill a less adaptable race.

After landing, the Samian pilot left his ship and came over to Aaron's headquarters in his own specially designed vehicle. It was a tubular contraption with lightweight toothed wheels that could climb a modest slope. The Samian sat in the midst of a nest of webbing. He looked like a large side of bacon smoked to a mahogany color. It was difficult to consider him a living creature, much less an intelligent one, since he showed no differentiation into specialized parts. A muscular chunk of dark muscle, the Samian had no visible limbs, no apparent way to manipulate matter. Aaron could see the silver filaments that ran through the webbing binding the Samian to the chair. He had heard that Samians were able to control the electrical outputs of their bodies from many locations on their skin. This made it possible for the Samian to communicate directly with the small computer located beneath his chair. The computer itself ran on an Allison-Chalmers weak force multiplier.

Samian transport chairs took many forms and varieties. The most interesting question about them, however, was who had made them. The Samians hadn't permitted any surveys of their home worlds. But it was difficult to see how, given their physical structure, they could sustain a technological civilization without someone or something acting for them as their hands. For that matter, how, without limbs, could they build their spaceships? Or perhaps the question was, *who* built their ships? There were many unanswered questions about the Samians.

"I am very glad to meet you, Aaron Bixen," the Samian said, setting off the sound impulses of the voice-maker built into his chair. "I am Octano Halfbarr. I am at present a male and will remain so for the next two months. I have come here bearing a Council message. But I am also here in friendship, since you are my nearest non-Samian neighbor and it is proper for neighbors to meet in person.''

That meant that the Samian was from Leuris, next planet out from the sun after Aaron's own world of Sestes.

''You are most welcome,'' Aaron said.

''I have come to tell you that there will be a General Council meeting seventy-two hours from now. The presence of all planetary Council representatives is urgently requested.''

''I'm afraid this is not the most convenient of times for me,'' Aaron said. ''Harvesting has just begun in this hemisphere. We are lightly populated. Everybody is needed. Is the matter so urgent?''

''You must judge for yourself,'' Octano said. ''It concerns the expedition to the planet Myryx.''

Myryx, the fifth and final planet from the sun, had not been populated when the first Erthumoi and the first Samians settled in this Minieri system about three hundred years ago. Neither species claimed Myryx. It was considered to be of no value. The galaxy was full of planets that came closer to fitting the requirements of one of the six civilized races. Many marginally suitable planets were ignored, since there were more than enough first-rate planets to suit the population requirements at this stage of the civilized species' expansion through the galaxy. Myryx might have remained in that category indefinitely. But then just two years ago the Cleatis expedition discovered the vast deserted ruins of the civilization on Myryx that came to be called Alien City 4. This was the fourth find of its kind, proof that there had once been a seventh civilized race, which had vanished a million years before the first of the present-day six intelligent species ventured out into space.

Aaron said, ''My son, Lawrence, is with the investigative team on Myryx.''

''So I was told at Council headquarters,'' the Samian said.

''Why did the Council send you here?'' Aaron asked. ''What has happened on Myryx? Is my son all right?''

''I think there is no cause for alarm,'' the Samian said.

"But the Council wants to discuss the matter with you themselves, in person."

Aaron thought for a moment. "I'll need to activate a farm manager program. Then there is someone I must talk to. After that I am ready to go with with you."

"I will wait in the ship," the Samian said. "I regret having been the bearer of ambiguous tidings."

It was a stock apology among the Samians.

After activating a standard big-planet computer management program to take care of things in his absence—better than he could himself, if the brochure could be believed—Aaron telephoned Sara, Lawrence's wife. He arranged to see her at her farm immediately. He went there in a hopper, whose long jumps combined with a shallow glide to cover distances quickly on this large, hilly, underpopulated planet. Lawrence's farm was smaller than Aaron's, about the size of Italy on the home planet Earth. Since Sara had no interest in farming beyond growing tomatoes for her family's consumption, Aaron farmed the land for her. The computer didn't mind the extra work and it was only right with Lawrence away.

Sara was waiting for him at the door of the farmhouse. She was a small, graceful woman, dark-haired, with high cheekbones and an exotic tilt to her eyes. She was on her fifth life cycle, which made her older than Aaron. But age wasn't judged in terms of single life spans anymore. It took quite a few life cycles before age began to show on an Erthuma. And then cosmetic surgery was always an option.

"Do you think you'll see Lawrence?" Sara asked.

"That's hard to say. It's possible. I'll certainly try. Is there any message you want me to give him?"

Sara thought for a while, then shrugged. "No, nothing special."

Aaron said, "You're his wife, Sara. Won't you at least send your love?"

"What should I tell him? 'Stay as long as you want at the fascinating alien city, Lawrence. Take a year or two; what does it matter to your wife all by herself on this goddamned farm the size of Italy?' "

"I know it's difficult for you," Aaron said. "Just you and the child and the robot servants on this big farm."

"Lawrence said other Erthuma settlers would come here and we'd have neighbors. But they haven't. Why?"

"There are a lot of places for Erthuma to go in the galaxy," Aaron said. "And only a limited population to go to them. In fact, new territories are opened every day. But population increase is not sufficient to keep up with them. The result is, we Erthumoi are spread thin."

Sara was not impressed. "Lawrence should have thought of that before he brought me away from my home world of Excelsis. I'm used to people, laughter, a good time. Now I don't even have Lawrence. What's so interesting about Alien City Four, anyhow?"

"I don't know, Sara," Aaron said. "I haven't been there myself and the reports are fragmentary."

"You haven't been here much, either, Aaron," Sara said. "You're not being very nice to your daughter-in-law, are you?"

"I can assure you, I meant no offense. It's just that there's been so much work to do . . ."

"You must think I'm vain and stupid," Sara said. "You and Lawrence are both so serious-minded. It would be a waste of your time to spend much of it with an empty-headed lady like me."

"Sara, please! The truth is quite the opposite."

She looked at him sharply. "What do you mean, Aaron?"

Aaron suddenly realized he had said too much. "Nothing, forget it."

"You're trying to tell me something, aren't you?"

"Not at all," Aaron said, his voice carefully unexpressive. "Don't get any ideas, Sara."

"Are you trying to tell me you've never thought about you and me, Aaron?"

"You're an attractive woman. Of course I've thought about you. But anything between us is unthinkable. You're my son's wife. And please stop laughing."

"Oh, Aaron, if you only knew how silly and pompous you sound, saying those old-fashioned things. They don't mean a thing anymore! I was sure you wanted me. The way you used to look at me whenever Lawrence and I came to visit. You don't hide your interest very well, do you?"

"I suppose not," Aaron said. He knew the cause of his restlessness. His own wife, Melissa, had been off-planet for almost six months, retraining on the Erthuma planet Elsinore in the newest developments in her field of tide pool ecologies. He missed her badly. But it was necessary that they part. For beings who lived the equivalent of a dozen or more old-style human lifetimes, separations and reeducations were necessary. Aaron and Melissa were, by mutual consent, on their fourth term of marriage. It was something to be proud of. Though it didn't help much at the moment.

"I'm going to give Lawarence your love," Aaron said firmly.

"Sure," Sara said. "And while you're at it, maybe you'd like to take a little of it yourself."

"Please get hold of yourself," Aaron said. "I'm sure Lawrence will be back soon."

"And that'll make us all very happy, won't it?" Sara said. "Good-bye, Aaron. Good trip. Hurry back."

The flight to Stillsune, the other Erthuma planet and home of the Council, was uneventful. Aaron had wanted to question his Samian companion about the Council's deliberations about Myryx, and how Lawrence fit into that. He did not, though. The planet was only hours ahead. He would soon know whatever there was to be known about this affair.

When he reached Stillsune, the capital city of Laxiheetch was different than he had remembered it. It had been a sleepy place back then. Now he noticed the new buildings, the roads, the ornamental fountains. He wondered where the money for all this had come from, because the population of Stillsune was not much larger than it had been a decade ago.

The government buildings on Stillsune occupied most of the downtown blocks. Aaron went to the discussion hall where the delegates for the Erthuma Association were meeting. There were guards at the door. They looked over Aaron's identification, checked his retinal prints, finally let him through.

Within the discussion hall it was bedlam. Several speakers were trying to expound their points of view simultaneously. The master-at arms, with his red sash of office and his side arms, stood near the door with folded arms.

"Aaron!" That was Matthew Bessemer, a fat miner with an enormous walrus moustache from the far side of Aaron's home planet. "It's about time you got here! We were expecting you days ago."

"What's going on? What's the problem?"

"It's evident that you haven't stayed in touch with the situation on Myryx."

"What's there to stay in touch with? It's a deserted city. People are studying it. I'm told it could throw some important evidence on the Seventh Race."

Aaron was referring to the mystery of the disappearance of what was apparently the first intelligent race to emerge in the galaxy. This event, it was theorized, took place an almost inconceivable length of time ago. According to the artifacts discovered in the alien cities, this society had been further advanced than any of the civilized races who came after them. It was hard to reconcile the great antiquity of the race with the rest of the facts. They must have been active not long after the universe was born.

"You're sadly out of date," Matthew said, "if you think those are still the major developments on Myryx."

"Has Lawrence been up to something? He never tells me anything about how the investigation is going."

"None of them do," Matthew said. "As soon as a man gets into the alien city he gets closemouthed and possessive. This is true of investigators from the other species, too. Although the Council is financing their researches, all of them become secretive, unwilling to tell us what they've found; they're always pleading the need for more evidence."

"Surely you have something to go on?"

"We do have one Cephallonian report. It has disturbing implications."

* * *

Seashaws, a Cephallonian female from Lyrix, was the first to make a report of Alien City 4 from the point of view of her aquatic civilization. She took passage to Myryx in an Erthuma ship equipped with water tanks which had temperature and turbulence controls for maximum comfort. The ship was also equipped with ample supplies of the many varieties of the small fish and seaweed which the Cephallonians find delectable. The passage was expensive, but much of Seashaws's fare was paid by her principality of Thurune, for whom she was preparing a report on Myryx.

"Right this way, madam," the young Cephallonian crew member told Seashaws as she entered the ship, moving carefully in her unwieldy water-filled armor. "You'll find it all right once you're in the tank."

The Cephallonian was not wearing the water-filled armor that Seashaws had always thought was necessary. Instead he made do with a perspex helmet and mask, with a water-recirculation cylinder on his back. She wondered how he kept his skin sufficiently moist to prevent lesions in the hot dry air of the ship. Some sort of oil, she supposed. He certainly looked in very good condition. Then she was ashamed at herself for thinking such a thought and hurried to the tank as fast as dignity would allow. But she cast a glance back over her shoulder before she slid in.

She was more than a little giddy with the excitement of it all. It was only the third time she had ever been out of her native planet's water, and this was the first hyperjump she had ever made. She tried to calm herself, taking refuge in the nice little cave at the bottom of the tank. She arranged her swim bladder for zero gravity and hung in her cave, watching the TV monitor show a documentary on the lives of fish on different planets. It was the Cephallonian equivalent of soap opera, and usually it fascinated her. Not now, however. For once, real life was taking up all of her attention, driving out of her mind even normal speculation on the sexual preferences of the young crewman who had showed her such courtesy when she boarded.

"Oh, thank you," she said to him again, when the ship reached Myryx and he accompanied her as the crane assisted her to the surface. He helped her leave the crane's platform, and politely wished her the best of luck when they reached the little dock with the sloping ramp, where she would leave behind her helmet and proceed under her own fins to the water level of Alien City.

"It is a very great pleasure to serve one as beautiful as you," the crewman said.

Although it was no more than a standard galantry, nevertheless, Seashaws's heart leaped. She had been lonely of late. It had been hard to leave behind her two mates—big, surly Graver with the tender heart, and young Suddrix, the thrillingly beautiful young male whom she had won in the last city courtship lottery. Would they still be waiting for her when she returned? It was true that her relatives were keeping an eye on both males. Even so, Cephallonian males were known to be fickle creatures who combined a love for headstrong adventure with an attention span in matters of love that fell far short of female Cephallonian expectations. This discrepancy was a topic to be presented to the entire Cephallonian electorate for possible biological reengineering.

"Do you return to the ship at once?" she asked.

"My name is Trusknier," he said. "No, as a matter of fact, I've decided to stay here on Myryx for a while."

"Is that a fact?" she said saucily. "And what will you do here? Examine the ancient vanished civilization?"

"Seashaws," he said, pronouncing her name with the intonation of expectant intimacy, "I am not a scholar. I am simply a normal young Cephallonian male whose interest has been aroused by a maiden whose beauties deserve telling."

Thus began one of the formal courtship rituals of the Cephallonians. But Seashaws, thrilled though she was, yet clung to her sanity. This was no time to get mixed up with some fellow who was probably no better than the ones she already had. And besides, she was here for a serious purpose: to bring back word of the early findings of Alien City to the Ladies Club of Greater Truax, the municipality on her planet where she served as lecturer in popular exobiology.

"I have to investigate this planet," she said. "But maybe later . . .

"Yeah, right," he said, and swam off with a flick of his tail. Seashaws was aware that she must have given him the impression that she was uninterested, when actually he had read it wrong; her nuance had been intended to signify that beneath her apparent casualness she'd like to see him again. It was really annoying how you could miss communication like that, even if you were of the same species, or maybe especially when you were of the same species. But maybe that's how it always was when one of you was female and the other male.

Dorsal fins stroking smoothly, she descended into the water. Or began to. Then she was caught up at once in one of the unusual features of the underwater alien city. There was a sudden onset of turbulence, which threw her around severely without actually damaging her. When it was over she found herself at a very great depth, having been taken there somehow by the turbulence. She didn't understand how it worked, but it was pleasant to be at the bottom starting back up, since, for the Cephallonians, going from the top to the bottom requires a lot of energy and is like climbing a mountain for Erthumoi.

She began to glide upward, and she noticed that the water was springlike and sparkling, and shot through with dancing lights and dots of color. It was the sort of water you'd like to live in forever, but that was not to be; she continued upward and came to the next level, which was rose-tinged, melancholy, and given to encouraging cosmic thought of the deepest and most exquisite variety. After that she came to the third level, which was aquamarine and was shot through with golden specks that hinted at glory. On the level above that, the colors were blue-gray and indigo, streaked with lighter bands of mauve, and being here brought on a sensation of ecstasy, something which rarely happened at home, where all the levels of the water were much the same. And then, to make it all the better, she saw a flash of light and a sensation of shape, and she saw the young Cephallonian male swim past her, eyes shining, waving a flipper in a beckoning gesture that she found nearly irresistible. But resist it she did, because there was something about that young male that had brought worry to her, and fear. Something in his eyes foretold that she might not arise from the depths if she went down there in search of him. She didn't know if it were true, but it scared her enough to make her return to the surface at once, ask to be taken away from underwater Alien City, and file her report.

"That's a strange story," Aaron said. "The Cephallonians seem to pick up out-of-body experiences in the alien city. We know so little about the spiritual aspects of our fellow civilized races. I wonder if there's a parallel between their experiences and ours."

"There seems to be some evidence to support the view," Matthew said, "that the fundamental organization of life is identical in all species, no matter how different they may be. That's not to say that there's a point-to-point correspondence between the one and the other."

"True enough," Aaron said. "It's still a conjecture, this so-called similarity between species. But a persuasive one. Have other species experienced this feeling reported by Seashaws?"

"One of the Locrians spoke of a city which is not apparent to Erthuma eyes. The Locrians are the most visionary of the species. It's that huge single eye, visionary equipment if there ever was any. That eye can look into and through anything. Like some sort of X ray, I suppose."

"I know about the eye," Aaron said. "What are you trying to say?"

"Have you ever wondered how, to an eye like that, the alien city must appear? A Locrian reported that to his three-dimensional and stereoscopic vision of his inner eye, Alien City is like no other sight he has ever seen. Not even on his home planet. He said the alien city reveals itself to his view as three-dimensional architecture of the most beautiful and ethereal sort. They can see it; we can't.

Interesting, eh? Even the Crotonites, who are not noted for their sensitivity to landscape, have remarked on a strange feature of Alien City. They say the air there appears to be denser in some places than in others. It's the sort of thing a flying species would be bound to notice. They claimed that the densities have shape and meaning, though they couldn't tell me what that meaning was."

"Don't we have any reports on what Alien City is like to an Erthuma?" Aaron said.

"All the Erthumoi who have been there have proven maddeningly reticent. Even your son, Aaron. Lawrence phones in from time to time, and always sounds well. But he never talks about what is happening or how he feels."

"Is it possible that he has been taken over in some way?"

"He gives no sign of being under someone else's control. Or if he is, he shows no signs of knowing it."

"Surely you can get a straight answer out of some of them," Aaron said.

"I hasn't worked out that way. Some of the early investigators have vanished, you know."

"I didn't know that," Aaron said. "Lawrence never reported it to me."

"It's an ambiguous situation," Matthew said. "Some of the investigators seem to have vanished. But we can't be sure even of that. We don't know if they've been killed or just gone native. And if killed, by whom? There are many ambiguities running through the whole program, Aaron."

"Why don't you send in another team of investigators?"

"The situation is not sufficiently clear-cut to permit that. The investigation of Myryx is no longer directly under our control."

Aaron stared at him. "Now that *is* news. How could you permit control to slip out of your hands?"

"Don't take that tone with me, Aaron," Matthew said. "It's easy enough to criticize when you stay out of the battle and judge from afar. You have not even seen fit to inform yourself about what has been happening on Myryx. I hear it's a nice farm you've got there on Sestes. Big as an entire country back on Earth, that's what they say. I hope it stands you in good stead if the situation on Myryx comes apart on us.''

Aaron thought that Matthew was overreacting. But he realized he didn't have the right to say so since he didn't know what, exactly, Matthew was reacting to. The man was right; he had absented himself from the struggle. He had thought that giving a son to the mystery of the alien unknown was enough for one family. He'd had to do his son's work as well as his own. There had been plenty on his own world to claim his attention. But even though that might all be true, it didn't excuse him from informing himself about these issues.

''Let's back up a little,'' Aaron said. ''I haven't paid much attention to Myryx or Alien City since Lawrence went there two years ago. What has been happening that I should know about?''

''That's a little difficult to sum up in a sentence. But I'll try. Basically, a lot of people have been coming to Myryx. Not just Erthumoi from our two planets; also representatives of the other species. At first it was only Naxians. Then the Cephallonians set up a tank hotel. The latest arrivals on Myryx are the Samians.''

''I might have expected that. A Samian brought me the message from the Council.''

''I know the fellow you're talking about, Octano Halfbarr. What else did he say?''

''He implied, even if he didn't directly state, that the Council will request me to go to Myryx, presumably to say something on their behalf to Lawrence. The Samian seems to expect to go to Myryx with me.''

''Yes,'' Matthew said. ''I suppose you noticed how the Samians have been changing recently.''

''I can't say that I've noticed much,'' Aaron said. ''I've been curious about them, however. I think we all have. You and I have commented on how there's no apparent correlation between the Samians' almost nonexistent manual skills and their exquisitely engineered ships.''

''Quite right,'' Matthew said. ''It's possible, of course, that they had manual skills many ages ago, and lost them through atrophy. I don't believe that myself, but quite a few people do. As though spaceship construction was a skill a species could outgrow!"

"They have the so-called magnetic function," Aaron said.

"Yes, I know. They can make themselves part of things. An interesting skill, but a long way from being able to use an arc welder. Or to make an arc welder, for that matter. And now they have become extremely interested in the alien city on Myryx. You might think it doesn't matter what the Samians are interested in, so negligible are they as a species. Some of the thinkers from the Humanoid Institute think differently, however. It is believed by some—a minority view, I'll admit, but an alarming one—that the Samians may be the most formidable competition to mankind among the civilized species."

"Because they seem so inoffensive?" Aaron asked. "That's carrying paradox a little far, isn't it?"

"Look beneath the obvious paradox, Aaron. How did a species like the Samians ever get as far as they did? They seem to have no real strengths. Physical strength, yes. But that seems almost negligible, something of no worth in this age of manipulated megaenergies. They are not particularly fast thinkers. They have little ability at locomotion or manipulation. They have no apparent skills. They can't swim by their own powers or fly; they can't throw a baseball. They're pitiable, laughable."

"I agree," Aaron said. "How can anyone hold a different view?"

"Species have different strategies for surviving against nature and their fellows. How did the Samians get as far as they have? They seem no better equipped than flounders."

"This is rhetorical," Aaron said.

"I have no proof to offer. I can only tell you that the philosophers of the Humanoid Institute have asked us to take a much closer look at the Samians."

"What is it the Council wants me to do?"

"They will make it formal at the meeting later. But it's better for you to know now, so that you can accept or decline later on the basis of exact information. We want you to go to Myryx and take in the situation for yourself.

Then we want you to proceed to the alien city and meet with your son Lawrence, and the others."

"So I had imagined."

"We want you to take the Samian with you."

"To what end?"

"Study him, Aaron. I can assure you, he will be studying you."

"And what am I supposed to say to Lawrence?"

Matthew thought awhile before answering. At last he said, "You are a man of our generation. You know our views and we know yours. The people of the expedition to Alien City are young, visionary. We want you to go to their city as the representative of the rest of us. See what they're up to. Tell us about it. And if the situation seems out of hand or dangerous to our species— "

"This seems to be very wild talk," Aaron said.

"These things must be said. You must look over the situation, tell us what you think."

"And if I think the situation is dire?"

"More than one philosopher," Matthew said, "has come up with the view that the humanoid race would be better off if Myryx and its ancient city never existed; that the best thing that could happen to Myryx would be to see the entire planet fly apart in a near-instantaneous atomic explosion."

"I hope you are not advocating it," Aaron said.

"I? Certainly not. I only tell you how far we will go to protect our kind. You, Aaron, must let us know what kind of a threat, if any, exists for us on Myryx."

"Well, and suppose one does? Whoever's plot it is, he'd know enough to neutralize me before I could send off a message with warning. It's not inconceivable he's done that with Lawrence."

"We have considered the possibility. Please hold out your hand. Take it. Aaron, you are now in a position to do something about it if your feel the Erthumoi are in danger."

"What is this? What have you given me?"

"It is a bomb. You know how these are operated."

Aaron looked at the tiny object in the palm of his hand. "Fusion?" he asked.

Matthew nodded.

"What range?"

"It'll take out everything in the alien city."

"Take this thing back!"

"You would let your own race go to destruction?"

"It wouldn't come to that. You're being alarmist."

"You've heard some of our speculations on the Samians. Do you deny the possibility of a conspiracy against our species?"

"No such thing is happening."

"But if it *were* happening, do you believe it ought to be stopped? Suppose we could convince you that an alien influence is poisoning your people, undermining their morality, making them less and less fit to survive in the galaxy along with the other species. Suppose that, if you permitted this state of affairs to continue, your species' survival would be adversely affected, doomed to extinction. Assuming that, would you still refuse to carry a bomb? Would you still say, 'I can't be bothered with dirty little practicalities like killing aliens to preserve my own kind'?"

"You are sounding very extreme," Aaron said. "But if you really think it possible that such a threat against us might exist . . ." Aaron put the miniature bomb into a pouch at his belt.

The council room itself was not very large. It had a long oval table in the middle, under a bank of lights. There were fifteen Erthuma delegates present, two of whom were from the ancestral planet itself, the Earth of song and legend. They took no part in the discussion that followed. Aaron supposed they felt too distant from events in the Minieri system, and wisely left discussion to those who were directly affected by what happened at Myryx.

"Tell us, Aaron," said Clarkson, the chairman, a fair, portly man from Magister II, one of the largest of the humanoid associations, "what is your own opinion of what Matthew told you earlier?"

"I don't know what to think," Aaron said. "The situation appears to exist in a considerable degree of ambiguity."

"And how does one handle that?" Clarkson said.

"One tries to gather information in order to dispel the unknowns," Aaron said.

"That is the sort of answer we hoped to hear from you," Clarkson said. "There are quite a few elements in this situation—Myryx with its uncertain new status; the alien city, which we seem to learn less about every year; Lawrence's disturbing silence; why the city exists; and why the Samians, among others, have taken a lively interest in this project."

"I know very little about these things," Aaron said. "It would perhaps be better to send one of yourselves."

"We don't think so," Clarkson said. "We have argued about these matters for a long time. We consider ourselves too close to see the big picture, if there is one. You are known to all of us. We respect your intelligence. You will see the situation for yourself, and take what action seems best to you. We would like to be a part of the decision process, of course. But we know this might not be possible. There are many immediate decisions that may have to be taken. There may be no time to consult with home authorities. Nor may the home authorities be competent to act, since they won't be in the picture. You are our general, Aaron, you lead our armies. Maybe the first thing you have to find out is, are we in a war?"

Aaron agreed to visit Myryx, acting on behalf of the Council along the lines he had discussed with Matthew.

There seemed nothing more to say, and the meeting was brought to an end. Aaron's work seemed clear-cut enough to him. He was to look into certain matters on Myryx with a view to deciding what they meant for the entire humanoid group. And to take action. As simple as that.

Why hadn't Lawrence stayed in better contact with him and with the Council? Why was he so evasive when it came to explaining what work he and his committee were doing?

His thoughts jumped so quickly to his son that Aaron became aware of his own unconscious assessment of the situation. *Lawrence is involved in my decision. Lawrence is the key to the mystery.*

* * *

Aaron gave the command that set the Council ship *Artemis* on its way. They had already gone by shuttle to point omega, as the jump-off spot for hyperdrive operation was sometimes called. Point omega was the closest to a mass you could come yet still enable the hyperdrive to work. Ships driven by hyperdrive proceeded along an invisible network of point omegas.

It was a point of courtesy for Aaron to come to the main control room to accompany the Samian on this jump. Aaron preferred hyperjumping alone. Although there was no discernible transition, except for a flickering of lights and a sense of a geometric pattern of thin curving lines hanging in front of his eyes, he still considered it a private moment. The transition from *here* to *there*, almost instantaneous in the special universe in which hyperjump operated, was perhaps the closest analogue to death that a human could experience and still live to tell of it.

"Ready?" Aaron asked Octano Halfbarr.

"I think so," the Samian said, the translating machine accurately picking up the faint sense of doubt which had to be present in any creature taking his first hyperjump.

"There's nothing to it, really," Aaron said.

"I have heard," the Samian said, "that it affects some individuals more than others."

"That is true."

"That Samians are more prone to hyperjump side effects than the other species."

"By a few percentage points, yes," Aaron said. "But it is not an appreciable difference."

"I have heard that even death is not unknown as a side effect."

"I have heard that too. Perhaps you should have considered all of these points before volunteering for this flight."

A ripple passed over the surface of the dark bronze slab of bacon sitting in its net of webbing. Aaron could have sworn the creature had shrugged.

"Are we underway yet?" the Samian asked.

"We have been for several minutes."

"And you didn't tell me?"

"I thought it better for your peace of mind that I did not."

"Perhaps you are right," Octano the Samian said. "So. I have made my first hyperjump and I am alive."

"Right. Maybe the next time you'll even think of it as fun."

"Fun," the Samian mused. "Yes, I remember from my indoctrination lectures. Your species attaches quite a lot of importance to having fun, do you not?"

"I don't know that I would put it exactly that way," Aaron said. "I would say that as a species, we Erthumoi have a well-developed sense of play."

"And that is another of those important words that we Samians need to study. 'Play.' We have always considered it an overdetermination of the work function. But evidently it is more than that."

"Are you really interested in this idea of play?"

"Oh, yes," Octano reassured him. "It is important for us to understand it. Our experts agree that play is indispensable to the growth of higher intelligence. We are not ourselves a playful people. But surely we can learn, and the way to that knowledge is through experimentation."

"You are not like any other Samian I've ever met," Aaron said. "You are playful while denying it. This is not what your species is noted for."

"I suppose not. We must have seemed quite doltish at first, when we initially encountered the other intelligent species. We lack the quick ability at repartee that enlivens the thought processes of you Erthumoi, for example. We have noted how quick, nervous, and aggressive you are. Yet you are more than that, somehow. We had to take stock of ourselves, ask how we were doing in the great competition between species."

"That's the second time I've heard that idea recently," Aaron said. "Do you really think interspecies competition is necessary?"

"I wouldn't know about that," the Samian said. "What I do know is that it takes place whether one wills it or not. Each of us wants to be the inevitable form that intelligence will take. Ultimately, each species desires to be god. No one wishes anyone else any harm, but obviously my species can't be god as long as your species is claiming the title."

"I must tell you," Aaron said, "that I find all this talk of competition for highest intelligence and for longest survival to be depressing. Maybe life is nothing but the successful living of it, but it still bores me to hear it."

"That's quite an interesting thing to say," the Samian said. "I thought you Erthumoi were devoted to the concept of species survival at all costs."

"Where did you hear that?"

"It is common knowledge."

"It is not correct."

"Of course you would say that. The point is, a contest of sorts is going on between my kind and yours, and mine isn't doing very well."

Aaron was feeling more and more uncomfortable. He had enough work ahead of him without having to hear this sniveling, especially when it was just like the sort of stuff Council members like Matthew had been trying to feed to him.

How long would he be closeted with this creature? Days at the least. Weeks more than likely, perhaps even months. It had to be established at the start that either of them could speak his mind. If the Samian couldn't take it, it was time to find out about it now, not after they had come to Myryx.

"Perhaps you haven't done too well in the contest between all intelligent species," Aaron said. "But considering that you're starting out without any manual dexterity at all, you're really doing very well."

The Samian was silent for a moment. Then he said, "People usually don't allude to the fact that we have no limbs, fingers, toes, or even tentacles. It isn't polite. It's like pointing at a hunchback's hunch, to use an example culled from your own literature."

"I could also point out," Aaron said, "that not only do you Samians not have manual dexterity, you also don't have any vocal apparatus. A small synthesizer is producing your voice. Is that your idea of intelligent?"

The Samian said slowly, "I think this is what you Erthumoi call humor. Or am I mixing it up with candor?"

"They often go together," Aaron said. "But in this

case, you're quite right. We all have our problems, Erthumoi, Samians, Naxians, Cephallonians, Locrians, and so on. I suppose even the mighty Seventh Race had their difficulties, too; otherwise, why did they vanish?"

"I must confess," the Samian said, "that much of what I was saying to you was also what we Samians consider humor. I appreciate your own effort in that direction. It makes it less difficult for me to say that we Samians have been trying to remodel ourselves. We are very good at self-engineering, you know. It takes a long time before an idea lodges with us, but after a while we take it up with tenacity. Seeing how fast other species were, we retooled our synaptic responses. We also introduced a mild taste for aggression into our somatotype. Anything to get back into the competition, as it were."

It was strange for Aaron to hear these ideas come from an individual shaped like a large, slightly irregular rectangular oblong, or parallelopiped, of bacon, colored a dark brown or a bronze, and with very little about it with which to individuate.

Aaron wrote to Sara:

By the time we reached Myryx, you can imagine the state we were in, Octano Halfbarr and I. Trying to be good fellows toward each other, each trying to display the frankness of his character, and neither of us sure what the hell was going on. And the officers of *Artemis,* Captain Franklyn and the others, were no help. I suppose they had ferried diplomatic missions composed of more than one species before. They conducted themselves toward the Samian and me with strict impartiality. You could see they didn't want to get involved with either of us. Octano and I were getting a little tired of each other, too. I confess I never became accustomed to talking to a person who resembled a side of bacon. I suppose his view of me was equally unflattering.

And then Myryx came up on the horizon, and it was time to thank the officers of the *Artemis*. They were going to stay with the ship, keeping it in geosynchronous orbit, while the Samian and I descended to the surface. In my innocence I asked Captain Franklyn if we would be brought down directly to the alien city.

"I'm afraid the situation is a bit more complicated than that," Franklyn said. He seemed absurdly young to be given the responsibility of piloting an official ship equipped with hyperjump and all the latest communications equipment. But then, they say that the young have the quick reflexes necessary in matters of moral judgment as in matters of physical danger.

"More complicated?" I asked. "What could be complicated about dropping us off at the alien city?"

"There are formalities to be gone through," Captain Franklyn said. "You must go through the official channels."

"How could there be official channels?" I asked. "No one claims possession of Myryx."

"I'm afraid that has changed recently," Franklyn said tactfully.

Aaron and the Samian both elected to descend to the surface of Myryx by spinner. Aaron knew that spinner descents had been written about extensively as a source of extraordinary insight. There was something about the slow undulations of the pod, turning and twisting in the glow of twining gases, that was hypnotic without being enervating. By the time they reached the surface, both Aaron and Octano were feeling mild and peaceful, and certainly in no mood to cope with a half-regiment of belligerent officialdom. When the bureaucrats finally accepted the fact that the Erthuma and the Samian were representatives of the Council, their attitude became more reasonable.

"I know that we have no right by charter to operate a Customs and Immigration Service on Myryx," the tall, florid human who called himself Captain Darcy Drummond said, "but something had to be done to maintain law and order and public confidence. I don't think you know what a strange situation Myryx is in. Three years ago there wasn't anybody here. Not even me, truth be told. Then the Sarpedon expedition arrived and discovered Alien City Four.

And then people started arriving. Not just Erthumoi. Individuals from all the Six Races came here. From the beginning a series of compromises had to be made on this world which is owned by none, yet which plays host to the Six Races. For example, we maintain as much water as land out of respect to the aquatic races, and we keep the atmosphere as thick as possible to aid the fliers. Naturally we can't give everyone what he wants, since some of the demands are mutually contradictory. And there's no changing the gravity. Still, in spite of inconveniences, the species come here and adapt.''

''The alien city draws them,'' Aaron suggested.

''Of course. But the alien city is also an excuse for a get-together, a symbol of the need for intelligence, on its highest level, to recognize the commonality of all thinkers.''

There was a great deal of such talk. The officials seemed to feel a need to justify their existences and inflate their own sense of self-importance. Aaron wondered if there were not something unhealthy about their excitement, something sickly about their feeling that they were living at the center of great events.

Aaron thought he was not entirely himself at this period. It was strange, this feeling of self-alienation. Although he expected his mood to pass quickly, nevertheless, it persevered. He began to wonder why the Council had trusted him to pass a judgment on events too complex for him to be certain about. Were they merely trying to take the necessity of choice out of their own hands?

It wouldn't have been so bad if he hadn't felt physically unwell. He hesitated to say that he was sick. Is there something else that can afflict the body and is neither a state of being sick nor of being well? Aaron was afraid he was going to find out.

The officials found a room for him in the Hotel Sola. It was evident that someone had just vacated it. The bed seemed to have been hastily stripped, and the mattress was half off the frame. Under the bed he found a doll. It was a harlequin about half a foot tall, with bandit mask and Spanish floppy hat. And there was another doll behind the curtains, a fat little pig doll made of straw and covered with calico. Aaron sat down on a little stair beside a window, winded from the climb up here, but eager to get to work.

Just then there was a little knock at the door and a girl came through, about ten or eleven, smudgy round face, big pouting lower lip.

"Did I leave my doll in here, sir?"

"Is it one of these?"

She came and looked at both dolls. Then took the fat little pig doll and ran out of the room.

There were a lot of flies in the room. Aaron put in a requisition for the necessary things to bring his situation up to galactic standard. Because even a newly-discovered and as yet but imperfectly explored alien planet is required to keep up to the standards of hotel keeping. There can be no traveling around the galaxy in anything like security to say nothing of comfort if minimum standards are not met. And if minimum standards are not met in this, how will mankind handle the big challenge, the long-awaited extragalactic trips?

Aaron went down for dinner soon after that, almost tripping on the dark stairs over half a dozen dolls of various shapes and sizes, all sharing the qualities of indiscernibility and ubiquitousness.

And from then on, Aaron could go no place without stumbling over dolls. They came in a never-ending series of names, shapes, and numbers; thousands of them; some of such classical shapes as Donald Duck and Mickey Mouse; some of them from the Cephallonian Toy Conglomerate. What were they doing here? Did they mean something? It was inevitable that Aaron should ask himself: Is someone toying with me?

Aaron said, "Why don't you tell me about the old civilization?"

"Haven't a clue, old boy," said Octano.

"Tell me who you are?"

"Just another creature, old boy."

"A different species?"

Octano leaned back his head and laughed. It was only later that Aaron found the first of the great doll factories where gnomelike people manufactured the endless assortment of dolls that threatened to contaminate the previously agreed-upon reality. The dolls were an insult to common sense. Maladaptive transformation. They had to stick around and watch. The gods were capricious—simulators of intelligence rather than users of it. In terms of intelligence, they were like great winged dinosaurs in the days before true birds.

"You humans think the intelligence is inevitable," the Samian said. "But I can assure you, nature tried many different experiments. The last word isn't spoken on intelligence yet. It seems to be holding its own, but you can never tell. The universe isn't biased. It's as likely that nothing will work out as that everything will. I mean that as a matter of logic; you can expect things to work out about as often as they don't. Not even reality escapes the dichotomies."

"What could control the universe, if not intelligence?"

"You seem to think it important that things be understood. Why should it be? What does it matter to events if there's someone there to understand them?"

The dolls kept on reappearing, and they depressed everyone.

The powers that be had no choice in the matters. It didn't matter that things had run down. It was important to keep the dolls in mind by gentle nudging of their handles. That's how the human felt, besieged by strange and uncomfortable thoughts. For some, it began to look like not such a bad idea to get back to the home planet for a while. There are more dangers out there than being ripped with a laser. In the future, between the stars, there will be terrors as great as the spaces they signify. And then Aaron remembered to continue, to pick himself up wherever he found himself, and, taking matters in hand, tried to get to the heart of the matter. Trying to resolve it.

Sometimes he knew what he meant; other times he couldn't be sure. He was in the Sola, which had the curious property of appearing simultaneously familiar and exotic; like a drunken uncle returning from distant ports, perhaps. It was just before the monsoon rains, and the countryside around the alien city glowed with a sort of incandescence. The skinny juniper trees, planted at intervals along the long, bone white roads, drooped in a heat so ubiquitous as to take on hierarchical dimensions. Or was that the arrack talking through him? He hadn't even noticed when he'd begun drinking the stuff, probably soon after his arrival at the control point in Myryx, outside the alien city. Perhaps he hadn't even known at first it was alcohol, or whatever it was. Something to kill yourself with, a voice within him said. He didn't recognize the voice as his own. But whose could it be?

It was strangely difficult to keep in mind what he had come here for. Of course, that was because he was sick. But what would he be doing if he weren't sick? He supposed it was being sick that prevented him from knowing. And being sick prevented him from making much sense out of his talks with Sara. Because she started to visit him. But he knew that was impossible. Sara wasn't here; Sara was on the farm slightly smaller than Italy. Growing runner beans. Raising her child. What was its name? Waiting for Lawrence, or for him?

Sara started having conversations with him. He knew she was not really there. But this made it no easier. She seemed to be there. Tall, grave, gray-eyed. Her full underlip. Wisps of electric black hair escaping the clasp. A scent of the sea about her. Aaron worried about his sanity, but not much; he was too sick to worry.

"You see the problem?" Sara asked him.

"No, I don't see a thing," Aaron said. "Tell me what is happening. What does it mean?"

"Poor Aaron," Sara said. "Which is more important, what is happening or what it means?"

"But aren't they the same, what a thing is and what it means?"

"He's been asking to see you," Sara said.

"Who? Is it Lawrence?"

"No, I'm afraid not," a familiar voice said.

The Samian came into his room in his own special little tubular car. To Aaron he looked like something much better than a side of bacon. Without getting all Disney about it, he looked like a person. Someone you could get to like.

"Greetings," the Samian said. "How's tricks? I have been studying nonchalance. I am not so bad at it, do you think? But I do want to know if your health is improving."

"It is indeed," Aaron said.

"I had a slight indisposition myself," the Samian said.

"Indeed?"

"Yes. It colored my perspective for a while."

"But now?"

"I am ready to continue on to Alien City, if you are. I have obtained the necessary papers. Our departure awaits only your word."

"Let's take off in the morning," Aaron said. But it was not to be as simple as that.

In the morning, Aaron turned up at the Stromsky Gate which was the nearest point to Alien City. There were several Erthumoi around, as well as a few of the other species too. The gate through which he was to pass was high, made of wood, reinforced with strips of hammered iron. He wanted to ask someone why it was called the Stromsky Gate, but everyone seemed to be in a rush. And yet, no one wanted to allude directly to the journey Aaron was about to take. They said, "You'll be all right, no doubt," and looked away, in a manner which left no doubt what they thought of the safety of this enterprise. And he asked what was wrong, but in vain; they pretended not to understand: nothing is wrong; go right ahead.

"Where is the Samian?" he asked. But everyone became suddenly evasive— What Samian? Who are you talking about? No one wanted to discuss it, until one young man, little more than a child, said, "Your friend will catch up with you later." And that answer raised almost more questions than it answered, but there was no time to go into it. Someone threw open the gate; willing hands pushed Aaron toward the opening; and then, suddenly, just like that, he was through.

Even with this step taken, a step that should have been definitive, Aaron knew he wasn't all the way into the alien city. He had a small apartment. When he walked into Alien City, he seemed to be at the outskirts. Just ahead of him was a tall stone arch, a sort of gate, he supposed. Looking through it, Aaron could see a tangle of streets. Cobblestoned; yet he had the impression that the builders had used their materials for aesthetic purposes. Cobblestones give a nice feeling, especially when they are shining after a rain. And everyone likes the clop-clop a horse's hooves make as they cross cobblestones. It is a nice protected feeling you get in this place. Alien City is not so alien after all.

"Who are you?" Aaron asked.

"I'm Miranda," the girl said. She was small, tanned, and her hair was a bright tangle. Her mouth was small, kissable. Humans have to think in these terms, Aaron thought, trying to forgive himself for his sexual attitude.

"And this is Alien City?" Aaron said.

"Yes. Well, no, not exactly."

"Where is it then, exactly?"

"They call it an interface zone. It's not the same as the rest of this planet. But it's also not exactly what Alien City is, either. Here you will have a chance to rest, acclimatize yourself, so to speak."

"But I'm in a hurry," Aaron said. "The Council sent me. I'm supposed to look over this place, come to some conclusions."

"Yes, I understand," Miranda said. "What would you like for dinner?"

"I'm not hungry," Aaron said. But he realized that he was, and Miranda must have known it too, because she ignored his words and led him inside one of the houses whose bay windows beetled out onto the street.

Within he followed her through several rooms to a dining area in back. Here at a small table a white tablecloth had been set, and there were silverware and napkins.

Just beyond, in the kitchen, Aaron could see pots steaming on a wood stove.

"Can you tell me what this is all about?" Aaron asked.

"First eat," Miranda said. "There's plenty of time for explanations later."

The food was good. There was a cured ham, fresh eggs, a homemade loaf of bread. The butter seemed fresh churned. There was milk as well as a steaming coffeelike substance in low cups. Miranda wouldn't sit down herself. She hovered over him, however, making sure that he ate his fill, and occasionally darting into the kitchen for something she had forgotten: stewed fruits, preserves, biscuits.

After he had finished, Aaron had questions to ask. But Miranda looked out the window and suddenly saw someone coming down the street. Her expression brightened.

"Oh, look," she said to Aaron. "It is Mika, my uncle. He will bring us news of the Darfid."

"The what?" Aaron said.

"I forgot. You don't know the Old Tongue. Darfid refers to the meeting of the Lords of Diet."

"What does that mean?"

"It will all become clear to you," Miranda said. "Come, let us greet my uncle."

Mika seemed to be quite an old man. Aaron estimated that he must have used up his allotted cycles and be running on reserve now. On his own world of Sestes, Aaron had occasionally seen one of the very old ones. People looked at them with awe.

There was no reason why Aaron should have found himself with Miranda and her uncle Mika, but that was what had happened and he had to accept it, for the present, anyway. It was time to take stock of his situation. He was within Alien City, he thought, though he wasn't sure. It was important for him to find out. He suspected he wasn't really in Alien City because he never saw any of the others. There were supposed to be others here. He wanted to ask Miranda and Mika about the others. But it was curious, whenever he thought about asking them, they seemed to be absent. Miranda was always going into the fields outside the city walls. They were rolling meadowland,

and she must have kept a vegetable patch there, because she always returned with delicious things to eat. And Mika, where did he go? Aaron had the feeling that Mika went deeper into the city, to a bar somewhere, a tavern, where he drank with his cronies. Aaron didn't know why he never brought those cronies to the house so that Aaron could meet them, too.

It was nice to live with Miranda. Sometimes Mika stayed over, too. There was a little bed out back in the shed. The weather was mild, so it never bothered Mika to sleep out back. But Aaron preferred it when it was just him and Miranda. Then she would sing him those strange, sad old songs of hers. Sometimes she recited poetry to him in a language he did not recognize. Sometimes they went to the woods beyond the city for nuts and mushrooms. There were squirrels in the woods and bright yellow pumpkins in the fields. There was something strange about it all, but Aaron wasn't sure what it was. Whenever he tried to think about it, his head started to hurt. He wondered sometimes if he was going crazy. But that was so unpleasant a thought that his mind quickly veered away from it. He thought, if I'm crazy, it's best not to know.

"Miranda," he said one day, "when do I get to see my son?"

She looked at him, startled. "What are you talking about?"

"My son, Lawrence. He's in Alien City. I want to see him."

"You must have it wrong, Aaron. You're too young to have a son."

He stared at her. He understood that if he agreed with her, it would be true. He was tempted. Imagine being able to regain all those lost cycles! But he couldn't let himself do it.

"I have a son, Miranda. He must be older than you."

She flashed him a look. "That shows how much you know about it!"

"When can I see him?"

"Aaron, I must warn you, you're ruining everything."

"I don't see how. I'm just asking about my son."

"Reality is not what we deal with around here," Miranda said. "Is love so meagre, then, that you give it up in order to ask foolish and mundane questions? Where's Uncle Mika? He could explain it to you better than I."

"Yes, where is Mika?" Aaron asked.

"Oh, I'm here, I'm here," Mika said, appearing suddenly in a corner of the room and hastily buttoning up his fly. "Do I never get a moment's peace, not even for a naturalistic bit of business like this?"

"What's going on here?" Aaron asked him. "Who are you people?"

"He's seen through us," Mika remarked to Miranda.

Now that he looked more closely, there was something curious about both of them. Maybe it was the way the dancing candlelight of the little cottage seemed to seek them out, as though those fiery points of light loved them. Perhaps it was because they seemed so perfect, yet perfect in a nonhuman way, like something that lacks the flaws that would make it truly loveable; perhaps it was the way their figures wavered in the flickering lights, Miranda in her long peasant skirt, Mika in his blue serge pilot coat. The light from the fireplace danced around them, and then Aaron noticed that he could see through them, as though they were figures on an isinglass screen.

He mused about the strangeness of that time, when the thought of unreality first came on him, when he realized that perhaps he was not well yet. It seemed to him that he had to get out of there.

He had to leave the cottage, which had been more homelike than home itself, far behind.

And what was more horrible than that was the fact that this did not even dismay him. It seemed to him perfectly right and proper that Miranda and Mika should have something otherworldly about them. This feeling on his part alarmed him even more than his insight as to their transparency. It opened up many possibilities: that he was going crazy, or had gone; or worse, that he wasn't crazy, and that in some incomprehensible way, Miranda and Mika were as they were meant to be. For it seemed to him now that they might not even be humans. All the evidence at this point seemed to say that they were aliens, perhaps the original inhabitants of the city, and that they had taken this way to present themselves to him, so as not to alarm him and bring him slowly into their construct.

He began to search for ways of getting out. He didn't let on to them, but it seemed to him now that there was something horrible about the cottage, something distressing and unfamiliar about its inhabitants. He found himself wanting to study their faces more closely. He began to detect a faint wavering of their outlines when he glanced at them out of the corners of his eyes. But he couldn't be sure.

He decided he would have to be guileful, indirect. In the morning he began extending his habitual walks. Always going a little farther. It was important to do it this way if he were to ever hope to get away. And at the same time he knew that he was acting thoroughly crazy; there might be nothing in this; he might be making it all up.

Nevertheless, he continued extending his walks, and nobody commented on it. And then, one morning, when his walk had brought him to a little bridge across a stream, he crossed it. Looking back, the landscape seemed in some subtle manner to have changed. He knew then that it was time to continue, away from the cottage, on to what lay ahead.

Aaron walked across the fields. He wasn't sure in what direction Alien City lay, but he had an intimation that this was the right direction. After a while the fields gave way to second-growth woodland. Thin shoots of young trees stretched ahead of him interminably. He could hear the scolding sound of crows in the branches. They peered down at him with an air of indifferent evil. The day seemed to extend forever, low sun white in a white sky, black branches cutting across his vision, tangling his thoughts. He became very tired but he knew he mustn't stop. Not here, not now. His feet sank into the thin mud which the trees sat upon, and sometimes he could feel something below him, something lumpy and unmentionable. He didn't care to investigate, to see what it was, but hurried on. And the sun sank no lower in the sky. He could feel the presence of an ancient evil, or so it seemed to him. This was an accursed land. He wondered from time to time where he was, then reminded himself not to ask that question. He must not give up his certainties, even if he was wrong. Especially if he was wrong. He had to go on, and he did go on, until suddenly it was all over and he had arrived at the place he had been going to.

When he finally came to the alien city itself, he didn't recognize it at first. His mind was full of how other illustrious cities of the past have looked after excavation. Ur of the Chaldees, Babylon, Knossos, Thebes, Karnak, these were on his mind. Ruins give a feeling of antiquity and strangeness, and he had expected to find this in the alien city on Myryx, too.

And of course it was like nothing he had seen before. It didn't even seem strange. What was strange about this alien city was its familiarity.

He only began to know about this after establishing his second house. This was the ramshackle little hut on the edge of the swamp. He could look across the swamp and see the spires and towers of the alien city. Sometimes he could see people moving down the streets. But that was on the far side of the bog. There seemed no way to get there. The bog was treacherous; a pole pushed into it would continue down, finally getting lost in the muck that formed the bog's bottom. Aaron didn't like to think about what might be buried in the bog. He thought of skeletons with grasping fingers, corpses with dripping hands and mouths livid and set awry, and he stayed far from the swamp. From time to time he would put himself together and try to march around the bog. But he always gave up after an outing of half a day or less, around one side of the shore or the other. It seemed to him that he wasn't intended to go to the city at this time. Why else would it be so difficult? He had to wait, that much was obvious, or that much he could talk himself into. And all the time he was ashamed of himself as a quitter. But he also knew that profound changes were taking place in him, and that he couldn't hope to understand what had happened until it was finished happening.

And then there was a certain darkness, a wavering wall of uncertainty. It had been interesting, living here for a while in the limbo. The limbo was a good place.

After a while the problem came to consume all his waking thoughts. How was he to cross the bog and get to the alien city? He couldn't think of anything else. It became necessary to concentrate all thoughts on that one thing. And therefore it was not surprising that his world temporarily fell apart when something happened to vary the routine. He wasn't sure when he first heard the noise. He was too busy thinking about how to get across the bog to worry much about what sounds might mean in the little hut where he resided. Given his circumstances, it was both easy and accurate to lump all sounds together under the heading, "alien sounds." And then to ignore these.

But certain sounds are difficult to ignore. Dry scratching sounds in the walls, for example, and the scurrying of some dry-skinned creature in the crawl space of the ceiling. He found after a while he was reacting to the sound without actually registering it. Somebody was putting him to a great deal of trouble. It occurred to him to trace out the sounds, but he didn't think, not at this point, that there was any point to it. Why bother to learn the meaning of sounds in a place you are about to vacate, as soon as you figure out how to cross the bog?

Time passed, there in the little hut. The waters of the bog reflected steely clouds in the sky. In the evening there was rarely a true sunset. But sometimes the sky would light up with neurotic oranges and dubious purples. The light here was not on a human scale. It could even be considered pretentious. But he grew quickly to love it, so that, for years after, it would remain the signature of this place.

"Mr. Aaron? Are you awake?"

Aaron sat up. Somebody had whispered to him, there in the dark, in the small hours of the night, in his hut on the edge of the alien city.

"Who is it?" Aaron asked.

"You don't know me," the voice said. "But I'm a friend."

It was a firm, deep voice, and it led Aaron to think that it belonged to a large, burly man. Or possibly some other species. What did it want?

"What is it?"

"We have something to show you."

"What is it?"

"Come this way; see for yourself."

"I'm not going anywhere," Aaron said, "until you explain what you're talking about."

"You are here to investigate the Samians," the voice said. "Is that not correct?"

"Yes. But I don't see—"

"I can show you things that will tell you volumes about the Samians. Don't waste this opportunity. Come with me."

That let a lot of things open, and Aaron would have liked to pursue a few of the avenues which the voice had opened up. But there had been a certain urgency in his voice. On the other hand, Aaron was full sick of the bog, which rarely changed and had little wildlife around it to keep the gaze entertained.

Aaron stood up cautiously in the dark. The lights didn't seem to be working. A very small hand crept into his own. It was like a child's hand. Except that it seemed to have too many fingers. Not that he was prejudiced. It was simply something to note. He turned and followed the gentle tug of the fingers, toward a wall which dissolved and became a long corridor, dark but not quite so dark as the room had been earlier. He continued down it. It was a long time before he saw a dot of light at the end of it. He continued to walk and the dot grew in size. Far ahead he could see a glowing rectangle of light. This would have to be a doorway. He wondered if he had gotten through into the alien city after all. Could this have been his guide? He looked down and saw a very small rectangular figure. It looked a great deal like a Samian, only much smaller, and it had tiny arms and legs. Each leg terminated in a foot with seven toes, and each hand terminated likewise in a hand with six fingers.

"Who are you?" Aaron asked. "And where are you taking me?"

"This is the inspection," the small parallelepipedon said. "You should know that. You are the inspector."

"I am?" Aaron said.

"Of course. You were told by the Council to keep your eyes on the Samians, lest they prove a threat to the future of the humanoid race. Is that not so?"

"It's so," Aaron said, "but how did you know?"

"Our spies are everywhere," the parallelepipedon said. "Come, we have put out all the evidence for you."

"Evidence? What evidence?"

"Evidence as to the true intentions of the Samians."

Aaron could see hundreds of the little parallelepipedons. It was evident at once that they were closely related to the larger Samians.

As their spokesman, P. Samuelson, said, many ages ago the two races had been unified. Then the winds of change came. Separate religious holidays were declared. After that, the smaller pipedons found that a decree passed in the dark and sub rosa had declared the smaller ones second class citizens, to be known hereafter as the Underclass. Some of the smaller pipedons thought it was a pretty-sounding name, but the more intelligent among them soon put them straight. "Can't you see what they're trying? They want us to do all the work. That's why they're growing themselves without limbs!"

The larger pipedons were elusive when asked why they were breeding a generation without arms or any means of manual dexterity. The depth of their plot began to show itself when a warehouse full of indentured smaller pipedons, stacked one atop the other like leathery pancakes, was found, all awaiting their being sent to suburbs for indentured servanthood. They had been drugged. Upon revival, they said they had been promised a trip to a beautiful country where all living things lived together in peace. This was naive of them, but not criminally so. They mentioned a certain stranger who had made these promises—a big fellow the size of a rack of bacon, with a shifty expression. Since no one could prove that the larger pipedons were capable of any expression whatsoever, the case was dismissed.

Yet the trend was clearly established. The larger pipedons, actuated by whatever obscure survival energy, continued to breed out the use of limbs in favor of the new doctrine of psychic homogeneity. And more and more favor came to be found in the doctrine of spiritual immobility.

This was a time of great enthusiasm among the Samians. It seemed to them that willingly giving up the use of limbs was a great step toward true spirituality. It didn't occur to them, however, that all that they used to do for themselves was now done by the humble small parallelepipedons, who, more and more, were relegated to a backstage existence.

In vain did the smaller parallelepipedons point out that they had all the attributes of Samianhood. Nobody was listening. The Samians declared that the smaller Samians were "parts of the Samian body" and not autonomous creatures at all. According to this doctrine, anywhere a Samian found a smaller Samian he could claim him or her as his or her property, an autonomous part of his or her body that had somehow gotten loose.

Since the Samians knew this wouldn't go down well with the other civilized races, they bent every effort to keep anyone from finding out the Samian-Samian situation.

"As a rule," Samuelson said, "they don't let us off the home planets. But when this expedition to the alien city on Myryx came up, the Samians knew they would have to make an effort. In order to safeguard the future, you see."

The parallelepipedons had to be brought along by the big Samians in order to perform all the tiny functions that their hereditary drive toward immobility made impossible. The little fellows could scratch obscure itches. And do many other things. They had, unique among living species, two opposable thumbs. Nature had given them profligate dexterity.

Aaron felt like hell for the little oblongs, but it was difficult to figure out what to do for them. The Samians' doctrine of *primo inter pares* seemed only sound to groups which held on to their hegemony by a thread. Suppose all the organs could have a local intelligence and a way to express it? It has been an old humanoid fear for years. How many fables there have been about old doctor stomach.

Aaron made the mistake of expressing some of these views. The atmosphere at once became unpleasant. The small parallelepipedons moved toward him, clicking their long nails together in a menacing manner. Their very smallness, which had rendered them helpless before the larger Samians, like Pygmies encountering Watusi in a surrealistic replay of *King Solomon's Mines,* at this moment rendered them dangerous in the extreme to Aaron. He backed away, breathing shallowly to avoid taking one up the windpipe. It was just at this moment that the rescue team, headed by his buddy the Samian, came breaking into the bunker and set Aaron free.

"It's a crude attempt at blackmail," the Samian said. It was several hours later. Both man and Samian were taking their ease in a small audience chamber. The Samian listened as the man told his tale.

Aaron was a member of the Third Exodus. The first, the Jews from Egypt; the second, the Earthians from Earth; the third, the Erthumoi from Earth'n. It was the Third Exodus that Aaron belonged to. His parents had lived all their lives on Artemis V. Nothing changed much there. Not even the arrival of the six civilized species changed the level tenor of Artemis life. Aaron was eager to get away from the planet. His father was a religious man, but it never took on Aaron.

The early history of humanoid expansion was dictated by the convenience of setting up hyperjump points. It became increasingly difficult to set these up in the intense galactic core. As new worlds were discovered, the Erthumoi spread out to occupy them. This proved impossible, however, since the demands for new world populations far exceeded the ability of the species to breed sufficient volunteers. Sometimes whole worlds were occupied by only a single family or two, in an attempt to establish an

Erthuma presence and legal claim upon those worlds, and in hopes that a population would be attracted.

Aaron's father was a drygoods salesman on Kitanjar, a small green-and-black world in the general direction of the center. He was a hard man, and filled with old-fashioned views. He never really believed in the existence of the other civilized races. He thought it was a device of the devil for glorifying animals. Aaron's mother had been a channel swimmer. She was also an amateur watercolorist of some note. She left Aaron's father for unspecified riots in the year of the bipolar explosion, and moved to Syringin II with her son. Aaron lived there with her until she died when he was fourteen.

He left the school system the following year, and went to Sestes. He became a farmer on one of the quietest and least populated worlds in the galaxy, and this may be said to have helped him breed a certain independence of judgment that must have influenced his final decision in the Alien City 4 matter.

To Alien City 4, the strange place on the planet Myryx, Aaron has come. He wants to get in contact with his son, Lawrence; but even this is not a primary goal. In some fashion which he barely understands, Aaron has been searching for this place all his life. For the alien city is, paradoxically, the only place that is familiar and dear. This sounds paradoxical, but perhaps it isn't, really. In order to grow up, Aaron, like everyone else, has to give up the secret place. It has been the subject of a thousand comparisons. It can be compared to a secret garden, the one which, if our intimations are correct, we used to play in when we were young. It is strange that the most alien place should also be the most familiar. But so it is. And in finding this place, in a sense Aaron has come home.

But how is he to explain this to the others? He doesn't want to do what Lawrence did—give up even trying to communicate to others what is happening to him. This time he has the real thing, the objective correlative, the answer, the solution.

But what is he to say about this place? When the spirit is

right, any place is good. Alien City has views and aspects, the looking at which is a sacred matter. Here a man can have two things usually incompatible: to be home and to be abroad; to live in the strange and in the familiar simultaneously.

The city is filled with wonders, but they seem only normal when you are on the inside. Such matters as food and drink are no problem. They just come up when the time for them is there. This is so with everything; all of it is so easy and natural. That is the greatest thing about Alien City, how natural it all is.

Aaron saw Lawrence on his third day in Alien City. The first day was spent finding a place to sleep and then collecting the sleeping bags and other gear necessary. There was no furniture in Alien City. From the size of the rooms, you could guess that the aliens had been scaled to nearly our proportions. Though somewhat larger, and with a longer stride, to judge by the distance between flagstones on the long sloping ascents to the upper chambers. It was not so much a city as a single house of many rooms, with open spaces where you could assume that markets had been. There was no sign that these aliens had been a violent people. Although there was a certain amount of ornamentation on the walls, it was strictly geometric. There were no representations of the human form that Aaron saw, nor, he learned later, had any been discovered. It was found later, however, that one symbol recurred frequently in some of the other deserted cities. This was a flying snake, an old symbol on Earth. But this one had curious bends and twists to his tail, and his wings were broad with long finger feathers, as can be observed in certain raptorial birds. But basically the aliens didn't go in for much ornamentation. It was hard to figure out what the city had been intended for. It seemed to be more than shelter and sustenance. Although there were several thousand rooms in the city, maybe more, none of the doors had any external indication of a lock. Nor had the searchers found any sign of kitchens, larders, places to store food. Nor were there any restaurants. It seemed that the Seventh Race's ideas of what a city was for were very different from those of Erthumoi.

"What's this?" Aaron asked.

"We call this the central promenade," Lawrence told him. "It occupies a midpoint of the city."

"What is its significance?"

"We have no idea," Lawrence said.

"I don't know why you haven't communicated some of these discoveries to the Council."

"It's difficult to know what to say about this place," Lawrence said. "So much of it is nuance. You get a strong feeling about the aliens, but there's nothing to point to where that feeling comes from. Do you feel it, Father?"

"It would be impossible not to," Aaron said. "But this is natural. It is the sort of thing men felt when they uncovered the tombs of ancient Egypt on Earth, or the tombs of the Sultai on Amertegon."

It was natural to feel awe in the presence of the very old. The feeling of antiquity here was palpable.

Lawrence said, "I want you to meet Moira. She is helping me in my investigations."

Moira was a small, dark-haired girl, somewhat stocky, with an open, frank, cheerful face. She wore blue jeans and a man's large, baggy sweater. She wore sandals. Instead of a purse, she carried a knapsack. Her face was innocent of makeup. She was wide-eyed, and her features were harmonious rather than beautiful.

"I am very pleased to meet you," she said to Aaron, shaking his hand. "I have heard a great deal about you. Lawrence thinks very highly of you, you know."

Aaron hadn't known. He thanked her and stole a glance at Lawrence. His son was scribbling down a note and hadn't seemed to hear what Moira was saying.

They proceeded deeper into the city. There were fewer lights here. Aaron had a sense of growing antiquity as they continued. The shapes as they went deeper became more angular, more stylized. The corridors took odd little jigs and turns for no apparent reason. And the lighting effects became more elaborate. The sense of mystery deepened, although as yet Aaron had seen nothing he considered extraordinary.

"This next will interest you," Lawrence said. They went through a pair of open double doors, down a short flight of steps, then around another corner. When they were on a straight course again, Lawrence brought them to an abrupt halt.

"Here's what I wanted you to look at," Lawrence said.

The next revelation is even stranger. At first, wandering around Alien City, it seems a bunch of rather static wonders. Interesting, of course, but no different from any other alien city, not qualitatively different, that is, from what has been known before.

But gradually, there is a realization that Alien City 4 is something more than a diorama of marvels. Aaron has the glimmering recognition that the place is not dead, not inert. Something is happening here. Something is happening in response to the movements of others. In some sense, the city is like a teaching experiment. That is what Lawrence knows, and it is what Aaron is finding out.

"I could have sworn that doorway wasn't here before."

Lawrence nodded but made no comment.

"Is that true."

"You'd better find out for yourself, Father."

Aaron knew that he had been going to the third door on the left. Just a little while ago, it had been locked. Now, when he came back to it again, it opened to his touch.

"Did you change the door setting?"

Lawrence shook his head.

"Somebody must have. It was locked before. Now it isn't."

"No one has touched it. We have encountered this phenomenon before. The doors open when the city thinks you're ready to go through them."

To prove this, Lawrence went up to one of the doors and tried the knob. It was locked. He gestured to Aaron. Aaron tried the door and it came open.

"It must know that I have already eaten," Lawrence said. "So it sees no reason to open the door for me. You, however, have not had either breakfast or lunch. It is more than ready to feed you."

Aaron tried the door again, then cautiously slipped through it. After a moment, Lawrence turned the knob three times. This time the door opened for him.

"Where'd you pick that up?" Aaron asked.

"Trial and error. I found that after the first override, the city is more than willing to let me through. I have to insist on it; that's the only thing. It's perfectly willing to let me through if I'm determined."

Aaron looked around. The room was obviously a dining room. There was a marble and wood table and four chairs. There was a considerable setting of napkins, glassware, and china. And there were several large dishes in the middle of the table. When Aaron lifted their lids, a delicious aroma came forth. There was nothing alien about this food. It looked to Aaron like beef stew with potatoes and carrots. Not very exotic grub, but good sustenance.

"Who produced this food?" Aaron asked.

"The food simply appears."

"Is it always the same?"

"Not at all. The city cycles its food. It hasn't repeated itself yet. Sometimes there's an Oriental food, sometimes Russian, sometimes Latin American. And sometimes there is something we don't recognize. But we eat it anyhow, and it has never done us any harm."

There were other things which were not so familiar. The dolls, for example. That was a puzzler. They appeared everywhere. Dolls, none more than eighteen inches in height, and always elaborately dressed. Some of the dolls were made of rags, but some were elaborately made of white and blue porcelain. Sometimes they had eyes made of precious stones. These dolls were ubiquitous; sometimes there were a few, other times many more. Aaron could never find the reason, the principle, behind the dolls. At times there were no dolls at all. Then suddenly there would be dozens, hundreds of them. Aaron tried to keep lists, trying to work out what brought along the dolls. But he could never get it right.

* * *

"Sara! What are you doing here? I thought you wanted no part of this."

"I suppose I can change my mind."

"Certainly, no doubt of that. But *why* have you changed your mind?"

"That's my business."

"And have you seen Lawrence yet?"

"Not yet. All that doesn't seem as important as it did before I came here."

"But of course it's important!" Aaron said. "You must speak with Lawrence immediately. I know he'll be delighted to see you."

"Why don't you stop trying to be so stinking nice?" Sara said. "Things have changed. We'll have to see where we go from here."

Somehow Lawrence and Sara didn't come across each other. Aaron didn't think they were avoiding each other, yet they never seemed to meet. It was impossible to tell which was avoiding the other. It seemed almost natural, the way they never happened to meet. But it bothered Aaron. It bothered him also that Sara didn't seem interested in him. What had happened? Why had things changed so drastically?

The Samian said, "How are you, my friend?"

Aaron sat up. He had been spending more and more time recently lying down and contemplating the ceiling. Of late it had seemed that he had a great deal to think about. He wasn't sure what it was, nor was it difficult. He felt very calm these days, and, in general, quite optimistic. But there was something else involved, too, and this was what the Samian was picking up. All was well with Aaron, especially since the nightmares had stopped. For a while the Samian had been nervous about his friend. Aaron had been muttering about tiny Samians rebelling against the larger ones. The Samian couldn't imagine where his friend got such ideas.

"I'm fine," Aaron told him.

The Samian could hear the guarded note. He was finding a number of curious things going on. There was quite a number of the six civilized species inside Alien City. They seemed to be intent on exploring. Yet they were imprecise as to what. At the entrance to Alien City, messages were piling up. Some of them were from the Council, who were bombarding Aaron with queries, as before they had questioned Lawrence. But Aaron, like his son, didn't have time or inclination to answer. The Samian tried to talk him into replying. "These Council people, they're going to think it odd."

"I know," Aaron said. "But it can't be helped."

"You could tell them something," the Samian said. "It wouldn't kill you, would it?"

"I don't know," Aaron said. "I'm not sure."

The Samian began to wonder again if something were wrong with Aaron; perhaps, he thought, something was going wrong with everyone here. In fact, he had to ask himself if he were all right.

This sense of uneasiness went back to the humanoid centers. People were beginning to ask questions about Alien City. There had been no reply so far. Then Matthew, on behalf of the Council, told Aaron that they would have to come themselves, since Aaron couldn't seem to get himself together.

"How do you feel about that?" the Samian asked.

"It's probably for the best," Aaron said. "There's a lot going on here. In one sense, the original inhabitants of this city are not dead."

"Is that a fact?" the Samian said.

"Oh, yes. Haven't you figured it out yet?"

"I'm afraid not," the Samian said. "But then, we Samians are the second most recent and least sensitive members of the civilized races."

It is curious how the other civilized species, with the exception of the Samians, have been reacting to Alien City. More and more of them have been coming to Myryx. There is a considerable colony scattered over several square miles outside Alien City. Each species has set up its own life-style. There is a certain penalty against some of them;

the fliers, because the atmosphere lacks neon, the Cephallonians and the others because of their own limitations. Myryx is basically an oxygen-breather's place with light gravity. The others have had to struggle along as well as they could. Special constructions have been set up. An entire water world was set up by the Cephallonians. Some of the fliers, the Crotonites, have set up special habitats. Within a sealed district, they have been able to increase the thickness of the atmosphere so that it affords some lift for their wings. There's little they can do about the lessened gravity, however. Yet the planet of Myryx is forgiving even in that, as they seem to adapt to it. This is the closest to a universal planet for all species that has yet been found. Only the Samians have been staying away.

Octano Halfbarr, the Samian, has been alarmed by all this. He intends to inform his people that it's not safe in this place.

"Hello? Gwinfar?"

Neutronic communication is so close to simultaneous that only a quibbler would say it isn't immediate. Octano finally is able to speak with his clan chief, Gwinfar.

"What's going on in this world?" Gwinfar asked.

"It worries me," Octano said. "None of the other races seem to think much about it. At first they were really interested in investigating me."

"Whatever for?"

"They seem to have some sort of delusional system going. Or maybe it's the effect of Myryx."

"What sort of delusional system?"

"They feel that we Samians are harboring some deep secret."

"Hah! If only we were!"

"Yes, that's exactly how I feel. But they don't seem to understand that we're just about as simple as we seem. They look for some kind of mystery about us."

"Does it seem to correspond to what they call 'paranoid thinking'?"

"I didn't want to say it, but yes, it does," Octano replied.

* * *

Back at the Council meeting room on the main planet of the Minieri system, Matthew was alarmed. Later he could trace the precise beginning of his concern. It was when the Samian sent his report in and asked for assistance.

"He must have directed his message through the wrong channel," St.-Fleur said. "Why should a Samian request this meeting of us?"

"No," Matthew said, "it can't be a wrong channel affair. It's got our identification marks."

"This request of his for secrecy," St.-Fleur said. "I don't like it. It binds us in complicity with him."

"We need to find out what's on his mind. You know as well as I do that something untoward is happening here. If Octano can throw any light on it, we need to use him."

The meeting took place on Hester, a moon of the second humanoid planet. Although Hester was airless, a conference facility had been set up in one of the impact craters that dotted the side the little moon kept faced toward its primary. Not far from the conference room was an automated amusement facility. There was no sense in leaving living personnel on the planet, because trade wasn't swift enough to justify the expense. But the automated amusements did well enough for the low density population situations that usually came up on Hester.

Straight ahead was the zero-grav roller coaster with its intricate twists and turns. There were the stark shapes of the other amusements—tribute to man's ancient preoccupation with his own proprioceptive centers. The quick food stands were closed up now, but when St.-Fleur approached, the sensors picked up his arrival and the lights flashed on. They were genuine neon, ancient symbol of an old-time lurid civilization. Music started up too, beamed directly to their helmets. And then the mechanized voice of the huckster:

"Step up, ladies and gentlemen; step up and take your chances. Pin the tail on the wonky. Shoot down the sad old saber tooth. Run against the windrows of the sun. Quaff lethal beverage in zero time and enjoy the sense of accomplishment that comes from outrage. Don't be nervous; step up, boys and girls; take fun, enjoy pleasure!"

"This is quite unpleasant," St.-Fleur remarked to Matthew. "Do these things always go on this way?"

"I'm afraid so," Matthew said. "Newest thing, you know."

"But why should this sort of thing be popular?"

"Difficult to predict what direction the mass taste will take. It has been proven, I believe, or at least so I learned in psych class back in university, that the taste for the degraded does not exist in isolation but is in reaction to the desire for the good. Whatever the reason, mankind has a need for these sleazy places. There is a theory that nothing human is alien or unnecessary."

There on the airless moonlet, the amusement park games and rides arced high, silhouetted against the sky, lying in the great crater of crushed white stone with hard needle points of stars above. The two men walked through the deserted amusement park trying to devise their next move.

St.-Fleur said, "This might not have been a good idea, Matthew. We may have overstepped the legitimacy of our quest."

"We need to find out whatever we can," Matthew said. "We should be willing to go anywhere to find out what's happening on Myryx."

"Except going to Myryx itself," St.-Fleur said.

"We've already discussed that."

St.-Fleur adjusted the oxygen flow across his nose and mouth. "It wouldn't be a good idea to go to Myryx. You agreed to that yourself, Matthew."

"Under duress."

"No matter; you did agree. We didn't twist your arm. And it's only reasonable, Matthew. We don't know what's going on on that ambiguous planet. Whenever we send anyone, he fails to stay in touch. Aaron is only the latest."

"We could send someone else," Matthew said stubbornly.

"I know you'd like the job yourself. But to what end? If you stopped communicating too, we'd just lose another important Council member."

"All right," Matthew grumbled. "But where is he?"

"Across there," St.-Fleur said.

Matthew looked. Across, on the distant side of the amusement park, just up from the fenced-in space where the asteroid miners used to park their vehicles, something was moving. It proceeded parallel to them for a while, then turned and headed directly for them.

St.-Fleur drew a bell-shaped revolver from his belt, but Matthew put his hand lightly on the older man's shoulder.

"Take it easy. It's Octano, the Samian."

The Samian was in his tubular vehicle. A vat of gases was stored at his feet. The colored gases percolated out, flowing across the featureless slablike front of his body. The body, a dark side of meat, seemed to have no animation. All signs of life came from the repeater board in the tubular ship. From the flash and intensity shift of the LEDs, Matthew could tell that the Samian was disturbed.

They exchanged cautious greetings. Then the Samian said, through his translating machinery, "I'm glad you've come. You know I've come here to talk to you about Aaron."

"I fail to understand," St.-Fleur said, "why you didn't present your request through official channels."

"This is a little too serious for that. The situation on Myryx has many baffling aspects. I think you should hear me out."

"But why have we come here?"

"You must know how it is," the Samian said. "The governing board of the Samian Confederacy is not at all sure what the situation on Myryx means. But we can see one thing. Something is happening on Myryx which is having profound effects on the species that have gone there to investigate. The effect is especially profound on the Erthumoi."

"Why would the council of the Samian Confederacy object if you told us that?"

"You know very well," the Samian said, "that beneath the cloak of good manners and evenhandedness, my race, like all the others, conceals its fears and its competitiveness. We say there's no interspecies struggle, but that's just standard piety. Although the galaxy is wide beyond our power to grasp, we still are all trying to be number one in it."

St.-Fleur said, "You are unusually frank."

"Why not? I do not share this view with my fellows. I want my people, the Samians, to endure, of course. But we are at a disadvantage in the sort of game that is taking place on Myryx."

There was some more discussion on these lines. It appeared to Matthew that the Samian was attempting a new approach to the ancient program of competition between species. He could not be sure; this could be a subtle attempt to undermine the Erthumoi somehow. He puzzled it out, there in the brilliantly lit but deserted amusement park, on a moon that had been bypassed by the waves of interplanetary commerce. One thing was certain; he had to find a way to learn what was going on with Aaron. Especially now, since the latest reports had shown over a dozen ships heading for Myryx. The people aboard were tourists, and they were made up of four of the six species.

"Are you saying that the city itself is responsible?" Matthew asked.

"I didn't want to say it. But you have said it. Now you must consider whether it could be true or not."

Matthew thought it over. The city was not deserted; but personnel did not return, nor did they maintain communications. Was the city built as a trap? It was known that other intelligent species came there. . . .

It took Aaron a long time to get to sleep that first night. He realized as soon as he got there that the city was living, functioning, after all these millennia. It seemed ridiculous to ask himself, what for? There was no way he could know the purpose of the alien builders.

It was strange, there in the guest house. It was a long shadowy room, with a central walkway and tatami-mat rooms on either side. The lighting still worked, too: just raise your finger and up came the lights. He had eaten earlier in the communal messhall. Dinner he had taken only with humanoids. It's too difficult to share a meal with some species that eats crankcase grease or its moral equivalent. He finished and went for his bath. This was set up so that, after he stripped, he went down a long metal tube, slid down it into the water. It seemed to Aaron an unnecessarily dramatic way of getting into the water, but he didn't seem to have any other choice.

In he went and he plunged down into the water in a dense cloud of white bubbles. There was something a little odd about the gravity around here; he was descending very slowly, and all around him were brightly colored strands and wafteroons of kelp and other long floating things, some of them with what looked like brilliant feathers, others with tiny scales.

Shapes floated through the water at him, other humanoids, he realized. As he watched, a Cephallonian swam past, looking very sure of itself; then a Naxian, somehow stroking through the water, went by looking no less sure than the Cephallonian. The water he had dived into was lit from below, and the water was very clear. Aaron didn't find it strange to continue descending, dropping down in a cloud of bubbles past other swimmers, toward the lights below that seemed to recede as he approached them. It didn't occur to him to ask how come he was able to breathe underwater. If you find that you can, why ask?

He continued descending, and he had no impression of pressure, nor of breathlessness. He saw others in that brightly lit cone of light-filled water, old friends and new, old lovers and lovers yet to come, and they all waved at him as he continued going down.

Then he was at the bottom, and he saw a little round opening at the very base of what he could see now was a large glass flask. He swam through it, and abruptly he was on the surface again, shaking water out of his hair and eyes, and looking ahead of him at a small beach, gleaming white and silver over floodlights set into the rocky walls that surrounded it.

There was a man swimming beside him, unnoticed before. Aaron had never seen him before, but the man waved to him with enthusiasm, and with every sign of knowing Aaron and expecting to be known by him.

"I'm very sorry," Aaron said, after he and the man had both climbed out onto the beach. "Am I supposed to know you?"

"Not yet perhaps," the man said. He added something that Aaron didn't catch. But Aaron found he understood anyhow. Even a few unintelligible words served to awaken in him a vision of the meaning of the speaker's words. Though putting those meanings into words was something else again.

Then the figure was no longer there, as happens with figures in a dream, where exits and entrances are no problem, and the continuations are obscure. The point was, of course, that everything was very simple; take the scales from our eyes, very easy, this is the gift, the first gift from those who have gone beyond.

There is knowledge that sticks to the mind no longer than Chinese food is said to stick to the stomach. So it was that even though Aaron understood everything, it was only for an instant. Then the dream, which he already knew was to be considered an alternative, was ended, and it was time to start the next thing.

"Are you feeling better now?" Sara asked.

Aaron opened his eyes. He was in what looked like a very old room, built of stone pieces crudely joined together. There was a high, raised, canopied bed, and that is what he occupied. There was a brisk fire in the fireplace. Standing in front of it, her hands clasped behind her back, tall and slim, was Sara.

"What is it?" Aaron asked. "What are you doing here?"

"You had a close call," Sara said. "Do you understand how our very possibilities could be in a state of mutability?"

Aaron hadn't thought about it before. Now the proposition forced itself on him. Yet how could it be that the inner thrust of the humanoid race could itself be subject to change and flux? It was like finding out that the background, which you had considered stable, had suddenly flung itself into a series of wild transformations. Not merely the figure, the ground, too. Of course Aaron was vaguely aware that quantum mechanics should have prepared him for that. And if nothing else, man's ancient doctrine, called under many names, but revived most recently as chaos theory, told him the vanity of the objective.

* * *

"What are you thinking about?" Sara asked.

"It's strange," Aaron said, "that no name has ever been found for the possibility we are discussing. It's a kind of death of the dream. I hate these vague terms, but how do you speak of it? I'm afraid it's just one more idea that doesn't quantify."

"Don't get scared," Sara said. "You're doing fine."

Maybe he was, but he couldn't feel it. Aaron knew of this, but he had never encountered it himself—this sharp, sudden, crucial crisis of faith, in which not just oneself as a man is in doubt, but the validity, the usefulness, even the beauty of everything. And there had been epidemics of this sort of thing on other worlds, sudden and unaccountable die-offs, when beleaguered portions of the general population suddenly gave it up. We have seen the future and it is not us. And he wondered if it was possible that Myryx, the alien city, generated such a mood, produced such a poison.

What had he dreamed? He sat up suddenly. Yes, he had it! The information death of the universe. For information is a kind of energy, too, and it follows its own internal rules. For an information universe to be established, there must be a user of the information. Thus information is always duoform: one who sends; one who receives.

"This isn't strictly true, of course," Aaron said. "We know very few of the properties of information. What we can conjecture is that death may be a multileveled thing. There is death on every level. Dead is dead, but it can come to you on many levels. Information, yes, there is information which is incompatible with the concept of information as we, as science, understand it. We cannot understand that which refuses to share our realm of discourse, and someday this will undermine us."

"How long has he been going on this way?" Matthew asked.

"For the better part of two days," Dr. Franz said. "He said he had to talk with you, and then he lapsed into incoherence."

"Information is a true substratum," Aaron said. "You can cut off a chicken's head; that's one way of destroying him. But you can also deny him existence and that's another way. There are many roads to inner mysteries and they are never apparent from the viewpoints of other inner mysteries."

Easy now, Aaron thought. Pull yourself together. Take stock of the old think piece. Something to be done, but difficulties in your path. Here in this charming city. Where the blue of the something. No. Don't play around with it. They disapprove of levity.

"Good afternoon, Aaron."

"Good afternoon, Miss Marcheck."

Vague glimmerings of old maid fussiness. Behind us, the stars, eternal backdrop, go on eternally. He remembered a long time ago. It had been different. But here? Forlorn! The very word is like a bell. Get hold of yourself.

The masters passed up and down the ranks of students. The students remained very quiet. The masters had not a hair on their heads. But then he forgot; they had all been shaved; it was preparatory to the next stage.

"Just ease yourself out of it, Aaron."

They were talking about his body. Just ease out of it, indeed! Like to see them bloody try. Nonetheless, it was happening. "Let the body fall away." No letting about it; it did so anyhow, didn't it? Yes, but we have to agree, anything to keep them quiet, the masters; why was it always like that?

Wavering doubts, dreams, blown foam, the end of the old days. Why were these hands around him now? Was he drowning, or did they fear he didn't know how? That's it; he knew he had something to say, but no, he wasn't going to say it now.

Stand him up; give him room.

Yes, dreary sort of place, they were lapping up the booze, the sweet oblivion, or not so sweet; didn't make no matter, don't mind.

The hyperjump ship should be back. What is it to be alone here on the station? They usually didn't leave people alone on the hyperjump point. Limited air, food, water. Nothing to do. Wait until the next ship comes along. And how soon will that be? Aaron pulled the jacket more closely around him. At least his main requirements were taken care of. But what did that matter; he was cold, cold, and there was no warmth in sight.

Still they couldn't just let him die here, could they? He was aware that he was not having these dreams for the first time. He was remembering what had happened the first time. It had all happened before. Or was that merely what they wanted him to believe?

Aaron sat up abruptly. He felt clear, lucid for the first time in a long time. He was in a large, elaborately decorated room deep within Alien City. It was a room of marble and porphyry. On the mantel were old bronzes. There was a mosaic on the floor. It seemed to depict a sun goddess. Aaron himself was clad in costly robes. He was wearing a long silk robe of many colors. He was holding an orb in one hand, a scepter in the other. His gaze was fixed on the doorway. He couldn't see how the place was lighted. The lighting seemed to emanate from the stone and marble. But it was not as though it was a quality of those materials. Rather, something was moving along the corridor, something that seemed to be composed of pure light.

The light flowed along the corridor, entered his room, stopped. He could see it, wavering lightly in front of him, a dim flame twisting slowly, about six feet high. Within the turnings of the flame he thought he could make out features. After a while he could recognize them: they were Miranda, Mika, many of the others he had met.

"Who are you?" he said to the flame.

"I'm glad to see that you can speak reasonably with me," the flame said. "I am what they used to call the spirit of place."

"Could you explain that a little further?"

"In every spot, there is that which is the spirit of that spot. When the place dies, so dies the spirit of it. But the spirit can be reborn in other places. I have been reborn."

"Are you the spirit of what we call Alien City?" Aaron asked.

The flame flickered and wavered in what was unmistakably a nod. Aaron realized that it wasn't actually talking.

Rather, words were appearing in Aaron's mind as if the flame were speaking.

"How should I call you?" Aaron asked.

"You may call me Gea," the flame said. "I am the spirit of place."

"Gea," Aaron said, "what can you tell me about yourself? What is going on? What have you come here for?"

"I've been waiting for someone to recognize me," Gea said. "I had to show you a lot of things, Aaron, before you knew me for what I am. Do you know now?"

"Yes, I know," Aaron said.

"I have had to show you miracles," Gea said. "I have had to demonstrate to you all manner of strangeness. Only in that way could you become convinced."

"Are you purely spirit?" Aaron asked. "Or do you have a corporeal aspect?"

"I am physical as well as spiritual," Gea said. "Where I am, all three elements—physical, spiritual, mental—are all aspects of the same reality. This energy is eternal and indestructible; yet its specific form can be destroyed. I have preserved myself throughout these years to be ready for my reentry onto the galactic stage."

"I understand," Aaron said.

"I do not claim to be God," Gea said. "But I am something more than man, something more than the other species. Are you ready to serve me, Aaron? You are my prophet."

"I am ready," Aaron said.

"What a wonderful day of destiny this is," Gea said, "not just for ourselves, but for the entire human race. It is the time that mankind has long dreamed of. The time of guidance and care. I will take care of my own, Aaron, never fear. I have already shown you a glimpse of what is possible. It remains for us to finish this stage. Then we can go on to where the destiny of the race takes us."

Lawrence had been standing by helplessly during this conversation. He seemed to be bound by invisible bonds. Not for the first time he tried to pull himself free. It is only a trick, a sort of hypnosis, he told himself. He pulled against the restraints, but he could not budge. It had been like this for a long time. There was nothing he could do against it now.

"Father!" he cried. "Do you know what it is that has us?"

"Of course I know, Lawrence," Aaron said. "It is what we have always wanted, always dreamed of. A guide, one who will help us through the dangers that the universe presents."

"No, Father, you've got it wrong!" Lawrence had more to say, but sudden agonizing pain stopped him before he could go on. He wanted to warn Aaron: This thing meant nothing good for them, and certainly not for the human race. But there was nothing he could say.

"It's all right, Lawrence," Aaron said. "Gea and I understand each other. Gea, I want you to send my son and the others away from here. You and I need to talk, to plan our moves."

"I do the planning," Gea said.

"Of course you do," Aaron said. "But I can be a help. There are things you haven't learned about us yet. Ways of handling us which will suit your goals."

"Very well," Gea said. "You Erthumoi are more stubborn than I believed possible. But if at least one of you will listen, will obey me, then all is not lost."

"I am that one," Aaron said. "I greet you, Master."

Father! The word screamed against Lawrence's brain, but he couldn't pronounce it. He watched, sick to his heart, as Aaron groveled in the dirt in front of the flame.

"Send them away," Aaron said. "And let us begin our plans."

Lawrence felt himself lifted, borne away. He underwent a moment of vertigo. Then he awoke and found himself back on his ship. It was the original ship that the expedition had brought to Myryx over a year ago. Now, for the first time, he was able to work the controls. He lost no time in removing the ship a safe distance from the planet. Then he got on the communicator fast.

With his communicator set to transmit everything to Lawrence's ship, Aaron followed the flame deep into the interior of Alien City, to the shrine room he had located below the main level. It was deserted, a long, low-ceilinged place lit by flaming torches set into wall embrasures. The others had left, commanded to do so by Gea. Now Aaron was alone with the flamelike spirit.

The flame, substance of the creature who called himself Gea, was changing now, becoming silvery and waterlike, then changing again to a deep metallic purple red. The shapes and colors flowed ceaselessly, and Aaron didn't understand what generated its changes. As soon as he thought he could grasp it, it flowed and became something else. Aaron wondered if this might have been the origin of the shape-changer myths that mankind had had for so long. For all he knew, this fiery, slippery creature might have been the original Proteus, old man of the sea and of change.

"Mobility is strength," Gea said, "and I have many transformations. The others were too timid. They couldn't stand to look at me and behold man's next becoming. I could never trust them. You are wise to serve me, Aaron, although for a while I worried about you."

"Are all of your shapes elemental?" Aaron asked. "Or can you show me one of your human forms?"

"I can take any shape I want," Gea said. "But why a human one? That is the only time I'm vulnerable."

Aaron said, "We will want to make statues of your human form so all mankind can see."

"That's a good idea," Gea said. His surfaces flashed and flowed. He was for a moment the source of all light in the room, an explosion of silent color and brilliance. Then the light faded and there stood before Aaron a gigantic man with godlike proportions. He looked to Aaron like a huge Michelangelo sculpture, or perhaps one of the great chryselephantine statues of Zeus.

"This is classic, one of my forms that mankind has always enjoyed," Gea said. "This was one of those I wore before the cataclysm."

"What cataclysm was that?" Aaron asked.

"Atlantis," Gea said. "That was when the Antagonist bound me and sent me out here."

"Tell me more," Aaron said.

Gea looked at him suspiciously. "I wonder about you, Aaron. What are you?"

"Your prophet," Aaron said.

"Are you really? Humans lie so readily."

"I am, for sure," Aaron said. "And here is my proof." He removed the bomb from his pouch. As he had suspected, Gea did nothing to stop him.

Gea merely looked at him. There was sadness in the classical features, the short, heavy beard, the hyacinthine locks. Gea said, "How quickly the cycles turn!"

Aaron said, "Was this how it ended last time?"

"This is always how it ends. Aaron, don't do it. We can work together, shape the human race into something really noble, something godlike."

"You poor fool," Aaron said. "Don't you realize that the human race doesn't want and doesn't need anyone to shape it?"

A silent and rosy glow mounted against the blackness of space. The light spread for a moment, then faded away.

"It's over," Lawrence said.

Matthew said, "How long were you under that creature's power?"

"We succumbed almost from the first," Lawrence said. "He kept on showing us miracles, strange ways of being, different modalities of consciousness. He never seemed satisfied. The other investigators and I fought him all the way. It took my father to pretend to join with him, and then pull the pin."

"So that's what one of the ancient ones looks like," Matthew said. "It seems hardly possible that that creature was one of the ancient Seventh Race."

"I doubt very much that he was that," Lawrence said. "We'll never know for sure, but my impression is that Gea is of a race of galactic creatures, powerful but not particularly intelligent. Perhaps he's the last one of his kind. Certainly he's the only one we've seen. I think he takes refuge in deserted cities. Like bats and snakes hide out in caves. He's a predator, and he's got a few tricks up his sleeve, but he can be killed."

"What was all that he was saying about Atlantis?" Matthew asked.

"I don't know," Lawrence said. "It seemed to be something about being bound to a spot. Like Prometheus and the rocks of the Caucasus. And his story has aspects of the Christ myth, too. Though in this case he would be Lucifer. There *was* something devilish about him, wasn't there?"

"I think so," Matthew said. "It's an interesting analogue. I think it's the first time mankind, or any other species, has encountered anything like this. It argues the possibility that other such creatures might exist in the galaxy. Some of them in deserted cities. Others, who knows where?"

"It's something to watch out for," Lawrence said. "But we'll have to take that up later. Now I have to go."

"Where, in such a rush?"

"To see Sara. Gea made it impossible for me to talk to her." He moved toward the door and then stopped. "I only wish my father were here to see this."

THE BURNING SKY

POUL ANDERSON

Ilis never quite slept. After dark the towers and slipways of its centrum flared with light, pulsed with traffic, life that the free city, largest on Ather, drew unto itself from the whole planet and beyond. The harbor district lay quiet, though, watercraft and machines waiting for sunrise. Walls along the docks lifted sheer, their darknesses blocking off all but sky glow. Thus eyes found stars above the bay. Past full, the bigger moon was nonetheless rising bright enough to throw a bridge over the waves, which they broke into shivers and sparkles. Smells of salt, engines, cargos drifted cool.

Harul Vargen stopped before his apartment building. "Here we are," he said needlessly. Was it shyness that thickened his accent? Ordinarily he spoke fluent Merse. The vague illumination showed him tensed within the gray tunic and breeks of a Comet Line officer. "The hour's gotten later than I expected. If you'd rather postpone the—the conference—"

Laurice Windfell considered him. He stood a head taller than her, with the slenderness, sharp features, fair complexion of his Brèttan people. As was common these days on Ather, he went beardless and kept his hair short. Those blond locks had thinned and dulled, furrows ran through brow and cheeks; he must be far overdue for a rejuvenation. She hadn't ventured to ask why. The eyes, in their deep sockets amidst the crow's-feet, remained clear, "No," she said, "I think we had best get to our business," putting a slight emphasis on the last word, lest he misunderstand.

It had, after all, been a pleasant evening, dinner at Bynen's, liqueurs, animated conversation throughout, that continued while they walked the three kilometers to this place. They discovered a shared passion for Ather's wildernesses; he sought especially to explore the Ronaic Alps, and had had some colorful experiences there. Otherwise he said little about himself, nothing about his past. However, she felt she had come to know him well enough for her purposes. Several personal meetings, after her agents had compiled a report on him, should suffice. They'd better. Time was growing short.

"Very well," he agreed. "If you please, milady." The door identified him and retracted. He let her precede him into a drab lobby and onto the up spiral. It carried them to the fourth floor.

Admitted to his lodging, she glanced about, hoping for more clues to his personality, and found disappointment. The living room was small, aseptically clean, sparsely furnished. While she had gathered he was an omnivorous reader, it seemed he owned nothing printed but drew entirely on the public database. A half-completed model of a sailing ship, probably one that had plied the seas of ancient Earth, was the only sign of other interests. Well, maybe he'd picked these quarters because a transparency offered what must be a spectacular daylight view of bay, headlands, and ocean.

"Please be seated," he urged. "Can I offer you a drink?"

Laurice took a chair. Like the rest, it was rigid. "Just cofftea," she said. "No sweetener."

Vargen raised his brows. "Nor brandy? As you wish. I'll have a snifter myself, if you don't mind." The dossier related that he drank rather heavily, though not to the point of impairment and never in space. He shunned psychotropes. His occasional visits to Chlora's Bower hardly counted as a vice in a man unmarried. The girls there found him likable, yet none of them had really gotten to know him, any more than his shipmates and ground-side acquaintances had.

He stepped into the cuisinette. She heard a pot whirr. He came back carrying a goblet half full of amber liquid. "Yours will be ready in a couple of minutes," he said, and sipped. The motion was jerky. "Would you care for some music? Only name it."

"No, thank you," she replied. "Nice in the restaurant, but pointless now. Neither of us would hear, I think."

He tautened further. "What do you want with me, Milady Windfell?"

Her hazel gaze met his blue. "First and foremost," she told him, "your pledge to keep everything secret. I've satisfied myself that you can. Will you?"

"I take for granted this is . . . honorable," he said slowly.

She stiffened her tone. "You know my father is Davith, Head of our House."

"Indeed. And I've heard about you." A lopsided smile creased the gaunt face. "When a member of one of this world's ruling families seeks me out, talking about a possible service but not specifying it, I do a bit of inquiry on my own. I found a couple of men who've gone exploring with you. They spoke highly." He drew breath. "You have my promise. Absolute confidentiality until you release me from it. What do you want me to do?"

Despite herself, she felt her pulse quicken. "Don't you think you're wasted as mate on a wretched ore freighter?"

His expression blanked. He shrugged. "It's the best berth available. At that, you remember, I had to work up to it. There isn't much space trade hereabouts."

The thought flitted unbidden: No, there isn't, as isolated as we are on this far fringe of Erthuma settlement. Not that distance matters when you hyperjump. But after two centuries, we are still not so many on Ather, and most of us are conservative, inward-looking, preoccupied with our local affairs. The other planets of Florasol suffice us. Even I and my comrades find exploration ample for lifetimes among the immediate neighbor stars.

Is that what called you to us, Harul Vargen? Our loneliness?

"Once you had a command," she threw at him. "It was a fully robotic vessel. How would you like it again?"

He stood unstirring.

"That was long ago," she pursued, "but we, my associates in this enterprise and I, we don't believe you've lost the skills. A little practice should restore them completely. If anything, to be an officer with a live crew, as you are these days, is more demanding, and your record is good."

He kept his countenance locked, but she barely heard his question, and it trembled. "What ship do you mean?"

"The *Darya,* of course. Windfell only has one of that kind." Few Houses possessed any; they cost. "We sponsor scientific expeditions, you see. I'm no cosmonaut myself, but I can assure you she's a lovely, capable craft."

"I know." He stared beyond her, drank, and asked in an almost normal voice, "Why do you want me? You have your qualified people."

"Three," stated Laurice. "Feru Windfell is currently undergoing rejuvenation. The other two are from client families, perfectly fine except that—Olwar Mihelsson is a blabbermouth. You can trust him with anything except a secret. Sora Tomosdaughter's husband is one Bern Ironhammer. I don't say she would betray our confidence to him and his House, but . . . best not subject her to a conflict of loyalties, right?"

He seemed to have quite regained his balance. "Since we're being so frank, what about me? The Comet Line belongs to the Huldrings, after all, and the Windfells have been at loggerheads with them as often as with the Ironhammers or any others."

"You're a resident foreigner. You owe them no fealty and they've had no oaths from you. Take an unpaid leave, and you're a free agent. Afterward, I expect we'll offer you something permanent." Laurice softened her words. "Not that we ask any betrayal. We simply don't want outsiders thrusting in—at least not till we understand the situation ourselves."

His glance went to the transparency and the stars that

the lighting hid from him. "Does that include Erthumoi everywhere? The whole Six Races?"

She nodded. "Aside from the Naxians, those of them that already know, and are concealing the truth. Whatever it is. Something tremendous, we believe. Potentially—explosive? For good or ill, not anything we want irresponsibly released."

His dryness was a challenge: "Especially not to rival Houses."

Anger flickered. "We're no saints in Windfell. But I don't think you, either, would like this planet if the balance of power lay with a religious fanatic like Anlus Huldring or a clutch of reckless commercialists like the Seaholms."

He cocked a brow. She practically heard him refrain from saying: So you deem them.

"And as for the galaxy at large," she continued, striving for calm, "six spacefaring species make things precarious enough. Just look at what the business about the Forerunners is causing—tensions, suspicions, frantic competition to discover more. No, we intend to proceed with every possible precaution. There may well be danger anyway, danger enough to suit the rashest rattle-brain."

He grinned. "Which you assume I am not."

The abrupt lightness of his manner eased her. He can handle people pretty well when he wants to, she thought. Excellent. She laughed. "Explorers have an old, old saying that adventure is what happens to the incompetent. What we intend is simply an investigation. Once we know more, we'll decide what to do next." Sobering, she finished, "My father has been the Head of his House, with as strong a voice in the World Council as any, for nearly two hundred years. Ask yourself, hasn't he proven out? A hardheaded realist, yes, but concerned with the welfare of Ather more than of his kin or clients, and with civilization as a whole over and above that. Will you put your faith in him or in a coven of snakes?"

Vargen frowned the least bit. She suspected he found her language objectionable, as a person might who had fared widely about and dealt with many different beings.

"Oh, I'm not parochial," she said quickly. "Contrariwise. In fact, we were alerted to this by a Naxian, and it-he'll travel with us."

"Us?" he murmured.

Blood heated her face. "If you accept the mission."

"I rather think I will." He inhaled a fragrance from the cuisinette. "Your cofftea's ready, milady. I'll bring it."

Taking a datacard out of her sleeve pocket, she put it in his terminal. "This has been edited, but only to bring time-separate parts together and cut out nonessentials," she explained. "It's our basic record of the encounter."

A woman appeared in the screen, seated at a desk. She was a sister of Laurice's, but well-nigh a stranger, born eighty years earlier and, newly rejuvenated, looking girlishly younger. The image showed date and time in one corner. Behind her, a viewscreen displayed the mining camp she superintended. Beyond it, rock and ice lay in a jumble to the near horizon. The moon's gas giant primary hung as a crescent in the darkness above. Florasol, shrunken by remoteness till the disk was barely perceptible, gleamed near the edge of its ring system.

"Janya Windfell, wedded to Elfer Ullosson, calling from Isrith," she proclaimed. The name of her present husband wasn't necessary to identify her, but she always made a point of using it. He was among the House's most prominent clients, chief engineer at the base and, at home, grown wealthy from his investments. "I have immediate need to speak with the Head, communications enciphered."

The screen blinked, the time indicated was half an hour later, and she was saying as crisply: "A strange spacecraft has arrived unheralded and taken up orbit about us. The pilot, who claims to be alone, sent a request for tight-beam laser contact. I obliged. It is a Naxian, asking urgently to be put in touch with the leadership of our House. Yes, it seems to understand Atheran sociopolitics fairly well and to be aware that operations on Isrith are Windfell's. That may be why it sought us instead of somebody else, this chance for secrecy. It doesn't want anything made public." She hesitated. "I have no experience in dealing with nonhumans. Nobody here does. Pending your orders, I've restricted news of its arrival to those few who already know, and have activated the censor program in all transmitters. Rumors are flying. I have no idea how long the Naxian will wait. Please advise me."

The scene cut to a magnified image of the outsider vessel, a black blade athwart stars and Milky Way. Vargen whistled. "Naxian, for sure," he said. "Scout type, small, high-boost, maneuverable. However, if one of them singlehanded her, it was pretty desperate. The best of their automatic systems don't compare to the average of ours, you know."

"Daring more than desperate, I'd say," Laurice murmured. "You'll see. Watch."

Davith Windfell's fine-boned visage took over the screen, against a backdrop of his study, swirl-grained wainscot, an antique table, shelves of codex books and memorabilia that had been in the family for generations. She thrilled to the steadiness of his voice. "The Naxian doesn't want to talk through hyperspace. Fears the neutrino beam being tapped. Well, it could be, and our ciphers probably are not very secure. So we require a personal representative of the House, and time is lacking for consultation. Therefore I am appointing Laurice Windfell envoy plenipotentiary. Although she is young, her part in explorations of planets in this galactic vicinity has given her as much knowledge of nonhumans as anyone on Ather seems likely to possess. She has also demonstrated self-control and sound judgment, alike in emergencies and in ordinary difficulties. I have every confidence in her."

Dad thinks that of me!

The screen showed Laurice in the command cabin of a courier boat. In Vargen's apartment, she observed herself observing herself as if another person were yonder, and thought, Why? Do I want to know how he sees me?

The rush to make ready and be off had told on her. Instead of a glittery flowrobe, she wore a coverall, rumpled, smudged here and there. The auburn hair wasn't netted in gold but, under low acceleration, hung sweat-lank past her ears. Still, she thought, she was very much a woman of her world, not tall but full-bodied, supple, tawny of skin and high of cheekbones, short-nosed, heavy-lipped, stubborn-chinned. A fair-sized number of men found her attractive. . . . Stop that! she silently snapped.

The pilot looked into the pickup and said: "I record my understanding of my assignment just prior to medicating, getting into the flotation tank, and ordering top boost for the passage.

"I've never met a Naxian before, and only talked casually with people who have, but naturally I've been interested and studied up on them. Now I've brought along a database and will be accessing it en route. Transit time, about sixty hours, should let me learn something, though I'd better arrive reasonably rested and fresh. Better try to avoid preconceptions, too. However, I can't help guessing. Since that may influence my actions, I'll enter my thoughts at this point.

"I doubt we've got any subtle scheme under way. We're as alien to the Naxians as they are to us. What buttons could they single out to push? Oh, they do have their ability to read emotional states, but that's on an individual basis. It doesn't tell them how groups of us will react to something.

"I also doubt we've got a criminal trying for a haven. Not that we can be very sure what constitutes a crime among them. But anybody smart enough to make it here must know we won't risk provoking an interstellar incident for nothing. We'll need to be convinced it's worth our while to help.

"Nevertheless, this isn't exactly a usual way for a stranger to show up. My guess is that our visitor has come on behalf of some faction. The Naxians are no more united than we Erthumoi."

The image smiled. "Don't worry. I won't embroil us in a civil war of theirs. I couldn't if I wanted to. I'm really only empowered to ask questions and make suggestions. Believe me, I'll think hard before I do either."

The screen blinked. The time displayed was two and a half standard days later. Laurice floated weightless. She had spruced herself up. "I've proposed to the Naxian that we rendezvous elsewhere,'' she said, and projected the coordinates and orbital elements, a million kilometers from the giant planet. ''It has agreed. That should enable Janya to damp out rumors and gossip on Isrith. Please inform her. She might tell the troops this turned out to be a stellar survey expedition from so far off that its database didn't include the information that this system has been discovered and colonized by humans; and it went on its way feeling embarrassed. Plausible. The galaxy is so big, so full of stars.''

Vargen chuckled.

He leaned tensely forward when the other ship swelled in view. Running commentary described the matching of velocities and the extension of a gang tube. Laurice appeared, spacesuited, an automatic camera on either shoulder.

''I'm crossing over like this,'' said her voice. ''Not that the air or the temperature or anything would kill me, but . . . well, just in case. The suit is reinforced, and I've got a blaster in my oddments pouch.''

''That much was beamed back to my father,'' she said in the city. ''The rest had to wait till I returned to my boat—no, I misspoke. All I sent then was word that I was safe and things looked interesting. The real information, I wasn't about to trust to any transmitter.''

An interior flashed before her and the man. In its cramped austerity it seemed almost familiar, until one noticed the details. The Naxian poised free-fall at the center. The sinuous body, dull red, as long as a man's, was half coiled. It had extruded two stubby pseudohands, which clutched a standard model simultrans over which the blunt head swayed. Behind that snout the eyes glowed quite beautiful, like twin agates. The simultrans rendered purring, rustling sounds into flat Merse: ''Well be you come, Erthuma. Have you immediate desires that I might perchance fulfill?''

Laurice's helmet included a sonic unit. ''Can we get straight to business? I don't want to be discourteous, but I don't know what's polite in your society. My database told me that if we both belonged to the Naga nation''—the simultrans turned that human name into the appropriate hisses—"we'd spend the next hour exchanging compliments. I'm willing, but not sure how."

Again Vargen chuckled.

"I am not a member of it myself," the Naxian said. Did the vocal tone carry wrath or sorrow or eagerness? "And I will gladly go by the straightest tunnel, the more so when I sense that, beneath a natural wariness, your intentions are honest. Names first? I often designate myself Copperhue. I function as male."

"Laurice Windfell. Female. I . . . imagine you know what my name signifies."

"Yes. You belong to that one of Ather's dominant consanguinities." It was the best rendition the machine could make of a word in that particular Naxian language, which attempted to describe a concept perhaps unknown to any Naxian culture. "The one that I sought."

"Then you know more about us than I do about you."

"I was here briefly, three rejuvenations ago. That was as a crew member of a ship conveying an expedition sent to gather information about what was then a new colony."

"Yes. I've studied the accounts. Your people's only visit, wasn't it?" Locrians, Cephallonians, Crotonites, and Samians had come similarly for a look, found no threat nor any particular promise to them, and gone away again.

"Correct. Since then, of course, much has evolved. I have striven to bring my information up to date. Travelers often take along databases about their homes. A copy is an appreciated gift or a trade item of some value."

"I know. But why did you care about us especially?"

The coils slithered around, whispering along the glabrous hide. "The second planet of this sun would be quite hospitable to my species."

"Venafer?" Laurice's image registered surprise. That hot, cloudy world of swamps and deserts? "Well, yes . . . I suppose so . . . but there must be plenty more in the galaxy, some of them better, that you haven't settled yet, or even found."

"True. However, I pray you, consider *who* will take them. S-s-s-s—" Copperhue's head struck at air, to and fro. Little protuberances like claws formed down its-his length.

"House Windfell doesn't own all Venafer," Laurice said. "Nobody does."

"Correct." The head grew large in sight, drawing near her helmet. Fangs glistened, eyes smoldered. "But your consanguinity is uniquely qualified. First, it does own the large island on the planet that you call New Halla." It-he must have put a special entry in the simultrans's program. "Territory of scant or no use to you, originally claimed for prestige and on the chance of mineral resources, retained merely because of inertia and, s-s-s, pride. Second, as of recent years you have maintained exclusive operations on the moon Isrith. This gave opportunity for a discreet approach. I realize my plan is hopeless unless we, your people and I, can suddenly present the galaxy with an accomplished fact."

Laurice's tone grew strained. "What do you want?"

"The island. What else? I have considered how the transaction may be done. Pay me a sum equal to the agreed-on price for the land, with an option to buy it. Leave the sum in escrow until I have fulfilled my part of the bargain. I will know whether your chieftains intend to abide by this and, afterward, whether I have truly met the terms as they understand them. My researches lead me to expect they will be honest."

"You're asking . . . a great deal."

"I offer much more."

"What?"

Copperhue hooked its-his tail around a stanchion. The long body swayed and rippled. "I cannot precisely tell you, for I myself do not know. But it is of the utmost."

"For God's sake! Get to reality, will you?"

The undulations went hypnotic, the words sank to a breath. "Hearken. I am a cosmonaut of the Python Confederacy, as you name it. It embraces eight inhabited planets, their suns lying about seventeen hundred light-years from this. You have heard? Yes-s-s.

"During the last several of your calendrical years, its Dominance has repeatedly dispatched expeditions elsewhere.

They are totally secret. Nothing whatsoever is said about them. Key personnel return to live sequestered in a special compound. I have gathered that they enjoy every attention and luxury there, and are well satisfied. Ordinary crewfolk of the several ships go more freely about on their leaves, but may not speak to anyone, no, not nestmates or clones or even each other, of what they have done and seen.

"That is easy to obey, for we know well-nigh nothing. Our vessels leap through hyperspace to someplace else. We lie there for varying times while the scientists use their instruments and send out their probes, operations in which we do not partake. All we perceive is that we float in empty, unfamiliar interstellar space until we go back. Ah, but the feelings of those officers and scientists! They flame, they freeze, they strike, recoil, exult, shudder; the glory and the dread of Almightiness are upon them.

"And at home, I have once in a while come near enough to certain of the Dominators that I sense the same in them. Not the awe, no, for they do not venture thither themselves, to yonder remote part of the galaxy; but their inward dreams grasp a pride and a hope that are demonic." (What did that last word really mean in the Naxian tongue?)

In free-fall there is no true over or under. Nonetheless, Copperhue loomed. "Is this not a sufficient sign that something vast writhes toward birth?" it-he demanded.

"I-I can't say," Laurice stammered. "You, how and why did you—"

"They knew I was unhappy, until presently, slowly, I went aquiver," Copperhue said. "Well, my race has learned dissimulations. I led them to believe that I suffered private difficulties, hostilities, until I began seeing ways whereby I might cope. They expected little of a humble crew member, therefore suspected little. Meanwhile, I took my surreptitious stellar sightings and made my calculations.

"And at home, I plotted with others. Jointly, they raised the means to obtain this spacecraft and send me off in it, all under false pretenses. Our need is that great.

"Here I am. I know, quite closely, where and when the

monster thing is to happen. It will be soon. What is this worth to you and your kindred, Erthuma?"

The day before departure Laurice spent with her parents. They were at the original family home, on Windfell itself. Small, a stronghold as much as a dwelling, Ernhurst offered few of the comforts, none of the sensualities in mansions and apartments everywhere. Yet Davith and Mair had refrained from enlarging it, and often returned there. It held so many memories.

From the top of a lookout tower Laurice saw immensely far. Southward the downs rolled summer-golden to the sea, which was a line of gleaming argent on that horizon. Wind sent long ripples through the herbage; cloud shadows swept mightily over heights and hollows. It boomed and bit, did the wind, but odors of growth, soil, water, sunlight brought life to its sharpness. Northward the land climbed toward hills darkling with forest. Far and far beyond them, the snow peak of Mount Orden shone in heaven. Other than the estate, its gardens, and beast park, the sole traces of man lay to the west, toylike at their remove—a power station, a synthesis plant, and the village clustered around them.

"Oh, it's good to be here again," she sighed.

"Then why are you so seldom?" her father asked quietly.

She looked away from him. "You know why. Too much to do, too little time."

His laugh sounded wistful. "Too little patience, you mean. You're trying to experience the whole universe, and you not yet forty years in it. Relax. It won't go away."

"I've heard that aplenty from you, when Mother hasn't been after me to settle down, get married, present you with another batch of grandchildren. You relax, you two. *That* won't go away. My next cycle, or my third, I'll be ready to start experimenting with domesticity."

"If you live till you reach an age for rejuvenation." She sensed how he must force the words out. "Ordinarily, yes, we'd be content to let you enjoy your first time around in freedom, like most people. But your youthful enthusiasms are not just intellectual or artistic or athletic, and your idea of a youthful fling is to hare off and hazard your life on some weird planet. . . . I'm sorry, my dear. I don't want to nag you again, on this day of all days." Her right hand rested on the parapet. He laid his left over it. "We're afraid, though, Mair and I. How I rue the hour I asked you to go meet that Naxian. Ever since, you've charged breakneck forward."

She bit her lip. "You could have taken me off the project. You can still."

Aquiline against the sky, his head shook. "And have you hate me? No, I'm too weak."

"What? You?" She stared.

He turned to smile at her. "Where you are concerned, I am. Always have been, for whatever reason."

"Dad—" She clung to his hand.

He grew grave. "I do have to talk with you, seriously and privately. This seems to be my chance."

She released herself, stepped back a meter, and confronted him. He had now put the well-worn importunities aside, she knew. Doubtless he had only used them as a way into what he really had to utter. Her heart knocked. "Clearance granted," she said, and realized that today this was no longer one of their shared jokes.

"You're bound into an unforeseeable but certainly dangerous situation—"

"No, no, no!" she protested automatically. "Must I explain for the, it feels like the fiftieth time? The environment's safe. Copperhue saw no special precautions being taken."

"But Copperhue did learn that an extraordinary event will occur there in the near future. Who knows what it will involve? If nothing else, the Naxians won't be overjoyed when outsiders break in on their ultrasecret undertaking. Their resentment might . . . express itself forcibly."

"Oh, Dad, that's ridiculous. They're *civilized*."

"There are Naxians and Naxians," he declared, "just as there are Erthumoi and Erthumoi. The rulers of the Python Confederacy are not the amiable, helpful sorts who lead most of their nations. It isn't general knowledge, because we don't want to compromise our sources, but some of our intelligence about them makes me wonder what we may have to face, a century or two from now."

She didn't care to pursue that. The immediate argument was what mattered. "Anyhow, we'll be in clear space. If anything looks threatening, we'll hyperjump off in a second. No, a millisecond. *Darya* computes and reacts faster than any organic brain."

"Understood. Otherwise I'd never have authorized the venture. But you in turn understand—don't you?—you can't depend on the ship to handle everything, especially not to make the basic decisions. If she could do that to our satisfaction, among those countless unknowns, she wouldn't need a master, nor even a scientific team aboard. Laurice, the more I've considered your choice of personnel, the more I've discovered about them, the less happy I've become."

She clenched her fists. "Copperhue? It-he's got to come along. Guide, advisor, and, well, hostage for its-his own truthfulness. Yes, we know very little about it-him, but that's hardly its-his fault."

"Copperhue worries me the least," Davith replied. "Why did you co-opt Yoran Jarrolsson?"

"Huh? You know. He's an able physicist, specializing in astronomical problems. Bachelor, no particular attachments, easily persuaded to join an expedition whose purpose he won't learn till we're in space. If anybody should be loyal to us, that's Yoran." You made him what he is, Dad, recognized talent in a ragged patronless kid, sponsored him, funded him through school, got him his position at the Institute."

Davith frowned. "Yes, I assumed as much myself, till it occurred to me to order an inquiry. I'd lost touch with him. Well, it turns out he's not popular—"

"Abrasive, yes. I've generally gotten along with him. Consulted him about stuff relating to various explorations, you remember."

Davith's lips quirked a bit. "You don't feel his arrogance, as his inferiors do." Earnestly: "Also, I suspect that—never mind. The fact is, he is . . . no gentleman. Less than perfectly honest, in spite of that raspy tongue. And I daresay an impoverished childhood like his would leave many people somewhat embittered, but most wouldn't make it an excuse for chronic ill behavior."

"As long as he can do the job—"

Laurice broke off, went back to the parapet, gazed over the vast billows of land. After a moment she said, "I think I know where part of his trouble stems from. He's a scientist born. Nature meant him to make brilliant discoveries. But there aren't any to make anymore, not in fundamental physics. Nothing new for—centuries, is it? The most he can do is study a star or a nebula or whatever that's acting in some not quite standard way. Then he puts the data through his computer, and it explains everything in conventional terms, slightly unusual parameters and that's all. When I hinted we might be on the trail of something truly strange—you should have seen his face."

"Scientific idealism or personal ambition?" Once more, Davith sighed. "No matter. Too late now in any event. I'm simply warning you. Be careful. Keep on the watch for . . . instability. If he proves out, fine, then I've misjudged him; no harm done."

Laurice turned to face him again. "Have you anything against the rest of the team?"

"Newan, Enry, Thura? Well, you told me he nominated them to you, but otherwise— No, they appear sound enough, except that they lack deep space experience."

"*Darya* and Captain Vargen supply that."

She saw the change in him. It was as if the wind reached in under her coat. "All right, what is it, Dad? Speak out."

"Harul Vargen," he said bleakly. "Seemed to me, too, as good a choice as any, better than most. But why did he abandon his career, drift away, finally bury himself among us? That's what it's amounted to. If he's certificated for robotic ship command, he was near the top of his profession. Here, the best he might ever get was a captaincy on some scow of an interplanetary freighter—until you approached him. What happened, those many years ago?"

Laurice stood braced against the stones. Their hardness gave strength. "None of our business," she replied. "A tragedy he doesn't want to talk about, probably not think about. My guess—a few words that slipped loose a couple of times, when we were sitting over drinks—he does drink pretty fast—I think he lost his wife. If they'd been married a long time, maybe since his first cycle, her death would hit hard, wouldn't it?''

''Not that hard, that permanently, if his spirit was healthy,'' Davith said. ''Why has he postponed his next rejuvenation so long? Another two or three decades at most, and it will be too late, you know. I wondered, and got background information on him. He's making no provision for it, financial or otherwise. How much does he want to live?'' He raised a palm. ''Yes, of course I had no legal or ethical right to pry. To destruction with that. My daughter's life will be in his hands.''

''Not really.''

''By now he's integrated with the ship. Her skipper. His orders will override anyone else's.''

Defense: ''Yes, down underneath, he is a sad man. I think this voyage, this fresh beginning, may rouse him out of that. But mainly—Dad, I haven't survived so far by entrusting myself to incompetents. Look at Harul—at Vargen's record, just in this system. The *Arinberg Castle* wreck, the Bannerport riot. Both times he earned a commendation. No, whatever his emotions are, they don't cloud his judgment or dull his sense of duty.'' Laurice felt the blood in her face. She turned into the cooling wind. It tossed her hair.

''I took that for granted, given the facts,'' Davith pursued. ''But were they sufficient? Finally I sent an agent to Bretta, Vargen's home planet.''

She gasped. ''You did? Why, the—the cost—''

''It was your life.''

She flared. ''And you didn't see fit to tell me.''

''I did not,'' he replied. ''You'd object. Even if you promised to keep silent, I feared you'd let something escape to him.''

We know each other too well, Dad and I, she thought.

''Well,'' Davith continued, ''the spoor was cold, and it led off Bretta, and the upshot is that I only got the report yesterday. I think you'd better hear what it said.''

Her neck had stiffened till it was painful to nod. "Go ahead."

He regarded her with a pain of his own behind his eyes before he asked low, "Have you ever heard about the Novaya disaster?"

"No, I— Wait." She groped among shards of recollection. "I think I read something once. An asteroid strike, was it?"

"In a way. Novaya's far off, but at the time, the news flashed across the Galaxy. It was well before you were born, though, and other events, looking bigger in their perspective, soon pushed this down to the bottom of our general consciousness."

Remorselessly: "Erthuma-colonized planet. A large asteroid was perturbed into a collision orbit. It happened suddenly and unpredictably. The asteroid passed near a gas giant with many moons. Chaotic events occur sometimes in celestial mechanics, as well as on smaller scales. Factors are so precariously balanced that an immeasurably small force can make them go one way rather than another. This asteroid was flung almost straight at Novaya.

"Almost. It plowed through the atmosphere. That would have been catastrophe enough, the shock wave, a continent ignited, but the friction slowed it into capture. An eccentric, decaying orbit, bringing it back again and again. At each approach, more broke off, huge chunks crashing down on unforeseeable spots. They touched off quakes and volcanoes. The tsunamis from ocean strikes were nearly as bad. A war passing over the planet would have done less harm than that asteroid did, before the last fragment of it came to rest.

"Meanwhile, naturally, as many people as possible were evacuated. Temporary shelters were established on the Novayan moon, to hold the refugees till they could be transported out-system. Spacecraft shuttled between planet and moon. An appeal went out, and ships arrived from far and wide to help. Yes, some of them were nonhuman.

"Your friend Vargen was among the newcomers. He commanded a robotic vessel chartered by the Galactic Survey. Her owners put her at the disposal of the rescue effort. For a short while, Vargen was a busy ferryman.

"Then the asteroid returned. The next bombardment began. He got in his ship and fled. Raced out of the gravity well, sprang through hyperspace, slunk home to Bretta.

"He could offer no excuse. The owners fired him. His wife left him. He went on the bum, drifted about for decades, living hand to mouth off odd, unsavory jobs, now and then wangling a berth in a ship that'd take him to some different system. Finally, when he reached Florasol, he pulled himself together and got steady employment. But his promotions—I've verified this for myself—they haven't been due any particular ambition on his part. He's merely moved up the seniority ladder.

"That is your captain, Laurice," Davith finished.

She stood a long while mute. The wind skirled, the cloud shadows hunted each other across the downs.

"I'm afraid it's too late in this case, also," she said finally, dully.

"No, we can replace him. Olwar or Sora aren't really totally unsuitable. Or I can look outside our House."

She shook her head. "Any replacement would take too long. Ship-captain integration. Copperhue keeps reminding us that the climax will come soon. Any day now, perhaps. If we showed up afterward, could we discover what the Naxians did? Besides, it's a cosmic-scale thing. The environment later may be lethal."

She attempted a grin. "Anyhow," she said, "aren't you glad we've got a cautious man in charge?"

Schooled in public impassivity, he still could not entirely hide from her what he felt. It was well-nigh more than she could bear.

"Come on," she proposed, "let's go down and say silly things at Mother, the way we used to, till lunch."

The ship accelerated outward, seeking free space for her leap across light-years. Aft, the sun dwindled. Forward and everywhere around, night glittered with stars, the Milky Way was a white torrent of them, nebulae glowed or reared dark across brilliance, sister galaxies beckoned from across gulfs that imagination itself could not bridge.

In her saloon, revelation. The physicists—Yoran Jarrolsson, Enry Bobsson, Newan Lucosson, Thura Halsdaughter—stared over the table at Copperhue. After a moment their eyes swung toward each other's, as if for comfort or comradeship. Watching in a corner, Laurice saw lips move silently and caught Yoran's muttered, amazed obscenity.

The team chief recovered his wits first. But then, he had always kept his associates dependent on him. He leaned forward. "Have you no clues to what the object may be?" he demanded.

Coiled on the opposite bench, head uplifted, the Naxian considered before responding. "None that appear significant. We common crew were seldom allowed as much as a look out; viewscreens were kept blank most of the time. I obtained my star sightings, from which I later calculated the location, when I went forth in a work party to retrieve a probe that had failed to dock properly with our ship."

Yoran's dark, hook-nosed features drew into a scowl. "How did you take the measurements, anyway?"

"I had fashioned an instrument while home on leave, and smuggled it aboard in my personal kit. On a prior trip, despite the unfamiliar shape of the galactic belt, I had recognized certain navigational objects, such as the Magellanic Clouds. When this opportunity came, I withdrew from my gang, telling them I had spied what might be a loose object, missing from the probe. When out of sight, I quickly made my observations and discarded the instrument. The numbers I stored in my mind. I had been confident such a chance would come, because the probes frequently had difficulty with rendezvous."

"Yah, your Naxian robotics aren't worth scrap. And we're supposed to proceed on your memories of your amateur star shooting?"

"We've satisfied ourselves that the data are adequate," Laurice declared.

Yoran glanced her way. "Uh, sure. Sorry, milady." Half ferociously, he turned back to Copperhue. "But did you never see or overhear anything? Did you never *think* what this might all be about?"

"The Dominance knows well how to keep secrets. Given

our species's ability to sense emotional states, perhaps it has developed a few methods slightly better than you conceptualize."

A shame, Laurice thought, that the simultrans just gives out unemphatic Merse. What's Copperhue really saying with overtones and body language?

"But you must have speculated," exclaimed Thura.

Yoran threw her a glower. "I'll handle this discussion," he said.

Well, Laurice thought, everybody babbling at once would make for confusion and wasted time. Nevertheless—

She admired how Copperhue remained dignified. Or did it-he not care whether the bipeds were polite? "Since the location is in interstellar space, the phenomenon is presumably astronomical," the Naxian said. "The probability of someone having come upon it by accident is nil, considering the volume of space involved." Was that a studied insult? Certainly Yoran flushed. "Doubtless something was noticed from afar. Most likely this was in the course of a general astrographic survey. The Python Confederacy, like most nations that can afford to, has mounted several during its history. They do not significantly overlap, as huge as the galaxy is. One of these ships detected some anomaly, such as a peculiar spectrum, and went for a closer look. The report that it brought back caused the Dominance to make this a state secret and mount its own intensive investigation."

Yoran tugged his chin. "Well, yes, your reasoning is, uh, reasonable. Have you any further thoughts?"

"Mainly this. Given the character of the Dominance, I am sure that its members hope for some outcome, some discovery, that will greatly strengthen the Confederacy and therefore themselves. It may be scientific, it may be economic, it may be something else. I do not know, and doubt that they know, yet. But in their minds, the possibility justifies the effort—which is, actually, a modest investment, a small gamble for perhaps a cosmically large stake."

Yoran straightened on his bench, as if he were a judge. "And you're betraying your people?"

"They are not my people," Copperhue replied, its-his natural voice gone soft.

Laurice stirred. "That will do," she ordered. Things looked like they were getting nasty. The expedition could ill afford quarrels.

Yoran shifted his glare to her. "Milady, I've had a hard life," he said. "I've learned lessons a patron like you is spared. A traitor once is apt to be a traitor twice."

"Our comrade's motives are honorable," she clipped. "Watch your language. Remember, it's going into the log."

Embarrassment yielded visibly to relief among the subordinates when Yoran hunched his shoulders and growled, "As milady wishes. No offense meant." And maybe, she thought, that's true. Maybe he does not perceive his own boorishness.

Newan plucked up courage to say, "I beg milady's pardon, but what's this about a log?"

"A robotic ship records everything that happens on a voyage, inboard as well as outboard, unless directed not to," Laurice explained. "It isn't normally a violation of privacy. We have very little of that anyway, while we travel. As a general rule, at journey's end the ship edits everything irrelevant to the mission out of the database. But we can't foresee what may teach us something that may be valuable in future operations. Psychological stresses are as real as physical, and as dangerous, when you're bound into places never meant for humans."

Had Vargen been listening outside, or did he chance to enter at that moment? His body filled the doorframe vertically, though its jambs stood well apart from him. "Pardon me," he said in his usual mannerly style. "I know this has been a big surprise sprung on you four and you have a sunful of questions; but we're just a couple of hours from hyperjump, and I need to make a certain decision first. Would you come confer with me in my cabin, Copperhue?"

"Indeed." The Naxian slithered off its-his bench and flowed to the captain. They departed.

The rest gaped after them. "Well," said Yoran. "Isn't he the important one? What might this decision be that we commoners mustn't hear about?"

Why does that irritate me? wondered Laurice. Aloud, curtly: "I daresay he wants to consider possible hazards, without groundsiders butting in. You, sir, might best be preparing yourself and your team for your job, once we've arrived."

And what will mine be? she thought, not for the first time. What's waiting in space for me? I'm only a planetarist. And even that title is a fake. I don't do geology, oceanography, atmospherics, chemistry, biology, ethology, or xenology. I dabble at them all, and then dare call myself a scientist.

She rose to her feet. I help get the specialists together, and keep them together, and sometimes keep them alive. That's *my* work. That justifies my being here, though I had to force it every centimeter of the way.

Yoran got up too and approached her. His squatness barely reached above her chin. As he neared, he made a dismissing gesture at the others. They didn't leave, but they sat where they were, very silently.

"Maybe I could put a few of our questions to you, Milady Windfell," he said.

"Certainly," she replied. Be friendly. After all, it was she who had brought him into this, and for justifiable reasons. She knew him to be able, quick-witted, fearless. That she sympathized with him, felt sorry, would like to give him a shot at his dreams—these things were beside the point. Weren't they? "I'll answer as best I can."

He cocked his head. "But we are under confidentiality. There might be some advantage to our House."

She picked her words with care. "Possibly. Still, you know Windfell isn't interested in conquering anybody. We simply want to . . . stay on top of whatever wave we'll be riding. Keep the power to make our own fate."

"Of course. But then why are you willing to cede New Halla to that snake?"

"We won't necessarily. An assembly of the House will judge how much Copperhue's help was worth to us." I never felt more proud of what I am than when it-he agreed to trust our honor, it-he who can feel our feelings. "We will take good faith for granted and into account. The island would be no great loss to us."

"But why does it, uh, it-he want the place?"

"Well, you see, Copperhue is a . . . crypto-dissident in its-his nation. I don't entirely understand the situation. Maybe no human can. But it seems—we've verified—there's been a movement among the Naxians, starting several centuries ago. The 'trans calls it the 'Old Truth.' A religion, a way of life, or what?" Laurice spread her hands. "Something that means everything to its believers. And that doesn't fit well into most Naxian societies. It's been generally persecuted, especially in the Python Confederacy, where it was finally forbidden altogether. Copperhue's lineage is one of those that pretended to convert back to orthodoxy, but has maintained the rites and practices as best it can in secret, always hoping for some kind of liberation."

Yoran gazed at a bulkhead. "I see. . . ."

"New Halla would be a haven for the Old Truthers," Laurice proceeded. "They aren't so many that they need more, and probably quite a few couldn't manage to leave their planets anyhow. But Copperhue does have this idea of a refuge for them."

"Yes." The black eyes caught at hers. "They'll be under Atheran sovereignty. We'll be their protectors. And they'll multiply, and move into other parts, and eventually our evening star will be full of snakes, won't it?"

"How would that harm us?" she retorted. "They'd acquire any further land legitimately. We've made sure that their principles are decent. I should think there'd be pretty wonderful potentials in having beings that different for our friends and neighbors."

"Well—" The hostility dropped away. He shivered. "Maybe. Who knows? You understand, milady, don't you, I'm concerned about our House. It's mine too. I'm only a client, adopted at that, but I belong with Windfell."

Pushy, she thought; and then: No, that's unfair. Isn't it?

Encourage him. "Leave politics to the patrons, Yoran. Look to your personal future. Why would the Pythons be so interested in this thing ahead of us, if they didn't believe it may lead them to something really new? Something as revolutionary as, oh, quantum mechanics or nuclear fission and fusion or the unifying equation."

She saw the pallor come and go in the blue cheeks, the hair stir on the backs of his hands. "Yes," he said hoarsely, "yes, that's possible, isn't it? Thank you, milady."

Again his gaze sought hers, but this time half in worship. Well, she thought, I've known for years he's in love with me.

"Stand by for hyperjump." The ship's voice filled her cabins and corridors with melody. Laurice had a moment's envisionment of her as the stars might see, a golden torpedo soaring amidst their myriads.

"Ten, nine, eight—" sang the countdown. It wasn't necessary, only a custom followed when time allowed. That sense of oneness with history, clear back to the rockets of antiquity, gave heart on the rim of enigma. "—five, four—" Laurice tensed in her safety harness. The console before her seemed abruptly alien. She, the fire control officer? A jape, a sop. *Darya* alone could direct the weapons she carried. "—two" Well, but somebody had to decide whether to shoot and at what, and Vargen would have plenty else occupying his attention. "—one—" Besides, Vargen was a coward.

"—zero."

And the viewscreens that englobed Laurice showed a sky gone strange.

Inexperienced, she lost a second or two before she saw the differences. Stars in space were so many, unwinking diamond-bright; constellations became hard to trace. Moreover, the distances she had hitherto traveled, to suns near hers, changed them but little. Now she had skipped over—how many light-years had Copperhue said? Fifty-four thousand, seven hundred and some. To the other side of the galaxy's heart.

Acceleration had terminated shortly before transit through hyperspace. The ship fell free, at whatever velocity her kinetic and potential energies determined. It couldn't be high, for an instrument revealed that she had not generated an exterior force field to screen off interstellar atoms. Nor did there seem to be any other radiation hazard. Weightless, Laurice revolved her chair three-dimensionally and studied her new heavens.

Odd, she thought, how familiar the Milky Way looks. Some differences, this bend, that bay, yonder silhouette of the Sagittarian dust clouds; but I expected it to be quite altered. And Copperhue didn't mention red stars. How many? A score at least, strewn all around us— "Damn! I clean forgot." Sweat prickled her skin. "Any trace of Naxians?"

"None," replied the ship.

Her muscles eased. "Well," she said redundantly, "our navigation data aren't what you'd call precise. We'll have to cast around a sizable region till we find what we're after, close enough to identify it."

Vargen's command over the intercom was otherwise. "Captain to science team. Start your studies."

"What?" responded Yoran. "We can't be anywhere near our goal. Commence your search pattern."

"I'll give the orders, if you please. We're not going to hyperjump about at random till we have some idea of what this part of space is like. I want at least a preliminary report within an hour. Get busy."

Captain Caution, Laurice thought. But it does make sense, I guess. She touched her own intercom switchplate. "Fire control," she said. "I'm obviously no use here. May I be relieved? I could give a hand elsewhere."

"Perhaps." Vargen sounded skeptical, as well he might. "Stay aft of the command sector."

Why, what will you be doing that nobody else should interrupt? "Aye, aye." Laurice unsecured, shoved with a foot, and arrowed toward the exit. A dim circle of light marked it, for it was part of the simulacrum system. When it retracted for her, she passed through the galactic band into a prosaic companionway.

Motion in zero gravity was fun, but now she sped on to business—to find Copperhue and put certain questions to it-him. The Naxian occupied one of the crew cubicles. It was unlocked. Entering, she found it empty, save for the few curious objects that were personal possessions.

Hmm. Would the wight crawl around idly under these

conditions? No, it-he was a cosmonaut and knew better. Just the same, Laurice searched everywhere she was permitted to go. It took a while to establish that the Naxian must be forward with Vargen.

Why? Well, it-he did go reticent after that private talk of theirs. What are they hatching? Let's try the physics lab. I barely glanced in earlier.

There Laurice found confusion, Yoran's three assistants struggling with apparatus that wandered perversely from them. The chief was shouting at the intercom: "—weight! These people can't work in free-fall!"

"Then they'd better learn," Vargen's voice snapped.

"God curse it, do you want a quick report or don't you? Nobody else is here to detect us, unless you've brought along some phantoms of your own."

After a moment during which the whirr of the ventilators seemed loud: "Very well. One gee in five minutes."

Yoran switched off. "Treats us like offal. What's he think he is, a patron?" He noticed Laurice. "Oh. Milady."

"I'll help you get your stuff together before the boost," she said. "Not to let it crash down helter-skelter." Skillfully, she moved about, plucking things from the air. "I didn't know you three lack this training," she told them angrily. "I took for granted you had it. What possessed you to choose them, Yoran?"

The man's tone went sullen. "I made sure they aren't subject to spacesickness. That would have been adequate, if our dear captain showed some common sense. Why should we conduct these studies? Elementary, routine procedures. The ship can perfectly well do them. Bring up one or two robot bodies from the hold, if necessary."

"This tests how well you'll perform when we need procedures that are not routine," Laurice replied. "Well, I'll give you three some basic drill as soon as may be, and hope for the best. But Yoran, I'm very disappointed in you."

She wondered how much rage he must suppress in order to mumble, "I'm sorry, milady." The wondering was brief. A thought came to the fore instead. Test—

Countdown gave warning, power coursed silent through

the engine, the deck was once more downward and feet pressed against it. Having nothing better to do, Laurice sat in a corner and watched the physicists work. She confessed to herself that Yoran got things organized fast and thereafter efficiency prevailed. Spectroscopes, radio receivers, mass detectors she recognized; others she did not, but they spoke to those who understood.

Excitement waxed. "Yes, got to be masered— Three hundred twenty kilohertz— This'n's nearly twice that— And another—" Minute by minute, suspicion gathered in her.

Vargen: "You've had your hour. What can you tell me?"

Yoran muttered an oath and raised his shock head from the instrument over which he had stood crouched. "We don't need interruptions!" he called.

"I didn't say you must stop work. I only want to know what you've found out so far. You can keep on as long as needful."

Yoran straightened. "That may be some while." His tone gentled, with a tinge of awe. "This is certainly . . . a very peculiar region. Radio emissions from—a number of sources, we haven't established how many but they're in every direction. Mostly coherent waves. Frequencies and intensities vary by several orders of magnitude. We've only checked two Doppler shifts as yet, but they show motions of kilometers per second, which I suspect are orbital. Many graviton sources are also present. I can't state positively that they are invisible accelerated masses. . . . Oh, we'll be busy here. Is this a natural phenomenon, or could there be artifacts of the Forerunners still operating after how many millions of years—?"

"What do you propose to do?"

"Keep studying, of course. Examine everything. We haven't even begun to search for matter particles, for instance. Neutrino spectra, perhaps? Captain, I don't want to make any hypotheses before we know a muckload more."

"Very well. Carry on." Vargen laughed. "Don't forget to fix yourselves a bite to eat now and then." He switched off.

He wouldn't crack a joke here, would he? Unless—

It shivered through Laurice. She rose. "Yoran," she said, "would you analyze one or two of those red stars?"

The physicist blinked. "Huh? Why, they're just dim red dwarfs, late M types, milady. You'd need amplification to see any that are more than three or four light-years off."

"Please. I have a notion about them."

"But—"

Laurice put command in her voice. "I have a notion. You can do it quickly, can't you?"

"Well, yes. Automated spectroscopy." With visible resentment, Yoran squinted into a finder and operated controls on a box.

"Hasn't it struck you odd that we've got this many around us?" Laurice asked. "Not that I've seen any except the closest, as you said, but they imply plenty more."

"Red dwarfs are much the commonest kind of star, milady," Thura ventured. "They often occur together."

"I know," Laurice answered. "These, though, aren't enough to be a proper cluster, are they?" Of the usual sort, that is.

She saw how Yoran stiffened where he stood. Did he see what she was driving at? He stuck to his task regardless, until he could look up and announce: "This specimen is extremely metal poor. As much so as any I've ever seen described. Ancient—" His features congealed. "Shall we survey the rest?"

"I don't think that will be necessary." Laurice touched the intercom. "Captain Vargen, I can tell you what we . . . have found."

An astonished-sounding hiss bespoke Copperhue's presence at the other end. "Then do," Vargen said slowly.

Victory responded. "This is the remains of a globular cluster. Old, old, formed almost at the beginning, first-generation stars, when hardly any atoms heavier than lithium existed. Probably drifted in here from the galactic halo. All the big suns in it went supernova ages ago. The lesser ones evolved into red giants, sank down to white dwarfs, radiated away that energy too. Only the smallest and feeblest are still on the main sequence. Everything else is clinkers, cold and black, or at most emitting so little it's well-nigh lost in the cosmic background. Maybe a few neutron stars give off pulsar beams yet, but weak, and none happen to be pointed at us. More likely, I'd guess, they're also dead. Cinders, embers, ashes; let's get out of here."

Air whispered.

"The radio waves?" Vargen asked. She heard the strain.

"Beacons," she said. "What else? You'd need them to find your way around in this gloom. The debris may not be closely packed by planetside standards, but the risk of collision would be appreciable, especially when you hyperjump, if you didn't know where objects are. A higher risk would be coming out of a jump too deep in a gravity well, and blowing your engine.

"Somebody finds it worthwhile to mine the cluster. The ancient supernovae must have plated certain smaller bodies with a rich layer of rare isotopes. I daresay it's a Samian enterprise. This sort of thing fits what I've read about them."

Laurice glanced around. The three assistants had retreated toward the bulkheads. They looked alarmed. Yoran stood his ground, legs wide apart, shoulders forward, hands flexing at his sides. Lips had drawn away from teeth. Word by word, he spat, "You knew about this. You did not take us to our goal."

"I will, when your team is ready to cope," Vargen replied coldly. "Congratulations, Milady Windfell. I didn't expect my little puzzle would be solved this fast. Maybe I should arrange another practice session. Though it won't be as informative when you've been forewarned, will it?"

"You swine-sucker," Yoran said. "You smug, white-bellied snot-fink. If you think you and your snake bedmate are fit to command *men*—"

"Enough. Silence, or I'll order up the robots and put you in confinement. Go back to your duties."

Her exultation had vanished from Laurice. It was as if the frozen darkness outboard reached in to touch her. "Captain," she said, "you and I had better hold a conference."

He hesitated. "Immediately," she said.

The response came flat. "Very well. The ship has things under control." Aside from the people, she thought.

She turned the intercom off. "That's right, milady," Yoran snarled. "Give him his bucketful right back in his mouth. You've got the rank to do it."

"Have a care," she said into the smoldering eyes. "Without discipline, we're done for."

Striding the corridors, she worked off some tension and arranged some words. At the back of awareness, she was glad of the acceleration. Weightlessness made faces go puffy and unattractive.

Given *Darya*'s omnipresence, the captain need seldom occupy his own viewglobe. Laurice found him in his cabin. The ship must have announced her arrival to him, for the door retracted as she approached it, and he stood waiting. "Come in, please," he invited. She heard the tension in his voice, saw it in his visage and stance.

Copperhue uncoiled on the deck. "Best I betake myself," it-he said.

"No, I want to speak with you too," Laurice answered.

The head shook, solemnly imitating a human negation. "Not at present, honored one. Later, if you still wish. I shall be in my quarters." Holding the 'trans in three extruded flipper-arms, the supple form slithered past her. The door closed behind it.

Laurice stared after. "Why?" she asked. "If it-he meets Yoran along the way, there'll likely be an unpleasant scene."

"Naxians read emotions," Vargen reminded her. "Copperhue must deem we'll do better alone." His tone sharpened. "As for Yoran, I'm bloody sick of his insolence. Maybe you can warn him. If he pushes me further, I just might give him twenty-four hours of sensory deprivation, and hope to teach him some manners."

Yes, she thought, his type is bound to grate on you. I should have foreseen. Well, it's up to me to set matters right—or, at any rate, make them endurable.

Returning to him, her glance traversed the cabin. It was

larger than the sleeping cubicles, but mainly because it contained a desk, a four-screen terminal with associated keyboards, and access to a tiny bathroom. Otherwise it was monkishly austere, the bunk made up drumhead tight. His garb was a plain white coverall and slipshoes.

"Be seated, milady." He gestured at the single chair. When she took it, he half settled on the desk. His smile was forced. "Seated because I suppose we'd better allow our groundlubbers another half hour or so of weight to get their stuff properly stowed."

Nor did she sit at ease. She compelled herself to meet his gaze and say, "I know Yoran can be difficult, but he is able. On balance, I judged him the best person readily available for his tasks. I did not anticipate— Vargen, I must insist you show the understanding, the—the kind of leadership I thought you would."

His reply was low, almost subdued, but stubborn. "What have I done wrong?"

"This trick you played on us, with Copperhue's connivance. I mean to reprimand it-him as well. Frankly, I feel insulted. But it's the scientists whom you've wronged most."

"Milady, did you really think we'd be wise to plunge straight to an unknown destination without a single trial run? Now it's proven that we need a training period, if not a complete shakedown cruise."

"You know perfectly well, doctrine is that the moment we spot something we're not sure we can handle, we hyperjump away."

"We may not be able to, on half a second's notice."

"Yes, and strolling through Riverview Park at home, we may be struck by lightning. One can't provide against every conceivable contingency, not even by huddling forever in a hole." Laurice drew breath. "This is getting beside the point." *It is getting closer to the basic truth than I want, God help me.* "We will have no more such incidents. Is that clear?"

Vargen frowned. "Milady, I am the captain. My duty is to follow my best judgment."

Davith might have uttered those words, with the same

gravity. Yes, and as Vargen said them, he looked much like the Head. For an instant, Laurice's eyes stung, her heart stumbled. She pulled her body straight and replied, recognizing that she spoke too loud and fast, "You're in command of the spacecraft while she's underway. She and her robots obey you. The rest of us must not obstruct, nor refuse a legitimate order. However, it is the House of Windfell that sponsors this expedition and its policies that you are to execute. I speak for it. I have authority to direct us to any lawful destination, including directly back home; and upon our return, you are answerable to the House for all actions."

He folded his arms and leaned back a little. "Let's not fight," he said quietly. "Just what is your complaint?"

"I told you. Your distrust of us is bad enough. Don't you know how important morale is, élan, on every exploratory mission? The way you showed your attitude was downright humiliating. I can swallow it for the sake of peace; but then, it didn't touch me in my honor. Yoran is a proud man. He has a right to be infuriated."

"Proud? 'Overbearing' would be a better word; and he doesn't have the genuine worth that might excuse it. He's too small. He can't stand having his superiority called into question. Most of his tantrum was because you, the amateur, reached the truth before he did."

You see cruelly well, Laurice thought, but your vision is narrow. "You don't understand. And you've got to. Yoran's had to fight for everything, all his life. His parents weren't only poor, they were lowly, despised—patronless. As a boy he needed unlimited brashness, first to keep hope alive, then to bring himself to the attention of those high and mightinesses who could help him. In spite of his adoption, his scholarships, his accomplishments, he continued suffering scorn and discrimination. Professionally, too, he was always thwarted. He was born too late to become the great scientist he could have been centuries ago. Unless this voyage of ours— That's one reason I picked him, Harul. Don't ruin his dream!"

"Must everybody indulge him forever?" Vargen retorted. "Is he the single being alive that's had troubles and frustrations? A real man puts such things behind him, acknowledges his mistakes, and goes on."

"Like you?" escaped from her.

"What do you mean?" he cried.

He jerked to his feet and swayed above her. She must needs rise too. He had gone appallingly white. "D-don't be so self-righteous," she stammered. "You've made y-your mistakes. Everybody has."

"Mine?" It sounded as if he were being garroted.

I've got to retrieve this, oh, God, I didn't realize how woundable he still is. "Your, well, your record shows you gave up an excellent position once. You must have . . . had reasons."

His head sank. He turned from her. A hand dropped to the desktop and lay helpless. "You know them, then." The words fell empty.

I could bite out my tongue, she thought. Or should I? May it not be better to bring this forth, between the two of us, and I try to gauge how trustworthy *he* is? If I can. If I can. Dad, be with me, lend me your wisdom and strength.

"About Novaya, yes," she said.

He stared at whatever rose before him. "And still you kept me on?"

"We didn't find out till almost departure time, and Copperhue thinks the hour is late for us. Which is one reason this . . . delay . . . upset me. But I, I was willing to have you anyway, Harul. We'd gotten to know each other, at least a little. I'd like to hear your side of the story."

"Nobody else ever did. . . . Ha-a-ah!" he cawed. "Now I'm sounding like Yoran. Self-pity. No. There was no excuse. I ran away because I was weak. Couldn't stand it. How many might I have saved?"

She reached toward his back, but withdrew. "It was terrible, I'm sure."

"Blackened land, ash blowing on acid winds. Craters, trees strewn around them like jackstraws, kilometer after kilometer after kilometer, snags of wall above toppled ruins, a burnt-out city. The dead in their thousands—millions, we knew—animal, human, sprawled bloated and stinking till they fell apart and the bones grinned through—" Vargen checked the shrillness that had arisen in his voice. After a moment, he went on in a monotone: "But it was good when we helped survivors. Planetside vehicles, ground and air, located them and brought them to the spacecraft. Many were ragged, filthy, starved, sick, but they would live. I lifted my share of them to the moon, and came back for more."

He stopped. When the silence had lasted too long for her, she touched the hand that dangled at his side and whispered, "What happened then?"

He turned around. She looked upon despair. "The next lot of stones arrived," he said harshly. "They were strung out along the whole orbit, of course, so that the night sky was always full of shooting stars, except where dust or storms hid them. We'd get a major strike somewhere almost daily. But the bulk of them stayed clustered together. When that returned, the real barrage began again.

"The orbit was perturbed and the planet rotated, so new areas were hit worst at every such time. Now Suzda's turn came, a big, beautiful, heavily populated island off in an ocean that from above looked like blued silver. I was ordered to a certain town, unharmed as yet. Night had fallen when I landed. Another ship was already there. An awkward, crewed hulk, she was. But much bigger than mine, with a belly that could take a hundred. They were streaming out toward her. It was chaos. Not quite a mob scene, everybody seemed brave, struggled to maintain order, but nevertheless the mass swirled and eddied, yelled and moaned, mothers tried to pass small children along over the heads of people in front— The rescue operation always was badly confused, you see. There had been so little warning, and then volunteer vessels like mine kept appearing unannounced from across half the galaxy—do you see? Nobody here had heard I was coming. At least, nobody appeared to know. I wondered if anyone had even seen me land; it was some distance off, naturally. I debarked, hoping I could do something toward straightening matters out. I was shaken and sickened by what I'd seen earlier, but I did debark. I shouted and waved. 'Over here! This way!' "

He fought for air. She could not but take both his hands in hers and ask, "What then? What was it like?"

"Like the—the end of the world, the wreck of the gods, in—in some ancient myth." He groaned. "I was in a brushy meadow, near a road, several kilometers from the town. Its roofs, spires, domes stood black against the sky. The sky was afire, you see. Flames streaked over it, out of the west, from horizon to horizon. Hundreds of flames—the great fireballs, blue-white, tailing off in red and yellow, that left me half blinded, till I didn't know what was afterimage and what was rock booming in at kilometers per second—and the little devils, countless, zip-zip-zip, wicked for an instant across the dark, gone, but more were there at once, more and more. Only the night wasn't really dark. Not with all those thunderbolts splitting and shaking it, and a forest burning to the south, and— They roared, screamed, whistled. When a big one struck somewhere, I'd see a flash over the horizon. A second or two later the ground shivered under my feet, up through my bones and teeth; and then the airborne noise reached me, sometimes like a cannon, sometimes like an avalanche that went on and on, below that uproar overhead. The air reeked of smoke and lightning. And I knew I was defenseless. If anything hit anywhere near, by the sheerest blind chance, that ended my universe."

His hands were cold between her fingers. "You could face that," she foreknew.

"Yes." The tears broke forth. "Barely."

"But what happened next?"

"I—I—" He wrenched free of her. "No."

"Tell me."

He slumped onto the chair, covered his eyes, and shuddered.

"I hurried toward the crowd," she made out. "I waved and shouted. Several on the fringes, they saw, they moved my way. A girl ran ahead of them. She was maybe six or seven years old, light on her feet. I've wondered why she went alone. Got separated from her family in the scramble? There I was, as terrified as her, but she didn't know that. I was a man, holding out my arms to her, under that horrible sky, and at my back the ship that was life. She held a kitten to her breast—"

He wept, long, racking gulps and rattles, into his hands. "The strike— The town went up, a crash that deafened and staggered me, a blaze that rose and rose and lost itself in a black tree of smoke and dust— Fragments— They tore through the crowd like sleet. Those people that were making for me, they, they became . . . rags flung right and left. The little girl rolled over. She flopped into a bush. It caught fire. I ran to her and stamped at the flames. It'd been such a pretty dress. Her hair— 'Please, oh, please!' I think she screamed. The chunk had ripped through her. Guts slurped out. Her kitten was burned too. I put my heel down on its skull. It crunched. That was all I could do for her. Wasn't it? By then she was dead. A bolide trundled and rumbled overhead. Its light brought her face out of the shadows, in fits and starts, fallen jaw and staring eyes. She looked very much like my daughter the same age, my daughter who'd died the year before.

"I don't remember much else, till I was back in space, outbound."

Vargen raised his head, pawed at the tears, caught a breath, and said, saw-edged, "No excuses. I never made any. I had that much self-respect left me."

"We are none of us infinitely strong," Davith Windfell had told his own daughter. "Always the universe can break us. If we go on afterward, scars and all, it's because luck made us brave." She knelt to enfold the man who had opened himself to her.

The ship sprang to a known part of space. There she coasted while Newan, Enry, and Thura practiced in freefall. Violet and rose, a nebula phosphoresced across a fourth of heaven. Through its laciness gleamed fierce points of light, newborn giant suns and the coals that were stars still forming. Oh, no lack of wonders whereon to heighten skills!

Given intelligence and healthy reflexes, most Erthumoi soon learned how to handle their weightless bodies. Precision work was the hard thing to master. It began with always, automatically, making sure that objects would stay where you left them. Over and over and over, Laurice put her pupils through the drill, explained, chided, encouraged, demonstrated, guided. Then followed assignments in partnership with the three robots. Who knew but that the multiple manipulators and ship-linked but individual intelligences of Un, Du, and Tre would be needed?

"Time for lunch," she said wearily. "Meet again in half an hour. You're doing quite well. In fact, you no longer require me to hector you."

"Why, Sergeant Major, you sound downright human," Enry japed.

Laurice laughed. "I have reason. *I* won't be here next session. Seriously, I am pleased. Keep on as hard as you have been, get your efforts a little better coordinated, and we'll be in shape to fight mad tax collectors."

Their friendship felt like a warmth at her back as she left. Yes, she had driven them hard, but they realized why. House Windfell's clients knew that it traditionally expected more of its patrons than it did of them.

The whole cosmos was warm and bright. Flying down the corridors, Laurice whistled that bawdy old ballad "Two Lovers in Two Spacesuits."

She assumed Yoran would be at a rec screen, whether to play three-dimensional go against the ship or watch one of the loud, flashy musical shows he'd put in the library database. He wasn't, though. She inquired. "He is in the electronics shop," *Darya* told her.

"What's he want there?" Laurice wondered aloud.

Hitherto she couldn't have gotten a reply. The ship's capabilities weren't for crewfolk to spy on each other. Vargen had lately directed that she have the same full access as himself. It was just a gesture, impulsive, scarcely significant but endearing. She'd forgotten, and felt surprise at first when *Darya* said, "He appears to be writing a program. I cannot tell for certain, because he is using a personal computer he brought along, unconnected to my systems, and his body blocks the keyboard and display from my sensors. Do you wish a visual?"

"No, no. I only have to talk with him. I'll go in person." Laurice set off.

Already competent in zero gravity, he hunched at the middle of the compartment, legs wrapped around a stanchion, machine friction-hooked to his lap. It was a mini, useful enough when something more powerful wasn't available. He started when she entered and slammed the cover shut. She smiled. "Hullo," she greeted. "What are you up to?"

He swallowed. "Ah, uh, experimental procedure. I don't want to show it to anybody till it's finished."

"Why not use *Darya*'s systems? You'd finish in a tenth the time, not counting blind alleys that that gimcrack may let you wander into."

He flushed, then paled. How haggard he had grown, these past several watches. And solitary, silent. She almost missed his waspishness. "I don't choose to! When my program's ready, when I'm satisfied, I'll put it in the network."

And if it's a failure, there'll be no record of it. Nobody will ever know, not even the ship. You poor, forlorn devil.

Best avoid the subject. "As you like. I'm afraid you'll have to set it aside and rejoin your team, at twelve-thirty hours."

He glared. "Why?"

"They're ready to practice with you."

"And where will you be?" After a pause: "Milady."

"Elsewhere." It tingled through her skin. "I've given them their basic instruction. Now I should not be underfoot. It's your team. Get them into unison with you."

"I see," he said. "And you will be elsewhere."

"Look," she pointed out, as mildly as possible, "it shouldn't take long. I hope not. We don't want to come late for the big event. However, when you're prepared, we'll take two extra watches and rest before we proceed to destination. We'll do it under boost, so everybody can feel at ease while regaining some muscle tone. Captain Vargen thinks, and I agree, we'd better reach the scene in optimum condition. That'll give you time to complete this project of yours, if you want." And you will. You don't sleep much or well, do you?

"Captain Vargen." Yoran's attention went back to his computer. "Very well, milady. Now, if you will excuse me, I may be able to write this subroutine before completing my duties."

"Of course." If only I could share happiness with you who hardly know what it is. Impossible. So why mar mine? "Good luck." Laurice left him.

On her passage forward, she met Copperhue outside the galley. Enry, Newan, and Thura were in it, fixing their meal, but the Naxian was evidently through eating. By tacit accommodation, it-he did so alone. The two species didn't like the smells of each other's food. "Will you not join your fellows?" it-he hailed her.

Courtesy demanded she press palm against bulkhead and brake herself. "Later," she said. "I must report to the skipper."

The luminous eyes searched her. "You are hungry."

She laughed. It sounded the least bit nervous to her. "Does your emotion reading extend to that? Yes, I would like a sandwich, but it can wait."

The artificial voice lowered together with the sibilant purring. "Honored one, let me suggest you be more . . . circumspect. Feelings toward you have intensified."

Blood throbbed in her throat. "What do you mean?"

A ripple down the long body might correspond to a shrug. "I detect emotions, not thoughts, and with an alien race my perceptions are basic; nuances are lost on me. Still, I can identify joy, and rageful bitterness, and even amicable, slightly prurient curiosity. This enables me to make deductions that as yet are probably mere speculations in the minds of the rest." Those lips could not smile, those pseudopods could not embrace, and the speech was synthetic. Yet did she sense benevolence, concern, perhaps a kind of love? "None of my business, as your saying goes, especially when I am a total outsider. But I do pray leave to counsel discretion. We are embarking into mystery. We must remain united."

"Sufficient."

Copperhue flowed off. She looked after it-him till it-he disappeared around a corner, before she continued forward.

It-he's right, she knew. We have been careless, Harul and I. Well, it happened so suddenly, overwhelmingly. . . . No justification. We're not freed from our responsibilty for crew and mission.

On earlier expeditions she had stayed prudent, celibate except on the two she made in company with Tumas Whitewater, and there it was known beforehand they would be together. (They had talked eagerly about forging one more marriage bond between their Houses. That faded out with the relationship, in wistful but not unpleasant wise. He was too immature.) Planetside, you could be as private as you wanted, and in any event jealousy wouldn't create a hazard.

But damn it, Harul's the best lover I've ever had or hoped to have. Knowing, considerate, ardent. As fine a human being as I'll ever meet. Wise, gentle, resolute. He's come back out of the night—I raised him from it, he says—with a strength, a knowledge, beyond my imagining, I who have never been there. Dad and Mother won't be happy at first, but they'll learn, they too.

Meanwhile, yes, of course, we'd better see to our masks. If we can. How do you appear in public not radiating gladness?

Jump.

Brilliance.

Slowly, she eased. Nothing had happened. She floated before the weapons console in silence and the ocean of stars. Well, she thought, we knew Copperhue's fix was rough, and the smallest difference in astronomical distances is big beyond our conceiving.

She gazed about her. Now the Milky Way did have an altogether new shape, seen from its farther side, from within another spiral arm. Awe walked cold over her spine, on into arms and fingertips. She searched the strangeness for anything she might identify, as the Naxian had done. Magellanic Clouds, Andromeda galaxy, a few naked-eye sisters—clotted darkness shielded her from the blaze at the heart of her own galaxy and marked it for her—an obvious blue giant, maybe five hundred light-years away, might be in some survey catalogue—

"What do you detect?" Vargen breathed through the night.

"No radiations such as spacecraft emit," *Darya* reported. "An anomalous source at nineteen twenty-six hours planar, sixty-two degrees south. Radio, optical, X-ray; possible neutrino component."

Excitement pulsed in Vargen's voice: "That's got to be *it*. All right, let's aim the array."

"Request permission to leave my post," Laurice said.

"Granted," Vargen answered. "Come join me. We may want to swap ideas off the intercom, not to disturb the scientists."

You transparent innocent! Laurice thought. We could talk directly, cubicle to cabin. . . . Well, but if I know Yoran, he's now too engaged in his work to notice. . . . Never mind him. What better time to be at your side, darling?

She hastened. Glorious though the sight was, he had abandoned it for his quarters. The kiss lasted long. "Hold, hold," he mumbled when her hands began to move. "We'd better wait awhile. The team should have word for us in a few minutes."

"I know," she said in his ear. "Make some arrangements for later, though, will you? And not much later, either. Have I told you you're as good in zero gee as you are under boost?"

He chuckled, low in his throat. "The feeling's mutual. Uh, the ship—"

"Oh, *Darya* knows too, the way we kept forgetting she existed. And if we cut her off now, we might delay an emergency call. You won't tell on us, will you, *Darya*, dear?"

"I am programmed not to reveal mission-irrelevant matters to others than the captain upon command, and yourself," replied the sweet tones. "Those will be wiped upon our return, prior to logging the permanent record."

"Yes, yes. But it's nice of you to, well, care." Did the robotic brain? A philosophical question, never really answered. Certainly *Darya* was not, could not be voyeuristic. Still, her consciousness didn't seem completely impersonal and aloof. And—Laurice felt a blush—that unseen presence did add a little extra spice.

As if any were needed! She nuzzled. "You smell good," she murmured. "Clean but male. Or should that be male but clean?"

Half an hour passed. They required something to discuss if they were to stay chaste and alert. Vargen declined their search as a subject. "It is a capital mistake to theorize before one has data," he said. She got the impression he was quoting, perhaps a translation from an ancient writer; like her father, he read widely. Well, they had their future to imagine, and to plan soberly. They were quite aware that much of it would be difficult, especially at first, before he had once more fully proven himself.

The intercom chimed. They accepted. Yoran sounded almost friendly, or was that sheer exuberance? Whichever, Laurice was delighted to hear it. "We've got our preliminary data, Captain, milady. Something peculiar, for certain. I'd rather keep my ideas in reserve for the moment."

Vargen, too, showed pleasure. "What can you tell, in layman's language?"

"Well, actually there are two radiation sources. Radial velocities tremendous; you'd think they were quasars. Spectra indicate mostly hydrogen, some helium, traces of metals. In short, interstellar medium, but at sunlike temperatures. Each source appears to be rotating differentially, the inner parts at speeds approaching c, but we aren't sure of that yet. Nor of much else, aside from— It is extraordinary, Captain."

"Good work. I hereby become your errand boy. What do you want us to do?"

"Skip around. Get parallaxes so we can determine the location in space, transverse component of velocity, intrinsic brightness. Observing from various distances, over a range of a hundred parsecs or so, we can follow any evolution that's been taking place. That should let us figure out the nature of the beast."

Vargen frowned. Yoran's reply had been scoffingly obvious. Vargen's brow cleared. Laurice saw he was willing to overlook the matter. As keyed up as he was, Yoran doubtless bypassed tact without noticing. "Fine. Give me your plan."

"I'll develop it as we go along and collect more information. For the present, hmm, I must do some figuring. I'll get back to you with the coordinates of the next observation point in about an hour." The physicist cut the connection.

"An hour," Laurice said. "That'll serve."

Vargen blinked. "What?"

"An hour of our own. Let's take advantage. We may not have more for some time to come."

Fifty hours of leap, study, leap were unendurably long and unbelievably few. At the end, the travelers met in the saloon. Word like this should be face-to-face, where hand could seize hand. For it, they gave themselves boost, weight, that they might sit around the table at ease, perhaps the last ease they would ever know.

Yoran rose. Pride swelled his stumpy form. "I am ready to tell you what I have found," he said.

"After the Python Confederacy." Copperhue murmured the words, but forgot to keep the 'trans equally quiet. Well, Laurice thought beneath her heart-thumping, Children's Day morning expectancy, of course all beings want their races given all due honor, whether or not they like the governments.

Yoran surprised her with a mild answer: "True. And your people scarcely came upon this by last-minute accident. As long as they've been spacefaring, I imagine they found it hundreds of years ago. They—the rulers, that is—saw the potentialities, but bided their time till the climactic moment neared. Erthumoi couldn't have kept a secret like that."

Has his triumph made him gentler? wondered Laurice. I'm glad for you, Yoran.

"What are the potentialities, then?" Vargen demanded.

"I don't know," the physicist replied. "Neither do the Naxians, or they wouldn't be making such an effort." He paused. Something mystical entered his speech, his whole manner. "An unprecedented event, rare if not totally unique in the universe. Who can say what it will unleash? Quite possibly, phenomena never suspected by us. Conceivably, laws of nature unknown even to the Forerunners."

And what technologies, what powers might spring from those discoveries? went chill through Laurice. For good or ill, salvation or damnation. I can't blame the Naxians of the Python for wanting to keep it to themselves. I wish we humans could.

"Tell us what it is!" she blurted.

The three assistants shifted on their bench. They knew. Their master had laid silence on them. This was to be his moment.

He looked at her and measured out his words. "I can give you the basic fact in a single sentence, milady. Two black holes are on a collision course."

Copperhue hissed and Vargen softly whistled.

Black holes, Laurice evoked from memory. Suns two—or was it three?—or more times greater than Florasol, ragingly luminous, consuming their cores with nuclear fire until after mere millions of years they exploded as supernovae, briefly rivaling their whole galaxy; then the remnant collapsing, but not into the stability of a white dwarf or a neutron star. No, the mass was still too huge, gravitation overcame quantum repulsion, shrinkage went on and on toward zero size and infinite density. The force of gravity rose until light itself could not escape. . . . She had seen pictures taken from spacecraft at a distance and by probes venturing closer. The event horizon, the sphere of ultimate darkness, appeared seldom, and only when data processing succeeded. It was asteroid size, a few tens of kilometers across at most, and screened from view. For around it wheeled fire, the accretion disk, matter captured from space, spiraling ever faster into the maw, giving off a blaze of energy as it fell. . . . No transmissions had come from nearby. The stupendous gravity dragged at radio and light waves, reddened them, twisted their paths. Its tidal forces stretched a probe asunder and whirled the fragments off into the disk. . . . Most of the knowledge was to Laurice little more than words—quantum tunneling, Hawking radiation, space and time interchangeably distorted. . . .

I'm not badly informed for a layman, she thought. I remember Professor Arbureth remarking how much is still unknown to anybody in any of the Six Races. He opined that in the nature of the case it always would be unknown too, because there is no possible way for information to reach us through the event horizon. But if a pair of them crash together—

"That must be rare indeed," Copperhue said low.

"Unless at galactic center?" Vargen mused.

"Conjecture," Yoran snorted. "Yes, perhaps lesser black holes are among the stars that the Monster engulfs, but no probe has survived to tell us what's going on there. Here the event is out where we can watch it." He grew milder. "Also, this is not a simple linear collision, such as we believe we have some theoretical understanding of. That would be vanishingly improbable, two singularities aimed straight at each other. This will be a grazing encounter.

"From our observation of orbits and accelerations, we've obtained the masses of the bodies with considerable accuracy. They are approximately nine and ten Sols. That means the event horizons are about sixty kilometers in diameter. Calculation of closest approach—that involves some frank guesswork. We have good figures for the orbital elements. If these were Newtonian point masses, they'd swing by on hyperbolic paths at a distance of about thirty kilometers and a speed of about one-third light. But they aren't, and it'd be a waste of breath to give you exact figures, when all I'm sure of is that the event horizons will intersect. The ship has programs taking relativistic and quantum effects into account. I've used them. However, certain key answers come out as essentially nonsense. The matrices blow up in a mess of infinities. We simply don't know enough. We shall have to observe."

"Can we get that near and live?" Vargen asked.

"As near as the Naxians, I daresay." Yoran sounded boyishly bold and careless.

"How near is that, do you suppose?"

"Probably closer than humans would venture, if this had been our project from the beginning. We'd send in sophisticated robotic vessels. The Naxians will do their best with probes, but that best isn't very good. No nonhuman race's is. They all keep trying to copy from us, and never get it right."

"Every species has its special talents," Laurice interjected for shame's sake. She wondered if Copperhue cared, either way.

"Give me a figure, will you?" Vargen snapped.

"An estimate," Yoran replied. "It takes into account our advanced protection systems; we can fend off more than most ships. The Naxians must have some that are equally shieldable. Integrating the expected radiation over time around the event, and throwing in a reasonable safety factor, I'd undertake to keep on station at a distance of two hundred million kilometers, for two hundred fifty hours before the impact and maybe as much as thirty hours after it, depending on what the actual intensities turn out to be. That's far too deep in the gravity well for a hyperjump escape, of course, but I'd call the odds acceptable."

He spread his hands. "Granted," he went on, "the whole reason for the exercise is that nobody can predict what will happen. I make no promises. All I say is, if I were the Naxian in charge, I'd post four live crews at approximately that distance. Two on the coordinate axis through the point of contact, normal to the tangent to the orbits at that point and in their plane. Two on the axis normal to this at the same point. I'd put others elsewhere, naturally, but these four should have the best positions, if our theories correspond to any part of reality.

"And if I were that Naxian, I'd join one of those crews."

Laurice leaned forward. She shivered. "When will the encounter be?" she asked.

"If we jumped now to the vicinity," Yoran told them in carefully academic style, "we would observe it in a little more than eleven standard days."

"That soon," Vargen murmured into stillness renewed. "We barely made it, didn't we?"

He shook himself, straightened where he sat, and clipped, "Very well. Thank you, Dr. Yoran. If you haven't already, please put your data and conclusions in proper form for transmission. We've got to notify headquarters. What we've learned thus far mustn't be lost with us. Besides, I'll be interested in the exact information, the actual numbers, too." His smile was crooked. "Personally interested."

Laurice saw doubt on Enry; Newan swallowed; Thura laughed aloud. They foreknew. It was Copperhue who said, "Thereafter, do you intend that we shall seek the event?"

Vargen's head lifted. "What else? On Ather, they'd never outfit and scramble another ship in time."

"Humans won't get another chance," Yoran agreed, "and I doubt the Naxians will share what they learn."

Laurice paid him no heed. She caught Vargen's arm. "Yes, certainly," rang from her. "It's up to us. That's how you were bound to think, Harul."

Yoran stood where he was. He drooped, the glee drained out of him, as if somehow gravity had reached from the lightless masses yonder.

Neutrinos passed through hyperspace, across half the breadth of the galaxy. Their modulations carried the findings made aboard *Darya*. Laurice wished she could talk with her father when they were done, but haste forbade. The instruments gathered information at rates hugely greater than the transmitter could send it. Conveying all they had took several irrecoverable hours. For the same reason, the expedition would send home nothing but the new data from each stop along its course henceforward—and nothing whatsoever, once it was close to the black holes, until it was outward bound again.

Yoran spent the waiting period in the electronics shop. Laurice supposed he tinkered with something in hopes that it would ease his tension and . . . unhappiness? Or did the magnificence ahead of him drive out mortal wishes?

Newan monitored the reporting. Vargen studied the facts, with Thura and Enry on hand to answer questions. In the saloon, Laurice and Copperhue played round upon round of Integer until, at length, they fell into conversation. It turned to private hopes, fears, loves. You could confide to a sympathetic alien what you could not to any of your own species. "I look forward to your Venafer colony," Laurice said finally, sincerely.

The summons resounded. Crew took their posts. Countdown. Jump. A light-year from their destination, they poised.

Words reached Laurice in her globe as if from across an equal gulf. She had instantly established that no other vessel was in the neighborhood. Absurd to imagine that any would be, those few score motes strewn through the abyss. Why, for starters, consider that the light-year is a human unit, a memory of Old Earth like the standard year and day, the meter, the gram, the gee. Nobody else uses them. . . . Her eyes sought the predicted coordinates on the sphere. She couldn't tell whether she picked the two sparks out of the host that glittered around. Her fingers trembled a little as she set the console viewscreen to them and turned up the optics.

The breath caught in her throat. Magnified, amplified, two comets flamed before her. From their incandescent brows streamed flattened blue-white manes, becoming many-forked tails that shaded through fierce gold to a red like newly spilled blood. Fragments rolled behind, and she imagined the turbulence within, great waves and tides through the gas, lightnings, atoms ripped into plasma, roaring down to their doom.

And this is only how it was a year ago, she realized. The black holes were still well apart. How far did Yoran say? I forget. The span of a thousand average planetary systems? The accretion disks had just begun to interact strongly with the interstellar medium. Their bow shocks were mostly generating visible light. Later it shifted toward X rays, harder and harder.

"Next jump," Yoran called.

"Already?" Vargen asked.

The reply screeched. "Chaos take you, we haven't got a second to waste! Nothing registers here that we can't account for in principle. I've programmed everything for maximum data input and processing. Make use of it, you clot-brain!"

Hoy, that's far too strong, Yoran, thought Laurice, half

dismayed. Harul has every right to put you in confinement. Are you off your beam? Now, in these last, supreme days?

Relief washed through her when Vargen rapped, "Watch your language. The next offense, I will penalize."

She considered ordering the ship to show her the physicist. Maybe, knowing him, she could calm him down. The sense of deliverance mounted at his grudging, "Sorry . . . Captain. May we proceed?" She hadn't wanted to cope with him.

Darya knew the planned pattern in which she was to draw nigh. "Ten," she sang. Vargen must have given her a signal, not quite trusting himself, to speak. "Nine. Eight. Seven—"

At half a light-year, the comets burned naked-eye bright. Optics showed their tails contracted, thickened, drawn into intricate strands that looped around as if seeking forward to the hungry furnaces of the comas. Enry's voice was full of awe and puzzlement: "Sir, that looks almighty strange, doesn't it? I can't think how you'd get curvatures like that in the gas, at this stage of things."

"Nor can I," Yoran admitted eagerly. Rapture had eclipsed wrath. "The cosmos is running an experiment like none we've ever seen before or ever will again. I'd guess that mutual attraction is—was—appreciably distorting the event horizons. That'd be bound to affect magnetic fields and charge distributions. But we need more information."

Not that it would soon reveal the truth, Laurice realized. Understanding must wait upon months or years of analysis, hypothesis, tests in laboratories and observatory ships and brains, back at Ather and no doubt elsewhere among the Six Races. The task here set before Yoran's genius was to decide what sorts of data, out of the impossibly many his team might try for, would likely bear such fruit. "The polarizing synchrometer should—" The conversation from the intercom went out of Laurice's reach.

She tuned it low and made a direct connection with Copperhue in the saloon. Her yearning was for Vargen's words, since she could not have his presence. The skipper shouldn't be distracted, though, nor should the others be given grounds to suspect he was. Besides, she felt sorry for the Naxian, become functionless, restricted to whatever view *Darya* got a chance to project on a rec screen for it-him.

"How're you doing?" she inquired softly.

"We fare among splendors," she heard. "Is this not worth an island?"

"Yes, oh, yes." A thought she had not wanted to think pushed to the forefront. "Will your—will the Pythons really let us carry it home?"

"We have considered this before, honored one. The vessels on which I served were unarmed. The Dominators have no cause to expect us. The fleet come for the climax may include a few naval units of models suitable for rescue and salvage operations, should those prove necessary; but they are probably not formidable."

"I know. I remember. However, it's occurred to me—it didn't before, because on Ather we don't think that way—in a number of Erthuma societies, the military would insist on having a big presence, if only for the prestige."

"They do not think like that in the Confederacy either, honored one. There is no distinction between organizations serving the Dominance; they are simply specialized branches of the same growth. This means that commanders can act decisively, without having to consult high officials first. You see, their intelligence and emotional stability have been verified beforehand. I warned your father that I do not know what the doctrine is with respect to preserving this secret. But I doubt that orders read 'at all costs.' Additional combat vessels will scarcely be sent from afar, under any but desperate circumstances. That would mean leakage of the truth, from crewfolk not predisciplined to closeness about it. Besides, the Confederacy is as desirous of maintaining stability as any other nation is." Copperhue hesitated. "I do counsel that we avoid undue provocation."

"Well, you can advise the captain. Can't you?"

"I can try. Perhaps I shall bring you into conference, if possible. Your rapport with both him and me may enable you to make ourselves clear to one another."

It thrilled in her. "I can't imagine any better service. Thank you, old dear, thank you."

Jump went the ship in a while. And again, presently, *jump*. And hour after hour, *jump*, to a different point of view, to a new distance, but always nearer, *jump*, *jump*, *jump*.

Jump.

At one light-hour, the incandescence around the black holes made them the brightest of the stars. You could have read by that livid radiance. Their closeness was deceptive; *Darya* had emerged well off any normal to their paths. Yet even as Laurice watched, her unaided eyes saw them creep nearer. Chill went through her, marrow deep. Second by second, those colossal accelerations were mounting.

And what when they met? Yoran believed the masses would fuse. If nothing else could leave such a gravity well, how could the thing itself? But this was no simple, head-on crash, it would be a grazing blow. He said the case had been considered theoretically, centuries ago, but not as fully as it might have been, and had since lain obscure—probably in the archives of other races too—for nobody awaited it in reality. He spoke of problems with linear and angular momentum, potential fields, quantum tunneling by photons, leptons, baryons, gravitons. The event horizons should undergo convulsive changes of shape. Still more should the static limits, below which everything from outside was ineluctably hauled into orbit in the same sense as a black hole's rotation. These twain had opposite spins with distinct orientations. What wavelike distortions might their meeting send out through the continuum? Already, space-time around each was warped. In a black hole's own frame, the collapse to singularity was swift. To a safely distant observer, it took forever; what she saw was not a completed *being* but an eternal *becoming*. Yet if somehow the inside of it should be bared, however briefly, to her universe, there was no way even to guess what would follow.

"Emissions from spacecraft power plant detected," said *Darya*. "I estimate the nearest at fifteen million kilometers."

No surprise, here. Nevertheless Laurice knew guiltily that for a pulse beat she had let her attention stray from her guns. Vargen remained cool: "Any indications that they've noticed us?"

"None. They may well fail to. The background is high because of emissions from the search objects, and the Naxians have no reason to watch for new arrivals."

"Uh-huh. Hard to see how they can think about anything but . . . that."

Laurice allowed herself a magnified view. The optics must adjust brightness pixel by pixel before she could see any detail against the glare at either forefront. The comet tails were gone. Instead, changeable light seethed in a ring around each flattened fire globe. She thought she could make out fountains and geysers within it, brief saw teeth on the rim. Dopplering shaded it clearly toward violet on the one edge, red on the other, a whirling rainbow.

"Emissions indeed!" Yoran shouted. "God, these readings!"

Nothing dangerous to ship or crew. This puny radius, which would not have touched the Oort cloud of a typical planetary system, was still beyond mortal comprehension. You could give it a name and hang numbers on it; that was all.

"Yes, event horizons distinctly deformed," Yoran well-nigh crooned.

Laurice knew that his instruments saw what she could not. The sight before her, like every such earlier, must in at least some part be illusion. Gravity sucked matter in from every direction, while its colliding atoms gave off radiation that grew the more furious the deeper it fell; but as it neared the static limit, bent space-time compelled it into the maelstrom. Yonder coma was no more than its last clotting and sparking before it entered the accretion disk; the ring was no more than the verge of an inward-rushing cataract. Yoran's devices looked past them, through the ergosphere, to the ultimate blindness itself. And they had not the eyes of gods wherewith to do this. They took spectra, traced particles, measured mutable fields; from what they gathered, computers drew long mathematical chains of inference.

That process would not end for years, perhaps not for generations. The readouts and graphics that Yoran saw flash before him were the barest preliminary theorizing. They might be dead wrong. It was a wonderful mind that could, regardless, immediately grasp something of what went on.

Time went timelessly past, but in retrospect astonishingly short, until he said, "We're clear to move on, Captain."

Praise him, Laurice thought. He needs it. He's earned it. "Fast work," she chimed in.

His laugh rattled. "Oh, we could spend weeks here and not exhaust the material. But we haven't got them."

No, she thought, we now have days to reap a share of the harvest for which the Naxians spent decades or centuries preparing.

"Right," Vargen agreed. "I take it you want to go on to your next planned point?" Same distance, but directly confronting the impact to be.

"No. I've changed my mind, on the basis of what I've learned in the last few stops. The latest input seems to confirm my ideas. We're going straight in."

"What? Immediately? You know we're close to the boundary for hyperjump, given masses like those."

Once inside it, we run strictly on normal drive, till we've gotten remote enough again. We're committed.

"Yes, yes, yes." Laurice heard how Yoran barely controlled his temper. "But *you* know, or should, contact will take place in a hundred and seventy-six hours. I want to be at the two hundred million kilometer radius I calculated was safe, before that happens, in time to set up experiments I've devised. How fast can you get us there, ship?"

"At one gravity acceleration, with turnover, considering our present velocity, that will require eighty-eight hours, plus maneuvering time," *Darya* told him.

Laurice visualized him shaking fists in air. "You can boost higher than that. A lot higher! We've got medications against excess weight. We could even go into the flotation tank."

"Such a delta vee would dangerously deplete our reserve. Does the captain order it?"

"No," Vargen decided at once. "One gee it is. You can still observe as we go, Yoran."

"But—" The physicist gasped in a breath. "Can't you understand? We've got to be close in, and prepared, for the main event. I expect fluctuations in the metric, short-lived superparticles, polarized gravitons, superstrings— Aargh! Time's grown so scant as is. If you hadn't farted it away, everywhere else in space—"

"Most of what we lost was because the people you chose turned out to require training," Vargen interrupted stiffly. "Prudence demands we don't squander so much convertible mass that we can't get onto emergency trajectories."

"Yes, you'll keep your hide safe, won't you, whatever else may be sacrificed?"

"That will do. If your considered judgment as a scientist is that we should head directly inward, I assume you don't want to dawdle here arguing. Give the ship the coordinates you have in mind. Crew, stand by for boost at one gravity."

Laurice and Vargen were in his cabin when the message came.

"To the captain," *Darya* said. "Incoming audio signal on the fifth standard band. Radar touched us sixty seconds ago and is now locked on. Code: 'Acknowledge and respond.' Shall I?"

Vargen disentangled himself and rose from the bunk. "Do, and relay to me, with translation. Surely a Naxian." To Laurice, wryly: "I knew this couldn't last. We're picking up more power plant emissions every hour. Somebody was bound to notice ours, and wonder."

She needed a moment more to swim up from the sweet aftermath of lovemaking. The warmth and odor of him still lingered as she heard "Ship *Green Pyramid,* Dominator Helix commanding and speaking, to vessel accelerating through sector eighty-seven dash eighteen dash zero-one." That must be *Darya*'s best attempt to render the coordinate system established for this locality, she thought. "You do not conform to the plan. Identify yourself."

"Captain Harul Vargen, from Ather, Florasol III, with crew on a scientific mission," the man stated. "We intend no interference or other harm, and will be glad to cooperate in any reasonable way."

The last drowsiness fled from Laurice. She glanced at her watch. Silence murmured. She got up too. The deck felt sensuously resilient beneath her bare feet, but remote, no longer quite real.

Twenty-eight seconds before response. If Helix hadn't hesitated, its-his (?) craft was four million-plus kilometers away. "Your presence is inadmissable. This region is closed. Remove yourselves."

Laurice bent over the intercom control and pushed for Copperhue's cubicle. "We are not aware of any such interdiction," Vargen was saying. "By what right do you declare it? It seems to be in violation both of treaty agreements and general custom."

"Copperhue," Laurice whispered. "They're on to us. At least one ship. They command we turn back. Listen in, and tell us what you think."

"S-s-s," the fugitive breathed.

"The Dominance of the Python Confederacy has taken sovereignty," Helix said. "Under its policy and in its name, I order you to return to clear space immediately and hyperjump hence. Else you are subject to detention and penalties. I warn you, we have weapons. If necessary, we will use them, with regret but without hesitation."

"I should hope no civilized being would make a threat like that, without even having discussed the matter first," Vargen answered. "Certainly we require more authority than yours. What are your reasons for this demand?"

"It-he bluffs, I believe," Copperhue murmured. Vargen also leaned close to hear, flank to flank with Laurice. She laid an arm about his waist. "Tell it-him that the Houses of Ather would have known if any such claim were registered with the Diplomacy Guild."

She noticed the time lag had grown. *Darya* was outrunning *Green Pyramid*, if "run" made sense when you spoke of coordinates, vectors, fields, and their derivatives in three-space. Evidently Helix thought that switching over to hypertransmission would be more trouble than it was worth. Or did it-he welcome these moments, to consider what to say? "The Dominance is concerned about safety." Was it-he trying to wheedle? "A cosmic cataclysm will soon take place. You are not prepared for it."

Vargen straightened and grinned. "Oh, but we are. That's why we're here." He went on as Copperhue had advised, finishing with: "Since no claim has been assented to, we have as much right as anybody. They know on Ather where we are, and that you are here. I don't imagine your superiors want an interstellar incident."

Dismay and rage hissed under the incongruous mellowness of *Darya*'s translating voice. "How do you know? What spies have you set on our sacred Nestmother?"

"To the best of my knowledge, none. And I wouldn't call the concealment of a scientific treasure trove a friendly act. Nor do I suppose the Six Races, including the other Naxian nations, will so regard it. I repeat, we mean no harm or interference. We hope your chief of operations will contact us when your officers have conferred and decided on a proposal intended to be mutually satisfactory. I respectfully suggest, and ask you to convey the suggestion, that they start thinking at once."

"Good," oozed from Copperhue's cubicle. "Firmness and correctness, after Helix faltered in both. The grand commander should well evaluate the playback of this conversation."

"Signing off, then," the Naxian captain said grimly. "You shall receive more soon." Laurice heard an abrupt absence of background sounds she had not noticed before.

"You did it! Whee, you did!" She leaped at Vargen, threw her arms about his neck, kicked heels in air. "I love you!"

"We've just begun," he cautioned, "and God knows what'll happen next." She let go and he activated the general intercom. "Attention. Urgent news."

"We're busy, for Founder's sake!" Yoran exclaimed, obviously from the main lab.

"Too busy for the Naxians?"

"Huh? Oh. Carry on, you," to the assistants. "A minute . . . All right. Tell me."

Vargen did. "We're leaving them behind, you say," the physicist answered. "They're doubtless unarmed anyway."

"Unless that fellow was lying, they do have some combat-worthy units. And hyperbeams must be flying from end to end of their fleet."

"The farther in we go," *Darya* reminded, "the smaller the volume of ambient space and therefore the more difficult evasion becomes. It is certainly incompatible with keeping station."

"I'll bet you're better armed than anything they've got here," Yoran said. "Stand up to the stinking snakes. Make them crawl."

"Copperhue," Vargen sighed, "may we have your opinion, and your pardon for that language?"

"My guess is that naval strength is small and incidental, confined to two or three craft whose real task is to help out in emergencies," replied calmness—or steely self-control? "Granted, the command will consider our advent an emergency. If they do possess superior force, they will probably threaten us with it."

"They don't," Yoran said. "I swear they don't. Fight. Blow 'em out of the universe."

Laurice remembered violent deaths she had witnessed. It was like a benediction when Vargen responded, "Only in self-defense, and only as an absolute last resort. I don't want to hear any more such talk. Go back to your studies. Let me know if a worthwhile thought occurs to you." He switched off.

Turning to Laurice, he took her hands in his. "I'm afraid that henceforward we're on twenty-four-hour duty." He smiled the smile that was like Davith's. "Well, we did luck out on this watch." He drew her close. The kiss was brief and wistful.

"Memories to look at, whenever we get a moment to pull them out of our pockets," Laurice agreed. "We'll enlarge the collection in future." Abruptly she giggled. "Speaking of pockets, we'd better grab a quick shower and get dressed. It doesn't make any difference to the

Naxians, but we'd scarcely overawe our human shipmates as we are, would we?"

Ahead, the envelopes of the black holes burned hell bright, drowning naked-eye vision of everything else in the dark around them. Without magnification, they were still little more than star points. Incredible, that the masses of whole suns and the energies to annihilate them were rammed down into volumes so tiny. But from the outer edges of the disks, beyond the ergospheres, gas had begun reaching, like two candle flames pointed at each other. Sparks drifted off them and guttered out.

Elsewhere in heaven, from her control globe, Laurice saw the Naxian ships. They and *Darya* had matched velocities and now orbited unpowered, those three in linear formation, she some thousand kilometers from them, a separation that would increase only slowly for the next hour or two. Much enlarged, their images remained minuscule, spindle shapes lost in the star-swarm beyond.

Just the same, she felt very alone. Vargen was in his own globe. He had linked his communicator to hers, but no other human was in the circuit, nor was Copperhue. This connection would be audiovisual, and it-he had counseled against letting the Naxians know of one whom they must regard as a traitor. Yonder midges could spit lightnings and missiles. Her heart beat thickly.

The screen before her flickered. Its projection split into a pair. Vargen's head confronted that of a Naxian, whose skin was yellow with black zigzags down the sides. Was the same strain upon both faces? She couldn't read the alien's. Nor could she know what feelings were in the tones that went underneath *Darya*'s methodical running translation.

"Hail, Captain Harul Vargen," she heard. "I am Crystal That Sparkles, Dominator, in ultimate command of the Python Confederacy's astrophysical quest."

"Your presence honors us, madam." How does he know that creature's quasisex? she wondered. Well, in the past he dealt with members of all Six Races, and he's intelligent, observing—he cares—

"*Ts-s-s.*" A laugh? "You show us curious courtesy, sir. In total contempt of authority, you have continued on your way, forcing us to divert these craft from important duties. That makes hypocrisy of your assertion that you mean to create no disturbance."

"No, madam." Vargen spoke levelly, patiently. "As soon as your representative called for rendezvous at a point we agreed was reasonable, we commenced maneuvers toward it. I cannot see any need for you to send three vessels. One would have served, surely; or we could have talked by hyperbeam. Are you trying to intimidate us? Quite unnecessary. We're the same peaceful scientists we took you to be."

Now there's hypocrisy for you! whooped Laurice. A fraction of the sweat-cold tension slacked off within her.

Hairless head lifted on sinuous neck. "Police need weapons against contumacious lawbreakers. Indications were that your ship is of a heavily armed type."

"That is true, madam, but it doesn't mean we want to menace anybody or throw our weight around." No more than we've got to. "You have had a good look at us. If your databanks are complete, you've recognized the model and know more or less what firepower we carry. You should also know why. This vessel is for exploration, where unpredictable demands on her can always come out of nowhere."

"You do not need nucleonics against primitive natives, sir, and when have starfarers attacked you?"

"Never, madam." Thank whatever god— "And we devoutly hope none ever will." —made those terrible devourers up ahead. "Certainly the owners, the House of Windfell, have no such intention. But an expedition just might run into, ah, parties willing to violate civilized canons. Far more likely, of course, nature may suddenly turn hostile. Antimissile magnetohydronamics deflect solar flare particles. A warhead excavates where a shelter is to be built. An energy beam drills a hole through ice, for geologists and prospectors to reach the minerals beneath. Besides work like that, this ship took a large investment. People protect their investments."

"Your best protection is to depart, sir. This vicinity will soon be unpredictably dangerous." Does it-she have a dry sense of humor? wondered Laurice. Well, Copperhue does.

"We're prepared for that as fully as I'd guess you are, madam. This situation is unique. We can't abandon our mission without betraying our race." Vargen raised his brows and smiled—for Laurice. "Unless the Dominance plans to share everything you discover with the rest of the civilizations."

Crystal's head struck back and forth, at emptiness. "How did you learn of us?"

"I'm not at liberty to tell you, madam, assuming for argument's sake that I know. But we've transmitted home the data we acquired along the way. You'd expect us to, wouldn't you? The basic secret is out. Why not let us carry on our observations in peace—or, better yet, join you in making them? Think of the goodwill the Confederacy will earn throughout the galaxy."

Silence seethed. Had the black holes moved perceptibly closer? Less than two days remained before the crash.

"No," fell from Crystal. "I . . . have no right . . . to grant such permission. This was our discovery. We staked our efforts, our lives, for cycle after cycle. Yes, you have stolen something from us, but the great revelations you shall not have. Turn about, sir, or we must destroy you."

"Can you?" Vargen challenged. "And firing on us would be an act of war, madam."

"Sir, it would not. Ather would feel aggrieved, but be a single planet against the Confederacy. No other nation would be so lunatic as to fight about an incident so remote in every sense of the concept. The Diplomacy Guild would arbitrate, an indemnity might be paid, and that would be that."

It-she understands politics, Laurice thought. And . . . I wouldn't spend lives and treasure myself, over something like this. Maybe, in a hundred years, when the Pythons have powers nobody else does, maybe then I'd be sorry. But today I'd just hope that things will work out somehow.

"Therefore," Crystal continued, "I urge you, sir. I implore you, not to compel us. Be satisfied with what you have. Go home."

Vargen made it-her wait for an entire minute before he replied, "Madam, with due respect, with sympathy for you in your dilemma, your demand is unlawful, unreasonable, and unacceptable. The right of innocent passage and access to unclaimed celestial bodies is recognized by every nation of the Six Races. I have no intention of heeding your demand, and do not believe you have the power to enforce it."

"They are small units," *Darya* had said. "Their combined firepower barely approximates mine; and I am a single vessel, self-integrated, with stronger defenses and more acceleration capability. They could perhaps take me in a well coordinated attack, but I estimate the probability of that as no more than forty percent."

"And supposing they did wipe us, you'd get one or two of them first, most likely, wouldn't you?" Laurice had pointed out. "That'd be a big setback to their whole operation. I'm sure those three are all the armed craft they have here. They aren't meant for guardians, they're for possible rescue or salvage work, and they must have scientific assignments of their own as well."

"Right," Vargen had said. "They'll be making the same calculations."

The image of Crystal's head leaned forward, as if trying to meet the man's eyes. "Would you truly be so barbarous as to initiate deadly violence?" it-she asked low.

"We'll go about our business, and defend ourselves if assaulted," Vargen declared. "After all, madam, a government that really upheld civilized ideals would not have kept a discovery like this hidden. It would have invited galaxywide cooperation, for everybody's benefit. Please don't speak to me about barbarity."

Silence and stars. Is Crystal ashamed? Poor being. But dangerous, because dutiful.

"We don't want to disrupt your work, or anything like that," Vargen continued. "Nor do you, madam. In spite of everything, you are civilized too." No matter those aspects of your society that drove Copperhue to seek refuge, and caused you to conceal these wonders. "Can't we compromise?"

Silence again. Laurice's knuckles whitened above the weapons console.

"It appears we must," said Crystal, and Laurice's hands lifted through weightlessness to catch at tears.

Again *Darya* decelerated toward her destination.

Vargen, Laurice, and Copperhue entered the saloon together. The physicists were already there, aquiver. Yoran leaped to his feet. "Well?" he cried.

"We have leave to proceed," Vargen told them.

Enry gusted out a breath. Newan and Thura raised a cheer. "Marvelous!" Yoran jubilated. "Oh, milady—" He saw her face more closely and broke off.

Vargen moved to the head of the table. His companions flanked him. "It was a tough bargaining session," the woman said.

"I know," Thura mumbled. "It went on and on. And when boost came back, and we didn't know where we were bound—"

"You'll have your shot at our target," said Vargen. He sat down. The rest who were standing did likewise. Copperhue coiled on the bench. The captain's gaze sought Yoran's.

"I couldn't push my opposite number, Crystal That Sparkles, too hard," he went on. "It-she must have been in contact with whatever superiors at home could be reached immediately, and some kind of hurried decision must have been made. It obviously left Crystal with some discretion, some choice. That's usual for Python officers in the field. And mainly, no reinforcements could reach it-her in time. Even if they jumped at once, it'd take them too long to cross the normal-drive distance. The black holes would already have met, and meanwhile we could be playing hob with the Naxians on the scene. And in fact, *Darya* hasn't detected any new arrivals, which she could do. Still, Crystal surely received orders not to give away the store."

"An officer of the Confederacy who shows cowardice is strangled," Copperhue said. "One who shows poor judgment is ruined. Over and above these considerations is nest honor."

"So I mustn't leave it-her with no choice but to attack," Vargen continued. "That would mean a certainty of heavy loss to the Naxians and a better than fifty percent chance of losing everything; though if we won, we might still be crippled. And while the political repercussions wouldn't be catastrophic, they'd be troublesome. On the other hand, Crystal couldn't, wouldn't, meekly stand aside and let us take all the forbidden fruit we might.

"The fact that we had already taken a good deal, and passed it on to Ather, weighed heavily. What I had to do was give Crystal a way to cut its-her side's losses. We dickered—"

Yoran's fist smote the table. "Will you get to the point?" he yelled. "What did you agree to?"

Vargen squared his shoulders. "No cooperation, no information exchange," he said. "That was too much to hope for. But we may take station at the minimum safe distance you want. Congratulations; they'd arrived at almost the identical figure, and had more and better numbers to work with. They have four live-crewed ships there, on the two orthogonal axes you described.

"We must not come any nearer to either axis than—the Naxian units equal about one million kilometers. We must not enter the orbital plane of the black holes at all."

"What?" Yoran sprang back to his feet. He leaned across the table, shuddering. "Why, you— That plane's where the most vital observations— You clot-brain! Didn't you ever listen to me? A rotating black hole drags the inertial frame with it. Those two have opposite spins, differently oriented. Cancellations, additions—the whole tendency will be for things to happen, unprecedented things, exactly in that mutual plane— And you threw this away for us!"

"Quiet!" Vargen shouted. Into the rage that choked and sputtered at him, he explained in a voice gone flat: "I did know. So did Crystal. I asked for a place farther out on the axis in the plane, or at least somewhere in it. It-she refused. We went around and around, with me offering different versions, and always it ended in refusal. I couldn't stop to consult with you, if I'd wanted to. Frankly, I was amazed to get what I did. The minimum radius, only a million kilometers north of the plane. Not quite twenty minutes of arc to sight down along. Does it make any serious difference?''

''Yes,'' Yoran said as if through a noose. ''Plane polarization of generated gravitons is likely, and who can foresee what else? It—it—Captain, you've got to renegotiate. You must.''

''No,'' Vargen stated. ''I can't risk it.''

''The balance in Crystal's mind is certain to be fragile,'' Copperhue added. ''It-she may well decide that an attempt to alter the agreement shows bad faith, and feel compelled to give us an ultimatum, that we depart or fight.''

''Then, by God, you give the ultimatum yourself!'' Yoran flung forth. ''They'll back down. You admit you were surprised at what they did concede. They *are* weaker than us. We can destroy them, do our research, and be safely homeward bound before they can bring any real warship to bear. And they know it.''

''If I knew for sure we'd win any fight without damage to ourselves,'' Vargen said, ''I still would not risk killing sentient beings for as little as this.''

''Little, you call it? Little? You idiot, you idiot, you—traitor to your race—''

Wrath flashed up in Laurice. She slapped the table. ''That will do, client,'' she called. ''Hold your tongue, or else if the captain doesn't confine you, I will.''

The eyes into which she looked seemed glazed, blind. ''Yes, you would,'' Yoran raved, ''you, his slut. Do you imagine we haven't seen you two smirk, sneak off, and come back smarmy enough to gag a disposal?''

It isn't the loss to his science that's driven him over the edge, she understood, appalled.

Worse came after: ''Oh, you've got fine taste in men, you do. You pick the great Harul Vargen, the one who ran away at Novaya. Have you heard, shipmates? They were evacuating people from a meteoroid bombardment. He lost his nerve and bolted. Now he's so very tender of lives. How many did you leave to die on Novaya, Vargen?''

He stopped, stared past them all. A convulsion went through him. He fell back on the bench and buried face in hands.

Silence lasted. His breathing hacked at it. Nobody else moved. Vargen's features had stiffened and bleached, like a dead man's.

At last, hearing it as if a stranger spoke far away from her, Laurice said, "That's what you did in your spare time. Worked out a program to slip into the ship's network. To listen to us, what we discussed in private. And to watch? Isn't that correct, *Darya*?"

"I have been unaware of it," the robot brain answered. "I would be, if the program was cleverly designed. Let me search. . . . There is a new file. Access is blocked to me."

"I would kill you," Laurice said. How calm she sounded. "But it isn't worth the trouble it would cause. And my hands would always be soiled. The authorities will deal with you when we return. Go to your cubicle. Rations will be brought you. You may visit the lavatory at need. Otherwise you are quarantined for the duration of this voyage."

Yoran raised his head. Tears whipped down the coarse cheeks. Sobs went raw. "Milady, I crave pardon, I did wrong, scourge me but—but don't deny me—"

"I told you to go."

"Wait." No robot spoke as mechanically as Vargen did. "We do need him. For scientific purposes. Without him, we could not learn half as much. Can you continue in the laboratory, Yoran? If your performance is satisfactory, we will consider entering no charges against you."

Does a tiny, evil joy flicker? A trial would bring everything out in public. "Y-yes, sir," Yoran hiccoughed. "I'll do my best. My humble apologies, sir."

I may have to let you go free, Laurice thought. You'll have your professional triumph. But never a place on my world. You'll dwell elsewhere, anywhere else. Aloud: "*Darya,* knowing about the illicit program you can screen it off, can't you?"

"Certainly," said the ship. "I will take precautions against further tampering."

"Not needed, I swear, not needed," Yoran mouthed.

Laurice ignored him. "Good, *Darya,*" she said. "Save the program itself. We might want it for evidence." Her glance swept around the table. "Shipmates, I'll be grateful for your discretion after we return. Meanwhile, I trust you will carry on, setting this deplorable business aside as much as possible. Now I think Captain Vargen and I deserve some privacy. It's still several hours to destination. We aren't likely to meet trouble en route." She rose. "Come, Harul."

She must pluck at his sleeve before he got up and followed her.

In his cabin she turned about to cast herself against him. "Oh, darling, darling. Don't let it hurt you. You mustn't. That horrible little animal. Can't gnaw you down. You're too big."

He stood moveless, looking past her. She stepped back. "Harul," she pleaded, "what does it matter if they know? They also know what you *are,* what you've made of yourself s-s-since then. I do. That's what counts. Isn't it?"

He hugged himself and, momentarily, shivered.

"You didn't run because you were afraid," she said. "You couldn't stand seeing the pain, the death. Isn't that right?"

The reply came rusty. "Is it?"

"And, and you've lived it down, whatever it was. You've become strong and brave. A man for my pride, Harul."

"Have I?"

"I'll show you!" Again she embraced him, arms, hands, lips, tongue, body. After a while he began to respond.

She led him to the bunk. Nothing happened. He tried, but nothing happened.

"It's all right." She held his head to her breasts. "I understand. Don't worry. It's only natural. Come on, boy, cheer up. We've got a job waiting for us. The two of us."

Oh, damn Yoran Jarrolsson. Damn him down into the bottom of a black hole.

The ship took station. Maintaining it was a delicate, intricate balancing act, when the ambient gravitational field constantly changed as the two masses hurtled inward. Those ever-shifting linear accelerations gave no weight that flesh and blood noticed, but sometimes you felt it a bit when the hull rotated.

Oddly enough, or perhaps not, her people worked on in almost normal fashion. Yoran spoke softly and avoided Laurice's eyes on the rare occasions when they met in a corridor. An assistant fetched food and drink for him to take among his instruments. Those three persons likewise were seldom away from the laboratory, never for long. What they did, what unfolded before them, was all-absorbing, overwhelming. She blessed it.

Mostly she, Vargen, and Copperhue watched the drama roll onward. *Darya* supplied not only exterior views, modified as desired, but graphics and commentary to the rec screens, adapted from the ongoing analysis of the computers. Laurice was soon wholly caught up. Vargen continued generally silent. But what can you say in the presence of inhuman might and majesty? She saw his tension lessen, until at last he smiled once in a while or his fingers responded when she caught his hand.

She had taken an opportunity to draw Copperhue aside. "How is he doing?" she asked, and trembled.

"He approaches calm," the Naxian said. "The shock was savage, like a half-healed physical wound torn open. However, he is not shattered. Given peace, inner peace, he should regain his sense of worth. It may be the stronger for this." The serpent body flowed through the air and curled lightly around her. "Until then, his strength comes from you."

She hugged it-him and laid her cheek against the dry, cablelike suppleness. "Thank you," she whispered.

With detectors and optics she found the scientific vessel occupying the fluctuant point that Yoran had desired. Vargen beamed a greeting—"out of curiosity," he said. How wonderful that he began again taking some interest in things. The craft turned out to be Helix's *Green Pyramid*. Amusing coincidence. No, not unduly improbable. The Naxians couldn't have dispatched a large fleet if they wanted to preserve secrecy. Traders, diplomats, outsiders of every kind would inevitably have noticed something afoot and started inquiring. Besides, if each vessel had half *Darya*'s capabilities, ten or fifteen should be ample. They must be that many, however, to contain the large scientific teams—twenty to fifty individuals per hull, she guessed—that made up for the relatively primitive robotics and automation.

If only we'd come with more of our own, Laurice thought. Well, we'll bring home enough knowledge that the Confederacy never will spring a surprise on the galaxy. . . . She grimaced. "We" in that context meant Yoran. She must admit it. She did not like it.

Green Pyramid had a partner, or guardian, or both. Crystal's flagship, whose name *Darya* rendered *Altitude,* maintained at a few kilometers from her. Probably specialists aboard conducted experiments of their own. Certainly she was where she was, after a rapid reshuffle of plans, to make sure that the Erthumoi observed the terms of the truce. Alone, she couldn't stop them, but by harassment she could make a breach pointless.

All vessels hovered isolated. Because it would interfere with various delicate instruments, transmission through hyperspace was stopped; and what did anybody have to say over the lasers? Paradoxically, the muteness made Laurice feel closer to yonder beings. Her folk would keep their promises. So would the Naxians. As the judgment instant neared, you forgot your merely mortal quarrels.

Shrouded in fire, the black holes sped to their destiny. Minute by minute, second by second, they swelled in sight, blazed more wildly brilliant, roared the louder throughout every spectrum of radiance. The disks were whirling storms, riven, aflare with eerie lightnings. Vast tatters broke off, exploded into flame, torrented back down or threw red spindrift across heaven before vanishing into vacuum. It was as if the stars, their light rays bent, scattered terrified from around those masses. Afloat in the captain's globe, Laurice heard the blood thunder in her ears like the hooves of galloping war-horses. And yet this was only a shadow show. To have seen with your bare eyes would have been to be stricken blind, and afterward die.

She gripped Vargen's hand. It was cold. His breath went harsh. The sky had burned over Novaya too; but not like this, not like this.

The black holes met.

Nobody in real time saw that. It was too swift. At one heartbeat they were well apart, at the next they blurred into streaks, and then light erupted. White it was at the center, raw sun stuff; thence it became night violet, dusk violet, day blue, steel blue, gold yellow, brass yellow, blood red, sunset red. Outward and outward it bloomed. The fringes were streams, fountains, lace in a wind. They arced over and began to return in a million different, pure mathematical curves.

"I didn't know it would be beautiful!" Laurice cried.

Force crammed her against her harness. Her head tossed. With no weight for protection, dizziness swept black across vision and mind. Another, opposite blow slammed, and another. The metal of the ship toned.

"Graviton surges," she dimly heard Vargen gasp. "Predicted—uneven—hang on—"

The waves passed. She floated. The noise and giddy dark drained from her head. He, in his chair, strained toward her. "How are you, darling?" The words quavered. "Are you hurt?"

"No. No. I . . . came through . . . intact, I think. You?"

"Yes. If you hadn't—" He mastered himself. "But you did. It was a, a wave of force. The physicists didn't expect it'd be this strong, with this short a wavelength. Most of it was supposed to spread out in the orbital plane— Look. Look."

The fire geysers rained back toward what had become a single fierce, flickery star. As they fell, their lovely chaos drew together and made rivers of many-hued splendor. The flows twisted, braided, formed flat spirals that rushed inward, trailing sparks. A new accretion disk was forming.

Elsewhere, though, half a dozen blobs of dancing, spitting luridness fled from them.

The light played unrestful over Vargen's face, as if he were a hunter on ancient Earth, crouched above his camp fire in a night when tigers and ghosts prowled. "Report," he said at the general intercom. "Everybody. *Darya*?"

"All well," the ship said. Her serenity was balm. "Minor damage, mostly from a blast of lasered gamma rays that struck well aft. Nothing disabling or not soon repairable. Interior background count went high for half a second, but the dose was within safe limits and the count is down to a level acceptable for twenty watches."

"We'll be gone well before then," Vargen promised. "Uh, crew?"

The replies babbled, joyous, one (never mind whose) half hysterical. No harm sustained.

"How'd the observations go?" Vargen asked tartly.

"We won't know for weeks," Yoran answered. "That flood of input— But it seems like every system functioned. I do believe we . . . we have a scientific revolution at birth."

Laurice's attention had stayed with the mystery. "It seems to be dimming," she ventured.

"It's receding fast," Yoran said. "The resultant momentum. But, I'm not sure yet, but I think the tensors aren't quite what relativity would predict. Something we don't understand came into play. Certainly that gravitational effect exceeded my top guess by orders of magnitude. Captain, we will follow the star. Won't we?"

"Of course," Vargen replied. "For as long as feasible. Taking due precautions. Positioning ourselves here, we took a bigger gamble than we knew. I don't want to push our luck further."

"Nor I, sir." Yoran laughed like a boy. "Not with everything we've got to carry home!"

They've forgotten their feud, Laurice thought. I have too. At least, it doesn't matter anymore. Probably it will again, when we are again among human things. But today it's of no importance whatsoever.

Carry home . . . Yes, this precious freight of knowledge. There must be more data aboard now than we could transmit back in days, maybe in tens of days. We have more in our care than just our lives.

"Those fiery clouds that got ejected," she asked, "why weren't they recaptured?"

"The energies released caused them to exceed escape velocity from the vicinity of the ergosphere," Yoran said. "I'm half afraid to calculate how much energy that was. The ergospheres themselves, like the event horizons, went through contortions as they met and fused. Space-time did. I don't know what happened in those microseconds. Maybe we never will." Awe shook his words. "For an instant, the gates stood open between entire universes."

"The hints alone should reveal a new cosmos to your minds," Copperhue murmured.

Laurice nodded, dazed more than comprehending. "But what, now, holds the clouds together? Why don't they whiff away, evaporate?"

Yoran laughed afresh. "Do you take me for an oracle, milady? At this stage, we can only guess. Magnetic bottle effects, conceivably, as in ball lightning. Or maybe each is the—the atmosphere around a new-formed mass. Yes, I think that's a bit more likely. But we'll find out."

"Those masses would need to be planet-sized," Vargen said low. "That gas is incandescent hot. It'd never stay around anything less. As if . . . this union tried to beget worlds—"

"Signal received," *Darya* broke in. "Audio on the fifth standard laser band. Code: 'Distress. Please respond immediately.' "

A dream hand caught Laurice around the throat.

"You know where it's from?" she heard Vargen snap.

"Yes. The Naxian ships just south of us. One of them." If *Darya* has to correct herself, is she frightened?

"Acknowledge and translate, for God's sake!"

Laurice had an impression that the hisses and whistles beneath the impersonal robotic voice were equally calm. "Crystal That Sparkles, commanding *Altitude*, beaming to Erthuma vessel *Darya*. We request information as to your condition after the event."

"We're in good shape," Vargen said. "You?"

"Not so," came after seconds of time lag. "We and *Green Pyramid* were tossed together, too fast for effective preventive action. Both ships are disabled. Casualties are severe."

"A gravitational vortex," Yoran said raggedly. "A potential well, an abnormal local metric, expanding principally in the main inertial plane. It didn't flatten to the ordinary curvature of space-time till it had passed you." Laurice thought he found refuge in theory. Did he utter mere guesses? Belike he did. Who was sure of anything, here?

Her eyes tracked the dwindling star that was not a star. It gleamed exquisite, like a ringed planet seen from a distance, save that it was also like a galaxy with a single spiral arm. There passed through her: If Harul hadn't settled for less than we wanted, *Darya* too would be drifting helpless, a wreck. I might be dead. Oh, he might be!

"We're sorry to hear that, madam," Vargen said. "Can we help?"

"I do not know," Crystal answered, "but you are our single hope. We have contacted our nearer fellows. Ordinarily we could wait for them. However, observation and calculation show we are on a collision trajectory with one of those gaseous objects spewed from the fusion. We shall enter it in approximately four hours and pass through the center. At its speed, that will go very fast. But radiometric measurements show temperatures near the core that even in so brief a passage will be lethal. No Naxian craft is close enough, with sufficient boost capability, to arrive before them."

Stillness descended. The time felt long until Vargen asked, slowly, "You have no escape? No auxiliaries, anything like that?"

"Nothing in working order," said Crystal. "Else I would not have troubled you. We realize that for you, too, a rescue may well be impossible."

"We can cross the distance between at maximum boost, ten Erthuma gravities, with turnover," *Darya* said, "in approximately one hundred and fifty minutes. To escape afterward, we should accelerate orthogonally to the thing's path, but at no more than five gravities, since you have injured persons with you and the hale will have no opportunity to prepare themselves either. This acceleration must begin no later than half an hour before predicted impact, if we are to avoid the hottest zone. Before we start, my crew must make ready; otherwise, at the end of the first boost they will be disabled, perhaps dead. Allowing time for that also, we should have half an hour, or slightly less, for the transfer of crews from your vessels to me.''

In short, Laurice thought, the operation is crazily dicey. No. We can't. The odds are too big against us.

Her gaze went to the clouds. She didn't know which of them was the murderer on its way, but they seemed much alike. Faerie nebulosity reached out around a glowing pink that must be gas overlying the white-hot, ultraviolet-hot, X-ray-hot middle. As she watched, small light streaks flashed from it and vanished. Meteors. No, they must in reality be monstrous gouts of fire.

''I see,'' Crystal was saying gravely. ''Our hope was slight at best. Since those are the actual parameters, the risk is unacceptable. I would make that judgment myself, were situations reversed. Thank you and farewell.''

''No, wait!'' Vargen clawed at the locks on his harness. ''We're coming. Crew, prepare for ten gee acceleration.''

Is this possible? ''Harul, you can't mean that,'' Laurice protested.

His look upon her was metallic. ''You heard me,'' he said. ''All of you did. Get into the tank. That's an order.''

The chamber was completely filled and closed off; should a sudden change of vector occur, slosh could be fatal. The salt water was at body temperature; apart from their sanitary units, skinsuits served only modesty. Afloat, loosely tethered, breathing through air tube and masks, you might soon have drowsed, were your faring peaceful. Not that comfort was complete. The liquid took weight off bones and muscles, it helped keep body fluids where they belonged. Yet heaviness dragged at interior organs, while nothing but medication held pain and weariness at bay. Eventually you must pay what your vigor was costing you, with interest.

A low, nearly subliminal pulse throbbed through Laurice. *Darya* could not hurl herself along at full power without a little of that immense energy escaping to sing in her structure. Hands and the minature control panel on which they rested were enlarged in vision, seemed closer than they were. Yet shipmates on every side had gone dim, half unreal, in a greenish twilight.

Talk went by conduction from a diaphragm in the mask. After the scramble and profanity of getting positioned were done and boost had commenced, silence replaced a privacy that no longer existed.

Laurice broke it first. "Captain," she said stiffly.

Vargen never took his eyes off the single viewscreen, before which he was. "Yes?"

"Captain, I petition you to reconsider. I believe the others will join me in this."

"I do, sir!" She had not expected shy Newan to speak up. "The science we're losing, that we might do every minute if we weren't idled here."

"The science we *will* lose, sir, if we don't survive," Thura chimed in. "That all the human race will."

"The chances of our survival are poor, you know," Laurice said.

"A crazy gamble," Enry felt emboldened to add, "and for what? For some snakes that did their best to keep us away."

"Mind your language," Vargen reprimanded in an automatic fashion. "Yoran, have you any comment?"

"Well, Captain, uh, well," the physicist replied, "of course, when you commanded, we obeyed. We're no mutineers. But it's not too late for you to reconsider and turn back, sir. Your impulse was generous—fearless, yes— but thinking it over, wouldn't you agree we have a higher duty?"

"Copperhue? . . . No, I forgot, your simultrans wouldn't work here." Laurice thought fleetingly how lonesome that must feel. Vargen turned his head. "But you have picked up a little Merse, I believe. Nod if you vote for us going on, wave your tail if you vote for us going back."

After seconds had mounted, it was the tail that moved.

Vargen barked a laugh. "Unanimous, eh? Except for me." He stared again at the viewscreen. From her post, Laurice saw it full of night; but he must be watching the flames. "However, I am the captain."

She summoned her will. "Sir," she said, "I have the authority to set our destination. It is in safe space."

"I have the authority to overrule you if I see a preemptive necessity."

"Crew may lawfully protest unreasonable orders."

"If the protest is denied, they must obey."

"This will mean a board of inquiry after the voyage."

"Yes. After the voyage."

"If the captain shows . . . dangerous incompetence, the crew may relieve him of his duties. The board of inquiry will decide whether or not they were justified. It is a desperate measure."

"How do you propose to carry it out? This ship is programmed to me." Vargen raised his voice, though it remained as cold as before. "*Darya,* would you remove me from command of you?"

"No," came the level answer. "What you attempt is exceedingly difficult and may fail, but success is possible, and it is not for me to make value judgments."

"Values," Vargen murmured. "Everybody always told me what value sentient life has. The old, old saying, 'Greater love has no man than this, that he lay down his life for his friends.' Don't you agree any longer? Have your beliefs suddenly changed? We are seven. There must be ten or twenty times that many aboard those ships. Civilized spacefarers go to the aid of the distressed. We shall."

Sharply: "My judgment is that we can do it, provided we keep our heads and work together. Otherwise we doubtless are doomed. I assume you are all able, self-controlled people when you choose to be. Very well, we'll now develop a basic plan of action. As we approach, I'll contact Crystal again, learn in detail what the situation is as of that time, and assign tasks."

"No, please, sir," Yoran stammered.

Laurice unclenched her jaws. "You heard the captain," she said. "Let's get cracking."

The sky burned.

A fireball glared lightning colored. It would have been blinding to behold, were it not shrouded in a vast nimbus that glowed blue, yellow, red with its own heat. Smoke streaked the vapors, ragged, hasty, as the thing whirled. Currents twisted themselves into maelstroms. The limb of the flattened disk faded toward darkness. Tongues of flame leaped from it, arced over, streamed sparks behind their deluge. At the equator, many broke off and sprang free, cometary incandescences. Those that were aimed forward ran ahead of the mass that birthed them. Right, left, above, below, they passed blazing around the ships. They would not gutter out for thousands of kilometers more.

If any of those thunderbolts hits us, we're done, Laurice knew.

Spacesuited, she clung to a handhold near the portside forward airlock and waited. A viewscreen showed a pale ghost of what lay ahead. *Darya* maneuvered now at fractions of a gravity, but shifts in direction brought momentary dizziness, as if chaos reached in to grab at her. The Naxian craft were outlined black across the oncoming lightstorm. Their impact had driven plates and ribs together, formed a single grotesque mass, two boughs reaching from a stump. It wobbled and tumbled. Shards danced around.

A fire tongue streaked, swelled, was gone. It had missed *Darya* by a few hundred meters. At Laurice's side, Vargen caught a breath, half a cry. In her audio receiver it sounded almost like the scream of a bullet. Through their helmets she saw sweat runnel down the creases in his face. "You shouldn't be here," she told him. "You belong in the command globe."

He shook his head. "The ship c-can cope. We need . . . every hand."

At least, she thought, he has enough sense left to refrain from boasting he won't send crew into any danger he won't meet himself. The hazards are much the same wherever we may be, with that ogre booming down on us. But if he stayed behind, he wouldn't be out *among* the meteors. And he'd have an overall view; he might make the snap decision a robot brain wouldn't, that saves us.

No use. I've tried. He's determined. And, true, we're ghastly undermanned as is.

Laurice swallowed fear, anger, bitterness, and braced herself. They were about to make contact.

Weight ended. She floated free. Silence pressed inward, save for noises of breath and her slugging heart. Voices went back and forth, she knew, *Darya*'s and Crystal's or Helix's or whoever was in charge over there; but she wasn't in that circuit. The screen showed her the silhouette of an extruded gang tube, groping for an airlock. Wormlike, obscene, amidst the terrible beauty of the flames. To hang here passive was to lie in nightmare. How long? Seconds, minutes, years? It had better be less than half an hour. That was about as much time as they had before death became inescapable. Could she choke down her shriek that long?

How had anybody stayed sane at Novaya?

Contact. Linkage. Weight returned, low but crazily, sickeningly shifty as *Darya* matched the gyrations of the other hulls. The airlock valve moved aside. The mouth beyond gaped. Laurice pushed into the chamber before she should lose her last nerve. Vargen followed. They collided, whirled about in clownish embrace, caromed off the side. The valve shut. For a moment they were adrift in blindness, and she wanted to hold him close.

The inner valve opened. Air brawled down the gang tube. The compartment beyond lay bared to vacuum. Laurice let the wind help her along. Frost formed briefly on dust, little streamers that glittered in the beams from wrist lights.

She and Vargen came forth into a cavern. Air fled and light fell undiffused, hard-edged. Things sprang solitary out of shadow that otherwise engulfed sight—save where the hull was rent and stars marched manifold past.

The rotations of the conjoined wrecks caught at your blood and balance, cast you about. Space was too confined for safe use of a jetpack. You must somehow recover, compensate, be a master juggler; and the ball you kept going was yourself.

Yourself and others. Naxians in their long, many-jointed spacesuits waited for deliverance. Most tumbled helpless. A number were violently nauseated, their helmets smeared with spew on which they choked. A handful (pseudopodful, Laurice thought with a lunatic chuckle) of trained personnel were there to shepherd them as well as might be. The task was too much for so few. Victims, especially the injured, kept flopping and drifting away. The humans went after them.

Things couldn't be so bad at the waist lock. It was joined to an unruptured section. Clumsy though they might be, Yoran and his scientists could give the Naxian marshals some help. And elsewhere, *Darya*'s three robots flitted to a part torn entirely loose. They would break in and tow back those whom they found.

But this half of *Green Pyramid* had been barred from the rest. Damaged servos didn't allow personnel trapped in it to transfer to the middle and await rescue. Instead, crewfolk from *Altitude* must bring extra spacesuits and, as rendezvous neared, herd, drag, manhandle the people into this ripped compartment, the only one that *Darya*'s forward gang tube could reach when the middle one was engaged.

Laurice's light picked out a threshing, drifting shape. She went for it. Spin changed its path. She kicked against a crumpled plate, intercepted, clutched. Panicky, the Naxian struggled in her arms. "Hold still, you idiot," she groaned.

Noises she could neither understand nor imitate gibbered in her ears. Some that were calm and steady came to dampen them. The Naxian didn't relax, but stiffened, became a load Laurice could manage. She heard the Merse: "Honored one, I am informed that several victims are near the breach in the hull." Back aboard *Darya,* simultrans active, Copperhue was the living message switchboard.

Laurice bore her burden to the tube mouth and gave it

an impetus. The passage was already half filled with bodies. A Naxian officer at either end clung by the tail to a handhold and issued orders. Several at a time, the fugitives were passing into the lock and thus to the Atheran ship. Laurice kicked off toward the gap where the stars danced.

Hoo! Nearly went through it! She clutched a piece of metal in time and cast light rays about. The serpentine forms appeared in the glow, suits ashimmer. They had wrapped themselves fast to whatever they found, lest they be cast adrift into space.

"Copperhue," Laurice called, "tell them to link hands or tails or whatever and let go when I take the lead. I'll guide them to the tube—"

Heaven vanished in a burst of brilliance. For a moment there was no more night. Throughout the cavern, each being, body, bit of wreckage sprang forth into sight. They had no color; that radiance showed them molten white. Thunder crashed in Laurice's skull. The doomsday blow sent her off, end over end, barely aware. She heard a man howl and knew it was Vargen. Dazzlement blew in rags. As if she dreamt, there passed across her: very near miss. Electric field. Discharge. How close by now are we to the volcano?

Then a solidity captured her, and brought her to rest, and she heard, "Laurice, are you all right, oh, Laurice."

Slowly, she looked about her. The fire splash afterimages began to fade; she glimpsed stars. The ringing in her ears diminished. I'm alive, she knew.

"Get into the tube," Vargen chattered. "Back aboard *Darya*. I'll finish here."

"No," she said hoarsely. "You go on. Back to your work. We've damn little time left. I'll join you in a couple of minutes."

A sob caught in his throat. He released her and sped off.

Stars, Milky Way, sister galaxies shone in majesty. Among them the black hole and its disk were a jewel, minute and dwindling. Even the cloud from which *Darya* fled was now scarcely more than another gleam in the brightness-crowded dark. The crimson that for minutes had raged and roared about her was become a memory. She had radiated its heat into space. The brutality of five-gee boost lingered only in aches, bruises, exhaustion, nothing that a good rest wouldn't heal; she flew at gentle Erthuma weight.

Memory still echoed. Nor had the ship yet relinquished her booty. Snakelike bodies crowded the decks. Pungent odors and sibilant words filled the air. Laurice picked a way among them, bound aft. When she thought some hailed her, she responded with a nod or a wave and passed on. It was all she could do. They had their medics and others tending to the hurt among them. She was ignorant of their requirements, and in any case wrung dry, wanting no more than to creep into her cubicle, draw the bunk sheet over her, and sleep.

Her course took her past the laboratory. Yoran saw and shambled to the door. "Milady," he called in an undertone. She heard urgency and stopped. He beckoned her to enter. They were alone there, the others having gone to their own places. His back was bent and fatigue showed leaden in every gesture. Nonetheless the ugly face grinned.

"What do you want?" she asked.

He rubbed his hands together. "I wanted you to know first, milady." He leaned close. She was too tired to draw back. He spoke in a near whisper, although no Naxians were in this corridor and probably none but Copperhue knew any Merse. "As we were finishing the evacuation, milady, I saw one of them carrying a data box, and what'd be in it but their observations? Different model from any of ours, but it had to be a data box. Things were crowded, confused. I shoved in and slipped it right out of that ridiculous false hand. The bearer didn't notice; walking wounded. Nobody did. I've got it here, and I'm about to copy off the file. Then I'll leave the box for them to find, as though it got dropped accidentally. But when the stuff's translated, we'll know what they found out, at least this part of what they did. So our efforts paid off that much, didn't they, milady?"

You little tumor, she thought. I shouldn't accept this.

But I suppose I must. Maybe I should even congratulate you.

He peered at her. "I did well, don't you think, milady?" he asked. "You'll put in a good word for me when we get home, won't you, milady?"

"I'll stay neutral, if I can. It's up to you." She turned and left.

Copperhue, bound forward with its-his personal kit, met her farther on. They halted. "How fare you, honored one?" it-he greeted. Under the 'trans, did she hear concern? "I have not seen you since you went to aid in the rescue."

"I'm all right," she said. "Everybody is, or as much as could be expected, I guess. You?"

"Sh-s-s, I hold back. The Naxian officers know that a member of their race has been aboard this ship, but they know no more than that. Captain Vargen agrees it is best they not meet me. On his advice, I seek the number two hold."

Slightly surprised, Laurice noticed herself bridle. "I should hope, after what we've done, they won't cause trouble."

"No, but why provoke emotions? I can bide my time. Soon we make rendezvous and transfer our passengers. After that, in view of our condition and the delta vee we have expended, Captain Vargen says we shall go straight home. Surely other researchers will come from Ather, and from many more worlds."

"I don't imagine those Pythons are so grateful to us they'll make their discoveries public."

"Would you in their place, honored one?"

Laurice laughed a bit. "No, probably not." Though in the long run, now that the great secret is out, everybody will know everything that can be known about it.

She stroked Copperhue's head. "Go rest, then," she said, "Pleasant dreams."

"I fear yours will not be," it-he replied.

Her hand froze where it was. After a space she said, "Well, of course you feel what I'm feeling."

"I feel that you are woeful. I wish I could help."

"And . . . and him?"

"He was full of pride and gladness, until there came a dread I believe was on your account. That was the last I saw of him, about a quarter hour ago."

"Don't worry about it."

"I do not worry much about you, honored one. You are undaunted. He— But go, since that is your wish. May the time be short until your happier day."

Laurice walked on.

In the crew section, the assistant physicists had already closed their doors and must be sound asleep. Deck, bulkheads, overhead reached gray and empty, save for the tall form that waited.

She jarred to a stop. They stood for a time. Air rustled around them. "Laurice," Vargen said finally.

"I should think you'd be resting or else in conference with Commander Crystal," she stated.

"This is more important." He made as if to approach her, but curbed the motion. "Laurice, why are you here? Why not the cabin? When you didn't show, I asked *Darya*, and—"

"If you please," she said, "I am very tired and need some rest of my own."

Bewilderment ravaged the haggard features. "Laurice, what's wrong? We saved those beings, we're safe ourselves, why do you look at me that way?"

Get this over with. "*You* saved them. It was your decison, your will."

"But—no, wait." He swallowed, straightened his shoulders, and said, "I see. You're angry because I put your life at risk. No, that's unfair. Because I gambled with everybody's. Including mine."

"No," she sighed, "you do not see. It's because of why you did."

He stared.

"Worse than staking us, you staked what we'd gained here for our people," she told him. "It was in fact a crazy thing to do, from any normal viewpoint. Maybe, morally, it was justified. Seven lives, a valuable ship, and an invaluable store of knowledge, against half a hundred other lives. We did win through, and I daresay we have gotten some goodwill that our leaders may find useful in future negotiations. But . . . Vargen, none of this was what you had in mind. Not really. Was it?"

"What do you mean?" she barely heard.

She shook her head, like one who remembers a sorrow. "You redeemed yourself. You met again with the terror you'd run from, and this time you overcame it, first in your spirit, then in reality. Even if you'd died, you'd have won what mattered, the respect of your peers back, and of yourself.

"I'd come to know you. Copperhue's now confirmed my understanding, but it wasn't necessary. I knew. What mattered to you above all else—the only thing that mattered—was your redemption."

"No," he croaked, and reached for her.

She denied the wish to lay her head on his breast. "Yes," she said. "Oh, never fear. You'll receive the honors you've earned, and I'll speak never a word against them. But I can't stay with any creature so selfish. Please leave me alone."

She dodged by him, into her cubicle, and shut the door. The light came on. She doused it and lay down in the kindly darkness.

ISLAND OF THE GODS

HARRY TURTLEDOVE

WAVES SLAPPED GENTLY AGAINST THE BOW OF THE galley *Hewnall* as it drew near the Island of the Gods. That was what the locals called it, at any rate; Terry Fischer thought of it as Laputa. The setting sun, a G-3 star the Azusans called Tonclif, silhouetted the artifacts, monuments, whatever they were, that the Hidden Folk had left on Laputa—and floating above it. That was how the island got its Erthuma name.

The Hidden Folk had been gone at least a million years. Their creations seemed as fresh as if they'd left yesterday and would be back tomorrow. Like all the remains of the Hidden Folk, they also remained maddeningly incomprehensible.

The merely human eye had trouble even grasping the proper proportions of some of those—things—ahead. Lines faded, twisted, shifted; curves bent in ways curves had no business bending.

Terry looked away, shaking her head. "This isn't what alien ruins are supposed to be like," she muttered, not for the first time. "Where's the big monolith that looks like the old UN building's granddad?"

"I presume this is the image to which you refer," the robot Chives said. It projected a scene from the immortal *2001*: man-apes capering around a black rectangular prism.

"Yes, that's it," Terry said. "Now turn it off, if you please. You're making the natives restless." Several crewmales had stopped rowing to gape at the picture hanging in the air. The rowmaster hissed at them. They got back into their rhythm before the oars fouled.

"My apologies," Chives said. The still from *2001* vanished. The star called Tonclif glittered off the coat of green enamel that gave Chives its name. Rather more to the point, the paint job made the robot the same color as the Azusans, and made them less nervous about it. Not that it much resembled them otherwise: they were man-sized bipeds, yes, but dinosaurian, with clawed hands, forward-slung torsos, and long, stiff, spiky tails to counterbalance the weight of those torsos.

They were also primitives, Terry thought with faint contempt. The *Hewnall* was as fine a machine as they could build, yet the Greeks had sailed better when their fleet beat Xerxes' at Salamis. But for Laputa and its other chief oddity, Tonclif IV might have been one of the many worlds that, while they housed intelligent life, were hardly worth visiting.

Lorah chose that moment to come spiraling down from what Terry kept wanting to call the Crotonite's nest. His wings were too weak to let him fly in Tonclif's atmosphere, but he still made a fine sailplane. He landed just in front of Terry, folded those batlike wings over his back. His small black eyes glittered as he peered up at the human.

"What was that picture you were looking at?" he demanded. His short beak and the breathing tube that ran into the corner of his mouth from the tank strapped on his chest made his English hard to follow, but Terry had grown used to it.

"A scene from an old film—a piece of visual fiction," she answered.

"Fiction," Lorah said scornfully. "This is another word for lies."

"No, this is a tale known not to be true," Terry said. "It was an early imagining of what contact with a more advanced species might be like for humans."

"You see the reality before you." Lorah preened his fine gray hair. He turned, used one of his two stubby arms to point to the great masses floating above the island they were approaching. "You also see proof ahead that the Hidden Folk were winged, as we are. Why else would they have built as they did? Surely no dirt-hugger would have felt at ease so far off the ground."

"Oh, I don't know," Terry said easily. "The human name for this place comes from an island that floated in the air in one of our fables."

Lorah hissed at her. Crotonites had moods, and reveled in them. Terry was briefly glad she had got Lorah annoyed. In a perverse way, he would be happier on account of it.

"More lies. More human frivolity," he said after another sip on the supplemental oxygen heavily laced with ammonia and hydrogen cyanide that let him survive in what was, to him, an unpleasantly thin atmosphere. "The Hidden Folk, I assure you, had no use for lies or frivolity."

"To be perfectly accurate, we have no idea what the Hidden Folk had uses for," Chives said. "By 'we,' I include not only Erthumoi but all six starfaring races currently inhabiting this galaxy."

If the Crotonite had hissed at Terry, he snarled at the robot: "I do not care to discuss the matter with an overautomated bottle opener."

None of the other five species with advanced technology had gone in for developing artificial intelligences. The big, slow Samians found the concept vastly amusing. Crotonites tended to look on it as a perversion of both machinery and intelligence. Crotonites, Terry thought, tended to look on everything they hadn't come up with for themselves as a perversion of one kind or another.

"Chives is right, Lorah, as I'm sure you know quite well enough," she said sharply. "If we were sure of anything much about the Hidden Folk, we wouldn't need to keep exploring sites like this one in the hope that one day parts of them would start to make sense."

"They make sense enough to my people," Lorah retorted. "It is you other races whose brains are stuck down in the dirt with your bodies and cannot soar toward the truth."

"Your comment reminds me of a tale in my database,"

Chives observed, his voice electronically smooth as always: "the tale of the mentally defective Earthman who could not recognize his own illness, but instead projected it outward, saying to his only friend, 'Aye, the whole world's mad save me and thee, and I have my doubts about thee.' "

Terry knew Chives was not programmed to be deliberately insulting. Its database was so large, though, that everything anybody said reminded it of a story. Since by human standards Crotonites were self-centered and rude, the stories they made it recall also ran in that direction.

Before Lorah went from snarling at Chives to screeching at it, the Azusans distracted him by starting to screech themselves. They had formidable teeth for an intelligent species, Terry thought—as they hooted and pointed, she was reminded of nothing so much as a pack of *Deinonychus* that had just spotted some large, lumbering herbivorous dinosaur to tear and rend.

"What's happened?" Terry called. Chives translated her words into the Azusans' language. She kept repeating herself, and Chives kept getting louder, until the locals finally paid attention to her.

"That ship beached there in the harbor." The *Hewnall*'s captain was a stalwart male named Ekrekek. He kept the claws on his index fingers filed to needle points. The left one sparkled now as he stabbed it out toward the offending vessel.

Terry looked at the ship. It looked like a ship, longer and broader than the *Hewnall,* perhaps, but just a ship. She carried some lightweight binoculars on her belt. She looked at it through them. She still couldn't see anything wrong with it. "What about it?" she asked.

Ekrekek made a series of noises like something going badly wrong inside a steam engine. "Expletives," Chives said helpfully. After a while, the captain began mixing in a few words that were not expletives: "That's a tail-biting, nest-robbing, egg-sucking Gormanian ship, that's what about it."

"Oh," Terry said, and then again: "Oh." The pack of *Deinonychus* had not spotted prey after all. They'd spotted rivals. Tonclif IV was one of the handful of worlds in the galaxy with two intelligent species. Saying Azusans and Gormanians did not get along was like saying magnesium oxidized rapidly when heated: It was true, but it didn't convey the full flavor of the reaction.

That was so most of the time, at any rate. Terry said, "Is this not the Island of the Gods? No one fights on the Island of the Gods."

Gormanians and Azusans agreed on that. It was about the only thing on which they did agree. The island they called the Island of the Gods lay about midway between the continents where their two species had evolved. They'd both discovered it about the same time. The awe the remains of the Hidden Folk raised in them was enough to overcome even the hatred they felt for each other.

But now, Ekrekek said, "It is our time, my people's time, to visit the holy island. The Gormanians have no business setting foot there for the next two moons. We would be within our rights to slay them."

For the past hundred years and more, the six starfaring races of the galaxy had upheld and strengthened the truce the two local species had worked out on their own. That was only partly altruism: Research on the Hidden Folks' artifacts went more smoothly if the locals were not busy killing each other. The easiest way to keep Azusans from fighting Gormanians was never to let the twain meet. Fortunately, their religious calendars made it practical for each species to visit the island exclusively for half the year.

Terry wondered why the Gormanian had come here now. She said, "Surely only an emergency would have made that ship land on the Island of the Gods out of season."

"And so?" Ekrekek answered. "They have transgressed, and we will make them pay for their transgressions." He wore only a series of belts. Some were decorative; some, along with his gilded tailspikes, showed his rank; some were for hanging things on—the Azusan equivalent of pockets. From one of the latter he took a bronze-headed axe and waved it about. His sailors screeched. They brandished weapons too.

Lorah spread his wings. With them folded on his back, he looked small and unimpressive. Now they enfolded him like a cape, lending him a presence he had not had before. He did not need Chives to translate for him; he spoke Azusan himself, and sarcastic Azusan at that: "You, my good captain Ekrekek, are an idiot."

"And you are a liar," Ekrekek retorted, his manners bad as the Crotonite's. "The gods decree that we kill the sixlegs where and when we find them. Finding them on the gods' own island in our proper time can only mean a gift from the gods of their blood."

"Their gods bid them slay you," Lorah answered, "and from the size of their ship as many of them are here as of you. How do you propose to return to Azusa with most of your crew slain? Do your gods bid you to slay yourselves to no purpose?"

"Anyone who dies killing a Gormanian assures himself a joyous afterlife," Ekrekek said. Even so, he lowered his axe, though he did not let go of it.

"That may be," Chives broke in, "but are you, are any of you"—it rotated its metal head through three hundred sixty degrees to look at all the sailors; the Azusans stared and muttered to themselves—"so eager to enter the afterlife at this moment?"

"Keep quiet, contraption," Lorah said. "I am doing well enough on my own."

While Ekrekek still looked defiant, Chives's remark had its effect on the Azusan captain's crew. Suddenly they seemed to remember that, while they were going to fight the Gormanians, the Gormanians would also fight back.

Terry watched Ekrekek gauge his males; he seemed to be making the same calculation she was. She said, "For all you know, shipmaster, the Gormanians may already be in ambush among the wonders on the Island of the Gods, ready to take you by surprise after you land."

"They will be sorry if they try," Ekrekek said. Terry's heart sank. Getting caught in the middle of a batch of battling primitives was not why she'd come to Tonclif IV. Then the captain of the *Hewnall* went on, "But we will stretch a point for the sake of you off-worlders. So long as the cursed sixlegs do not attack us, we will not bare our weapons against them."

Some of the sailors hissed angrily at that. Ekrekek shouted them down. "He says he is the captain, and they will have to fight him before they can get to the Gormanians," Chives translated for Terry. She knew she wouldn't want to take on Ekrekek, not without a neuronic whip tuned to his species—or maybe a portable rocket launcher.

Lorah said, "Folk from any truly intelligent race would learn a language for themselves instead of giving the work to an unreliable machine."

"Oh, shut up," Terry muttered. The other five starfaring peoples were all better linguists than humans. That was true of Crotonites even without the brain amplifiers they had implanted when they needed to carry several extra languages around for a limited time, as Lorah was doing now. Terry stifled the urge to tell him to place the amplifier in a body cavity for which it had not been designed.

Chives drew a flare pistol from the pocket in his right thigh and fired it up and out, being careful to miss the *Hewnall*'s rigging. As the brilliant red flare slowly descended toward the sea, Lorah screeched, "What did you do that for, you—" English invective failed him; he squawked something offensive in his own language. "I think the salt spray is corroding your circuits."

Unlike Terry, Chives had no temper to lose; none had been programmed into him. She envied him for that. He answered calmly, "The flare will let the Gormanians know our ship carries off-planet folk. That should make them less eager to attack these Azusans on sight."

"I hope so," Terry said. She carried nothing more lethal than a stunner that could not outrange a Gormanian crossbow. She did not think Lorah bore any more dangerous weapons. No one was supposed to, not on worlds with intelligent but low-tech natives. Of course, Crotonites were almost as good as humans at getting around rules they didn't care for.

The *Hewnall* glided into the habor of the Island of the Gods. Chives fired off another flare, blue this time. Lorah said nothing, by which Terry concluded he'd decided it was a good idea.

The ship grounded with a jolt. Terry grabbed a rail to keep from being pitched over the side. Ekrekek shouted orders. Azusans sprang down onto the sand. Others pitched ropes to them. They dragged the *Hewnall* further out of the water so it would not refloat at high tide.

"The crew of the Gormanian vessel is being very quiet," Chives observed. The other ship was beached three or four hundred meters away from the *Hewnall*.

"You're right. They should be paying us some attention, shouldn't they?" Terry brought her binoculars up to her eyes again. The Gormanian ship seemed to leap closer. She could spell out its name in the syllabic script the Gormanians used: *Agwadulsi*. She could not see anyone aboard. She said as much.

"You must be wrong. Not even barbarians would be stupid enough to abandon their ship without leaving so much as a sentry behind," Lorah said. "Perhaps this is especially true of barbarians, in fact, as they often need to make sure they are not about to be attacked."

"I would have thought the same." Terry did not like agreeing with the Crotonite about anything, but had no choice here. "But I saw what I saw. Look for yourself." She held the binoculars out to him.

"I don't need your toys." Lorah used one of his short, feeble arms to wave the binoculars away. He peered toward the *Agwadulsi*, boasting, "Eyes modified in the genes serve me better."

"Eyes modified in the genes won't see anything if there's nothing to see," Terry said.

Lorah did not answer for some little while. Then, grudgingly, he admitted, "I also see no one. Perhaps the Gormanians observed our approach and are hiding on the deck below our level of vision."

"That is unlikely on two counts," Chives said. "First, Gormanian ships are not often constructed with such a deck. Second, I make no infrared signature that would indicate the presence of any warm-blooded life-forms aboard. From some of the hasty lashings I observe, and the missing section of rail, I would say this ship has recently encountered heavy weather. Whether that is germane, I could not speculate."

The Crotonite took no notice of the robot. From that, Terry concluded he could not argue with Chives. Chives might be an artificial intelligence, she thought, but it was not a petulant one. Such musings vanished in her greater concern: "Where *are* the Gormanians?" she said.

No one had an answer. Terry and Chives walked down the gangplank. Her boots dug into fine gray sand. Lorah scrambled to the top of the rail and glided down beside her. However much he despised humans—which went double for human-built AIs—he preferred civilized company to that of the locals.

Some of the Azusan sailors, spears and axes at the ready, advanced on the *Agwadulsi*. After a cautious pause, one of the Azusans cast a looped line until it caught on a belaying pin. Tails flailed as a couple of sailors scrambled up the line onto the Gormanian galley. When they reappeared, they spread their hands in a very humanlike gesture of bewilderment.

"The ship *is* empty, then," Terry said.

Chives translated the remark for Ekrekek, who was standing close by. The Azusan captain let out a baffled hiss. "What are the stinking sixlegs playing at?" he demanded. "We have only to burn their ship and sail off to put them in desperate straits. They are vile, but they are not stupid. Why do they leave themselves vulnerable to us?"

"If we knew, we would tell you," Terry said, though she doubted Lorah would tell anyone not a Crotonite anything of any importance if he could help it. No, she admitted to herself, that was not entirely true. "We depend on you, after all, to return us to our base on Azusa."

"Will I be able to?" Ekrekek asked. "Can I be sure the accursed Gormanians have not found some sorcery that lets them turn themselves invisible so they can fall on us without danger?" He stuck out his long, bifurcated tongue in an apotropaic gesture.

"There is no such a thing as magic," Lorah said contemptuously.

"Of course there is," Ekrekek told him, shocked. "How else to account for things like you?"

So there, Terry thought. Before she could answer, Chives said, "Good captain, you surely know that the inside of the eye must be dark to see. If the Gormanians made their flesh invisible, light would strike their eyes from all sides and they would be blind. That, then, is a magic you need not fear."

"It may be so," Ekrekek admitted after pausing for a while to work through the robot's logic.

An Azusan came dashing back from the *Agwadulsi,* his torso held almost parallel to the ground and his tail stuck straight out behind to balance him. "Captain, a scent trail from the sixlegs' ship leads into the jungle. We find no other traces of their reek. For whatever reason, they all seem to have gone that way."

Ekrekek's tail lashed back and forth. "Something mad, but something all the same. Very well." He glanced at the sky. Light was fading fast. "Come morning, we—some of us—will follow. The Gormanian stench will not have vanished by then, and I do not care to enter the jungle in the dark. When we can see as well as smell, we will learn what evil reasons they have for disturbing the Island of the Gods." He turned to Terry, Lorah, and Chives. "Will you accompany my males? Seeing you among us might make the Gormanians less willing to attack from ambush."

"Yes," Terry said at once. Lorah also agreed, though more slowly and less enthusiastically.

"You track by scent?" Chives asked Ekrekek the next morning as an armed Azusan party, and the off-worlders with it, headed down a trail through thick green-blue vegetation. The captain did not risk his whole crew; about half waited back at the *Hewnall.*

"My nose is not keen like a ftorek's," Ekrekek answered, "but I can pick up the dead-meat stink of a sixlegs well enough. Don't you smell it yourself?"

"I have no sense of smell," Chives said. "I was not built with one." Ekrekek stared at the robot, perhaps out of pity for its lack, perhaps because it spoke of itself as being built rather than born or hatched.

When Chives relayed the conversation to Terry, she sniffed the air, trying to pick out the odor Ekrekek had described. Maybe the Azusans' noses were better than they thought, or perhaps the trail they were following was to her swallowed up by all the other unfamiliar scents in the jungle, for she noticed no smell like the one the captain had mentioned.

Nostrils low to the ground, the captain and his crewmales moved confidently down the narrow paths that meandered, seemingly at random, through the jungle. The leafy canopy overhead blocked off the sun so well that Terry did not know in which direction they were going until she checked her wrist compass.

The jungle plants were not much different from the ones that grew near the Azusan port out of which the *Hewnall* had sailed. The ocean currents flowed from east to west, from Azusa toward Gorman, so few if any Gormanian plants had ever established themselves on the Island of the Gods.

The animals, what little Terry saw of them, were also related to those of Azusa: four-limbed, scaly, often erect on their hind legs. Between the Island of the Gods and the continent of Gorman lay Tonclif IV's equivalent of Wallace's Line: a stretch of deep ocean that had been deep ocean for several hundred million years, preventing any interchange of land fauna until the Azusans and the very different Gormanians discovered one another.

The Azusan band came out into a clearing. Even so, no sun shone overhead: One of the Hidden Folk's huge floating mysteries blocked it from view. Another, smaller, noncomprehensible object sat in the center of the clearing.

Terry raised her camera, took a holo of it, then shifted from still to vid and walked all the way around it, photographing as she went. As was true of all Hidden Folk gadgets, this one showed no sign of wear. All its edges were sharp, all its colors bright and unfaded. Ground-covering plants grew up to it, but not on it or over it. If it was for anything more than keeping itself tidy, though, no one knew what.

"You have a curious ritual," Ekrekek said when Terry returned to the band. "Our worship is simpler." He and his sailors saluted the artifact as they might have a superior officer, then walked around it to follow the Gormanians' odor trail.

"We must stop to make a thorough examination of this tool of the Hidden Folk," Lorah said. "That, after all, is why we came to this wing-forsaken place. Stop, I say!" he shouted as Ekrekek prepared to press on.

"Lorah, that whatsit has been sitting there for close to a million years," Terry said. "It's not going to up and run away while we're finding out what happened to the Gormanians."

"I suppose not," the Crotonite admitted with poor grace. "But it remains galling to have to bypass the mission for which we have traveled so far."

"Yes, I know. At a first quick look, that one reminds me of Hidden Folk remains on Bongliich III and Rop and maybe Mopona II. Those are supposed to be late sites. If this is another one, it might help us figure out in which direction the Hidden Folk pulled out of the galaxy, if not why."

"The why is simple," Lorah said, fixing her with his usual stare of dislike. "They were sickened by the evolution of so many wingless races here, and withdrew in disgust."

Terry did not bother to reply. Crotonites were even fonder of writing racially flavored history than humans ever had been. They took the stuff seriously, too, no matter how nonsensical it sounded to everyone else in the galaxy. Terry supposed that being the only starfaring species with wings gave them a skewed view of things.

Being winged also left Lorah slow and clumsy on the ground. Without his supplementary atmosphere, he would not have lasted long on Tonclif IV. Even with it, he kept falling to the rear of the Azusan troop. Finally, Ekrekek snapped, "If you cannot move more quickly, starfarer, we will leave you behind alone."

"Would you like me to carry you?" Chives asked the Crotonite. "Your weight would not impede me to any great degree."

Terry expected Lorah to snarl and say no. Instead, he opened his mouth wide, the Crotonite equivalent of a big smile. "Certainly. It will be a pleasure to see a machine employed as a machine, rather than fancying itself an intelligent being."

"I am designed to do my best to ameliorate the inefficiencies of organic life," Chives said, which made Lorah shut his jaws with a snap. Nevertheless, he let the robot lift him and carry him along.

Artifacts of the Hidden Folk appeared with greater and greater frequency as Ekrekek and his band pushed deeper into the jungle. Terry photographed each one as she hurried by; the Azusans began saluting without stopping. Most of the remains kept on reminding the human of Hidden Folk remains presumed to be late. Past that, no one resembled any other in anything save being both incomprehensible and apparently indestructible.

"How much further will you go?" Terry asked Ekrekek after several kilometers. "Do you want to risk being cut off from the *Hewnall*?"

"No." The captain's mouth gaped wider than Lorah's ever had; Azusans panted rather than sweated. "But the sixlegs, curse them, are moving toward the temples we have set up to the gods of the island, toward land upon which they have no business setting their stinking furry feet at any time of the year, let alone during a moon when their kind are not allowed here. We will punish them for that."

The Azusans and their off-world companions hurried on. The next object the Hidden Folk left behind was what looked like an empty plastic wading pool, save that its orange jagged wall surrounded a fifty-meter circle. A gap perhaps two meters wide let people enter that circle. After the ritual salutes, Ekrekek and his sailors cautiously went inside, Terry, Chives, and Lorah in their midst.

"What's the matter?" Terry asked when the Azusans began to mill about in confusion.

Ekrekek pointed to the ground. It was bare rock. It was, Terry thought, likely the same bare rock that had been there when the Hidden Folk did whatever they did to set this structure in place—as far as anyone could tell, they built for eternity. But the captain of the *Hewnall* did not care about that. "The trail—ends here," he said.

"But it can't," Terry protested automatically.

"But it does," Ekrekek said. "For all I know, the gods grew angry at the Gormanians for trespassing on holy ground and swallowed them up."

That remark made several of the sailors with him hastily scurry back out of the circle. It also made Terry's eyes go wide. "There's no record of any Hidden Folk artifact on Tonclif IV ever going active, is there?" she asked Chives and Lorah.

"None," the Crotonite and the robot answered at the same time. They both sounded positive.

"I didn't think so, either." Terry's voice was taut with excitement. Some things the Hidden Folk had left behind on other worlds and in space were still live (for all that anyone could figure out about Hidden Folk technology, that might have been literally true). They did what they did no matter what starfarers tried with them. Some were beautiful, some exciting, some dangerous—some all three at once. Assuming one lived to get them back to a civilized world, active Hidden Folk artifacts could make one—or even three—rich for life.

Assuming . . . Terry got out of the circle herself. If it had already disposed of a good many Gormanians, she saw no reason to doubt it might do the same to her. When Chives followed, Lorah said not a word in protest. She walked around the artifact, taking pictures.

A voice speaking Azusan—but not a hissing Azusan voice, rather one deep and throaty—called from the cover of the undergrowth ahead: "I have a good bow. I can slay several of you before you hunt me down. But I will speak to you of what I saw the gods do if you pledge not to harm me once I show myself."

Terry nodded vigorously. On Chives's shoulders, Lorah half spread his wings in a Crotonite gesture of agreement. But the decision was not theirs to make. They both looked to Ekrekek. The captain said, "Aye, come ahead, sixlegs.

I promise safe conduct for you. With so many of my folk here, one Gormanian is scarcely worth killing."

Bushes rustled. The Gormanian, still carrying a bow, but with no arrow in it, stepped out into the clearing. The dominant life-forms of Tonclif IV's western continent were hexapodal mammaloids: funny-looking centaurs, in other words.

That was close enough for government work, anyhow, even if the local's south end wasn't particularly horselike and his—no, her, for six bright pink nipples poked through the matted gray fur—torso even less humanoid. She said, "My queen will pay ransom for me. I am Gussaw, captain of the *Agwadulsi*."

"You are also on the Island of the Gods out of season," Ekrekek said. "Will your queen ransom such an oathbreaker as you?"

Some of Ekrekek's crewmales snarled at the Gormanian, hefted their weapons. Terry said quickly, "Let Captain Gussaw tell what happened to her crew. That is of interest to all of us."

"Thank you—off-worlder?" Gussaw's voice was unsure; starfarers had rather more to do with Azusa than Gorman. The centaur's round, shaggy ears twitched as her head swiveled to take in the human and then to robot and Crotonite. She went on, "Yes, I know it is not our time here, but we caught a storm and were forced to make the best—the only—landfall we could."

Ekrekek's tail lashed back and forth. "There looked to be damage," he admitted. "Whether it was true storm-hurt or applied with intention to deceive remains as yet unhatched."

"You are seeing threats where none exists, Captain," Lorah said. Terry squeaked, but managed to swallow her laugh. This sort of comment from a member of the most paranoid species in the galaxy? Lorah had to be even more eager to find out about the circle of the Hidden Folk than Terry was.

"When it comes to sixlegs, I always see threats," Ekrekek said.

"Scale-face, right now I am too tired and hungry to threaten anyone," Gussaw said.

Terry supposed it was inevitable that the Gormanians would have as unflattering a name for the Azusans as vice versa. She said, "Captain Ekrekek, could you or your sailors give Gussaw something to eat? After she's fed, I expect she will tell us what happened to the rest of her crew."

"*Feed* the Gormanian?" Ekrekek could not have sounded more scandalized if she'd asked him to mate with Gussaw. But he was not a fool, nor unadaptable. Though he hissed and spluttered to himself, at last he said, "Well, the situation is unusual, and I suppose we have to keep the sixlegs alive to ransom her. Sarriri, you have some meat there. Give the Gormanian a chunk."

Sarriri hissed too, but the *Hewnall* had a disciplined crew. The sailor cut some salt meat off the gray slab she carried, tossed it in Gussaw's direction. Gussaw's large round eyes were anything but delighted. "Lizard's meat," she said. Gormanians were omnivores, unlike the carnivorous Azusans. But hunger won over distaste. Gussaw needed to do more chewing than, say, Ekrekek would have, but the meat vanished quickly all the same.

"Now you will talk," Ekrekek said the moment Gussaw was finished. To back up the captain's words, several sailors raised weapons.

"Put those down," the Gormanian said wearily. "You do not need them. I said I would talk, and I will. We beached here, let me see, four days ago. I sent teams into the forest to cut timber for repairs. I knew those could only be rough, but they would have let us sail back to Gorman. Things went well enough the first day, but that night we started seeing lights in the woods."

"Lights in the woods?" Ekrekek echoed. "Don't be absurd. Your pirates were the only people here. What could make lights in the woods?"

"They came from the gods' things here," Gussaw answered, "from this one that swallowed my crew and from the others as well. Some shone blue, some orange, some the purest white. Once we even saw for an instant a flash of white light form that magic floating thing there." The Gormanian raised a four-fingered hand, pointed to one of the Hidden Folk's airborne structures that had been defying gravity for a thousand millennia now.

Defying gravity was all it had been doing, though, so far as anyone knew. And for all anyone knew, the grounded artifacts here hadn't done anything, either, except to stay perfectly preserved—which, Terry supposed, ought to count for something.

Before she could speak, Ekrekek said, "Now I know you lie, sixlegs. The gods' things do not glow, they simply are." That was what she had been thinking, though put in more hostile terms.

"Tell me where my sailors are and I will admit I am a liar," Gussaw said. "Till you can do that, would you not say that listening and learning seem a wiser course?"

Ekrekek took a step forward. "Don't do anything you'll be sorry for later," Terry said quickly. She put her hand on the hilt of her stun pistol.

"How could I be sorry for killing a Gormanian?" Ekrekek said. But he checked himself. "Still, the sixlegs may possibly know something worth telling. Go on, sixlegs. So, you say the gods' things glowed in the night. I am not sure I believe this but, as you say, I do not know where you have hidden your sailors, either. Tell me about them. Tell me what made you so stupid as to take your whole crew off the *Agwadulsi* and send them traipsing through the jungle. If your kind were all such great fools, we would have exterminated you as soon as we met you."

Terry gulped at the Azusan's casual wish for successful genocide. Again, though, he'd found an insulting way to ask an important question. Had Terry commanded the Gormanian galley, she would have left at least some of the sailors behind there.

Gussaw said, "Scale-face, there you have me. When morning came, we all felt the urge to go into the woods, and we all went. No one thought anything of it. Looking back, we should have." The Gormanian used both hands to try to comb the matted hair on her flanks. "Looking back, we were crazy to do what we did, but we did it."

"You were crazy, aye," Ekrekek agreed, "but *why*

were you crazy?'' His tail went back and forth, back and forth like a metronome.

''That I do not know,'' Gussaw said.

''Psychic compulsion?'' Terry wondered out loud. Some of the Hidden Folk's devices played with the minds of intelligent beings. The ones that did, though, did so all the time. As with the lights Gussaw had talked about, this sudden activation of a new effect in the previously dormant artifacts—if that was what had happened—would be something new.

''Do you want me to translate that?'' Chives asked. ''The best I can do is a phrase that really means something more like 'mind magic.' ''

''Never mind, then,'' Terry said. ''Just tell the Gormanian to go on.''

Chives did. Gussaw gave the robot another curious stare before continuing, ''As I said, we went into the woods. We did not seek my race's temples here, or even those of the Azusans, though we might well have done either, I suppose.'' Her ears flapped, perhaps a gesture of annoyance or perplexity. ''In any case, we kept on until we found ourselves inside that circle there. And then''—that ear-flap again—''my crew was gone.''

''Were you inside the circle too?'' Lorah asked. Terry's mouth was already open for the same question.

''Yes, I was,'' Gussaw said. ''Why I was not taken, only the gods know. I felt a biter crawling here''—she pointed to a spot between the second and third nipples on her right side—''and looked down to catch it. When I looked up again, everyone was gone. I stayed near the circle in the hope they would come back again. But you are here instead.''

''Where were you standing?'' This time Terry got the words out first.

''I can show you,'' Gussaw said after Chives translated. ''Are you sure you want to go into the circle with me, though? You—or I—may vanish as my crewfolk did.''

''I was inside once, and it didn't take me,'' Terry said with more confidence than she felt. ''I'll try it again if you will, Gussaw.''

"I will stay outside," Lorah declared. "If you do vanish, human, someone from a civilized race should witness it and bring word back to the rest of the starfaring peoples."

"I am adequate for that purpose, if you feel the need to examine the site of the unexplained phenomenon at first hand," Chives said.

"Never mind," Lorah said at once, so quickly that Terry laughed. No one had figured that physical courage would be necessary for this mission.

As she stepped toward the circle, though, the laughter faded. She found she had to will each foot forward. "I hope the snark's not a boojum," she said.

"Indeed." Chives was not built to nod, but he put that tone into his voice.

"More human unintelligibilities," Lorah complained.

Up close, Gussaw did have a distinct odor. Terry did not find it unpleasant, but it was different from the dry, musky smell of the Azusans. No wonder they had been able to track the crew of the *Agwadulsi* by scent.

Gussaw led her up to the opening in the Hidden Folk's circle. They both flinched as they went through. "We're still here," Terry said when nothing untoward—nothing at all—happened. Chives raised his electronic voice to translate for Gussaw.

"So we are," the Gormanian said, and Chives turned her words into English. "Perhaps we even have some hope of remaining here—but then, my crew thought they did, too."

"Show me where you were when they disappeared," Terry said.

"Here," Gussaw answered. "I am certain of it. Do you see this red stripe in the yellow inner wall of the circle? I was looking at it just before I began to itch."

"I see it," Terry said.

Chives again did the translating. The robot had walked around the outer perimeter of the circle to a point just outside where Terry and Gussaw stood. Chives observed, "The red band extends completely through the wall."

"Does it? That's interesting," Terry said. Neither she nor Lorah had brought any fancy scanners to the island. So far as anyone knew, artifacts of the Hidden Folk were opaque to all the scanners the six starfaring races knew. But then, so far as anyone knew, artifacts of the Hidden Folk did not go around turning themselves on, either. Maybe scanners would have done some good. Since Terry didn't have any, imagining they would have done some good was easy.

She asked, "Are there any other red bands around this circle?"

Still perched on Chives's shoulders like an old buzzard of the sea, Lorah said, "Humans are surely the most unobservant species ever evolved. Your device carried me past one back here. Why did you not notice it too?"

The obvious retort was that the stripe was only on the outside part of the wall. But when Terry looked back, she saw that the obvious, unfortunately for her, was not true. The red line did extend all the way through. "I wonder if there are any more of them," she said.

Lorah let out a squawk of disgust. "You circled this object with your camera. Did you not bother to take your brain along as well, to observe and remember what you were recording?"

"I didn't know it was going to be important," Terry said lamely.

"And so you took no special notice." Had the Crotonite's eyes been less beady, he would have rolled them. "It never ceases to amaze me that humans are classified as an intelligent race, let alone that they somehow stumbled across the hyperjump."

"Merely because human intelligence differs from your own, Lorah, do not underestimate it on that account," Chives said. "Having no psychic powers to speak of and only an ordinary sensorium, humans were forced to become perhaps the most skilled artificers in the galaxy. The result was—"

"Abominations like you," Lorah said, effectively ending the conversation.

Gussaw had been impatiently shifting from foot to foot to foot to foot while the off-worlders bickered. Now she said, "Why does it matter that this red band is here and not elsewhere? Does the color of a wall make it something different from a wall?"

"I don't know," Terry said. "It may mean nothing at all. But seeing as it's the only clue we have, we probably ought to check it out." She peered over to the far side of the circle. Wide as it was, spotting a thin red line was not easy.

With his electronically amplified vision, Chives did a better job of searching than Terry could. "There are two more lines over there," it reported. "As nearly as I can determine, the four points at which the bands occur are separated one from another by ninety degrees around the circle."

"Which would lead us to conclude that they are probably not just incidental marks on the artifact, but probably relate to something important without it," Terry said. She felt foolish for using "probably" twice in the same sentence, but that was as sure as anyone could be when talking about things the Hidden Folk had left behind. She went on, "Gussaw, do you remember noticing those other three lines the last time you were inside the circle?"

"They were not here," the Gormanian said positively. Terry wished she knew how far she could rely on that. A lot of races had total recall; a lot that didn't, humans among them, often pretended to. She couldn't recall into which category Gormanians fit.

Then Chives said, "Those bands were not here the last time we examined the circle. Review of my data records shows that the only red line present then was the one by which we are standing now."

Terry felt the small, fine hairs on her arms trying to prickle upright. "Then this site's shown new activity just in the last couple of hours," she breathed.

"Activity perhaps designed to send us wherever the crew of the *Agwadulsi* went," Lorah said.

"No," Terry said. "You've missed something, Lorah—Gussaw says these lines weren't here when the Gormanians vanished. They have to be for something else."

"Whatever their purpose," Chives said, "I suspect we will not determine it today. And since you organic folk will soon require nourishment and then rest, the coming of night now upon us may be as good a time as any to suspend our operations for the day."

"The coming of night?" Terry looked up in surprise. How had Tonclif snuck all the way down to the western horizon? She wondered if everyone was as taken aback by sunset as she was. Evidently not: Ekrekek's sailors seemed to have been going about the business of setting up camp for some time.

Lorah, for once, looked to be as bemused as she was. "Let us continue working," he said. "I am not the least bit hungry or tired." As soon as the words were out of his mouth, he gave vent to an enormous yawn. "Well, perhaps the least bit," he amended, sounding as sheepish as a Crotonite could, which wasn't very.

"What have you learned?" Ekrekek demanded when Terry and Gussaw came out of the circle. "I see you have found the gods are no longer hungry, else you would have joined the rest of the Gormanians." The peculiar rhythmic hiss he let out was Azusan laughter.

Terry thought it in poor taste. She asked Ekrekek, "Have you ever heard of changes in any of the strange things here on the Island of the Gods?"

The captain laughed again. "No, no more than I have heard of them lighting up. That is why I think this sixlegs you insist on making much of is but spinning out a fine tale to keep us from doing to her as we usually do with Gormanians."

"But—the ransom—" Terry said.

"May the ransom's eggs all break. Roasting and slicing the sixlegs now would be more enjoyable than collecting money later. I know you think my people harsh for this, but ask Gussaw what she and hers would do to me if ever I fell alone into their claws."

Terry glanced toward the Gormanian. She was reluctantly eating another chunk of smoked meat, which Ekrekek's sailors had reluctantly given her. She looked sad, bedraggled, very much alone, and not in the least dangerous. Terry visualized her along with a few dozen more like herself, all of them well-fed and cheerful. Could they match the Azusans atrocity for atrocity? They probably could, Terry decided—reluctantly. Nothing in Tonclif IV's history suggested otherwise, anyhow.

With tropical abruptness, light vanished from the sky. Stars made strange patterns in the black dome of the heavens, patterns interrupted here and there by the floating artifacts of the Hidden Folk. Even uninterrupted, though, the constellations would have meant nothing to Terry; she was some thousands of light-years from home.

She turned to Lorah. "Are you close enough to your native world for the local stars to seem familiar to you?"

"No, though I must say many more of them seem to be visible here than on most worlds I've visited. I suppose that's mostly because the atmosphere here is so beastly thin. On most Crotonite worlds, stars are hardly visible from the ground."

"I never thought of that," Terry said. "Here we are, trying to unravel the riddles of the Hidden Folk, and we don't know nearly enough about one another. Intelligence is like that, I suppose—always pushing out into the distance without worrying so much about what's close at hand. If your people couldn't see the stars, I'm surprised you ever developed space travel."

Lorah spread his wings. "Don't forget that we always had flight. Going up and up was natural with us, and when we developed technology we used it to do more than we could unaided. We—"

The Crotonite's voice faded as Ekrekek and his sailors cried out. Close by them, the circle that had swept away the crew of the *Agwadulsi* began to glow a soft but piercing gold. Farther away and overhead, other relics of the Hidden Folk also began to shine. Gussaw shouted something, again and again. Chives translated for Terry: "I told you so!"

Terry had to admire Ekrekek for what he did then: He walked over to Gussaw and saluted her as if she were one of his own species. "I found lies when you spoke truth," he said. "It was so strange a truth, I could not believe it, especially since it came from an enemy. But I see it was truth nonetheless."

"You do not seek to trick me," Gussaw said slowly, half to herself, as if probing for hidden meanings in the Azusan's words. "You have no need to trick me, for I am in your power. So I see you are also speaking the truth. But that an Azusan should apologize to a Gormanian is as strange a truth as these lights we see now on the Island of the Gods."

"You are the enemy I know," Ekrekek said. "Of the gods and their toys here I know nothing. The danger they present may well be greater than yours. Until I know how great it is, I will act on that belief. As you say"—he opened his mouth wide to display those carnivore teeth—"I can do with you as I wish, when I wish. If slaying you seems to my advantage, I will slay you. But there is no hurry."

"For an Azusan, that's a miracle of moderation," Terry said when Chives was done translating. "Or, to be fair, for a Gormanian." She thought again about how Ekrekek would have fared alone with the whole crew of the *Agwadulsi*.

"Yes, it is remarkable," Chives agreed. "It would be as well if the allegedly more sophisticated and civilized starfaring races could also unite in the face of the unknown challenge the Hidden Folk represent, rather than having members of each species scheme for their own aggrandizement, often at the expense of others."

Chives was a diplomatic piece of machinery; it named no names. That was probably just as well, Terry thought. Crotonites despised all wingless races, which meant they despised all the other races in the galaxy that had discovered the hyperjump—Lorah was less xenophobic than most of his people. Humans were no mean connivers either, come to that.

Lorah said, "I observe no bands of anomalous color on any of the other Hidden Folk relics within my range of vision, and my vision can be amplified to the point where I would see them if they were of a width similar to the four red bands on the circle here."

Chives did not look around. Instead, it said, "Let me review my data store." After a moment, it went on, "You are correct. What significance do you ascribe to the fact?"

"I don't know." Lorah sounded anything but happy with the admission.

"I must confess it is not obvious to me, either," Chives said. The robot's voice was not programmed to show much emotion, but Terry did not think it was happy. It had been designed to be curious—or with a drive to collect and assess new data, which amounted to the same thing.

Terry said, "If the two barbarian races can work together here in the face of the unknown, Lorah, do you think we can imitate them, at least as long as we're here on the island?"

"Very well." Lorah still sounded less than enthusiastic, but went on, "The potential for learning here overcomes my distaste for cooperation, at least for the present."

Terry knew that meant he would do whatever he thought necessary as soon as they were off the Island of the Gods, but she'd known that all along. She slid her backpack off her shoulders, got out her sleeping bag. With a yawn, she said, "I'm not going to worry about anything till morning."

Lorah folded his wings about himself as if they were a cloak. Only the tip of his muzzle stuck out as he said, "For once, human, I cannot disagree with you."

"As I do not require sleep, I will continue to monitor the circular artifact until the two of you arise," Chives said. "In view of our present cooperation, Lorah, shall I provide you with a copy of my data record for the night?"

"Would you?" Lorah lowered his wings until he could peer out at the robot. "That would be uncommonly"—he hesitated—"forthcoming of you." He wouldn't say *generous,* Terry thought, not to an AI, or probably to anyone who wasn't a Crotonite.

"This is for the good of all," Chives said. After a moment, he added, "Who knows what the starfarers of the galaxy could accomplish if they worked together on all occasions as we do here? And not only we starfarers are cooperating now. Who would have imagined that Azusans and Gormanians could also perceive the advantages of at least postponing hostilities until a more propitious time?"

"Who would have imagined that a robot would end up turning social philosopher on us?" A yawn blurred Terry's words. She snuggled deeper into her sleeping bag and drifted off almost at once.

Tonclif was shining in her face when she woke. Local sunrise what not what had roused her; one of the arboreal jungle lizards hereabouts had a mating call that sounded like a giant breaking wind. Another machine-gun burst of reptilian pseudoflatulence made her snicker as she scrambled out of the sleeping bag.

Since the weather was tropically warm and she was the only human for several hundred kilometers, she hadn't bothered sleeping in clothes. She did wear them during the day; she needed shoes, and liked the convenience of pockets. Gussaw watched as she dressed. Chives translated the Gormanian captain's comment: "I see by your nipples that you are a true mammal, even if you have but two of them. Strange, then, that you should have come to the Island of the Gods with the scaly Azusans."

So much for the brotherhood of all beings, Terry thought. She answered, "I am not the same as an Azusan; I am not the same as a Gormanian. Should I despise you as the Azusans do, because you have six legs? Of course not. So why should I despise them because they have scales?"

Gussaw scratched her head and walked off. Sounding as wistful as a robot could, Chives said, "I wish the principle you propounded could also be extended from organic lifeforms to electronic ones."

"Humans think it can," Terry said. "We'd be lost without AIs, and we know it. If the other starfaring races can't see that AIs are people too, well, they're the ones making the mistake."

Lorah's hearing seemed as amplified as his vision. He looked up from the reptile meat he was devouring for breakfast and said, "I am forced to admit that this robot of yours has proven moderately useful. Still, I am of the opinion that machines should be tools rather than colleagues."

"In a word, nonsense," Terry said. She was just as glad when Lorah went back to eating: The argument about AIs had grown old for her, and she doubted that anything short of a miracle would convince the Crotonite to change his mind. A large miracle, she thought, digging through her backpack for a ration pouch. She could eat smoked lizard haunch if she had to, but it was bad enough to make even survival rations tasty by comparison.

She hurried back to the spot where Gussaw had been standing when the rest of the Gormanians vanished. The red band was still there. Since she had no fancy sensors, she took out an old-fashioned tape and measured it. "Three hundred seventeen millimeters," she said for the record.

Lorah and Chives were standing outside the circle by another of the red bands. Looking down at it, the Crotonite said, "This one is twenty-seven and a third *shalmoti* across."

"That works out to three hundred seventeen millimeters," Chives added helpfully.

They had spoken English. Gussaw asked Terry, "What are you talking about?"

Terry understood enough Azusan to follow that (she had not a word of any Gormanian tongue, and was glad Gussaw stuck with her captors' language). Still, she was pleased to see Chives put Lorah down and hurry over to translate for her.

"Most interesting," Gussaw said when the robot was done explaining. "So you and the winged one there do not use the same system of measurement?"

"No," Terry said with a rueful shake of her head. "My race spent hundreds of years getting to the point where we all used one system. Then we got into space and had to start converting all over again, because each species that travels between the stars has its own units for distance, time, and weight."

"It is the same here," Gussaw said. "Most Gormanians use the same set of weights and measures, but the Azusans have several different ones." The captain of the *Agwadulsi* walked partway around the circular relic of the Hidden Folk to another red band. "Now I would say that this line is about three *quatkuma* across. Ekrekek"—the Gormanian raised her voice to catch the Azusan's notice—"you're near that last band. How wide do you make it out to be?"

The captain of the *Hewnall* considered. "About four hands, I'd say."

"Ah, you're from one of the Azusan countries that—"

Gussaw's comment was left unfinished. Except for showing the red bands, the relic of the Hidden Folk had been altogether inactive while Tonclif was in the sky. That inactivity now ended. The bands began to glow, brighter and brighter. At the same time, the yellow of the rest of the circular wall faded until it was clear as air.

"Do you see that red square that's suddenly appeared in the center of the circle?" Chives said.

"All I see is rock and dirt," Terry answered.

"And I," Lorah said. "Human, I think your machine has need of repair."

"Interesting," Chives said. "I perceive the spot and you do not. Yet you should, for it radiates light at a frequency that your eyes can see and it is quite bright, I assure you—as bright as the red bands by which the two of you are standing." The robot raised its voice, shifted languages: "Gussaw, Ekrekek—does either of you see a red square in the center of the area inside this circle?"

"No," the Azusan said. The Gormanian added, "It looks the same to me as it did before."

Terry had the feeling that she was missing something, that someone should have been doing something that wasn't getting done. When she tried to put a mental finger on what was wrong, the idea slipped away. The harder she thought about it, the blurrier her wits became. That was annoying. After a moment, it was also familiar.

"A psychic compulsion field *is* operating here!" she exclaimed. "We ought to do something, but it won't let us figure out what."

"You are right." Lorah flapped his wings in frustration and waddled about close by the second pulsing red band. "How demeaning to be deliberately befuddled, as if I were an animal."

"I feel no psychic compulsion," Chives said. "Perhaps the field does not affect the electronic workings of an AI mind. The answer to our dilemma, in any case, would seem to be the investigation of that red square which I see and all of you do not. Your blindness, I conjecture, may well be another aspect of the mental field."

What the robot said made sense to Terry—but only for a moment. Chives's words slipped out of her mind even as she considered them. She wanted to ask the AI to repeat itself, but waited too long. She'd even forgotten why what it said was important. She saw Lorah open his mouth. The Crotonite shut it again, as if he too had lost track of what he wanted to say.

Chives felt no such mental qualms. The robot climbed over the now-transparent border of the circle, walked briskly toward the center. Try as she would, Terry saw nothing there but gray, boring rock.

With mechanical smoothness, Chives squatted, peered down. "I see," the AI said. "I am intended to stand within the square. Then this entire installation will do what it was built to do." Chives rose, took a step forward.

Terry cried out. Now she saw a beam of light shooting straight up from the ground. It bathed Chives in a fierce glow. Then Terry cried out again, along with everyone else, for the circle was no longer empty but for the robot. Dozens of Gormanians milled about inside.

They shouted when they saw the Azusans. The Azusans, most of whom had paid no particular attention to what the off-worlders with them were up to, shouted back and grabbed for their weapons.

Gussaw and Ekrekek locked eyes over the circle's wall—it was yellow again, Terry noted dazedly. Ekrekek's gaze broke away first. He whirled, yelled to his crewmates, "Hold up! Don't attack unless the sixlegs do! The gods have given them back—they're no longer fit meat for us to slaughter."

Gussaw bellowed at the Gormanians in their own language.

"The captain of the *Agwadulsi* says much the same thing to her crew." Chives's amplified voice overrode even the shouting locals as the robot passed Gussaw's meaning on to Terry.

"Find out where the Gormanians were when the circle took them away," Terry called to the robot.

"Finding out whether we are about to find ourselves in the middle of a battle strikes me as being of more immediate importance," Chives said.

"They can't fight now," Terry said, though she knew full well they could. But they didn't, at least not right away. The Gormanians' dramatic appearance was enough to awe the Azusans out of an immediate onslaught against their ancient foes. And the spectacle of two captains, one from each race, both crying out for peace, was a miracle hardly more credible than mammaloid centaurs springing from thin air. With Chives electronically bellowing for peace in both languages, and with the robot and the two off-worlders to keep the Gormanians off balance by their mere presence, no one made the first fatal move.

Terry scrambled over the waist-high fence and dropped down among the Gormanians. Chives hurried toward her to protect her if the locals showed hostility. She was glad to see the robot coming up, but not on account of that—at the moment, it hardly entered her mind. "Translate for me," she said to Chives.

"For one so easily damaged as yourself, do you think this the ideal moment to come into close proximity to locals who are both upset and armed?" Chives asked.

"Hell, yes. I want to find out what happened to them while it's still fresh in their minds. Ask this female here"—Terry paused to frame her question as precisely as possible—"what she felt when the circle took her away, what the place she went to was like, how long she thought she was gone, and how she came back here."

Chives emitted an eerily accurate imitation of a sigh. "Very well," it said, then began speaking the throaty language the crew of the *Agwadulsi* used.

The Gormanian next to Terry had listened in some impatience as two strange creatures spoke with each other in an unknown tongue. When one of them switched to her language immediately afterward, her ears furled in surprise. Then she spoke herself, loudly and volubly.

"Her name is Canlaster," Chives reported. "She says that she and her fellow sailors felt nothing out of the ordinary, but suddenly they were not here any longer. They were—someplace else, she says. She does not define it more closely than that, but I am compelled to be of the opinion that they were on another planet, either in this galaxy or another."

"Why?" Terry said.

"The sky was the wrong color, she says, and everyone felt too light, and the sun even looked the wrong color all the time—it was red or orange even at noon, not yellow."

"That's another planet," Terry agreed. After a moment, she went on, "But it's impossible! It would mean the Hidden Folk have a way to make a hyperjump straight off a planetary surface. By all the physics the six starfaring races know, you can't do that."

"Perhaps the Hidden Folk have not had the inestimable benefit of reading our physics texts," Chives said. Terry still wondered how they managed to program irony into AIs. The robot continued, "Days and nights both seemed too short, so Canlaster has trouble reckoning how long she and the other Gormanians were on this strange world. Her best guess, though, is not far from the length of time that Gussaw states had elapsed here."

"That has to mean the hyperjump, no matter what our physics books say," Terry said.

"I often wonder at the human ability to come to sweeping conclusions from completely inadequate data," Chives said. "Your speculation is possible, certainly, perhaps even probable, but by no means sure."

Terry knew the robot was right. She didn't care. Chives was welcome to call her conclusion a leap into the dark if it wanted to. She thought she was on target just the same.

Then something else occurred to her, something that filled her with awe. "Do you know what we did?" she said to Chives. "We made this device work—we activated it when it was dead."

"That does seem to be the case," the robot said. "Understanding precisely how we did it, however, will take more work."

Trying to understand gnawed at Terry as she and her off-world companions marched with the Azusans and Gormanians back toward their ships. The two species kept apart from one another, with the human and robot (the latter with the Crotonite on its shoulders) tramping between them and acting as a sort of spiritual buffer.

Ekrekek and Gussaw both seemed to decide to say something to the starfarers at the same time; the one hung back from his sailors while the other moved forward from hers. They eyed each other warily, but they both kept coming. Ekrekek spoke first: "How did the gods' creation first swallow the Gormanians and then restore them? You folk who travel between the stars are learned artificers—surely you must know."

"I wish we did," Terry answered, "but I fear I still cannot tell you. We came to your Island of the Gods to try to learn that very thing." We got more than we bargained for, too, she thought: did we ever! Aloud, she went on, "I saw what the circle did, but I could no more explain how it did it than I could tell you what this pillar here does." She pointed to what might have been a blue ceramic light pole a few meters to one side of the path.

As her finger went up and toward it, though, her jaw dropped. The pillar, which presumably had stood unchanging since the Hidden Folk set it in place for their own hidden reasons, suddenly turned as transparent as had the circular wall of the—the transporter, Terry thought. And, as with the transporter, four red bands appeared upon it, one above the next.

"It's active too," Terry whispered.

As if drawn by a lodestone, she stepped toward the pillar. Ekrekek and Gussaw followed her. Chives stood still until Lorah pounded on the robot's metallic cranium with both puny fists. "Go on!" the Crotonite squawked indignantly. "Do you want me to be the only one not in on this discovery?"

"Indeed not," Chives answered, stepping forward at last. "In fact, upon reflection I believe your presence may be required for any discovery to take place." Lorah preened at what sounded like a compliment.

"I see four red bands, each about the same width—" Terry began.

"The same three hundred seventeen millimeters we observed in the circle," Chives put in.

"Are they? I thought so." Terry went on, "They're separated from one another by clear areas about half as wide as they are." She turned to her companions. "Is that what you see too? Translate for the locals, Chives, and also let me know if you perceive anything I'm missing."

No one, the robot included, saw anything different from what Terry had described. "In this case, it appears the famous artificial intelligence has no special value," Lorah sneered. But he was still in the middle of his sentence when another red band began to shine above the four.

"As there are now five bands and five beings present, an obvious hypothesis is that one band is intended for each of us," Chives said. "Shall we test it?" He reached out and put a hand on the newly visible band of color.

Terry touched one also. The pillar was cool and smooth. From Chives's shoulder, Lorah bent down and set a hand on the red strip between Chives's and Terry's. Through Chives, Terry asked Gussaw and Ekrekek, "Will each of you touch a red band too?"

Ekrekek immediately reached out for one. Gussaw asked, "What will happen if I do?"

That, Terry thought, was what the ancients for some reason called the sixty-four dollar question. "I don't know," she said. "That's what we're trying to find out."

She did not need Chives to interpret Gussaw's skeptical grunt. Nonetheless, the Gormanian also extended a hand toward the pillar. In a sudden loss of nerve, Terry wanted to shout at her, to tell her to take her hand away. She wanted to jerk back her own hand, so the presumed five-fold circuit would remain incomplete. Who could say what the newly activated relic of the Hidden Folk might do?

Too late—Gussaw's hand flattened against the pillar. For a long moment, nothing happened at all. Terry wondered if even the Hidden Folk's marvelous machinery—if that was what it was—could wear out over the eons. Then all the bands of color flared so blindingly bright that her eyes squeezed shut of their own accord.

Looking at her watch afterward, she found that she and her companions were caught up in that flash of light for about a minute and a half. That never seemed right to her. Either the experience had taken no time whatever, or it lasted an eternity. A minute and a half of real time did not fit well with either view.

And yet, considering what the pillar of the Hidden Folk imparted, a minute and a half was not long to spend to acquire it. For by the time Terry's hand fell away from the pillar, she *knew,* at a level far deeper than words, what it was like to be a Crotonite, an Azusan, a Gormanian, even a robot. The closest she could come to describing the feeling was to compare it to the Naxians' empathic sense, which let them grasp emotions.

What she'd experienced surpassed empathy, though: For that timeless instant or endless minute and a half, she'd *been* Lorah, Ekrekek, Gussaw, Chives. She knew them as well as they knew themselves, and knew they knew her and one another the same way.

"How can we fight now?" Ekrekek said to Gussaw. The words were pacific; hearing the tone, Terry understood, as she would not have before, that the Azusan felt he had lost something of great price.

And Chives murmured, "So that is what the urgency of organic life derives from. Much about which AIs have only speculated now becomes clear." Remembering the clean, crisp, orderly confines of the robot's mind, Terry wondered how it would deal with everything it had learned. A pity Chives had not been designed to blush, she thought.

From the AI's shoulders, Lorah peered toward her. "Humans are very peculiar creatures," he said. Terry was sure he'd had the same gift of understanding the Hidden Folk had given her. It had done little to mellow him, though.

And that, she realized as she could not have before, was in keeping with what he was, with what Crotonites were. Physically weak, unique in the galaxy because of their wings, clannish among themselves but mistrustful of all other races, they could not help acting as they did. Terry was also certain that Lorah would indignantly deny she knew the first thing about him and his kind, no matter what wonders the pillar had wrought. That too was the Crotonite way.

Trying to make Lorah into something he wasn't could only be wasted effort. Instead, Terry said, "Now we've activated two Hidden Folk devices. We know the first one wasn't a fluke. Let's get back to the ship that brought us here, and then to our own starships. The research teams will start coming in droves after this."

On the beach that evening, the off-worlders stayed with the Azusans by the *Hewnall;* the Gormanians were a few hundred meters away near the *Agwadulsi*. Both Ekrekek and Gussaw had pledged to hold the truce until the ships went their separate ways. After the pillar, Terry was sure she could trust the captains. To help make sure none of the crewfolk on either side took things into their own hands, Chives walked to and fro on the beach between the two galleys, ready to shout out a warning at any sign of aggression.

Lorah said, "That we have succeeded is indisputable. *Why* we succeeded remains, in my opinion, as yet obscure." He took a noisy suck on his breathing tube.

Terry watched twilight fade from the western sky, watched the artifacts that floated above the Island of the Gods slowly begin to blend into the darkening sky. "Chives was a big part of it," she said. "When the compulsion field at the transporter befuddled the rest of us, Chives still saw what needed doing, and did it. And again at the pillar, that fifth band lit up when he drew close."

The Crotonite sniffed. "Despite all objections, you humans have insisted on bringing your AIs to Hidden Folk sites before. Up until this time, they have not shown themselves to be anything out of the ordinary in activating those sites. Keeping that in mind, I must say I find it hard to believe that our successes today are entirely attributable to the robot."

"No, but we wouldn't have made either gadget work without Chives." Terry paused thoughtfully. "Come to that, we wouldn't have made either one of them work without all of us. We had four people, each from a different species, close by red bands or actually touching them, and Chives to activate the transporter and to be the fifth at the pillar."

"Again, I am still tempted to ascribe this to coincidence," Lorah said. "Many examinations of relics of the Hidden Folk have involved more than one starfaring race; some have involved all six. Why, then, were we successful here where so many others have failed?"

Terry frowned. As she had while arguing with Chives, she felt sure she was right. Even more than Chives, though, Lorah had logic on his side. Or did he? "How many expeditions have included races that *don't* have starflight?"

"Not many, I would think," Lorah answered. "Most intelligent species without it are either low-tech like the ones here, or else have only used technology to do their best to destroy themselves, and thereupon renounced it."

"Exactly." Terry pounced: "So how many tries at cracking Hidden Folk artifacts have had more than one species of starfarer, more than one species of low-tech intelligent being, *and* an AI, all working together?"

The Crotonite was silent for some time. "That is intriguing," he said at last. "Can you propose any explanation as to why the Hidden Folk might have keyed their relics to respond only to such an unlikely combination?"

"Maybe, just maybe," Terry said. "Suppose you were one of the Hidden Folk, however many years ago they headed back for the Andromeda galaxy or wherever they came from. They must have known intelligent life would eventually arise here too, but what sort of intelligent life? They wouldn't be interested in species that never developed technology, and they wouldn't be interested in species which got along so poorly even with themselves that they ended up destroying their own planets."

"Not for long, anyway, in the latter case," Lorah said.

"No, not for long. And so maybe they rigged their artifacts to be able to respond only to a party that showed it was made up of races fully able to cooperate with one another no matter how different they were externally—and internally," she added, remembering the experience of the pillar. "Even different as to whether they evolved by themselves or were created, if you take Chives into account."

"The robot again," Lorah said disgustedly.

"Yes, the robot again. Discriminating against artificial intelligence is just as foolish and arbitrary as discriminating against a being for any other reason. And if the relics need two or more low-tech species to get them started, then under most circumstances that would be a pretty good indication that high-tech folk let less sophisticated races travel a great deal on their starships.''

''Which isn't so, not even slightly,'' Chives said.

''No, but this is Tonclif IV, with two low-tech species already in place. Not even the Hidden Folk would think that very likely, I suppose.'' Terry's eyes widened. ''Or would they? Doesn't it seem to you as though the disappearance of all the *Agwadulsi*'s crew except Gussaw was like a puzzle set up to see if we were smart enough—and cooperative enough—to figure it out?''

''Possibly,'' Lorah said. ''I would doubt some of your testing criteria, however—surely a prerequisite would be that at least one of the species involved in the investigation has wings, as the Hidden Folk themselves were surely winged.''

''Whatever you say, Lorah.'' Even having experienced it from the inside thanks to the pillar, Terry thought as little of the Crotonites' species-wide obsession with the overwhelming importance of flight as they did of humanity's penchant for building robots. She admitted to herself, though, that she could be wrong, just as Lorah had been—all she knew now was that she lacked the data to be sure, one way or the other. Time would tell.

Lorah suddenly hissed, as fiercely as if he were an Azusan. ''If all is as you describe, human, why should you be allowed to escape from Tonclif IV? Why should my people not gain the sole honor of contacting the Hidden Folk?''

Crotonites owned a richly deserved reputation for being underhanded. Lorah's starship was supposed to be no more heavily armed than Terry's. But what was supposed to be and what was sometimes weren't the same thing. Terry knew a moment of real fear, but then she began to laugh. Lorah squawked indignantly.

''It would matter to me if you blasted my ship as soon as we lifted off,'' Terry said, ''but would it do you any good in the long run? You might be rid of what I know, and humanity wouldn't find out about it, but you'd have to tell somebody, because I think you need another high-tech species as partner. And even the Samians, good-natured as they are, would ask questions you couldn't answer. Besides, where would you get an AI, except from humans? And you can bet humans would get very curious very fast if Crotonites developed a sudden, consuming interest in robotics. We may as well cooperate now, Lorah—we'll have to in the future."

"What a distasteful concept," the Crotonite muttered.

"That's what the Azusans and Gormanians think too," Terry pointed out. "They managed, though, when they really had to. I hope we will, when the time comes. If I had to guess, I'd say the Hidden Folk probably are to us as we are to the two species here. I just hope they're patient with us when we finally do figure out how to contact them."

"They'll need to be," Lorah said. "If they are that advanced, we won't be able to keep from resenting them at the same time as we learn from them." The Crotonite paused, then continued, "One more thing—"

"What's what?"

"I'll still bet you three *squantoken*—in your measure, about a tenth of a kilo—of gold that when the Hidden Folk appear, they'll have wings."

"You're on." Terry stuck out her arm. One of Lorah's small, weak grasping limbs stretched out to meet it. Their hands clasped. This was cooperation too, Terry thought, even in rivalry. "Good enough," she said.

"What?" Lorah asked.

"Never mind."

About the Authors

Poul Anderson

One of the most versatile writers in the history of the genre, Poul Anderson is equally adept at hard and soft science fiction, high fantasy, and sword and sorcery. He is also one of the most honored writers, having won seven Hugo Awards and three Nebula Awards for such wonderful stories as "No Truce with Kings," "The Queen of Air and Darkness," "Goat Song," and "The Saturn Game." His scores of novels included such masterworks as *Brain Wave* (1954), *The High Crusade* (1960), *Tau Zero* (1970), *Fire Time* (1974), *The Avatar* (1978), and *The King of Ys* (1986).

David Brin

The holder of a Ph.D in space science, David Brin has quickly established himself as one of the premier writers of hard science fiction. He won both the Hugo and Nebula awards for his first novel *Startide Rising* (1983), a Hugo Award for "The Crystal Spheres" (1985), and another Hugo for *The Uplift War* (1988). Other notable novels include *The Practice Effect* (1984), *The Postman* (1985), and *The Heart of the Comet* (1986, coauthored with Gregory Benford).

Robert Sheckley

Robert Sheckley debuted in the science fiction magazines during the 1950s, and his finely crafted, satirical stories were among the finest produced in that rich decade. The best of his early stories can be found in such collections as *Untouched by Human Hands* (1954) and *Pilgrimage to Earth* (1957). As a novelist in the science fiction field (he has also written excellent espionage novels), he is best known for *The Tenth Victim* (1966), which was a novelization of his short story "The Seventh Victim." Other notable novels include *Immortality Delivered*

(1958), *Mindswap* (1966), *Dimension of Miracles* (1968), *Crompton Divided* (1978), and *Victim Prime* (1987).

Robert Silverberg

One of the most esteemed and honored science fiction writers of his generation, Robert Silverberg has been awarded three Hugos and five Nebulas. It is likely that he has produced more noteworthy novels than any other writer in the genre—a few of his best are *Hawksbill Station* (1968), *Tower of Glass* (1970), *The World Inside* (1971), the magnificent *Dying Inside* (1972), *The Stochastic Man* (1975), *Lord Valentine's Castle* (1980), and *Star of Gypsies* (1986). His collaboration with Isaac Asimov, *Nightfall: The Novel,* is one of the most eagerly awaited novels of 1990.

Harry Turtledove

Harry Turtledove began his writing career under the pseudonym "Eric Iverson." His books combine his great knowledge of ancient history (he holds a Ph.D in history) with excellent writing skills. Dr. Turtledove's major work to date, a four-part historical fantasy series consisting of *The Misplaced Legion, An Emperor for the Legion, The Legion of Videssos,* and *Swords of the Legion* (all published in 1987) received widespread critical acclaim, as did his novels *Agent of Byzantium* (1987), *Noninterference* (1988), and *A Different Flesh* (1989).